WEB OF DECEIT

KATHERINE HOWELL

WITHDRAWN

Minotaur Books

A Thomas Dunne Book
New York

For Benette

A THOMAS DUNNE BOOK FOR MINOTAUR BOOKS.
An imprint of St. Martin's Publishing Group.

www.thomasdunnebooks.com
www.minotaurbooks.com

Library of Congress Cataloging-in-Publication Data

Howell, Katherine.
    Web of deceit / Katherine Howell. — First U.S. edition.
        p. cm. — (An Ella Marconi mystery)
    "A Thomas Dunne book."
    ISBN 978-1-250-05396-1 (hardcover)
    ISBN 978-1-4668-5678-3 (e-book)
    1. Policewomen—Australia—Sydney (N.S.W.)—Fiction. 2. Emergency medical
technicians—Australia—Sydney (N.S.W.)—Fiction. 3. Murder—Investigation—
Fiction. I. Title.
    PR9619.4.H693W43 2015
    823'.92—dc23
                                                                      2015035933

Our books may be purchased in bulk for promotional, educational,
or business use. Please contact your local bookseller or the Macmillan Corporate
and Premium Sales Department at (800) 221-7945, extension 5442, or by
e-mail at MacmillanSpecialMarkets@macmillan.com.

First published in Australia by Pan Macmillan Australia Pty Limited

First U.S. Edition: December 2015

10 9 8 7 6 5 4 3 2 1

ONE

In the ambulance's passenger seat, paramedic Alex Churchill checked his mobile. There was no text from Mia. He sent her another: *I'm calling Frances in five.*

'Sixty-three to Control.' The voice burst over the radio with the sound of screaming in the background.

The hairs rising on his arms, Alex looked through the rain-speckled windscreen. His partner, Jane Koutoufides, turned in the coffee shop and met his gaze. People in the shop around her stared at the portable radio in her hand.

'Go ahead, Sixty-three,' Control answered.

'Urgent backup, please. We have four code nines and one of those unconscious, six walking wounded, one car leaking fuel.'

The screaming grew louder. Alex had been there; he knew how it made you feel. He could feel it again now in the hammering of his heart.

'Copy that, Sixty-three,' Control said. 'I'll get rescue and more cars on their way.'

Alex leaned forward, ready to grab the microphone. In the shop, Jane moved towards the door. They'd heard Sixty-three dispatched five minutes ago to Botany Road, near the airport.

Although they were in Glebe, Alex had done longer runs many times. You never knew how many ambulances were tied up on cases between here and there. Jane was still looking at him. He glanced away. He understood her concern, but also felt belittled by it.

At the start of the shift, she'd said in a distinctly gentle voice that they could work however he wanted, swap roles back and forth between driving and treating as often as he liked, he just had to let her know. He'd nodded, uncomfortable. This was his second week back, and sure, on a shift last week he'd had a humiliating panicked few minutes at a car accident in which a twelve-year-old girl had been trapped, but he'd pulled it together. They'd got her out, she was going to be fine. He'd hoped that this morning – his first shift with Jane since – he could walk in like nothing had happened. But perhaps it was unreasonable to expect that. *She's just trying to be helpful.*

The seconds ticked by and Control didn't call. Alex knew there were crews on closer stations being phoned and dispatched. He gestured. Jane gave a thumbs-up and faced the counter.

Alex sat back in the seat. The psychologist had talked about bringing yourself back to the present, being aware of your sur-roundings and breathing. He put his hand on his stomach and took a deep breath. The rain had stopped and sunlight poured through a break in the clouds to sparkle in the drops on the windscreen. He stared at the colours. It helped.

He looked at his phone again. Mia was fourteen going on twenty-one, and she'd done this before: delayed texting him back even though she was already with her after-school carers, Frances and Donald. He remembered being fourteen and feel-ing like he was always being told what to do and when to do it, and finding little ways to exert his own bit of control. But rules were rules, and he'd seen too much to let them be bent.

Breathe.

Jane opened the driver's door and handed across his coffee. 'You okay?'

'Fine.'

Something crossed her face at his tone. She climbed behind the wheel, then nodded at the phone in his lap. 'No response from Mia-mouse?'

'Last time I called her that she said "I'm fourteen, not four",' Alex said.

Jane angled her cup towards him in salute. 'The joys of parenthood.'

'Yours were teens once,' he said, feeling better now they'd changed the subject. 'How do you survive?'

'It's like being a patient in a major trauma. Some of it you blank out, the rest of the time you take drugs.' She sipped her coffee. 'And you're in rehab for a long time afterwards.'

'That good?' Alex said. 'Perhaps I should have another.'

'Thirty-five,' Control said.

'Damn,' Jane said.

Alex grabbed the microphone as adrenaline thumped into his bloodstream again. 'Thirty-five's on Glebe Point Road.'

Not the screamers. Please.

'Got an MVA for you,' Control said. 'Car into a pole on Wattle Street, Ultimo, outside the park, opposite the school. Cross is Quarry. Person still in vehicle, query code nine.'

'Thirty-five's on the case,' Alex said.

'Damn,' Jane said again.

She dug a cardboard tray out of the centre console and tucked their cups into it while Alex clipped in his seatbelt, trying to calm his heart.

Jane started the engine and hit the lights and siren and pulled out into the traffic. Cars lumbered out of their way and the sun shone silver on the wet road. 'When we get there, let me know if you want me to treat,' she said.

He gave a terse nod. 'I'm guessing Mia's probably at a friend's.'

'Yeah,' she said after a moment, with a sideways glance. 'Probably. My kids were always doing that – nicking off somewhere after school and saying they forgot to let me know. You'd think the bullocking I gave them would make them remember next time, but it never did . . .'

He tuned her out as he pulled gloves onto his already clammy hands. Roads got slippery after rain. Skid, bounce up the kerb and into a signpost, minor damage, driver's freaked out and not got out of the car yet. The way the call-takers' computer system worked, they had to ask if the person was still in the vehicle, and if the answer was yes it automatically came through to the controller as a query trapped. Better safe than sorry, but it meant most code nines were fixed by merely opening a door. That's all it would be this time.

'We laugh about it now, of course,' Jane said, doglegging through to Bay Street and popping out halfway along Wattle. 'I tell them, wait till you have kids of your own, because then . . .'

Alex looked left and saw the accident: a silver late-model Mitsubishi sedan head-on into a power pole. Cars had stopped behind it and a couple of people stood by the driver's closed door. The powerlines were intact, nothing was on fire. The people by the vehicle looked concerned but weren't panicking. *It's okay.*

Jane pulled up next to the car. Alex saw a thirtyish man in a business shirt in the driver's seat, his hands white on the wheel, his forehead pressed to its top. There were no passengers.

'He in one piece?' Jane said.

'As far as I can tell.' Alex picked up the microphone. 'Thirty-five's on scene, will report shortly.'

'Thanks, Thirty-five,' Control said.

Alex grabbed the Viva out of the back and went to the driver's door. The window was up, the lock button down. He tapped on the glass, but the man gave no indication that he'd heard. His shoulders shook as if he was crying.

Alex checked the back door, but it too was locked, as were both doors on the passenger side. He started as a truck crunched its gears on the road behind him and covered it up by turning to the four bystanders. 'Has he been like this the whole time?'

'First he was looking around, all panicky,' a woman in her late teens said. She had a round face, wore jeans and a frilled white top and held a blue handbag by the strap. 'We kept asking him through the window if he was okay, whether he could get out, but he didn't answer. Then he just hid his face like that.'

The others nodded.

Alex looked up at the powerlines again, then down at the car. The bonnet was crumpled but not badly. It had been a fairly low impact. He shielded his eyes from the sun and leaned close to the window, peering into the car, checking what he could of the man's body. There was no visible blood. The dash wasn't pressing against his knees. The airbag had gone off and now lay sagging on his lap, but it was clean and bloodstain-free. He could hear the man's weeping. He rapped on the glass again.

'No joy?' Jane said behind him.

He shook his head. 'Ambulance,' he said, close to the glass. 'Will you please open the door?'

The man let go of the wheel and covered his face with his hands.

'Thirty-five,' Control called, loud and clear from the portable on Jane's hip. 'What's your status?'

Crap. Alex needed this guy to unlock the doors. Until then, they couldn't be completely certain that he could get out, and they were obliged to tell Control, who'd have no choice but to call for rescue, probably diverting them from the Botany Road job where they were really needed.

He knocked on the window with a hard fist. 'Mate, open your door.'

The man didn't move.

Jane leaned close to the glass. 'C'mon, buddy, we just want to make sure you're okay.'

Down the street, somebody blasted their horn and the man started and looked up. Alex felt the jolt of nerves too, but knocked on the window again. The man glanced at him, his face full of fear. Alex smiled and motioned for him to lower the window. The man stared wild-eyed past him at the people watching on the other side of the road.

'Thirty-five,' Control called again.

'We just want to make sure you're all right,' Alex said to the man. 'Then we'll leave you alone.'

The man said something, his voice muffled by the glass.

'Show you what?' Alex asked.

'He wants to see our IDs,' Jane said. She lowered her head as she undid the button on her shirt pocket. 'As if our uniforms and the whopping great truck behind us aren't enough.'

Alex got out his wallet too, and they held their ID cards to the window.

'Okay?' Alex said.

The man hesitated, looking past them again, then reached for the button by his shoulder. The rest popped up with it.

Alex opened the door. 'Do you have any pain? Can you move your legs?'

The man didn't answer. His face was angular, his eyes red from crying. He wore grey trousers and a blue business shirt, the sleeves roughly rolled up, the collar unbuttoned, no sign of a tie. His hands trembled on his knees and he smelled of sweat and fear.

'Sir?' Alex said, knowing how that felt inside, and sympathetic, but still aware of the people who were really trapped. 'What's your name?'

'I'm all right.'

'Can you turn sideways and put your feet on the road?'

The man did so easily, still staring at the people across the street. There was no hint of pain in the anxiety on his face.

Jane stepped away to tell Control they had good access and no backup was needed.

'Let me check your neck.' Alex leaned into the car.

'Don't.' The man's voice was full of panic. 'I can't see when you get so close.'

'I'll be quick.'

'I said don't.' The man dodged his hands and peered across at the crowd.

'Okay then, you keep watching and I'll reach in from behind you.' He opened the car's rear door and leaned in to examine the man's neck. His skin inside the shirt collar was slippery with sweat under Alex's gloves. 'Any pain? Tenderness?'

'No.'

Alex checked the man's head too. *See, you're managing fine. Everything's going to be okay.*

The way the man was acting suggested a head injury, but he had no swelling or lacerations. Alex pressed the man's scalp with his fingertips. 'Does this hurt?'

'No.'

Alex came back around to crouch inside the open driver's door. 'What's your name? Do you remember what happened?'

But the man's eyes were glued on something in the distance, this time further down the street. Alex glanced that way, but couldn't see anything other than the usual gawkers. 'How about we get in the ambulance? We can talk on the way to hospital.'

Still no reply.

'Sir?' He touched the man's hand.

The man flinched and tried to pull the door closed.

'Hold on a second, mate.' Alex glanced over his shoulder at Jane. Some patients responded better to men, some to women. It was worth a try.

Jane crouched inside the open door. 'Hi, I'm Jane.' Her voice was warm and calm.

Alex took the gear to the ambulance and stowed it, then stood listening to Jane murmur to the man and looking down the street to where the man had stared. There was nothing to see but people, some in suits, a few kids with their parents, maybe fifteen or so all up, and the number starting to dwindle as they realised there'd be no dead bodies or blood. His thoughts slipped to the night when there had been bodies and blood, but he caught his mind and hauled it back. *Stay in the present.*

Jane motioned him over with her head. She'd taken off her gloves and was holding the man's hands. He'd hunkered down into the seat and was peering up over the dash, not only at the shrinking crowd but in all other directions too.

'Marko,' Jane said to him, 'Alex is going to step in next to you and take your left arm. I'll be here holding your right. We'll stand up together, then walk across to the ambulance and climb in that door on the side.'

Alex stepped in close. Marko's eyes jittered to the open door then back to the street. Alex felt for him.

'Nobody can hurt you,' Jane said.

'He can see,' Marko said.

'Not once we're in the ambulance,' Jane said.

'It's dangerous for you as well,' he said.

'Nothing bad's going to happen,' Alex said. His own mantra. He hoped it sounded more believable to Marko's ears than it ever did to his own.

'You don't understand.' Marko pulled his hands out of Jane's grip. 'You're both putting yourselves in danger just by talking to me. You don't know what he's like.'

'Who?' Jane said.

'If I tell you his name things will be even worse.' He stared sideways down the street. 'He's probably watching now. He can find out things about you so easily. It's like he can read your mind.'

RPA had a good psych unit. They just had to get him there.

'So let's go,' Alex said. 'If things are that dangerous, we need to move.'

Jane took Marko's hand again, and he resisted for a moment then got to his feet and half-crouched between them.

Alex grasped his other hand. 'You're safe between us.'

'I'm not safe anywhere,' Marko said.

'You will be in a moment,' Jane said. 'Ready?'

They ran the three metres to the ambulance and Marko leapt inside. Jane followed him up the steps.

'I'll check the car,' Alex said.

She nodded.

Alex left the side door open so he could keep an ear on what was going on while he walked around the car. To trigger the airbag Marko would've had to have hit the pole at around twenty kilometres per hour. There was no damage apart from the crumpled front end, and no skid marks on the asphalt. He pressed the boot release button and looked in. It was empty.

The bystanders who'd been at Marko's window were on the footpath now.

'Did any of you see it happen?' Alex asked.

'I did, sort of,' the woman in the frilly top said. 'I was walking further down when I heard a horn blast, and I glanced around in time to see the car drive right up the kerb into the pole.'

'Could you tell whose horn it was?'

'No.'

'Did you hear any kind of collision before he hit the pole?'

'No.'

'How about the rest of you?'

'I was driving behind him,' one of the three men said. He wore navy blue workshorts and his knees and boots were crusted with dirt. 'A couple of cars back. It looked to me like he drove into it almost deliberately. I mean, he wasn't fishtailing or anything beforehand, the street's dead straight, and none of us were going fast. I don't know how he could've lost control.'

The other two men, older, grey-haired, in suits and ties, had been in buildings across the street and had come over at the sound of the crash to see if they could help.

'And none of you noticed any other vehicles that might've been involved?' Alex said. 'Or who blew their horn?'

'No.'

A marked police car pulled up behind them and two officers got out.

'Is the man all right?' the woman in the frills asked.

'Looks to be fine.' Alex smiled at them. 'Thanks for trying to help him.' They nodded, and Alex stepped away to speak to the police, listening on the way for the low murmur of Jane's voice in the back of the ambulance. There it was. She was fine. *And so am I.*

'Injuries?' the younger cop said.

'Possible psych,' Alex said. 'We're going to RPA. You want to speak to him before we go?'

The cop shook her head. 'We'll catch up with him there.'

Alex looked into the back of the ambulance. Marko lay on the stretcher under a blanket and Jane sat in the seat beside him, talking and holding his hand again. She smiled at Alex.

He nodded and shut the door.

The breeze rustled the leaves of the fig trees in the park and the sun was warm on the back of his neck as he walked around to the driver's side. RPA was just a few minutes away. Nothing bad had happened. He got behind the wheel, checked the rear-view and saw that Jane and Marko were still talking, then called Control and told them they were departing.

'Copy, Thirty-five.'

He started the engine and pulled out, looking over at the corner Marko had been so focused on. Now only a few people remained: a child in his father's arms pointing at the ambulance, two young women talking and looking past him towards the scene, a man with his hands in his jeans pockets and dark sunglasses covering his eyes. Alex waved to the toddler as he went past.

The lights at Bridge Road were red and Alex checked his mobile. No text from Mia. What did you do when they were like this? Eleven years of parenting her on his own and he still sometimes felt as lost as he had back at the start. There was a chance she was at Frances and Donald's place; they hadn't called to say she was late, after all. But with the way she'd been lately – with what had happened to him too – he needed to know for sure. He glanced at the lights and could see the oncoming traffic slowing. He was about to get a green. He'd have to wait and call after the case.

Five minutes later he backed into RPA's busy ambulance bay, turned off the engine and met Jane's eyes in the mirror. 'Stretcher?' Mobile patients often walked in.

She nodded.

He went to the back door, checking his phone again as he went, though he generally always heard a text arrive. Sure enough, the screen was blank. He lifted the door to see Marko had hidden himself completely under the blanket.

Jane tucked the case-sheet folder under her arm and climbed out the back and patted Marko's feet. 'Few clunks underneath you now,' she said, and she and Alex pulled out the stretcher then wheeled it into Emergency.

Two crews of paramedics with occupied stretchers waited ahead of them. Trudie, the triage nurse, a slender woman in her twenties with lots of make-up and jet black hair, frowned over a wad of paperwork. Marko lay motionless.

Alex spoke to Jane in a low voice. 'Mind if I step back out to check on Mia?'

'Go for it,' she said.

Outside the automatic doors, Alex called Mia's mobile. '*Hey, it's me,*' he heard his daughter say. '*You know what to do.*' Beep.

'You were supposed to text,' he said. 'We'll be talking about this tonight. Again.'

He hung up and rang Frances's mobile.

'Alex,' she answered. 'How are you?'

He could tell from her tone that everything was okay, and turned his face into the breeze. 'Checking in, you know how it is. She's there?'

'She was a little late, but she's here all right,' Frances said. 'Would you like a word?'

'One or two,' he said. 'Thanks.'

Mia came on the line. 'It wasn't my fault.'

'We have these rules for a reason.'

'It went flat,' she said. 'I told you I need a new charger.'

'I'm not going to argue about it now,' he said.

'How am I supposed to stay in touch like you want when I can't charge my phone properly? You expect me to do these things but then you make it impossible. It's not fair.'

He heard raised voices inside the department. 'I have to go. Do your homework and be good for Frances. We'll talk about this tonight.'

'Why do you always talk to me like I'm five?'

'I have to go,' he said again. 'Love you.'

She hung up. Alex put his phone away with his teeth on edge but the rest of him reassured and hurried back through the doors into Emergency.

'Let me go!' someone screamed further inside the department. 'Get off me!'

Jane stood by the stretcher with her hand on Marko's blanketed shoulder. As Alex came up, he heard her say, 'It's okay. Just somebody having a bad day.'

Marko clutched the blanket over his face. 'I shouldn't have come here.'

'It's all right,' Jane said.

Trudie sent the other paramedics and patients on their way and bustled over. 'What's up?'

Jane told her the story.

Trudie's frown deepened. 'Can he sit in the waiting room?'

Jane motioned for her to take a few steps away. Alex knew she'd be explaining the possible psych angle, out of Marko's hearing.

'Jane?' Marko said under the blanket.

'She'll be back in a moment,' Alex said.

'I'm sorry,' Marko said.

'You have nothing to be sorry for,' Alex said. 'This is our job.'

'Not about this,' Marko said. 'I'm sorry for anything that happens after.'

Alex put his hand on Marko's shoulder just as Jane had done. 'Everything's going to be okay.'

'I don't think it will,' Marko said. 'I appreciate that you're trying to make me feel better, but I truly don't think it will.'

Alex studied the blanketed form. He sounded less like a psych case now, but if that wasn't the problem, what was?

'Marko, what really happened today?'

'I can't tell you.'

'There's nobody here but you and me,' Alex said. Jane and Trudie were still talking down the corridor, and from Jane's pointed gestures Alex knew she was trying to persuade Trudie that Marko needed more care than being parked in the waiting room. 'Nobody can hear.'

Marko shook his head.

'Look at me,' Alex said.

'No.'

'Just for a moment.' Alex tried to ease the blanket down.

'Don't.'

'I want you to see that there's nobody else here, that you can trust me. I've been through some stuff too; I know how much people can help.'

'It's all useless,' Marko said. 'No one can help me.'

'We got you out of the car, didn't we? We got you here with no problems.' Alex tugged at the blanket again and this time Marko let go. 'See? Nobody here but us.'

Marko's face was pale, his cheeks wet with tears. 'You don't understand.'

'Try me, please.'

He shook his head and wiped his eyes. 'It's no good.'

The hopelessness in his voice touched Alex.

'Mate,' he said, 'people here really can help you. You just need to tell them what the problem is.'

'Mr Meixner,' said Trudie as she approached, Jane furious-faced behind her. Marko tried to pull the blanket back up but Trudie held it down. 'Do you know where you are?'

'RPA hospital,' Marko said.

'Do you know why you're here?'

'I was in a car accident.'

'What's the date today?'

'The twelfth.'

Trudie shot Jane a look. 'Seems perfectly with it to me.'

Jane's lips thinned further.

'Are you injured?' Trudie asked.

'A bit shaken up.'

'Are you thinking about hurting yourself?'

'What? No,' he said.

'You want to see a doctor?'

'He needs to,' Jane said.

'And the police will be expecting him to be here,' Alex put in.

Trudie didn't even glance his way. She grasped Marko's arm. 'Hop down. You can go to the waiting room.'

Marko resisted. 'He'll find me there.'

'See?' Jane said to Trudie.

'Nobody will get you,' she said. 'There's staff out there all the time and security is always close by.'

She tugged his arm and he slid off the stretcher.

'Surely there's somewhere in here he can stay,' Jane said.

'You want me to sit him on the floor by my desk?'

'If that's what it takes,' Alex said. They'd managed to bring Marko in; the least that could happen now was that he felt he mattered.

Trudie eyed him. 'I was kidding.'

'I wasn't.'

'This way,' Trudie said to Marko.

Alex looked at Jane, but there was nothing they could do. They watched Trudie walk the silent Marko to the doors leading to the public waiting area. When the doors closed behind them, Jane threw the case-sheet folder onto the stretcher mattress. 'He'll just get up and walk out of there. You should've heard what he was saying to me on the way. He reckons there's someone after him, that he saw this person in a car behind him and drove into the pole to get away from him.'

Alex wheeled the stretcher outside. 'That doesn't make much sense.'

'Exactly,' she said. 'That's what I pointed out to that woman. She said something about it sounding like a bad excuse for losing control on a wet road.'

'What's his medical history?'

'He said he doesn't have one.' Jane opened the back of the ambulance and sat on the step. 'But all that paranoia could easily be the start of some kind of psychosis.'

Alex's phone vibrated in his pocket. He took it out to see a text from Frances's number. *I want to be with mum.*

He froze.

'Everything okay?' Jane said. 'Alex?'

He fumbled the phone back into his pocket and tried to collect himself. 'Was he – did he say who it was that's after him?'

'He wouldn't say. He said we'd all be in danger if he did.'

Alex struggled to pay attention. 'He was saying similar things to me.'

'More proof of a developing mental condition,' Jane said. 'Who the hell's so powerful they could hurt not just him but us too? Only a psych patient could dream up someone like that.'

TWO

Jane checked her watch again. Ten to six. After leaving Marko in the oh-so-capable hands of Trudie at RPA Emergency, they'd taken a diabetic amputee from one of the wards all the way out to Nepean Hospital, and were now finally almost back in the city. She'd thought the timing would be perfect, they'd reach station right on knock-off, but then they'd hit this traffic on Anzac Bridge. Five minutes they'd been here and had moved only the length of the ambulance. Plus, judging by the radio messages flying back and forth, there was something big happening at Town Hall railway station. They hadn't been called yet, so she was crossing her fingers that it was under control, but when it came to knocking off you could never assume you wouldn't get another case. Not until you were walking out the station door, and sometimes the phone rang even then.

Alex looked across from the driver's seat. 'You all right over there?'

She tried to stop wriggling. 'I was really hoping we'd finish on time tonight.'

'Hot date?'

She laughed. 'Kids are in town.'

The words sounded fake, but Alex smiled and nodded. She'd lied so much these past few months. She'd been surprised sometimes how easy it was.

The setting sun turned the rear windows of the cars in front aflame, and the sky ahead was purple. Two vehicles along, a driver opened her door and stood on the sill, craning her neck to see the problem. Jane could've told her not to bother: she couldn't see herself – God knew, she'd been trying – and she was much higher up. There'd been no talk of an accident on the air, so it was either a breakdown or simply traffic. The Town Hall thing was too far away to be at fault.

She shifted in her seat again, then got out her phone. *Won't be finished on time*, she texted. *Typical. Sorry.*

A minute later the reply arrived. *Let me know when you're leaving.*

She texted back, *Will do*, then put her phone in her pocket.

Alex sat with his elbow on the wheel and his chin in his hand. She thought he looked anxious.

'Mia will be okay,' she said. 'I know that's hard to believe when you're right in the middle of it, but she's a good kid, and you're a great dad. Those things win out in the long run.'

'I hope so.'

'I know so,' she said. 'David was a little shit between fifteen and seventeen, and there was more than one night I lay awake terrified he'd end up in jail. Breanna was no angel either. Glenn wasn't too bad, thank goodness. But they're fine now. You just have to keep talking to her, keep those lines of communication open.'

'That's just the thing,' Alex said. 'She's become so secretive. We used to be such a team, we used to share everything, but now she hardly speaks even if I ask her a question.' The traffic ahead began to move and he put the ambulance into gear. 'I understand that a fourteen-year-old girl doesn't want to tell her dad about every aspect of her life, but it's like I'm the enemy and the tiniest scrap of information might get her killed.'

Jane nodded. 'I never told my parents a thing.'

'So what can I do? How can I protect her when I don't know what's going on in her life?'

'You have to trust her a little,' she said. 'Give her some space. Keep talking to her as if she is answering. At least that way she knows that if she does have a problem you're ready to listen.'

Alex didn't look like he believed her.

She reached across the cabin to touch his arm. 'I know the things you've seen, and I know how hard that makes it. But chances are, if you try to keep her locked off from the world, she'll work even harder to bust out and away from you.'

He didn't answer.

She hesitated. 'You'll be fine too. You did good today.' It felt condescending to say that when she was in no position to lead or guide. He was the one who'd had to cope alone at that crash the night she'd chucked a sickie; he was always focused on his patients while she often found her mind straying to the place she'd rather be. She kept seeing such doubt on his face though. If she didn't support him, who would?

He gave her a strange smile. 'I guess the bigger question is whether I can keep it up.'

'I think you'll do great.' *Oh man, just shut up!*

They were coming into the city now and the evening was settling into the streets. Drivers turned on headlights, and shopfronts cast a glow onto the crowds of pedestrians making their way home. They could be at the station in five minutes if they got all greens. With a tingle deep inside, Jane crossed her fingers that they'd sign off before another job came in.

'Thirty-five,' Control called.

'Dammit.' Jane grabbed the microphone. 'Thirty-five's on King Street in the city.'

'Thanks, Thirty-five. Sorry to do this to you but I need you to back up your nightshift at Town Hall train station. Patient's code four under a train, but the officers require assistance there.'

'Thirty-five's on the case.' She slammed the mike back on the dash. A body extrication could potentially takes ages. 'Dammit!'

Alex hit the lights and siren and hurtled right into George Street as Jane grabbed her phone and typed another quick text. *I don't believe it. Got a job, can't say how long.*

The road ahead was choked with cars and beyond them Jane could see multiple flashing lights and the tops of fire engines. The earlier radio messages hadn't given any insight into what was happening, just that multiple ambulances had been sent to the scene and most of them had cleared off empty not long after. Now they were all obviously tied up on other cases and unable to return.

Alex crossed to the wrong side of the road then swung into Druitt Street, flipped off the lights and siren and parked behind Thirty-six. Four fire engines and multiple police cars were lined up along the kerb. Further down two more ambulances sat with their back doors open, and Jane could see a couple of patients being treated inside. Pedestrians milled, cops trying to move them along. Despite all this, the air felt calm.

'Whatever happened, it's over.' She reached for the microphone. 'Thirty-five's on scene.'

'Copy that, Thirty-five.'

Her phone buzzed. *I can wait.* It buzzed again. *I want you.*

A thrill ran through her. *I want you too*, she sent back, then got out to grab equipment. The air was cool on her overheated skin. She just had to get through this job. How long could it take, really? Two hours? She could wait. She seized the Oxy-Viva and drug box.

'Kids'll have to cook their own dinner.' Alex hauled out the first-aid kit and monitor.

She smiled. 'Guess so.'

A stocky middle-aged security guard came up to them. 'This way.'

They followed his wide safety-vested back through the press of people, down the stairs, along the station concourse, then deeper and deeper into the system of grimy fluorescent-lit platforms, escalators and stairways. Police were everywhere. Jane could hear the muted rumble of distant trains in the tunnels and, as they descended another flight of stairs, felt the push of air in her face. The guard said something over his shoulder that she didn't catch. She glanced at Alex but he shrugged.

The next flight took them past more cops and onto a mostly empty platform. The air looked and smelled smoky, and firefighters in full gear and helmets crouched around something small by the far stairs. On the left side of the platform stood a train, doors closed, empty as far as Jane could see. Police talked with three people who she guessed were witnesses; the man and two women were dressed as if heading home from work, and had the stunned look she'd seen on countless people's faces before. Near them, a man sat on a bench with his head in his hands. The train's driver, judging by his uniform.

'This way.' The guard turned past the end of the railing and led them alongside the train.

Torch beams lit the darkness in front of the first carriage, and Jane heard their boss Ken Butterworth's voice down on the tracks. She put the gear on the platform and crouched on the edge. 'Partying again?'

Ken smiled wryly up from where he lay between the rails. 'Bloody back.'

His partner, Mick Schultz, injected the contents of a syringe into the IV cannula taped into Ken's wrist. 'Ten milligrams in. Partying soon.'

A cop standing near them held two torches on the scene. At the edge of the light Jane could see blood splattered on the train's silver metal and a grey-trousered leg with no foot on the far side of the track.

Behind her Alex said, 'Stretcher, spine board, what else?'

'Blanket to cover my face,' Ken said.

Alex went back up top to get the equipment. Jane lowered herself down onto the line then tried to brush the black dust from her hands.

'Give up now,' Ken said. His face relaxed, the morphine taking effect. 'It'll be all over you by the time we're done.'

'Great.' She looked at the leg. The body it was attached to was a dark shape in the shadows under the train. 'Suicide?'

'Not sure,' Mick said. 'The driver said he just appeared. When we first got here the place was all smoky, and I heard people saying there'd been a fire and everyone'd freaked out and tried to run and that maybe he was accidentally pushed.'

'Poor bastard.'

The top of the sock was intact around the leg's ankle, the exposed skin above it tanned with dark hairs. The wound was a clean line like a surgical amputation and she could see the leg in cross-section: the tibia and fibula stark white against the dark red tissue and yellow fat. She couldn't see the foot anywhere.

She turned to Ken. 'So what were you doing?'

'Jumped down and stumbled and that was it.' He blinked slowly and smiled.

She smiled back. This wouldn't take so long. They could have Ken in hospital in twenty minutes and get back to station ten after that, if they went hard. And as it didn't sound like a clear-cut suicide, the body would be someone else's to deal with after the cops had crawled all over everything. I'm coming, she thought.

Alex came back with the stretcher, spine board and four burly firefighters. He lowered the board to Jane, then jumped down onto the tracks himself. Jane laid the board on the rocks next to Ken, who was humming untunefully, and she, Mick, Alex and the cop, who'd put down her torches, rolled Ken gently onto his side and slid the board underneath his uniformed back. They strapped him securely to it, Ken giggling at their touch, then they lifted the board to waist height and walked to the platform. The crouching firefighters took hold of the front and helped slide it along, then Mick clambered up and coordinated the lift of the board up onto the stretcher.

Down on the track, Jane closed Mick's drug box and zipped up the Oxy-Viva.

Alex went to peer around the front of the train at the body. 'Poor sod.'

'I know. Especially as it might've been an accident.' She heaved the box and the Viva onto the platform. 'Apparently there was a fire and people panicked.'

'It wasn't a fire,' one of the fireys said. 'It was some kind of smoke device that someone dropped up the other end there.'

'Deliberately, you mean?' Jane said.

The firey shrugged. 'Idiots everywhere.'

'On a peak-hour platform too.' Jane scrambled back onto the platform and tried to brush off her hands. Her palms were black with train dust and there were smears of it on her shirt and trousers too.

Flat on his back on the stretcher, Ken said, 'Told you.'

'We got everything?' Mick said. 'Where's the lift?'

Jane slung the strap of the Viva over her shoulder, then heard a voice say, 'I was about here,' and looked around to see one of the witnesses talking to a uniformed police officer near the bottom of the stairs.

'He came barging through so hard that he caught my eye,' the man said. He looked to be around thirty, his clean-shaven face, neat navy suit and white shirt contrasting with the rough way his tie had been loosened and now hung at an angle from his collar. 'Then the smoke started, then I saw the guy go in front of the train.'

'The guy who'd been barging?' the cop said.

'No, the one from before. The one who pushed past me muttering about somebody being after him, somebody going to get him.'

A chill touched Jane's heart.

'First I thought the barger was just getting to a good spot

on the platform, to be ready when the train came in, but later I thought it was more. He had real purpose. And then he glanced up from under his cap and saw me looking at him.' He tugged at his tie. 'I don't know if I'm making much sense. It all happened so quickly. But somehow the way the first guy was saying someone was after him, then the second guy came through behind him –'

Jane dropped the Viva on the platform and jumped back down onto the line, grabbed one of the torches off the cop who was still standing there and rounded the front of the train. The torch beam lit up the grey trousers, stained with dust and grease and dark drying blood, but she could only see as far as the upper thighs; the rest of the body was under the train, twisted around and between the wheels. She squatted down and tried to find the man's face with the beam, her heart pattering in her chest, a whistling sound in her ears. Blood lay in clotted puddles between the rocks, and scraps of flesh were stuck to the under-carriage. She could see a stark white hand, but no face.

'What are you doing?' Alex said on the platform.

'Get the other torch and shine it in from the front.' She reached between the wheels.

Alex jumped down, then shone the torch in.

'Don't touch anything,' the cop said, crouched at Alex's side.

'Can you see his face?' Jane said. 'Is it him?'

'Who?' Alex said.

The wheel's edge cut into her shoulder, its flat surface cold against her cheek. She could see the back of his head. The hair was brown. She felt sick.

'You're not allowed to touch anything,' the cop said again.

Jane heard Alex moving on the rocks past the front of the train. She looked under it to see his beam cut off by the first wheels then shine again. The light flooded across the body, blinding her. Then he clicked it off.

'Alex?' she said in the quiet.

'It's him,' he said.

She stumbled around to where Alex was on his hands and knees on the rocks between the train and the platform. She pushed past the protesting cop and in next to him, held the beam of her torch as steady as she could and shone it between the wheels to see the dead white face of Marko Meixner staring back at her.

★

Detective Ella Marconi's phone beeped with a text as she entered Town Hall station half a step behind Detective Murray Shakespeare.

You can't just phone?

On a case, Ella sent back.

Dinner tomorrow then?

Let you know.

She switched the phone to silent. Her mother, Netta, was getting as obsessive about speaking to her live as she was about dinner invitations. It didn't stop Netta herself from texting as often as she wanted, of course.

Ella put her mother out of her mind and followed Murray onto the stairs. The call was an odd one: man under a train, and something about a smoke bomb and a crowded platform and a pushy guy wearing a cap. On the drive over, Murray had discussed at length his thoughts on whether it might be a homicide, a suicide or an accident, and the issues they needed to examine to work out which.

Ella had watched him talk and mused on his chattiness, his recent new enthusiasm about everything and a certain light in his eyes; and now, as they descended the stairs, she noticed that his hair was freshly cut across the back of his neck. Everything fell into place. The general level of intensity, the way he carried himself so newly tall and straight, the commencement of the use of cologne. There was no doubt about it: Murray had a girlfriend. She smiled. Good on him. She herself was spinning her wheels relationship-wise, but now was not the time to dwell.

They reached the platform, and she put on her cop face and looked around. A train sat stationary to the left, and the tracks on the right were empty. Firefighters were packing up gear, and uniformed cops stood with a small group of what Ella guessed were witnesses: three civvies, the train's driver, and two paramedics in dirty uniforms. The air smelled smoky and she could see a haze up high in the tunnels. She wondered what had really happened here.

A uniformed constable came towards them.

'What's the story?' Murray said, and Ella opened her notebook.

'Just before six the platform was packed, with trains due on both sides,' the officer said. 'The witness in the blue suit said that a man pushed through the crowd past him, muttering about somebody being after him. A moment later another man came pushing through, seeming very determined, and with a cap on. Then a smoke device was triggered, people shouted "Fire" and the crowd panicked and rushed the stairs. A train arrived then, and the same witness said the first man fell in front of it.'

Ella scribbled to keep up.

'What did the other witnesses see?' Murray asked.

The officer gestured at the group. 'Woman in the pink shirt also got pushed by a man in a cap shortly before the panic started. Woman in stripes says she saw the smoke gadget start up. Driver didn't see much at all, just sudden movement right in front of him. Paramedics say they took the dead guy to hospital earlier today after he crashed his car into a pole.'

'Head injury?' Ella said. 'Concussed and confused maybe?'

The officer shrugged. 'They said he was talking about somebody being after him then too. They thought he was a psych case.'

'Thanks,' Murray said.

The officer nodded and walked away.

Murray turned to Ella, all eagerness. 'Driver first?'

Ella nodded. The guy looked drained. It was the kind thing to do.

Murray beckoned him over.

'Detectives Shakespeare and Marconi,' Murray said.

'Troy Casey,' the driver said. His broad hands shook until he jammed them in his pockets, and he smelled of anxious sweat.

Murray asked him for his address and phone numbers, and Ella wrote them down.

'How old are you, Troy?'

'Thirty-one.'

'What did you see here today?'

'I was pulling in, normal speed, and as I got to the platform here I could see something was happening.' His eyes were red and his face strained. 'People were running, rushing away. And there was smoke too. I braked and just crossed my fingers that nobody tripped and fell. Then right here near the stairs I saw this flash of movement and heard the thud and knew somebody had gone under.' He shook his head. 'It's my third one this year.'

Ella felt for the guy.

'You couldn't tell if he'd jumped or fallen or was pushed?' Murray said.

'It was all too fast.' He wiped a trembling hand over his forehead and thinning hair. 'Just this flash and then the sound.' He shook his head again. 'Is that all? I'd really like to go home.'

'We might need to speak with you again later.'

'No problem.'

Ella shook his clammy hand and they let him go.

'Poor guy,' she said, when he'd gone up the stairs.

But Murray was already looking at the remaining witnesses. 'Next up, blue suit?' He beckoned him over before Ella could reply.

The man's name was Neil Furst. He was forty-three, worked in human resources, and lived in Bankstown.

'What happened here today?' Murray asked.

Furst described what the officer had summarised: the men pushing through the crowd, the smoke, the panic, the train, the death. His forehead was shiny, the skin around his shirt collar red, and Ella watched him pull his tie from side to side as he spoke.

'You sound like you think the second man was after the first,' Murray said.

'It did seem that way,' Furst said.

'In hindsight?'

'I don't know,' Furst said. 'It seemed strange from the outset. The way the second guy was coming through the crowd – he wasn't just meandering.'

'What did these men look like?'

'The first one was about my age, I think, brown hair, tanned. He was muttering, like I said. Looked a little wild-eyed.'

'Clothes?'

'Blue shirt's all I remember. Business-type shirt. It seemed a little at odds with how crazy the muttering sounded.'

'Did he have a briefcase or bag?'

'I don't remember seeing one.'

'And the second man?'

'Brownish cap pulled down low. Maybe greyish-brown. A nondescript colour, like it was badly faded.' Furst tugged at his tie. 'He had a shirt on, but I don't know what kind. The colour didn't jump out either.'

'It's okay if you don't know,' Ella said. 'No need to guess.'

Furst nodded.

'What else?' Murray said.

'He was a white guy. Couldn't see his hair. No beard or moustache.' He pulled on his tie again.

Ella's hand ached from writing so fast. 'How tall was he?'

'A little taller than me,' Furst said. 'Maybe five or ten centimetres. About a metre seventy. Or maybe eighty.'

'Skinny? Fat?' Murray asked.

'Average, I think. I'm sorry. I wish I saw more.'

'How long between the first guy and the second?'

Furst studied his watch. 'About three seconds.'

'And after that?'

'Like I said, I heard someone shout about a fire, and I looked that way —'

'Which way?' Murray said. 'Show us where you were standing.'

Furst moved closer to the steps and stood two metres from the edge of the platform. 'I was about here. The men were heading that way.' He pointed towards the narrow area of platform going past the stairs.

'Can you be sure they weren't going up the stairs?'

Furst hesitated. 'I guess not. That's not how it seemed though.'

'Then what?' Murray said.

'Someone yelled "Fire" down there.' He pointed towards the other flight of stairs. 'There was smoke too, suddenly billowing up, and people started shouting and pushing this way. I felt the wind of the train coming in, and it blew the smoke everywhere. I turned to head up the stairs myself and I saw the first guy right at the edge of the platform, and then as the train came in he went in front of it. The train driver braked, there was this God-awful screeching, and people rushed up the steps, tripping and falling on each other and screaming.'

'You definitely saw the man go in front of the train?' Ella said.

Furst nodded. 'I was on the stairs. I saw over the people on the platform edge.'

'Did you see the man with the cap?'

'I can't really be sure. It happened so fast, and people were shoving me from behind because of the smoke. I tried to stop but couldn't, and I almost fell.'

Ella looked at the steps. 'How far up were you?'

Furst went up a few and faced the train. 'About here.'

Approx five steps, she wrote.

'But you didn't see the man with the cap anywhere near him?' Murray said.

'I didn't see him anywhere,' Furst said. 'But maybe he took the cap off.'

Murray rubbed his chin in silence for a moment. 'Then what happened?'

'I got pushed along with everyone up the stairs, then managed to get out of the crowd and stop on the next level.'

'Even though you thought there was a fire?'

'I felt bad for the guy.' Furst glanced at the train again. 'I knew there was nothing I could do for him. I just wanted to – I don't know. Tell somebody what I'd seen.'

Murray nodded.

Ella could see past the railings along the narrow section of platform to the front of the train where torch beams flashed now and again from officers on the track. Back the other way, Crime Scene had arrived and were examining the smoke device. Between them, the two women and the pair of paramedics waited, the female paramedic checking her watch.

'Did you see the guy with the cap when you were on the upper level, or coming back down?' Murray asked.

'No. I did look, but I didn't see him.'

'All right.' Murray gave Furst his card. 'We might be in touch again, and in the meantime please call if you remember anything else.'

Furst nodded, then went up the stairs two at a time, taking a final glance back at the train before he disappeared on the upper level.

'Bit suspicious,' Murray said.

Ella looked up from her notebook. 'Him?'

'Didn't you notice how edgy he was? Tugging his tie all the time?'

She eyed him. There was keenness and then there was keenness. 'He'd just seen someone go under a train.'

Murray shook his head. 'I reckon it's more than that.'

Ridiculous. Ella turned away to look at the other witnesses. The female paramedic was checking her watch again. The male looked tired and pale, and the skin around his eyes was dark with rubbed-in soot.

'Paramedics next,' she said.

Murray called them over and introduced himself and Ella.

'I'm Jane Koutoufides,' the woman said.

'Alex Churchill,' the man said.

'You treated the victim earlier today?' Murray asked.

'His name's Marko Meixner.' Jane Koutoufides described how they'd been called to a car accident in Wattle Street that afternoon, how Marko had claimed to have driven into the pole deliberately to escape someone who was following him, how he'd had the doors locked and was too frightened to get out. 'We persuaded him it was best to come with us, and he ran to the ambulance and jumped in, then we took him to RPA. I told the nurse there about the things he'd been saying and that I thought he needed a psych assessment and careful watching, but she put him in the waiting room. That was the last we saw of him until we turned up here to help our boss who'd hurt himself getting down onto the line, and realised it was Marko under the train.'

'What things had he been saying?' Ella asked.

'That someone was going to get him, that it was dangerous for us to be talking to him, to be near him,' Jane said. 'I tried to get him to tell me more but he wouldn't.'

Alex Churchill nodded. 'I tried again at the hospital too, but he said it was useless, that nobody could help him. He sounded full of despair.'

Ella thought Alex himself sounded pretty low too. 'Did he have a psych history?' she asked.

'Not that he admitted to us,' Jane said.

'Did he suffer any sort of head injury in the accident?'

'He didn't have so much as a bruise.'

'The airbag had gone off, but otherwise it looked very low impact,' Alex said. 'The damage to the bonnet wasn't severe. There were no skid marks, and no damage to the back as if somebody had hit him. It looked like he really did drive himself into the pole.'

'Did he tell you who was after him?' Ella asked.

'He said he couldn't tell us, that it was dangerous for us to know,' Jane said.

'So he had someone in mind?' Murray said. 'It wasn't some random bad guy, or agent from the government, or whatever?'

'I got the feeling he knew who it was,' Jane said.

Murray glanced towards the train. 'And you're certain it's him under there?'

'We saw his face,' Alex said. 'There's no doubt.'

Ella circled RPA in her notebook. That would be the next step: to find out if he was assessed and what was found. Doctor Callum McLennan might be on shift. She felt a peculiar mix of hope and trepidation at the thought.

'What details did he give you?' Murray asked.

'His name's Marko Meixner,' Jane said again. 'He's thirty-five years old and lives in North Sydney. I can't remember his exact address, but it's on my case sheet up in the ambulance. I don't know anything else about him. He wasn't wearing a wedding ring, but some guys don't, do they.'

She sounded upset. Ella studied her, then looked around. 'North Sydney.'

'Yes.'

'This is the platform for the Bankstown line,' she said. 'He wasn't going home.'

Murray put his hands on his hips. 'So where was he going?'

★

The female witness in the pink shirt described the man who'd pushed her as wearing a brown cap, jeans and a black T-shirt. Her name was Jessica Sullivan and she was twenty-five years old and lived in St Peters. She carried a bright pink handbag tucked high under her left arm and held two paper bags from The Body Shop in her right hand. Her hair was tall and pink and so were her heels.

'He shoved right past me,' she said.

'Did you say anything to him?'

She shook her head. 'I thought he was crazy, and everyone knows you don't engage with the crazies. But he was gone in a second anyway.'

'Did you see much of his face?' Murray asked. 'Or his arms? Notice any tattoos, anything like that?'

'No,' she said. 'I only saw the side of his face, and it was for the briefest fraction of a second. He was white, and he didn't have a beard or a mo, but that's about all I could say.'

'What happened then?' Ella asked.

'Almost straightaway the smoke started. There was screaming and a mad rush for the stairs at the same time as the train came in. I went up the stairs too, then thought perhaps the crazy had something to do with the fire. I told a guard on the gates up there about it and she said I should tell the police. It was after that I heard somebody fell in front of the train. Was it him?'

'We don't think so,' Murray said.

'It was just some commuter?' She shook her head. 'That's awful.'

The witness in the black-and-white striped dress told them she'd been close to the spot where the smoke started. She was fifty-five, lived in Punchbowl, and her name was Sally-Anne Petrie. She smelled of cigarettes and breath freshener, and had a tiny red stone embedded in her left front tooth.

'I tend to notice things, you know? Things that would never register on anyone else's radar. So I'm standing there and I heard a noise like somebody dropping something plastic. I looked around and didn't see anything. But a minute or so later I smelled smoke and I looked around again and saw this funny tube-shaped thing and smoke was pouring out of the end. It looked plastic and I remember thinking, ah, that's what I heard being dropped. By then people were screaming and scrambling and I was trying to tell them that nothing's on fire, don't panic, but at the same time I was scared myself – who's to say that's not step one of a bomb and step two is a huge explosion?'

'Did you see who dropped it?' Ella asked.

'No,' she said. 'The platform was packed, and people were coming down the stairs and squeezing through the crowd all the time.'

Ella's wrist was aching now, her handwriting deteriorating.

'Then what happened?' Murray said.

'Everyone went charging in a panic up the stairs. I went too, then hung around up on the street until your fellas in uniform arrived, then I told them what I saw. They asked me to come back down and identify the thing, and here I am.'

As with the paramedics and Jessica Sullivan, Murray thanked her, gave her his card and told her they might need to talk to her again sometime. She smiled, the red stone glinting in the light, and went up the stairs.

Ella shook out her hand. 'Still think Furst is suspicious?'

'Just because the descriptions match reasonably well doesn't mean he's not up to something,' Murray said.

'Yeah, that's why he stayed around to talk to us.' But she remembered witnesses at another murder who'd waited in the blinding summer heat to tell a story she'd believed completely. 'Anyway, they all described the smoke bomb and the panic too.'

They needed to know whether Meixner had jumped, fallen or been pushed.

She pointed at the CCTV bubble overhead. 'Time to watch a movie.'

THREE

Grimy and exhausted, Alex walked from the car to their townhouse, his workbag over his shoulder and Mia stalking in silence behind him. He unlocked the door and held it open for her. She marched past without turning on the light and disappeared into the dark living room.

He closed the door, dropped his bag and switched the light on himself, wondering if Marko had a family; if somebody was waiting for him to come home or if the police had already told them. He'd been called to houses where such news had been delivered and people had collapsed; he'd delivered such news himself. The girl and her parents popped into his head: her grip on his hand, her mother's tears on his shirt. *Don't go there.*

His stomach rumbled. Frances and Donald had been kind enough to feed Mia but he needed to eat.

'Do you want a bit of toast?' he asked her.

'Yuck.'

He went into the kitchen and put the light on, then dropped two slices of frozen bread in the toaster. 'What did you have for dinner?'

'Chops and vegies,' she said. 'Yuck.'

'I hope you said thank you.'

She didn't answer.

Alex leaned back on the sink and rubbed his face with both hands. They smelled of alcohol handwash; he and Jane had used half a bottle each to clean off the railway grime. He was wearing his spare uniform from his locker at work; the dirty one was rolled up in his bag to soak later. There was a big pile of washing to do, and the dishwasher needed to be emptied, and he hadn't done the floors in a week. His plan this morning had been to get through the day. He'd done that, but still felt like he'd failed.

His stomach rumbled again, but he pressed the button to stop the toaster and went back to his workbag, then into the lounge room. He turned on the lamp to see Mia sitting sideways in an armchair, her legs over the side. She picked at her nails and didn't look up, but he saw her glance across out of the corner of her eye.

'Here.' He held out the phone charger he'd bought on his way to Frances's place.

She took it, still without looking up. 'Thanks.'

He sat in the other armchair and crossed his ankles. 'I got your text earlier.'

She shrugged.

'I understand how you feel,' he said. 'It's the same for kids everywhere. When things aren't going smoothly at home, everyone looks for a way out. And when you're stuck with the one parent all the time, you imagine it would be better to be with the other.'

'I'm not a kid.'

'Until you're eighteen, you're not an adult either.'

She shrugged again, a sharp dismissive move of her shoulders and head that had a practised air. He thought of what Jane said about keeping going.

'I know you imagine that being with your mum would be all roses, but you don't know her. She'd be like some random stranger on the street. You'd have as much chance of being happy with them, really.'

'No, I wouldn't,' she said. 'She's my mother. And I should be able to get to know her.'

'I agree,' Alex said. 'But she made the decision to leave, and she's made the decision not to keep in touch.'

Mia's cheeks were red, her eyes fixed on her nails. 'This girl at school said her dad has to send maintenance, and her mum knows where he is and what he's doing because of that.'

Alex's chest hurt. 'Sweetheart, your mum doesn't send anything.'

The last contact he'd had with Helen was when she stood in the bathroom doorway, suitcase in hand, and told him she was moving to Canada to meet up with an old boyfriend from school. He'd been on his knees by the bath and had reached out a wet hand. She'd turned away. Mia, three years old, No More Tears foaming on her head, had waved. 'Bye-bye, Mummy!' Helen had written three weeks later from Ontario, a brief note saying she was happy and hoped they were too. He'd sent photos of Mia and an admittedly grief-soaked letter to the return address, and got no reply. The next one he'd mailed was returned stamped 'addressee unknown'. When he'd still been in touch with Helen's sister, Mia's beloved Aunty Natty, before things had fallen apart on Mia's fifth birthday, he'd asked her to let him know if Helen ever got in touch, or to get Helen herself to call. Nat had promised. He wondered, not for the first time, where Nat was now, if she and Helen were in contact. Whether Nat had decided to abandon her promise after what had happened.

He rubbed his chest. 'I know you don't believe me, but I don't know where your mum is.'

Mia dashed tears from her eyes, her mouth set in an angry line, frown lines white on her red forehead.

'She's the one who's missing out here,' Alex went on. 'She's lived eleven years without you, without getting to know you and seeing you grow. If she doesn't want to be a part of that —'

'You're glad she's not here!' She was on her feet now, trembling. 'If she was here she'd let me do stuff and you wouldn't be the boss of everything! If she was here I might get to have a life, and you'd hate that!'

She rushed from the room and upstairs. Her bedroom door slammed.

Alex slumped back in the chair. She was right about one thing: he was glad Helen wasn't here. After the way she'd left, after she'd chosen not to keep in touch, after he'd picked himself up and made their little family work, he didn't want to share it with anyone. The two girlfriends he'd had for a month here and there over the years had eventually gone their own ways for the same reason. It was just him and his little girl – 'That's clearly all that matters!' one had flung at him. It was. So how hard was he supposed to search for someone who'd walked out on it?

Mia was wrong that he didn't want her to have a life though. Her life was the reason for the rules. He knew there was nobody to protect her but him. And while Jane had said he should trust her a little, it wasn't about trust. He'd seen what could happen, and he would never, ever forget.

*

In a stuffy control room at Town Hall station, Ella stood next to Murray behind a slope-shouldered grey-shirted security officer and watched CCTV footage.

First there was the dead man, Marko Meixner, pushing through the crowd. Three seconds behind him came a second man with a cap pulled low over his face. Ella saw the moment when he came past Neil Furst, recognisable by his suit, then the man kept on, leaving Furst standing still.

Showing on the next screen was Sally-Anne Petrie, also recognisable in the crowd by her clothes. She stood on the platform, looking bored. They'd seen her glance around forty seconds before, and now she turned as smoke started to billow up between people. The CCTV had no sound, but Ella could imagine the shouts as commuters rushed away from the smoke and panic ran through the crowd in a wave.

Earlier, after letting the witnesses go, they'd talked with the firefighters and looked at the smoke bomb, a short plastic pipe with holes punched in the sides and in the duct tape over the ends. Crime Scene had taken photos and were hopeful of lifting fingerprints from the pipe's surface. Ella wasn't so sure.

'Bombs like that aren't hard to make,' the fire officer in charge had said. 'Instructions are everywhere online, and there's nothing too complicated about the ingredients either. Kids are doing it all the bloody time.'

Ella focused on the next screen, where footage from a third camera was playing. This showed part of the stairs that Neil Furst had been forced up, and the narrow section of platform where Marko Meixner had gone in front of the train. She watched people rush up the stairs, some falling and disappearing from view under the crush.

'Lucky nobody else was killed,' the security officer said.

Other people fled along the narrow section beside the stairs, and Ella looked for a cap on a head or Meixner himself.

In the upper corner, the train appeared and in the next split second a body fell from the platform into its path.

'Go back,' she said.

The security officer clicked buttons and she saw again the commuters bolting along the narrow section.

'Slow it down just before the train appears.'

The people ran in slow motion. Women in dresses and suits and singlet tops, men in suits and T-shirts, a few people pulling children with them, then she spotted the slender figure of Marko Meixner moving as slowly as the rest. Nobody was wearing a cap, but it could have easily been removed. In the top corner, the train appeared again. She stared at Meixner and the people around him. The people rushed, and Meixner fell.

She let out the breath she'd been holding. 'You just can't see.'

'Replay it,' Murray said.

They watched it again, and again. Ella leaned closer but couldn't make out any more detail. She straightened and looked at Murray. He frowned.

★

Jane tapped twice on the glass pane by the doorbell. Footsteps. Door unlocked. Laird. That smile, and those arms.

The house smelled of dinner kept warm for hours and her stomach rumbled, but she led him upstairs first. In the glow of the lamps she studied his eyes, watched his clavicles rise as he breathed, the movement of his throat when he swallowed.

'What?' he said.

'Your ears are pink in the light.'

'Okay, weirdo.'

'It's good,' she said. 'It means you're alive.'

He took her hand and kissed it.

'I know these things,' she said.

'I believe you.'

The pulse beat in his neck. She laid her hand on his warm chest. His heart thudded under her palm and she could hear the air move in and out of his lungs. She blinked back tears.

He pulled her into his arms. She pressed her face into his neck and breathed in his fresh soap smell.

'Are you okay?' he said.

She kissed him, hard, and felt the build-up begin. She used to think people were lying when they said sex helped them after a bad day, but that was before she met this man. She felt now that they embraced in the face of death, pitting their life and energy against stillness and darkness, and the racing of their hearts and the sweat on their skin proved something that couldn't be proved any other way.

★

Ella squatted on the track in front of the stationary train and studied the mangled body of Marko Meixner underneath, a warm wind pushing at her back as a train approached on the other platform. Murray stood beside her with one shiny shoe on the rail. A crime scene officer lay on the black rocks and took photos, and a fire rescue team waited in silence on the platform for the go-ahead to begin extrication.

The scene officer got up. 'I'm all done.'

Ella stood too.

Murray said, 'Okay. He can come out.'

The rescue team climbed down with their equipment and a clean unfolded body bag. Ella scrambled back onto the platform, having no wish to watch Meixner being pulled from around the wheels, but Murray stayed.

She walked back towards the stairs, studying the platform edge. It was hard tiles overlaid with textured plastic squares patterned in such a way as to be recognisable to people with poor sight using a cane. She thought back to the CCTV and moved to the point from which she estimated Meixner had fallen, now two-thirds of the way along the first carriage. There were no signs on the ground to indicate what had happened, no scuff marks like you might see on a cliff edge if somebody resisted being pushed over. She looked into the carriage's dark and empty windows, then along to the front, trying not to imagine how it might feel to fall and know that this was probably it; how it might've felt if the force that put him there wasn't his own mind but a shove in the back.

'Ella,' Murray said, down on the track. He held a wallet open in a plastic evidence bag. 'The driver's licence says he's thirty-six and lives in Ryde.'

Ella flipped through her notebook to the details she'd copied off the paramedic's case sheet. Thirty-five, North Sydney. 'Maybe he did hit his head in the accident and lost a year.'

'The licence is three years old, and there's no change of address sticker on the back.' Murray clambered up onto the platform. 'Makes sense that he might've lied to the ambos. If he was as terrified as they describe, he might've worried who might overhear, who could get access to their paperwork.'

But terrified of who? Ella thought. The man in the cap? The voices in his head? Or something – or someone – else altogether?

★

They came out of the stairwell to fresh air and the flash of passing headlights. Full darkness had fallen while they were underground. The ambulances had gone and just one fire truck remained, the crew now helping the overall-clad government contractors load Marko's bagged body into their plain white van. Marked police cars with flashing hazard lights blocked the kerbside lane, their own unmarked one at the end of the line.

As they walked towards it, Murray handed Ella the bagged wallet and scrubbed at his palms with a handkerchief. In the plastic window she saw a photo of a smiling dark-haired woman – a woman who, no doubt, was wondering where Marko was. Years and years on the job, and it still made her uneasy to see pictures like this and know that in the next couple of hours they'd be knocking on the person's door, turning an ordinary day into the worst one imaginable and leaving nothing but devastation and questions in their wake.

They got in the car. Ella put the keys in the ignition but didn't start it. 'You going to call Langley?'

Murray refolded the handkerchief and wiped his fingers. 'I think this stuff's permanent.'

He dropped the cloth on the floor, then reached delicately into his pocket for his mobile. Ella heard Langley answer and ask where they'd been.

'We just got out of there,' Murray said. He gave their new boss a quick run-down. 'We're heading to the hospital now.'

'So you're thinking suicide?' Ella heard Langley say down the line. 'Classic paranoid-type thing?'

'Not necessarily,' Murray said, rolling his eyes at Ella. 'As I said, there was a man —'

'Pushing amongst a panicked crowed, yes, I heard you,' Langley said. 'Get the hospital's diagnosis then do the notification. Clock's ticking.' The line went dead.

'You'd think he was paying for the overtime himself,' Ella said.

She started the engine and watched the side mirror for a gap in the stream of headlights. Acting head of homicide Brad Langley was a numbers man: overtime, cases solved, man hours per case, detectives per shift. The fewer homicides that rolled down the chute, the more time detectives had to clear up older cases. He had every spare person digging into old files and re-interviewing key witnesses, chasing up evidence, following up whatever wasn't followed up before. The more cases he could slam the door on, the better his performance rating and the higher on the ladder he could climb. She missed her friend and usual boss, Dennis Orchard, currently acting up in counter-terrorism. He listened, and he cared.

At RPA, she parked in the police bay and they walked into the Emergency Department. Ella glanced around but couldn't see Callum.

Murray showed his badge to a young dark-haired nurse. 'We're here about a patient from earlier today, Marko Meixner.'

'Him,' the nurse said. 'I triaged him and put him out in the waiting room. He chose not to stay and left at some point in the next couple of hours. Why? What's he done?'

'Didn't he even see a doctor?' Murray asked.

'Look around,' the nurse said. 'We're overflowing with serious medical and trauma cases. A guy who runs his car into a pole and presents uninjured but perhaps depressed doesn't automatically get a bed and someone to hold his hand.'

'So he didn't see a doctor,' Ella said flatly. 'Did anyone else speak to him, other than you?'

'I guess reception out the front talked to him when they got his details. This way.' The nurse led them down a corridor. 'So what'd he do?'

'He's dead,' Ella said. 'Thanks for your help.'

They left her standing there and pushed through the double doors into the busy waiting area. Children wailed and parents shushed and rocked, teenagers huddled, one vomiting into a bucket, old people sighed and shifted on the hard plastic seats. Ella followed Murray to the desk, where he put his badge up to the security screen.

'We need to speak to the staff member who talked to Marko Meixner,' he said.

The grey-haired woman in her fifties frowned at her computer screen as she scrolled down with the mouse. 'That was me.'

Behind her, two other women worked at computers and a man talked on the phone. In the waiting room crowd, a baby's scream reached boiling point.

'Is there somewhere . . .?' Ella said.

The woman gestured for them to head through another door, where she met them in the corridor. Once the door closed most of the noise was shut out.

'I don't know how much I can tell you,' she said.

Ella got out her notebook. 'What did you and he talk about?'

'He said he was scared, that somebody was coming to get him.'

'Did he tell you that person's name?'

'No.' She twisted the blue lanyard that hung around her neck, making her ID card swing on its end. Ella saw that her name was Barbara Martin, her designation clerk level 3. 'He was very frightened though. To the point of distraction. I had to ask him a couple of times to tell me his address and next-of-kin particulars.'

'Which are what?'

'I'll just grab them.' She went back into the office area, then returned with a slim file. 'His date of birth's 12 August, he's thirty-five years old, he lives at 13 Helen Street in North Sydney, and his next of kin's his wife, Carla. He said he takes no medication and has no medical history. He said he'd never been to this hospital before, and when I put him into the system I saw that was right.'

It was the same wrong information that he'd given to the paramedics.

'He told you that?' Ella said. 'You didn't actually see anything with the information on it?'

'No,' she said. 'That's quite normal, if that's what you're asking.'

'Would you know if somebody with the same name but a different date of birth had been a patient here?'

She shook her head. 'But I can go and check now, if you like.'

'Thanks,' Ella said. 'Try 12 September 1977.'

Barbara went back into the office again.

'Two lots of lies,' Murray said.

'He must've been terrified,' Ella said.

'Or paranoid. Knowing Langley's luck, the date will match and we'll find out he's got a psych history as long as your arm.'

Barbara came out shaking her head. 'I even checked the name with the date of birth field empty. He's never been here.'

'Have you spoken to Mrs Meixner?' Murray said.

'No. I asked him if she knew that he was here, or if he wanted to call her and let her know, but he said it was too dangerous.'

'What did you do when he said that?' Ella asked.

'Well, after I finished I went out the back and said to Trudie, the nurse, that he seemed a bit off. She said she'd get to him.' Barbara twisted the lanyard up tight. 'At the time, I said to Mr Meixner that he was safe here, that nothing bad would happen, he just needed to be patient and he'd soon get to see a doctor.

I told him to take a seat and if he had any problems to come and see me again.'

'Did any police come to talk to him?'

'That's what made me realise he'd gone. I had to tell them he'd left.'

'What time was that?'

'About twenty past five. He came in a little after four. I know he was there at about quarter to five, when I went out to talk to a woman sitting nearby, but that's all I can really say.'

Ella wrote *4.45–5.20, left RPA.* 'What did you do?'

'I went back and told Trudie, but she was busy and just shrugged. It's not uncommon for people to leave, though usually it's after they've come up to the window five times and asked how much longer they have to wait.'

'Did you notice his behaviour while he was waiting?' Murray said. 'Did he talk to anyone? Cause any concern?'

'I didn't see him talking with anyone, and he certainly didn't cause any trouble,' Barbara said. 'He sat in the back corner and just huddled into himself.'

'And he wasn't assessed any more than what you've just said?'

She shook her head. 'He came in by ambulance, and Trudie checks those patients then decides where they're to go. Once she sends them out here, I or one of the other clerks get their details and put them in the system. Unless something drastic happens, like they collapse on the floor or start screaming in pain, they wait their turn.' She looked at them. 'Is Mr Meixner okay?'

'Unfortunately he passed away,' Ella said. 'We're trying to piece together why.'

Barbara covered her mouth. 'Dear God. That's terrible. I'm so sorry. I tried to help him. I could have tried harder with Trudie perhaps.'

'That's not the angle we're looking into.' Murray touched her arm. 'Thank you for your help.'

She went back into the office area shaking her head, and Ella shut her notebook. There was still no sign of Callum.

'How did Meixner get from here to Town Hall?' she said.

Murray nodded. 'We need to check the buses and taxis.'

They were outside and headed for the taxi stand when the Emergency doors slid open and Callum stepped out. 'Ella?'

'I'll just be a minute,' she said to Murray, and crossed the asphalt holding back a smile. 'How are you?'

The collar of his navy blue shirt was buttoned tight, the striped navy and gold tie pushed hard up against it. He smelled of hospital disinfectant. He smiled, but it didn't reach his eyes, nor last long on his face. 'Trudie said there's some trouble about a patient?'

'Not trouble as such,' Ella said.

'Some patient walked out of here and is now dead?'

'We're still putting the picture together, but that's how it looks.' She moved a little closer. 'How've you been?'

Callum opened and closed his hands by his sides. 'You know we can't stop people if they decide to walk out.'

'Nobody's saying your staff did anything wrong.' Ella lowered her voice. 'Are you okay?'

Callum frowned across the ambulance bay and didn't answer.

Ella hesitated, then touched his hand. 'What's going on?'

'Nothing.' He put his hands in his pockets.

'That's clearly not true,' she said. 'Are you pissed off that we didn't clear our questions with you first, or is it something else?'

He was silent for a long moment, looking everywhere but into her eyes, then he said, 'I have to go,' and went back inside.

Frustration bubbled in Ella's blood. She felt like an idiot standing there, unable to decide whether to follow him and dig out the truth or give up and walk away. She turned and headed for the car. Murray was leaning on the bonnet.

'How'd you go with the taxis?' she said before he could open his mouth.

'Spoke to the only driver there, showed him Meixner's driver's licence photo, but he didn't recognise him. We can call the dispatch centres from the office and find out if anyone picked him up, and check the buses on this route then too.'

Ella got behind the wheel and slammed the door.

Murray climbed in the passenger side. 'Everything okay with the good doctor? Had he seen Meixner?'

'No.'

'No to which question?'

'Meixner,' she said. 'Everything's fine.'

'It looked it,' he said.

She started the car with a scowl. She really liked Callum, and his behaviour stung. The night when he'd first invited her for coffee had seemed so full of promise. It was just before Christmas, almost two months ago, and she'd left her parents and Aunt Adelina watching slides of their New Zealand cruise, saying she had to go back to work. She and Callum had talked for hours, it'd been so comfortable and easy. Only once had she seen a cloud cross his eyes and wondered if he was thinking about his father, behind bars for the murder of Callum's cousin, the murder that she herself had solved.

Their second date in early January was good too, and she'd found he was a great kisser. But between then and their third date, a week later, his father's appeal had been dismissed, and when she'd sat across from him over dinner she'd seen that his eyes held nothing but clouds. They'd had coffee twice since, Callum saying he was too busy for anything more, but he was never really present, and the kisses were downgraded to pecks on the cheek. She was afraid that his father's guilt and her role in uncovering it might be obstacles too big for them to overcome. She understood how hard it must be for him; she could imagine that she too would find it difficult to be around someone who'd put one of her parents in prison. Not that she could imagine her parents ever killing anyone, but no doubt Callum had once felt the same way.

But it felt so wrong to lose that promise, those thrilling stomach butterflies, the easy conversation, and the shared dedication to work. That was an element of her personality her previous boyfriends had not been comfortable with, and she'd felt like this time things might be different.

'We going?' Murray said. 'Or are you going to stare all lovesick out the windscreen for the rest of the night?'

Unfortunately, after their second date she'd let slip to Murray where she'd been. She looked at him and noticed again his fresh haircut and the light in his eyes.

'What's her name?' she asked.

'Whose name?' Murray said.

'Is she in the job? Someone I know?'

He smiled. 'I have no idea what you're talking about.'

'Yeah, right,' she said, and drove out of the bay.

FOUR

Brad Langley stepped out of his office as Ella and Murray came out of the lift. 'Psych, right?'

'The doctor never saw him,' Ella said. 'There's no diagnosis.'

'There are other inconsistencies too,' Murray said.

Langley put his hands on his hips. He was tall, shaven-headed, with blue eyes a fraction too close together. He was known for favouring grey suits and white shirts, and had a rotating cast of ties in various shades of blue. He stared at them, then gestured briskly down the corridor. 'Get on with it then.'

He went back into his office and they walked to their desks. The office was empty, the other detectives gone for the night.

'I love bosses with that gentle touch,' Ella said.

Murray laughed. 'Coffee?'

'Of course.'

Ella sat at her computer and typed in Marko Meixner's name, then read her way through multiple screens with a shiver.

'Meixner's got no record, but he was a witness in a murder case seventeen years ago,' she called out. 'Short version is that he saw one Paul Mitchell Canning, aged twenty, kill one Karl Victor Grady, aged thirty-four, by hitting him with a star picket.'

'Jesus.' Murray put a brimming cup by her elbow.

'Canning and Grady were acquaintances who'd been drinking together when an argument began, which turned into a fight,' she said. 'Meixner was a taxi driver; he turned into the street where this was taking place at 1 am and saw it in his headlights. He called for police via his radio, then leapt from the car. It says here he shouted at Canning to stop, and when he didn't he threw himself over Grady's body to protect him. Canning threatened him and hit him once across the back, then fled.' She scrolled down further. 'Grady lived for a day, and was awake enough at one point to tell police what happened. Canning was located three days later, camping in the bush. He said, yes, he and Grady had been drinking and yes they'd argued, but then they'd gone their separate ways on the street. Canning's lawyer claimed that Grady was so badly injured, his memory had confused the drinking session with his grief-stricken friend with the assault. Meixner, meanwhile, had given a description that produced an excellent identikit picture, and he identified Canning from both a photo array and then in person in court. The jury believed him and Canning got twenty years with a non-parole of sixteen.'

'Seventeen years back,' Murray said.

Ella typed in Canning's details and her heart kicked up a gear. 'Released seven weeks ago.'

'Revenge would be sweet after a seventeen-year wait,' Murray said.

'Though kind of obvious,' Ella said. 'He'd know we'd look at him first. And what's he going to gain? Look at the risk. If he's caught, he goes back inside for another twenty, probably more.'

'Perhaps he felt it was worth it,' Murray said.

She saw there was a note attached to the file, and clicked to open it. 'Three weeks ago Marko went to Ryde station and told a Constable Luke Phillips that he was being harassed by Canning.' Her heart sped up even further. 'He said Canning had been lurking outside his apartment building, and once followed him for five minutes in the city. The officer wrote that he was agitated and panicky, and that he asked that Canning not find out he was talking about him.'

'Phillips look into it?'

'Yep.' She scrolled down. 'Spoke to Canning at his work, a boatyard in Neutral Bay. He said he didn't know what they were talking about. Had alibis for the times that Marko gave, from his employer and a couple of clients.'

'And during the conversation he probably found out who'd made the complaint.'

'No doubt,' Ella said. 'Phillips documented that he phoned Marko to say there was nothing to suggest Canning was doing anything, and certainly no evidence, and Marko asked him to look further into it anyway. Phillips told him there was nothing to look into unless something else happened, and for Marko to call back if anything else did happen. Marko hung up.'

'I can already hear what Langley's going to say,' Murray said with a sigh. 'Is there a mug shot of Canning?'

She brought it up. Canning had short brown hair combed to the right, brown eyes, and stared into the camera with a completely blank face. Ella had seen mug shots to make your hair stand up, criminals whose hate and fury burned from their eyes, but Canning looked like he was renewing his driver's licence, just one boring chore in a list of them he had to get done that day.

'Could he be more average?' Murray said. 'He might be one of a hundred guys on that platform today. Average build and height even. Bloody hell.'

Ella thought back to the CCTV. It was impossible to say whether Canning was the man in the cap. He'd hidden his face too well. They needed to look into more CCTV to see if there was a better shot of him.

'Meixner got a car?' Murray said.

She looked up Meixner's name in the RTA database. 'Nope.'

'It's probably in his wife's name,' Murray said. 'Cheaper insurance.'

Ella typed in the name Carla Meixner. No result. 'Either she doesn't have one or he lied about her name too.' She tried again with just the surname and the address. 'Here she is. Name's actually Chloe. Twenty-nine years old. Car's a white Honda.' She jotted down the rego, then entered it into the police system but it didn't appear. 'It's not showing as involved in an accident.'

'It has to,' Murray said. 'They took him to hospital so it would've been towed.'

'Unless he was driving a different car.' Ella searched for the entry about the afternoon's accident. 'It was a silver Mitsubishi, registered to a Daniel Truscott of Rydalmere. Listed as reported stolen at five-forty this afternoon.' She checked Truscott's record. 'Guy's clean too.'

Langley walked in. 'Who's clean?'

'The owner of the car that Marko crashed,' Ella said, turning to face him. 'Meixner was a witness in a murder case seventeen years back. Paul Mitchell Canning got out of jail seven weeks ago, and three weeks ago Meixner reported to his local station that the same man was following him, but the man had alibis and the officers could find no evidence.'

'More paranoia about being pursued,' Langley said.

'No reason it couldn't be legitimate,' Ella said.

'Except that no evidence was found, as you just said yourself. Did you check the mug shot? Does it match anyone on the platform?'

'It's impossible to be sure,' Murray said.

'You mean no.'

Langley loomed over them. Ella felt like a small child in trouble at school. She wished she'd stood up when he'd come into the room but then that might have seemed like she was jumping to attention. She felt his eyes on her and squeezed the arms of her chair. Murray was silent beside her.

'That's all you've got?' Langley said.

'For now,' she said.

'Get on with the notification then, find out what you can there. Look for psych medication in particular.' He snapped his fingers, the sound sharp in the quiet room. 'Chop chop.'

Ella stared at his back as he strode out, then swung in her chair to face Murray, her cheeks burning.

'Chloe, you said?' he asked after a moment.

Ella nodded. *Never mind Langley, think of the family.* She remembered the smile on the woman's face in the picture in Marko's wallet.

'No time like the present,' Murray said, but his voice was all false bravado.

★

Amy Street in Ryde was a series of unit blocks, the kerbs full of parked cars. Ella squeezed into a no-standing zone, and they got out to the faint sound of dance music and the squeak of bats in the trees. It was a little after ten, and Ella looked up at the night sky between the eucalypts and thought of the unsuspecting woman going about her life somewhere in this brown-brick building. They walked up the cement path of Number 18, carriage lights on ornamental posts lighting their way. Ella smelled the cool earth in the gardens and heard television laughter. The plastic evidence bag containing Meixner's wallet crackled in Murray's suit coat pocket and he put a hand on it.

The path split in two and a small sign on a post told them units 10 to 20 were to the right. They followed the path to a locked entry door. The space beside the button for Number 16 was blank, though most of the others had names printed on them. Murray pressed the button and they waited. Ella's heart felt squeezed.

'Yes?'

'Mrs Meixner?'

'Who's asking?' The woman's voice was firm, not frightened.

'Police detectives,' Murray said. 'May we come up, please?'

'Is this . . .' Now she sounded confused, worried. 'Is something the matter?'

'May we come up?'

A pause, then the buzzer sounded and the door clicked.

'Thank you,' Ella said in the direction of the speaker, and they went in and started up the stairs.

Chloe Meixner was waiting in her open doorway when they reached the second landing. Ella recognised her from the photo in Marko's wallet. She was short and slim, her dark hair back in a clip, her small hands cupping her tracksuited pregnant belly. Behind her stood another woman, taller but with the same features and the same anxious expression.

'Is this about where I've parked?' Chloe said, then her eyes searched Ella's and the colour left her face. 'What's happened?'

'May we come in?' Ella said.

Chloe moved back, her eyes huge.

They sat on a pale yellow lounge, Ella at one end, the woman on the other, and Chloe in between. Murray stood with his weight on both feet, clasping his wrist before him like a little boy.

'I'm Detective Murray Shakespeare, and this is Detective Ella Marconi.'

The TV behind him was paused on an episode of *Grey's Anatomy*. Lamps were on in the corners of the room, the curtains were closed, and the air smelled of satay chicken. The walls were covered in framed photos of Marko and Chloe: grinning in Times Square, outside the White House, in a gondola, pointing at the Eiffel Tower, on a green bridge Ella thought she recognised from a painting by Monet, on camels by the pyramids.

'Just to confirm, you are Chloe Meixner?' Murray said.

Chloe cradled her belly wordlessly.

'She's Chloe, and I'm her sister, Audra,' the other woman said. 'Just tell us what's happened, please.'

'I'm so sorry but we have bad news,' Murray said. 'Your husband, Marko, was killed tonight.'

'No,' Chloe said.

'We're very sorry,' Murray said.

'I don't believe you.'

Ella squeezed her shoulder. 'We're so sorry.'

'It's not true,' Chloe said. 'He's playing tennis.'

'How do you know it's him?' Audra said to Murray.

'It's not him,' Chloe said. 'It can't be. We're having a baby in four months.'

Murray took the bagged wallet from his pocket. 'This was in his pocket.'

'Someone stole it then,' Chloe said. 'Stole it then died.'

'The licence photo matches,' Ella said. Grief was tough to be around, but this was almost worse. 'And some paramedics who'd met him earlier in the day recognised him too.'

Audra tried to pull Chloe into a hug, but she stood and walked out of reach.

'I still don't believe you.'

'What happened?' Audra asked Murray, shaky-voiced.

'He was fatally injured when he fell in front of a train.'

'It's not true. He's at tennis and will be home any moment.' Chloe's face was pale, her eyes enormous and dark. She dug in the black handbag hanging on a chair and took out a mobile. 'I'll show you.' She dialled and listened. 'Hi honey, it's me. Call me back when you get this, okay? Love you.'

Audra started to cry.

'He's in the car with Henry,' Chloe said. 'They talk a lot and he wouldn't hear it ring, that's all.' She looked at the phone. 'I don't think I have Henry's number.'

'Chloe.' Audra got up and tried to hug her again.

Chloe pushed her away. 'Wait and see. Ten minutes and he'll be here. I guarantee it.'

Ella and Murray exchanged a glance. They had questions to ask anyway. Then they'd broach the problem again.

'Where does he play?' Ella said.

'Somewhere in the city, near the office,' Chloe said. 'Then his friend Henry drops him off. Henry lives at Epping so he's going straight past.'

'What's Henry's last name?'

'Marsden.'

'Does Marko have other close friends?'

She nodded. 'Tim Raye, who lives in Northmead now and works in real estate somewhere around there, and Lucas Ellison, who works in a bank and lives at Strathfield.'

'And where does Marko work?' Murray asked.

'Payton and Jones, in the city. He's a financial advisor.'

'When did you last speak to him?'

'Seven forty this morning, when we left for work. We go at the same time. He gets the bus into the city, I drive to Chatswood.'

She smiled. Audra put her head in her hands.

'What do you do?' Murray said.

'Payroll manager at Simpson Plumbing.'

Ella wrote all this down. 'How was he when you parted?'

'Fine. Great.' Chloe smiled again. 'He's been busy at work lately so has been a bit distracted, but otherwise everything's wonderful. I dropped him at the bus stop and we kissed and said have a good day.'

Ella said, 'Does he have any health problems? Take any medication?'

'He's on something for mild anxiety and depression. I can't remember what it's called. I'll get it for you.' She left the room.

Audra said, 'I can't stand this.'

'Sometimes it takes a while to sink in,' Ella said.

'And you're certain? It's really him?'

Ella nodded.

Chloe came back and handed Ella the packet. Citalopram. She wrote down the prescribing doctor's name too.

'How long's he been taking it?' Murray asked.

'Three or four years.'

'Did something happen then, triggering his problem?'

'We had a miscarriage, and it hit us both really hard, but even before then he had some issues. When he was nineteen, he saw a murder and had to go to court and testify. I didn't meet him until five years after that, but he still talked about it sometimes, and still had nightmares about it too.'

'How about in the last few months?'

'You mean because of the killer getting out of jail?' Chloe said. 'I was here when he opened the letter saying he might be coming out on parole. He started to freak out. I said he should tell them he was against it, but he ripped the letter to shreds and said that'd just be acknowledging it all over again, letting it affect his life again. I wanted to say that it was still affecting his life, it seems to me that it's never stopped affecting him, but he gets in these moods and he's so touchy that there's no point saying anything. That's marriage though, isn't it?' She sounded chirpy, and patted her stomach. 'Ups and downs, but you stick together.'

Ella didn't know where to look. 'So he never got in touch with the parole board?'

'If he did, he didn't tell me.'

'Did the prisoner ever try to make contact with him?' Murray asked. 'Send him a letter, anything like that?'

'No,' Chloe said. 'I'm sure he would've mentioned that. But you can ask him when he arrives.'

'Has anything happened recently that might make you think Marko was feeling threatened?' Murray said. 'Did he ever say he thought he was being followed, anything like that?'

'Before he went on the medication he used to say that,' Chloe said. 'It dropped off afterwards, and he'd only think it – or at least tell me – a couple of times a year.'

'How about lately?'

'No. But again, you can ask him when he gets here. Should be any minute now.' She glanced at the door.

'How were Marko's moods lately?' Murray asked. 'Say, since the letter?'

'Well,' Chloe said, 'we've both been under a bit of stress. He tends to worry about money, and more so lately because he wanted to be in a house before we had kids, but it's not going to happen and he feels bad about it. And also there's this guy at my work.' Her eyes welled up for the first time. 'This plumbing contractor, Simon Fletcher. It started about four months ago. For a while, he was just sending me flowers with no note and I thought it was Marko, but it wasn't – when I thanked him that first time, he got angry and upset. And then they kept coming. It was freaky. Marko wanted to go to the police, but we just told the florist near work not to deliver anything. After the first couple of weeks, he started mailing notes to work instead, saying things like he loved me from the moment he saw me, I was so beautiful, he knew we were meant to be together. He didn't put his name on them though, so I still didn't know. I was going to go to the police then, but this Fletcher came into the office and asked which of the bouquets I'd liked the best.' She shivered.

'What did you do?' Ella asked.

'I told him to get out. He said he just needed to express his feelings, and wasn't that what women wanted from men nowadays? I told him again to get out, that I didn't want his flowers, I wasn't interested, I was married. He said he respected a woman who respected her vows, then leaned over the desk like he was going to try to kiss me. My boss, Bill Simpson, came in and told him to get out, that he was fired from the job, and shoved him out the door. That was about six weeks ago.'

'Did you end up going to the police?'

She shook her head. 'There didn't seem much point. As soon as I knew it was him, it all stopped. And Bill improved security a bit so I felt safe there too.'

'Have you seen or heard from Fletcher since?'

'No,' she said. 'Could it be him who died and had Marko's wallet?'

'No, it's not him,' Ella said.

Audra hugged her knees.

'Has anything unusual happened recently?' Murray said. 'Hang-up phone calls, someone prowling the building? Damage to your car?'

'We have had a few hang-ups,' Chloe said. 'But we've had trouble with our line on and off for as long as we've lived here, so I thought it was just people trying to call and not being able to get through properly. And there was somebody lurking in the garden one night, but one of the other residents shouted they were calling the cops and whoever it was ran off. And the car's in the garage every night.' She peered at the clock on the wall. 'They must've hit some traffic.'

Ella said, 'Do you know a Daniel Truscott?'

'He and Marko work together.'

'Is there any reason why Marko would've been driving his car this afternoon?'

Audra said, 'I thought you said it was a train accident?'

'Marko had a minor collision in that car in Ultimo this afternoon. He was taken to hospital, all the while claiming somebody was after him,' Ella said.

'I don't understand.' Chloe frowned. 'Why would he have done that?'

Murray said, 'Is there any reason he might want to catch a train to Bankstown?'

'None that I can think of.'

'You don't have friends or family out that way?'

'Nobody,' Chloe said.

Audra said, 'Was it at Bankstown that, that . . .'

'No,' Ella said, then went on gently, 'Chloe, we need to ask you: has Marko ever tried to hurt himself?'

'No.'

'Clo,' Audra said.

'Oh, okay. Yes,' Chloe said.

'When was that?'

'Years ago. We've talked about it since though. After he started the medication he said he'd felt really low but he'd been afraid to tell me because he thought I might leave him. He said he realised it was the depression making him think that. I told him I love him no matter what, and that I always want him to tell me how he's feeling, especially if he feels so bad. I said we're a family, and nobody suffers alone. He said he once took an overdose of sleeping tablets, but that was before we met, and he woke up a day and a half later covered in his own mess. He said that before he started the medication he'd thought that maybe we'd both be better off if he was dead, but that he was afraid of pain and couldn't think how to do it, seeing as an overdose wasn't going to work. I made him promise that he would tell me if he was ever thinking about it again. He said he would. But since we found out about the baby, he's been completely thrilled. When we were at the twelve-week scan he said he couldn't believe he'd ever thought about killing himself, that he would've missed out on this, and how terrible that would've been.'

Audra burst into sobs and rushed from the room.

Chloe stared after her, then checked the clock again. 'He'll be here any second, I promise.'

Ella looked at Murray, feeling weak and useless and sick at heart. They were going to have to take Chloe to the morgue and let her see Marko's body for herself.

★

On the drive to Glebe Morgue, Chloe cradled her belly and sang under her breath. '*Hush, little baby, don't you cry.*' Ella saw in the rear-view that Audra sat with her head against the other door, wiping away tears and occasionally reaching out a hand that Chloe didn't take. The headlights of the oncoming traffic glared, and the car felt cramped and stuffy. Ella swallowed and reached for the aircon switch.

'*Daddy's going to sing you a lullaby.*'

Murray looked stiff and awkward in the passenger seat, and

they exchanged a miserable look. They'd updated Langley, who'd grumbled but was checking into Fletcher.

'Hush, little baby, don't you cry.'

Ella parked in the dark, quiet street at the back of the morgue and turned off the engine. They got out and crossed the footpath. Ella pressed the buzzer by the morgue door and a friendly faced young man in scrubs opened it.

'We need to see a body,' she said in a low voice. 'Meixner?'

He nodded. 'Come in. I'll get things ready.'

They went in and waited under humming fluorescent lights.

'Daddy loves you and so do I.'

Audra tugged Chloe's jacket tighter around her, but couldn't button it over her belly. Chloe pulled the jacket open again and smoothed her hands over her shirt.

'Chloe, honey,' Audra said. 'You know that Marko's not with Henry.'

'He is.'

'Then why hasn't he called you back?'

'Maybe they've gone to the pub. Pubs are noisy.'

'He doesn't go to pubs. You know that better than anyone.'

'They're stuck in traffic. There's been an accident and he's helping. He likes to help people.'

'Clo, look at me.'

'His phone's flat. He'll call when he can.'

'I'm trying to help you. You need to understand. Prepare yourself.'

'Daddy's going to sing you a lullaby.'

Audra turned to the wall in tears. Murray was staring at the fire exit map. Ella gazed at the floor, her heart aching.

The man returned. 'Follow me, please.'

They went in pairs down the corridor behind him. Audra tried to take Chloe's arm but she pulled away.

'Hush, little baby,' Chloe whispered. 'Daddy's stuck in traffic.'

Ella couldn't count how many times she'd done this, how many backs she'd stared at, how many times she'd held strangers while they wept. Hearing Chloe sing to the baby like this, though, put tonight in a whole different realm. She rubbed the unhappy goose bumps on her arms. Murray glanced over and gave her a tiny smile, as if he knew what she was feeling and was feeling it too.

They stopped at a curtained window. Audra pulled Chloe close, wrapping both arms around her. Chloe kept her face out of the hug and turned to the glass. The staffer disappeared into the room and Ella heard the click of the door closing, then the scrape of the curtain sliding back. Marko lay on a trolley with a sheet pulled up to his shoulders, hiding his injuries. His eyes and mouth were closed, his brown hair combed back, his skin pale. He looked younger than he had under the train.

Audra started to sob. Ella watched Chloe stare at him, her eyes wide and uncomprehending.

'Is this your husband?' Murray asked gently.

'No.'

'It's him,' Audra said. 'Oh God.'

'It isn't,' Chloe said. 'It's not. It looks like him but it's not.'

'Chloe –'

'It's not him! He's stuck in traffic!' Chloe smacked her palms on the glass. 'It's not him! Take him away! Don't make me look!'

'Chloe, it's Marko.' Audra put her hands to her sister's cheeks and turned her head to face her. 'It's him, baby.'

'No, no, no, no.'

'It's him.'

'No.' Chloe reached for the window as she sank to the floor. Her fingers left damp streaks on the glass. 'No.'

Audra dropped to her knees beside her. Chloe wailed in her embrace. Ella blinked back tears and saw Murray doing the same. The man inside the room hesitated, then drew the curtain closed.

'Marko!' Chloe screamed, then gasped and clutched her belly. Audra grabbed her arm. Chloe folded over onto herself and gasped again.

Ella's heart constricted and she turned to Murray, but he was already on his phone.

★

'Find who did this,' Audra said to Ella as the paramedics loaded the sobbing Chloe into their ambulance. The baby was fine as far as they could tell, and Chloe's pain had eased, but nobody was taking chances.

'We intend to,' Ella said. Beside her, Murray nodded.

Audra grasped their wrists. Her fingers were cold and hard as steel, her eyes even harder. 'Find who did this,' she said again. 'And make them pay.'

After the ambulance left, with Audra in the front seat, Ella and Murray got into their car.

'Marriage vows declare you're together until death separates you,' Ella said, her scalp tight and her skin clammy from all the tension. 'You think this Fletcher might've decided to help matters along?'

Murray called Brad Langley, and put him on speakerphone to summarise what Chloe had told them about Meixner and about Fletcher.

'A previous attempt and on medication?' Langley boomed. 'Sounds clear-cut to me.'

'We need to talk to this Fletcher and to Canning too,' Murray said.

'The wife know about Meixner telling police he'd been followed?'

'No, she didn't, but she's pregnant, so he probably didn't want to worry her.'

'Or he knew she'd recognise it as a sign that he needed to go to the nuthouse.'

Ella saw Murray's jaw tighten.

'How'd she take the news?' Langley asked.

'Not well,' Murray said. 'She's gone to hospital.'

Ella couldn't resist. 'I'm sure she'll feel better once we catch her husband's killer,' she said loudly.

'As I said, previous attempt and medication –'

'Yes, I heard you,' Ella said.

The line went silent. She squeezed her nails into her palms to stop herself digging the hole any deeper.

'So,' Murray said, in a conciliatory tone, 'we thought Canning first, then Fletcher.'

'Sounds like a job for tomorrow when you're on shift.'

Ella couldn't stand it. She got out of the car, shut the door, and walked into the centre of the empty street. Langley's penny-pinching attitude made her furious. Yes, they were on overtime, but this could be a murder just as easily as a suicide. Marko and Chloe and the baby deserved every effort. Finding the truth was what mattered. What better reason to spend money was there?

The high cloud in the night sky glowed with the city's lights. Out there somewhere was the man who may have pushed Marko into the path of the train. Almost six hours had passed already. It was plenty of time for that man to be getting rid of evidence, working out his alibi, putting lots of kilometres between himself and the scene, and they couldn't afford to let him have any more.

Murray got out of the car and leaned against the door. 'We can talk to Fletcher.'

'But not Canning? Jesus.'

'He said Fletcher's got convictions for stalking and assault, so he gave me his address and some names to rattle him with.'

That was good news, but still. 'He's forgotten Canning's conviction for murder, has he?'

'He said that because he's already been checked by the Ryde officers and had alibis for when Meixner thought he was being followed, he can wait until tomorrow.'

Ella glared up at the stars. 'Great.'

FIVE

Jane woke to the ringing of her mobile. She stumbled out of bed and groped in the darkness for her bag. The screen said the number was blocked.

'Don't answer,' Laird said from the bed. 'You know it's Deb.'

'The witch'll just leave me a voicemail.'

'Which you can delete. Turn it off and come back over here.'

'I have to get going anyway.'

He switched on the lamp. The ringing stopped and a moment later the message beep sounded. She scrolled through the phone's system and deleted it without listening to it.

Laird reached for her hand and she let him pull her back onto the bed, and kissed him, then got up again.

'You're cruel,' he said.

'Dayshift in the morning.'

'At least grant me dinner again tomorrow night?'

She smiled at him. 'Sure.'

She dressed and picked up her bag. He got up and pulled on boxers, then walked downstairs with her. The streetlight shone through the pane beside the door and she held him close and kissed him in the glow.

Outside, the street was quiet and cool, a breeze rustling the leaves of the trees in the gardens and along the footpaths. She shook off the irritation of the phone call and focused on how nice it was to be out at this time and to know that she was going home to bed. She didn't have to respond to anyone's call for help, she wasn't going to struggle on, exhausted, through the rest of a nightshift, then see the sun rise with gritty bloodshot eyes. She walked to her car swinging her bag and her hips, feeling Laird's gaze on her, and as she unlocked the door she waved. He waved back. She knew he stayed there watching as she drove off, and just before she reached the corner she put her arm out the window and waved again.

When she'd left Steve, she'd thought she was done with relationships. She didn't need anyone, she was happy and content on her own, and when a couple of her divorced friends got into it with new men she'd seen how the baggage on both sides tangled everyone up. Three months ago she'd met Laird, and changed her mind. They'd talked about baggage: she'd told him about Steve and Deb and the kids, he'd mentioned a long ago divorce and a more recent separation that was being kept quiet for his ex's sake. She was in LA, trying to make it as a fashion designer, and just didn't need the hassle, he said. Jane had Googled him a few days later and found a year-old photo of him and the blonde Lucille, and nothing since.

Because they both had to cope with the pressures of their work, him with the added stress of being high profile, they'd agreed to keep the relationship low-key and to themselves. It suited her right down to the ground, and something about the privacy made it all that much more thrilling.

Her phone rang again. Number blocked. 'Hag,' she said while it buzzed away on the seat. After a moment it stopped, then the voicemail beeped again. She lowered the window again and breathed. *Shake it off, shake it off.*

The drive from Laird's house in Bondi to hers in Maroubra took nine minutes on the quiet night streets. Traffic made such a difference in this city; a daytime run, even on lights and siren, could take double that. She found a parking space on the street twenty metres from home and walked under the streetlights along the footpath, then swung open the small gate to the path that led through her garden to her front door. Something crunched under her feet as she neared the patio, and she slowed. It was too dark to see, the shrubs she'd planted for privacy blocking the streetlights, and she turned the face of her phone to cast a glow on the path. Glass.

She looked up. The overhead light was smashed, the stained-glass panels in the front door also shattered.

The wrought-iron bars she'd had installed over the panels on the inside were intact, of course, as was the new lock. She unlocked it and stepped inside, careful of the shards on the tiles, and turned on the light. A sheet of paper rubber-banded around a rock lay in the mess. She closed and locked the door, picked the rock up and smoothed out the paper.

YOU HAD YOUR CHANCE. NOW KEEP AWAY FROM HIM YOU BITCH.

She re-scrunched the paper with a hard fist, then dropped it and the rock on the floor.

Steve's phone went straight to voicemail. 'You better sort your shit out,' she snapped. 'No more promises, no more gunnas. I swear, Steve, I don't care any more. This is it.'

She hung up and stamped upstairs to bed.

Whether or not she'd manage to sleep was another matter.

★

Simon Fletcher lived in Granville, in a narrow street between the railway line and the Great Western Highway. Most of the buildings were light industrial, with just four houses in a row remaining, all battered weatherboards, all in darkness. Ella drove past then turned around. A white work van with plastic piping strapped to the roof racks was parked at the kerb.

'I know that place.' Murray pointed to the house next to Fletcher's. 'Bikies used to live there. Real charmers.'

There was no sign of bikes now. Ella got out of the car. The front gardens of the houses were tall with grass and weeds, the roof lines were sagging, a smell like musty furniture in the air. Traffic droned on the main road and a train clattered past behind the buildings, but the houses were silent, almost eerily so. Her heart quickening in her chest, Ella found herself glancing along the street and around the overgrown gardens. Plenty of dark shadows. Plenty of hiding places.

The rotting ruins of a paling fence lay across the worn track to Fletcher's front door and she could see where it'd been trodden into the earth. They stepped onto the uneven floorboards of Fletcher's verandah, and Murray knocked on the doorframe.

Ella heard mutters inside the house, then a bare bulb burst into life over the door and cockroaches scattered across the wall. She touched her gun.

The locks turned, the door opened the width of the security chain, and one resentful eye looked out.

'Simon Fletcher?' Ella said.

'Yes.'

'Police,' Murray said. 'We need to talk.'

'Gawd's sake.' Fletcher closed his eyes, then took the chain off and opened the door. He wore baggy blue tracksuit pants and a paint-spattered, once-white T-shirt. He was about a metre eighty-five tall, had dirt-brown short hair and an average build. Ella thought back to the station CCTV. *Maybe.* 'Where were you this afternoon?' she said.

'On a job, then at the pub.'

'Can anyone verify that?'

'My offsider Daley, then the fellas at the pub.' He put a hand inside his T-shirt and scratched his stomach. 'What'm I sposed to have done?'

'What's Daley's surname and address?' Murray said.

'It's a bit late at night to go visiting, isn't it? Whyn't you let the boy get some sleep? Like you should be doing with me?'

'Just tell us,' Ella said.

Fletcher eyed her and said nothing.

'Or would you prefer to come to the station and have this chat there?' Murray said.

Fletcher sighed. 'His last name's Jones and he lives in a unit in Auburn. I don't know the exact place because he only just moved there.'

'And what pub were you at?'

'Thorn and Thistle in Pendle Hill.'

'What time did you leave?'

'I don't remember.'

'Was Daley there with you?'

'No, he was home with his girlfriend and baby.'

'Who'd you drink with?'

'Whyn't you just ask me if I did whatever it was then I can tell you I didn't?'

Ella said, 'Where's your job site?'

A cockroach ran out from a crack in the floorboards and Fletcher kicked it off the verandah with his bare foot. 'A building site in Seven Hills.'

'What time did you leave there?'

'Jesus, I don't know. Four?'

'Who hired you?'

'Fuck's sake,' he said. 'You want to know what time I took a shit as well?'

'Just the name of the person who hired you,' she said.

'Henderson Contractors, okay? Jesus.'

'So you left Seven Hills at four,' Murray said. 'Where'd you go then?'

'To Bunnings, then to the fucking pub,' Fletcher said.

'Times?'

'I don't know. Bunnings at twenty past, the pub at ten to? I don't know.'

'Got a receipt?'

'Pub doesn't give them.'

'Funny guy,' Ella said. 'From Bunnings.'

'I didn't buy anything. I was checking prices. As for what I did at the pub, I imbibed copious amounts of alcohol and participated in a number of games of pool. Happy now?'

'You miss your neighbours?' Murray said.

'Who?'

'Or do you all get together for a barbecue sometimes, talk about the old days?'

'The fuck are you on about?'

Murray tilted his head at the house next door. 'Bikers.'

'Noisy bastards, revving and music all hours of the night. Called the cops on them myself once. Plumbing's not just digging a trench, you know. I need to think. I need my sleep.'

Ella said, 'When did you last see Chloe Meixner?'

Fletcher put his hands on his hips. 'Ages ago.'

'When?'

'Whatever she says I did, I didn't.'

'When?' Ella barked.

'I don't know, six weeks? When Simpson kicked me out of the office.'

'When did you last try to contact her?'

'Same time,' he said. 'That was it. You think I'd try again when there are plenty more fish?'

'You put in a serious effort,' Murray said. 'All those flowers. Seems to me you'd be more determined after such an investment.'

'Whatever,' Fletcher said. 'I haven't been near her.'

'What about her husband?' Ella said. 'There he is, standing in your way. You ever met him?'

'No.'

'Didn't run into him tonight?'

'Fuck off.'

'You told her you liked that she respected her vows,' she said. 'But you also said she was meant to be with you. Don't expect us to believe that the thought of getting the husband out of the way never crossed your mind.'

'Youse are full of shit.'

'You have trouble letting go, don't you?' Murray said. 'The name Rosalee Griffiths ring a bell?'

Fletcher stared at him. Such piggy little eyes, Ella thought.

He said, 'That wasn't – that was a set-up.'

'You followed her from home to work and back again, and when you were sprung by her flatmate peeking through her windows you punched him out,' Murray said. 'You spent three months inside. Remember?'

A flush crept up Fletcher's cheeks. 'So what? I did my time, and that was ages ago anyway.'

'Four years,' Murray said. 'Doesn't fit my definition of ages.'

'I did my time,' Fletcher said again. He put his chin up and his shoulders back. 'I'm going inside. Unless you have a warrant, don't knock on my door or speak to me again.'

He slammed the door in their faces and the light over the door went out.

Ella stumbled along in the darkness behind Murray, across the broken palings and out to the footpath. 'You think he was the guy on CCTV?'

'He might be too tall.' He opened his door. 'We should talk to that offsider.'

'I agree, but I bet Langley doesn't.'

Murray got out his phone and called Langley. Ella crossed her fingers as he explained where things stood.

'I can't see any urgency on that,' Langley said. 'It can wait for your dayshift. Go home.'

Murray hung up. 'You hear that?'

'We sleep, and the clock ticks.' Ella rammed the key into the ignition. 'Great.'

★

The next day dawned grey and wet, and Ella got ready for work to the sound of the gutters overflowing onto the concrete paths below. She'd slept badly, but at least had been able to wake this morning of her own accord, not jerked from sleep by the blare of radios and shouted conversation of men on the building site next door. If this rain kept up, they might stay away for days.

She looked out the kitchen window at the sodden worksite. She missed the single-storey home that had been there before, and wasn't optimistic about what would replace it. The trend in the area was two-storey McMansions, all plaster facades and enormous windows. She didn't spend much time in her tiny backyard, but the thought of big tinted windows overlooking it got her back up.

The rain hammered the windscreen as she drove to the office, feeling bleak over the hours they'd lost and the restrictions Langley might put on them today. His focus on clearing older cases was insane; the warmer a case, the better the chance of solving it. The detectives on those older cases hadn't managed it then, so why take people off a fresh one to try again now? She stared at the queues of tail-lights and thought about Chloe and the child who would never know its father outside of photos and stories. Catching the killer wouldn't bring Marko back, but it was *something*. And that was the important thing, surely? It put her on the side of good in the world; it meant she was doing her best.

She wondered if that's how Callum felt when a patient died, that at least he was there, trying, doing his own best. She should call him. So he'd been cranky for no good reason last night – big deal. Life was too short.

She parked under the office building and dialled his number

as she walked to the lifts, a lightness in her chest as she listened to it ring.

'You've called Callum. Please leave a message.'

Voicemail. Dammit. She hadn't considered this. *Speak or hang up?* He'd see her number anyway. 'Hey, it's me. Just checking in. Hope all's well.' *What are you, a grandma?* She shut her eyes. 'I'll try you again later.'

She rammed her phone into her bag and punched the lift button with her fist. Yes, life was too short, but she also wanted to seem cool and in control. *Hope all's well. Jesus.*

The office bustled with people. Ella sat at her desk and phoned Audra. 'How's Chloe?'

'They've admitted her,' Audra said. 'Just to be on the safe side.'

'How is she otherwise? And how are you?'

'It's sinking in for us both.' Her voice cracked. 'Have you arrested anyone yet?'

'Not so far. The investigation's progressing though.' The words were hollow. She wished she could promise that they'd catch the bad guy soon. She wished they had more people so they had a better chance of doing so. 'I'll keep in touch.'

She put the phone down, then brought up the file about the murder Marko had witnessed. His statement included the investigating detectives' names: Michael Paterson and David Schuster. She opened the staff database and typed them in. Schuster had been killed in a car crash while on duty twelve years ago, but Paterson was a sergeant on the Central Coast.

She called his station and asked if he was there.

'He's off duty,' the desk officer said. 'Can I take a message?'

Ella gave her name and office and mobile numbers. 'It's about an old homicide case involving a witness named Meixner. Do you know when he'll be back?'

'I don't know. He's on sick leave.'

'Any chance my details could be sent to him in the meantime?'

The station would have his home and mobile numbers. Sometimes people would pass messages on, sometimes not.

'Is it urgent?'

'The witness is dead and I wanted to ask about the case,' Ella said.

'I'll see,' the officer said.

'Thanks.' Ella didn't feel hopeful. But she could always call back tomorrow, and the next day, and the day after that. At some point, either Paterson would come back to work or the desk officers would get sick of her and let him know.

Murray came over as she hung up. 'Langley wants a briefing. A proper one.'

She bounced a fist off the desk.

Ella had expected – hoped – the room to be full, but only four detectives looked up when she and Murray took their places at the head of the table. James Kemsley, John Gawande, George Lee, and Aadil Hossain. They were hard workers at least. She and Murray would need to wring every last bit of energy out of them to get as much done as possible before Langley decided to call them off.

And here he came now. He shut the door, then sat in a chair to one side of the room, shaved head shiny under the lights, tie a Greek ocean blue, legs in ironed trousers neatly crossed and hands clasped on his lap.

Ella opened the case folder and stuck Meixner's blown-up driver's licence photo to the whiteboard. 'Victim is thirty-six-year-old Marko Meixner, killed last night at 6 pm when he fell in front of a train at Town Hall station. Suffered major traumatic injuries. No cause of death yet; post-mortem's first thing tomorrow morning.' She described his earlier car accident and transport to hospital, and his apparent paranoia. 'The car he was driving belongs to a colleague, Daniel Truscott, who reported it stolen yesterday afternoon. He's yet to be interviewed.'

Murray summarised Meixner's leaving the hospital, getting somehow to the station, the smoke bomb and man in the cap.

'It was impossible to tell from CCTV footage whether he was indeed pushed or fell in the panic.'

'Or jumped,' Langley said.

'Yes,' Ella said, feeling the burn begin.

The four detectives said nothing and scribbled notes.

'Meixner was the star witness in a homicide case seventeen years ago,' Ella said, and described how Meixner had come across the two men fighting, how he'd tried to save the victim and was injured. 'Paul Mitchell Canning, twenty at the time, was convicted and jailed, and released on parole seven weeks ago. Three weeks ago, Meixner complained to his local station that Canning was following him. Officers spoke to Canning and found he had alibis for each occasion, and told Meixner there was nothing more they could do. Those officers, Canning himself and his parole officer are yet to be interviewed.'

'Last night we spoke to Meixner's wife, Chloe,' Murray said. 'He had a history of depression and anxiety, and was on medication. Years ago he attempted suicide, but Chloe is adamant that he would not have killed himself now. They're expecting a baby, and she said he'd even talked about how glad he was that his attempt hadn't succeeded because of how much he was looking forward to the new addition. Meixner's doctor is yet to be interviewed.'

The detectives turned pages in their notebooks and kept writing.

'Chloe also told us about some trouble she'd had with a former co-worker.' Ella summarised what Fletcher had done to Chloe, his past convictions for stalking and assault, and his response when they spoke to him last night. 'His offsider, Daley Jones, is also yet to be interviewed.'

She glanced at Langley, but the growing list didn't seem to be having any effect. He sat rubbing the fingertips of one hand across the knuckles of the other, his face empty.

'So this is where we are this morning,' Ella said. 'As you can see, there's plenty to find out.'

Langley got up and sauntered over to stand beside them. 'And here's the manner in which you'll do it. Lee and Hossain, you start by checking out Simon Fletcher's alibi. Talk to the offsider, then go to the pub. That shouldn't take you long because I doubt the clientele of the Thorn and Thistle are sympathetic to our cause. Don't worry about Bunnings for now, it'll take too long to check all their CCTV and watching it is probably unnecessary at this point. Then talk to Meixner's friends. Ask them especially about any recent mention of suicide.' He turned to Ella. 'You have their names?'

Ella nodded curtly. Talk about slanting the approach. But the detectives were smart guys: they could read between the lines.

Langley faced Lee and Hossain again. 'Then talk to Canning and ask the usual questions about where he was yesterday, then check with his parole officer about how he's doing.

'Gawande and Kemsley, call the taxi and bus companies and find out how Meixner got from RPA to Town Hall station and how he was acting on the way. Then go to Town Hall and watch more CCTV until you can see when he arrived, what he did, if the man in the cap is visible in any other frames with him.

'Marconi and Shakespeare, you check with Meixner's GP, then go to his workplace and interview his colleagues, including that Truscott. Ask again about suicidal references. He might've told someone he was depressed and thinking about ending it. People often do.'

Ella could feel that her face was set in a stony frown. She could hardly bring herself to nod.

'I'll get onto Media and have them put out a request for any witnesses to Meixner's car crash and from the train platform to come forward. I'll also check with the officers at Ryde, find out exactly how Meixner was acting when he made that complaint and how he responded when they said there was nothing to it.' Langley motioned the detectives to their feet. 'Priority is to rule out as many of these issues as we can, so let's get on with it.'

SIX

Doctor Elizabeth Hardy's receptionist barely looked at the badges that Ella and Murray held out. 'I'm guessing you don't have an appointment,' she said.

Ella raised her eyebrows. 'I said homicide.'

The woman wore a name badge labelled Hester. Her brown hair lay in flat curls all over her head and her shoulders were angular points inside her blue synthetic blouse.

'You see all those people?' She pointed past them at the waiting room, where two women and one man of varying ages sat watching them. 'They have appointments, and those appointments need to be kept. Doctor Hardy runs to an extremely tight schedule and this morning, in particular,' she glanced at the computer screen before her, 'she has not a single minute spare.'

'It's about a patient of hers,' Murray said.

His voice was still tight. They'd talked about Langley all the way here, and Ella had been impressed by his anger. It seemed the nameless girlfriend had ignited a new drive in him. Callum, on the other hand, was igniting nothing but frustration in her. No text, no call.

'In that case, privacy laws preclude her from sharing any information.' Hester paused. 'Unless, that is, you have a warrant.'

The pause was for effect; she knew perfectly well they didn't have one, because if they did it would be right in her face.

Ella eyed her. 'How about we ask Doctor Hardy herself if she can give us a moment?'

'That won't be possible,' Hester said. 'She's with a patient and cannot be disturbed.'

A young woman opened the front door and stepped in, bringing a gust of wind and the sound of pelting rain. Hester looked past Murray and Ella and smiled at her. 'Have a seat, thanks, Mrs Donaldson.'

Murray said, 'How about we wait here until she brings that patient out and ask her then?'

Hester turned even steelier. 'I promise you she has no time.'

'We like to give people the benefit of the doubt.' Ella smiled.

The phone rang and Hester picked it up and turned away from them to speak. 'Doctor Hardy's surgery, may I help you?'

Ella rested her elbow on the high counter and Murray tucked his hands in his pockets. Ella could smell his fresh cologne.

'How is she?' she asked.

He grinned. 'How's who?'

The door beside the desk opened and a crooked grey-haired man hobbled out on a walking frame, followed by a woman in her mid-forties with black hair tied in a tight bun at the nape of her neck and wearing a plum shirt with the sleeves folded up.

'See you next time, Mr Williams,' she said.

Hester was still on the phone, but on her feet and flapping a hand in the doctor's direction. Ella already had her badge out.

'Doctor Hardy? Detectives Marconi and Shakespeare. Do you have a moment to speak to us, please?'

Hardy glanced past them at Hester, then at the roomful of patients. 'One moment is about all I have.'

'Thank you,' Murray said.

Her office was warm and well-lit. It smelled of alcohol swabs and disinfectant, a smell Ella associated with Callum, and she felt a little pang.

They sat in chairs below sunny autumn prints, and Hardy went behind the desk. 'Which patient?'

'Marko Meixner,' Murray said.

'Is he okay?'

'I'm afraid he's dead.'

'I'm very sorry to hear that. Poor Chloe.'

'You don't sound surprised,' Ella said.

'He had a number of issues,' Hardy said. 'Was it suicide?'

'We don't know,' Ella said. 'Had he been suicidal?'

Hardy sat back in her chair and sighed. 'He'd been on anti-depressants for a few years, and I know he'd attempted suicide at least three times.'

'Three,' Murray said.

She nodded. 'Once with an overdose of tranquillisers; once he swam out to sea hoping to drown, but couldn't face it and came back to shore; and once he went to a national park near the Blue Mountains and set his car up to gas himself, but somebody happened along while he was still conscious and pulled the hose out and said they were calling the police. He gave up and drove back home.'

'When was that?'

'The first time was years ago,' Hardy said. 'Before he was my patient. He told me about it. The other two were in the last two years. I changed his medication a couple of times – anti-depressants have varying effects on different people – and lately he seemed better. I thought we had the dosage right.'

'Did he ever go to counselling or see a psychologist?' Ella asked.

'I suggested it each time, but he said he just wanted medication. Some people are like that. I can't force them.'

'Did he ever tell you what he thought was the cause of it all?'

'You mean the murder?' She nodded. 'I believe that he was predisposed to anxiety and depression though, and if that incident hadn't happened he would more than likely have developed both anyway.'

'Did he talk about the murder?'

'Now and again,' she said. 'That's one reason why I kept recommending counselling. He thought he should just be able to leave it behind, but as I told him, sometimes you need help to process things before you can do that.'

'Was he ever paranoid, thinking someone was out to get him?' Ella said.

'Not that I saw.'

'When did you last see him?' Murray asked.

She typed something into her computer and looked at the screen. 'Two months ago. He had an infected cyst on the back of his neck. I prescribed antibiotics and said to come back if it didn't heal within ten days. He didn't come back.'

'How was his mental state?'

'We talked about it briefly. He said he was feeling okay.'

'Did he talk about the murder that day?'

'No.'

'And nothing about him gave you concern?'

'Nothing. He was quiet and serious, but he always is. He was bothered by the cyst, but I didn't get the feeling that any-thing else was going on. I do sometimes, with patients. They talk about little problems, but you can see in their eyes there's something big they want to say. He didn't look like that.'

Two months ago was just before Canning was released from prison, Ella thought. Chloe had talked about Marko's reaction on opening the letter from the parole board, which would've arrived some weeks before that. It seemed strange that Marko would have told Hardy but not his wife about the other two suicide attempts, and then not mentioned the letter if it bothered him.

'Do you look after Chloe too?' Ella said.

'I do.'

'Do you think Marko was stressed about the pregnancy?'

Hardy smiled. 'He was delighted. They were both a little anxious, seeing as how they'd miscarried before, but otherwise they were thrilled.'

There was a tap at the door and Hester looked in, red-faced and frowning. 'Doctor –'

'Yes, I know. Just a minute.'

Hester withdrew and yanked the door shut.

'Is Chloe okay?' Hardy asked.

'She's in hospital actually,' Ella said. 'Just a precaution, I believe.'

Hardy shook her head. 'So sad.'

'Thanks for your time,' Murray said.

Out in the waiting room, Hester scowled at them as she thrust a cardboard file into Hardy's hand. 'Mrs Stubbs couldn't wait any longer, and Mrs Patel has moved her appointment to this afternoon.'

'Thank you again,' Ella said to Hardy, and they went outside to run through the rain to the car.

Once in, Murray slammed his door. 'Langley's going to be delighted. He'll say the crash into the pole was probably an attempt too, but Meixner chickened out at the last second, just like when he swam off the beach. Jump in front of a train and there ain't no way back.'

Ella brushed raindrops from her forehead and started the car. 'Maybe we'll learn something different at his work.'

★

Jane had left another message for Steve while sweeping up the glass and nailing plywood over the window holes before she left for work, then a further one while being jostled by wet umbrellas on the bus. Once at the station, she and Alex got a job the moment they signed on, so she didn't get a chance to make a third call until they pulled back onto station an hour later.

'Well, hello,' Steve answered.

'Thanks for ringing me back,' she said, her voice echoing in the plant room. She glanced inside the station. Alex was busy on the computer in the muster room.

'I thought you might've been sleeping before nightshift.'

'Yeah, that's why I keep calling,' she said. 'You sorted her out yet?'

'The timing wasn't right this morning.'

'You mean you're gutless,' she said.

'You sound like you think I'm not trying.'

'I know you're not.' She walked to the open roller doors. Tourists hurried from awning to awning along George Street. Rain dripped from the station's eaves. Seagulls whined in the grey sky and the damp air smelled of the briny, seaweed-filled harbour. 'Phone calls last night *and* smashed windows. You're doing nothing.'

'I'm sorry,' he said.

'Not good enough.'

'What can I do? I tell her nothing's happening. She doesn't believe me.'

'Go home sometimes,' Jane said. 'Like you should've done with me.'

'Janey,' he said. 'Janey, Janey. If I could have that time over again.'

'Don't be ridiculous.'

'No, I swear. It'd all be different,' he said. 'It's ironic, actually, that she thinks I'm seeing you, because it makes me think how great it would be if I was.'

'You're delusional.'

'If we got back together the kids'd be so happy.'

'It's been seven years,' she said. 'I think the kids have dealt with it.'

'No, listen, I've realised things. I've realised I can't talk to Deb like I can to you.'

'You didn't talk to me,' she said.

'She doesn't get me like you do.'

'You don't remember telling me in a fight once that I never got you?'

'I was crazy back then. I can see that now. And I can see the age gap is too much. It's as if she and I come from different worlds.'

'Whatever,' she said. 'Tell her to stop harassing me. Tell her where you go at night so she knows you're not with me.'

'How can I tell her that I'm –'

'I don't want to hear it,' she said. 'Sort it out with her or else I'll have to call the cops.'

'You don't need to do that. She's just stressed at work.'

'She's a receptionist, for God's sake.'

'Well, she finds it tough. And so she goes overboard some-times. She doesn't mean anything by it.'

'Bullshit.' The muster room door opened and Jane saw Alex look out. She lowered her voice. 'Fix it. This is your last chance.'

'Janey –'

She hung up on him and shoved her phone into her pocket. For years, Steve had chased after every girl who worked as his PA in his sheetmetal company, and by some miracle he'd never been sued. Deb had just been the last. To Jane's amazement, they got married and were still together five years later. When she looked back, she wondered why the hell she'd stayed with him for so long. Even the kids agreed.

'We all knew how unhappy you were,' Breanna had said over coffee soon after the wedding. 'I get that you didn't want to disturb my schooling, but some things are more important.'

Jane loved her kids. She loved that they were grown too, off living their own lives: Breanna with her delightful girlfriend, Alice, both of them graphic artists in Melbourne; David, a year older and single, working for the Commonwealth Bank in Adelaide; Glenn, two years older again, married and running a Cheesecake Shop franchise in Brisbane with his lovely Laura. Jane's friend Tracey Chapman – not the singer – whose own kids lived in the next suburb thought it was terrible, but for Jane it was great. The kids called on the phone most weeks, emailed now and again, and they all got together a few times a year. What more did you want? She'd raised them to go out into the world, not stay under her wing.

Alex opened the door again. 'Coffee?'

'Sure.'

She looked out at the wet street and the leaden sky and the wheeling seagulls once more, feeling like she'd drawn a line in the sand. Steve had his ultimatum now, and if he didn't tell Deb the truth about where he was spending his evenings, or at least persuade her he wasn't spending them in Jane's arms – a thought that made her shudder – he had nobody to blame but himself when the cops came calling.

Inside the station she found Alex in the kitchen, filling their cups. 'Sorry if I was yelling. Deb's been up to her tricks again.'

'She's persistent.'

'And deranged.' She got the milk from the fridge. 'I left him. Why the hell would I go back?'

Alex smiled. 'Hey, see the note Mick left on the table?'

Mick had scribbled that Ken had slipped a lumbar disc and would be in hospital for a couple of days while they decided about surgery.

'Ouch,' Jane said, as much for the nurses who'd have to look after him. He'd hate being stuck in bed.

There was an arrow on the bottom of the sheet of paper, and she turned it over. She looked at Alex. 'It's a girl. Mick and Jo are having a girl?'

He grinned. 'I rang him when you were outside. They had a scan, they're at twenty-four weeks and everything's fine.'

'That's fantastic.'

Mick and Jo had been trying with IVF for years. Jane wasn't surprised they'd held off telling people for so long.

'Do you remember seeing your own kids like that?' Alex said. 'I couldn't stop staring at Mia on the screen. The tiny face. The hands and feet.'

Jane nodded. 'They must be over the moon.'

'They're having a girl; Lauren and Joe had girls – there must be something in the water. You better watch out.'

'Oh, that's funny,' she said. 'Correct me if I'm wrong, because it has been a long time, but don't you need to have sex to get pregnant?'

'Don't ask me. I'm as dateless as you are.'

Jane took the cup he held out. You not only had to have sex, you had to be fertile, and she'd gone through early menopause two years ago.

'How's Mia today?' she asked.

'As delightful as she was yesterday.' Alex sat in one of the recliners and turned on the TV. 'Morning shows. What crap.'

She guessed he didn't want to talk about her. 'Don't grumble. If you found something you liked, the phone would ring.'

She sat on the arm of the other recliner and sipped. Alex flipped through the channels and stopped on a newsbreak that was talking about the death at Town Hall station last night. The newsreader said the family had been notified. Poor people, Jane thought. What a way to lose someone, and even more so if he was pushed.

'It doesn't sound like they know yet what happened,' Alex said.

An ad came on for the station's nightly news. Jane rested her cup on her thigh and watched, face carefully blank, as Laird looked seriously into the camera and spoke about the importance of the truth.

'Every time I look at that guy, all I see is ears,' Alex said.

'I've never noticed,' she said, the blood rushing up her throat.

'You met him at that awards thing, didn't you? What's he like?'

'Seems okay.' She lifted her cup to her mouth. 'We hardly spoke.'

Just enough to know they clicked and for him to get her number. It was when he'd called her the day after the bravery award ceremony, three months ago, that they'd talked. He'd asked how she was, mentioned that he'd seen the tears in her eyes when she'd received the medal for dragging the suicidal woman back from the edge of a roof, and next thing two hours had gone by. He'd invited her to his place for lunch the following day, they'd kissed over the salad nicoise, then spent the evening in bed. Jane's heart pounded so hard at the memory she could feel it in her face.

The job phone rang and she jumped up. 'Can you grab that? I gotta go.'

In the bathroom, she locked the door and ran cold water on her hands and wrists. *What are you, a teenager? You think of him and get all hormonal? Cut it out. Calm down. This isn't love. It's just a bit of fun.*

'Person fallen down stairs,' Alex called through the door.

'I'll be out in a second.'

She glared at herself in the mirror. *A bit of fun, nothing more. Pull yourself together.*

SEVEN

M arko Meixner had worked in an office on the fifteenth floor of a building in Kent Street in the CBD. The western side of the building would have a nice view of Darling Harbour, but Payton and Jones was on the east so the rain-streaked glass of its reception area looked onto other office windows and soaked roofs.

The PA at the desk studied Ella's and Murray's badges, then picked up the phone. 'Police detectives,' he said, listened, then put the phone down. 'Mr Weaver will be just a moment.'

Ella narrowed her eyes. If she was a civilian and detectives came to her office, she would be jumping right to it. 'What's he doing?'

'I'm not sure,' the PA answered.

Ella's phone buzzed. A text from her mother. *Dinner tonight?*

Don't know yet. I'm still on that case. As if she could've forgotten.

Please?

Ella sighed. *Okay. Unless I get overtime.* Fat chance of that.

Thanks. Lol.

Ella knew her mother meant 'lots of love' rather than 'laugh out loud', but it always made her smile. She put the phone away and next moment the door near the PA opened.

'Detectives, welcome!'

A tall heavy-set man crossed the carpet towards them. His hand was huge, damp and flabby when he shook Ella's, and she had to tilt her head to look him in the eye.

'Bill Weaver,' he boomed. 'Come through to my office.'

His office was timber-lined and leather-couched where it wasn't windows. His enormous black chair creaked when he sat down. He folded his hands as he faced them across a desk covered in papers and with the biggest computer monitor Ella had ever seen occupying one corner.

'How can I help you?'

'We need to ask a few questions about one of your employees, Marko Meixner,' Murray said.

'Yes, I notice he's not in today,' Weaver said. 'Is he in some kind of trouble?'

'Firstly, what kind of business is Payton and Jones?' Ella said.

'We're financial advisors and planners. Basically, we help people decide where, when and how to invest.'

'So Marko's role is what, exactly?'

'He talks to clients, finds out what they want and need, looks into their financial situation, helps them choose an investment strategy, and helps them alter that strategy later if their circumstances change.'

'How long has he worked for you?' Ella asked.

'Three years, give or take,' Weaver said.

'And before that?'

'With another company, I don't remember which. Doing accounts-type work though. This job was a promotion.'

'And you've been happy with his performance?' Murray asked.

'Absolutely,' he said, then asked again, 'Is he in some kind of trouble?'

'When did you last see or speak to him?' Ella said.

'Yesterday afternoon. I realised at about three that he wasn't here. He mentioned to me once that he has some issues, and is on medication, and I thought, well, perhaps he's had to go home. I would've preferred that he let me know, but sometimes sensitive people don't like to draw attention to themselves, do they, they prefer to simply slip away. Nobody else knew anything about it either. I'm surprised he hasn't turned up or called in today though.'

Ella said, 'How has he been lately? Has he mentioned any specific problems? Or have you been worried about his work performance?'

'I don't know that I feel entirely comfortable talking about this without his permission.' Weaver adjusted his hands on the desk. 'Is he in some kind of trouble?'

'We're sorry to have to tell you that he died yesterday,' Murray said.

Weaver stared at them. 'What?'

'We're sorry,' Murray said again.

'He's dead?' Weaver said, disbelief in his voice.

'Yes.'

'I don't understand. Was he sick? Did he have an accident of some kind?'

'We're not sure at this stage,' Ella said. 'We're trying to piece together what happened.'

Weaver took a folded handkerchief from a desk drawer and wiped his forehead, then leaned forward to his phone and pressed a button. 'Peter, can you come in here, please?'

The door opened and the PA stepped in.

'Tell everyone —'

'No,' Murray said. 'We'll need to speak to the staff ourselves.'

Weaver flapped the handkerchief at Peter. 'Bring me some water then.' He wiped his face again as the door closed.

'Are you okay?' Ella asked.

'I can't believe this. Are you certain it's him?'

Murray nodded.

'And what happened?'

'He was hit by a train.'

'Oh my God.'

'Did he have any particular friends in the office?'

'Uh, Denise, and I guess Roger,' Weaver said.

'Daniel Truscott?'

'Not that I'm aware.' He drew a deep breath. 'I'm having trouble taking this in.'

Ella could see that. Sweat was beading on his forehead and upper lip as fast as he could wipe it away, his cheeks were red and his jowls shiny. His eyes looked unfocused. He loosened his tie and popped the collar button, and pressed the handkerchief to the skin it revealed. She hoped he wasn't going to have a heart attack.

The door opened and Peter brought in a tray with three glasses and a jug of water. He put it on the desk, then hovered at Weaver's shoulder. 'Are you all right?'

'I'm okay, I'll be okay.' Weaver fanned his face with his hand. 'I just need a moment.'

It was too easy to picture him passing out and sliding off the chair onto the floor. Ella had done CPR on big guys before but nobody of this size.

'Would you like to lie down?' Peter asked.

'I'm fine, really,' Weaver said, but he didn't resist when Peter took his arm and helped him to his feet.

Ella grabbed Weaver's other arm and felt the heat and damp-ness of his skin through his shirt and suit jacket. He stumbled between them to one of the couches, then slid down onto the squeaking leather to blink dazedly at the ceiling.

'I'll be fine in a moment.'

'Maybe we should call an ambulance,' Peter said.

'No, I'm all right. It's just the shock.' Weaver fanned his face with both hands.

Ella drew Peter away. 'Marko Meixner died yesterday.'

'Oh no.'

'I'm starting to feel better already,' Weaver called to them. 'Don't ring an ambulance, for God's sake.'

'Maybe see how he goes while we talk to the other staff,' Murray said to Peter.

Peter nodded. 'I'll stay right here.'

★

Out in the reception area, Murray said, 'Denise first, then Roger?'

The main area of the office was open plan. Four men and two women sat at desks behind shoulder-high partitions. The woman who was closest turned as they walked in.

Murray held up his badge. 'Detectives Shakespeare and Marconi. We'd like to speak to Denise, please.'

The woman stood up, colour rushing to her face. The other staff stared.

'This way,' Ella said, and led her back into the reception area.

Denise Pham wore her black hair cut short across her cheeks. When she put her head down to cry, the ends swung forward by her temples. She was thirty-five and had known Marko for a year.

'How had he been lately?' Ella asked.

'A little quieter than normal.' Denise pulled a tissue from the sleeve of her grey blouse and dabbed her eyes. 'He's never been really lively, but the last few weeks he's been a bit more, well, withdrawn, I guess you might say.'

'Did you ask him about it?' Ella said.

'A couple of times I said, "Are you okay?" and he said he had things on his mind but nothing major. I thought it might be something at home and he didn't want to talk about it.'

'Do you know his wife is expecting?'

'Oh no, really? That makes it even more tragic.'

'Did you hear whether he told anyone else what was wrong?'

Denise shook her head. 'As I said, he's quiet. He doesn't share much at the best of times. He keeps his head down and buries himself in his work.'

'Did Marko tell you yesterday that he was leaving early? Or did you see him go?'

'No. I didn't notice he was gone until Bill came in asking about him. People often go out for meetings, so an empty desk is not unusual.' She dabbed her eyes again.

'Thank you,' Murray said.

Roger Saito sat down and wiped his palms on his knees. He was twenty-eight, he said, and had worked at a desk next to Marko's for two years. 'We'd chat a lot, mostly about work, but sometimes about other things. I like to surf, and he'd ask me how my weekend was, had I caught much in the way of waves.' He smiled and his dark eyes filled with tears. 'I can't believe he's dead.'

'Who was closest to him in the office, do you think?' Ella said.

'Me,' he said. 'I mean, because we sat together I talked to him more than anyone else. He was a bit of a loner. I invited him out to the pub and stuff a few times, but he wasn't interested. I think he spent most of his time with his wife. They were into travelling. Loved going overseas.'

'What else do you know about his life?'

'His wife, Chloe, works in accounts on the North Shore. They wanted to have a big family. He plays tennis one night a week at a court somewhere around here. I'm not sure where though. He loves his job, is right into it. He worked really hard.'

'Had you noticed any change in him recently?' Murray said. 'Say over the last couple of months?'

'He was a bit distracted,' Roger said. 'I'd see him sometimes staring off into space where before he'd always be typing or on the phone and going through documents. Or I'd say something to him and he wouldn't seem to hear me.'

'Did you mention this to him or anyone else?'

'I asked him if he was all right, but he just shrugged it off. I didn't tell anyone else. I thought if he's having a tough time that's his business. Besides, he's usually so completely focused, I felt like he'd earned a bit of time-out.'

'Did you know that his wife's pregnant?'

Roger glanced around. 'He did tell me but he asked if I'd keep it secret for now. He was over the moon about it. Couldn't wait to be a dad.'

'Did he ever talk about a court case he'd been involved in?'

'No.'

'You ever hear him mention the name Paul Canning or Simon Fletcher?'

'No. Who're they?'

Ella said, 'How was he yesterday?'

'Pretty quiet, but especially after this one phone call.'

'What phone call?' Ella said.

'He took a call and he sounded funny,' Roger said. 'I was doing some paperwork and the place was quiet, and I could tell that he'd lowered his voice. He sounded really serious.'

'What was he saying?' Murray asked.

'All I heard him saying was no. He'd be silent for a moment, as if listening to the other person speak, then he'd say no. Maybe four or five times. I assumed it was an angry client who hung up on him in the end, because next thing he put the phone down without saying goodbye or anything else. I glanced around and he was facing his monitor but not doing anything. Then I had a couple of phone calls to deal with myself, and I forgot all about it.'

'Did you get the impression that he was angry or upset?' Ella asked.

'It's hard to tell from one word,' Roger said. 'He clearly wasn't happy, but he didn't sound like he was on the verge of shouting at whoever it was.'

'Have you heard him get calls like that before?'

'No, but not all clients are happy all the time,' he said. 'I assumed it was simply that.'

'So what time did that call come in?'

'Around two, I'd say. Maybe two thirty.'

'And did he mention to you that he was leaving later, or did you happen to see him go?' Murray asked.

Roger shook his head. 'I don't even remember the last time I saw him. I guess at some point I noticed he wasn't here, but just assumed he had an appointment or something.'

'What's the phone system like?' Ella asked. 'Does each phone hold a list of numbers who've called it?'

'I don't think so,' Roger said. 'Some central phone hub might have them though.'

'Can you show us Marko's desk?' Murray said.

It was spotless and neat. Ella sat in the chair and surveyed the space. He had no Post-Its stuck along his monitor like Roger did at the next desk, no pens lying around. The keyboard sat square on to the monitor, the whole area dust-free, even between the keys. A diary lay to the left of the keyboard and she opened it at the ribbon. Someone had written *Call Nicky McLeod* in the space for 9 am that day.

'Is that his handwriting?' Murray asked.

'Yes,' Roger said. 'That's one of his clients. She's got some investments she's looking to roll over. She called this morning at 9.30 and I said it looked like Marko was off sick. She's calling back tomorrow.'

A tennis racquet and briefcase were tucked under the desk. Ella drew out the case and opened it. A softening banana lay in the bottom next to an empty manila folder, and three pens stuck out of the pockets inside the lid. She ran her fingers around the edges but there was no sign of anything hidden.

She opened the desk drawers. All three contained thick binders of information from various companies. She lifted them out and gave them to Murray to flick through.

'He doesn't seem to write much down,' she said.

Roger tapped the top of the monitor. 'All on here. You need to see?'

She nodded. If he willingly gave them access, they didn't need a warrant.

He booted up the computer and in a moment she was looking at a plain black desktop background with three columns of icons, mostly folders labelled with people's names.

'You recognise these names?' she said to Roger.

He nodded. 'They're all clients.'

'How do you know?' Murray said.

'Because I know. This is a small firm. We answer each other's phones. We help each other out. Marko and I've worked side by side for two years. He'd recognise all my clients' names, and I recognise his.'

Murray closed one binder and opened the next.

Ella looked back at the screen. She clicked on recent documents and went through them one at a time. All were about work: contracts, enquiries, tax issues. She opened his web browser and looked at the history, but again it was all finance-related.

Murray closed the last binder. 'Nothing.'

While the drawers were out she checked their sides and bottoms, then felt inside the desk frame itself. 'Nor here.'

She reinserted the drawers and Murray dropped in the binders. Ella closed the drawers, then looked around the office. The five other staff were watching, some wiping their eyes, some just staring with pale faces. They'd all obviously heard the news.

'Daniel Truscott?' she said.

A tall man with a freckled face and receding sandy hair stood up. 'That's me.'

They took him back to the reception area. Peter peered up from behind the desk, but lowered his head when Ella looked at him.

She faced Truscott. 'How well did you know Marko Meixner?'

'Not all that well,' he said. 'I gave him a lift home a few months ago when the trains weren't running, but that was the only time we've spent any time together outside work. I wouldn't call us pals.'

'Did he ask if he could use your car?'

'No. I only found out it was him who took it when I got a call from a police officer last night. He said that it'd been involved in an accident and Marko'd been driving it.'

'He'd never used it before?' Murray asked.

Truscott shook his head. 'I can only think that he took it because I was out at a meeting down the street for most of the afternoon, so he was able to take the keys from my desk. We have allotted spaces in the multistorey next door, so it wouldn't have been hard for him to find it.'

Across the room, Peter knocked at Bill Weaver's door.

Ella turned a page in her notebook and said to Truscott, 'There was nothing mechanically wrong with the car?'

'Not before he crashed it.' Remorse flickered across his face. 'Look, I didn't mean that. I'm sorry he's dead, but I'm not happy he wrecked my car.'

'Bill?'

Ella looked up at Peter's tone. He stood close to the door, as if listening, then knocked harder. 'Bill?' He tried the handle.

'Is everything okay?' she said.

'He's not answering his door or his phone, and I can't open the door.'

She crossed the floor and knocked. 'Bill?'

Silence.

She tested the handle. It turned. She tried to open the door, but something on the other side resisted.

'Bill, are you okay?' she said.

Peter and Murray put their shoulders to the wood beside hers and they managed to open up a gap of a few centimetres. Ella pressed her eye to the space and saw Bill slumped against the back of the door. 'Jesus. Push harder.'

'What is it?'

'Push!'

They pushed, but Bill didn't sprawl onto the carpet. Something was holding him in a sitting position. Ella slid her fingers into the gap and felt around the handle.

'Is there another way into here?' she asked.

'No,' Peter said.

'Go get me a knife. Scissors. Anything sharp. Then call an ambulance and the fire brigade.'

He ran off, and she looked at Murray. 'Weaver's hung himself on the handle.'

'What?'

'I can just reach it. I think it's his tie.'

The tips of her fingers slid off the smooth fabric. She had to press all her weight against the door to stop Weaver's bulk jamming it back on her hand.

'What's happened?' Truscott said behind them, Denise and Roger and the rest of the staff gathered around him.

''Scuse me, scuse me.' Peter shot through them all and thrust out a knife with a serrated edge.

Ella grabbed it and fed it into the gap and around the edge of the door. She shut her eyes to focus on the blade, felt it meet the taut cloth, and slowly, carefully, began to saw back and forth.

Somebody in the staff started to weep.

'Perhaps you'd prefer to return to your desks,' Murray said.

Peter darted back again. 'Ambulance and fire are on their way.'

'Fire?' Murray murmured to Ella.

'Chop our way in.'

She kept her eyes closed and her grip firm. If she dropped the knife . . . if they couldn't get in . . . and even if they could, how long had he been down? And then there was his size. None of the big people she'd done CPR on had been as big as him, and not one of them had survived. But she needed him to live.

What does he know?

Her wrist ached, her fingers throbbed. The fabric started to give way. She could almost feel the fibres snap one by one. She worked faster, harder. She turned her face the other way, and through the gap in the door could see the top of Bill's head, bobbing slightly from side to side in time with her action.

'Want me to take over?' Murray said.

She shook her head. Her cheek was against the cool timber of the door. Her hand and wrist were on fire. How much more fabric could there be?

Then the last fibres snapped and Bill slumped over on the floor. She dropped the knife, and Murray pushed beside her, but Bill's bulk pushed back.

'Peter, Roger, all you guys.'

They crammed in together and heaved. Ella hoped Bill's fingers weren't jammed underneath the door, but if they were it couldn't be helped. They needed to get in there and start CPR. The shoving pushed Bill onto his stomach, and Ella tried to squeeze through the newly widened gap, but it was still too small.

'Let me,' Denise said. She edged sideways into the space, straining to get through.

'Push,' Murray said, and they heaved again, and managed to hold Bill's weight back long enough for Denise to slip in.

'Can you roll him?' Ella said through the gap.

Denise grunted. 'He's too big.'

'How about grabbing his feet and swinging him around a little?'

She disappeared from view. Ella saw Bill's body shift a fraction and heard Denise grunt again.

'He's too big. I can't do it.'

Time was ticking.

Ella said, 'You have to.'

'Careful of your back,' Peter called.

Ella eyed him. They were trying to save a man's life, and he was being all workplace health and safety? *Or maybe he'd prefer Bill to stay silent.*

'Ready,' Denise said.

'Push!' Ella said to the door crew.

This time, between them, they opened the gap wide enough for Ella and she forced her way through. She seized Bill's right ankle and Denise grabbed the left.

'One, two, three,' Ella said, and they tugged the dead weight away from the door. He slid onto his back, and the door flew open and the staff poured in.

'Oh my God.' Peter dropped to his knees by his boss. 'He looks dead.'

Ella elbowed him out of the way. 'Go downstairs and wait for the ambulance.'

Bill's face was an ugly bluish-grey, and his motionless chest rose in a steep hill towards his belly. His eyes were open, staring, and it felt to Ella like he was watching her as she dug into his neck, trying to release the slipknot he'd made of his tie. She managed to pull it loose, then pressed her fingers into the dense flesh.

Denise waited, her shaking hands clasped over his chest, ready to do compressions. Murray hovered.

'I think he has a pulse.' Ella pushed deeper. It was so hard to know.

Denise felt his wrist and frowned.

'We need to start mouth-to-mouth anyway,' Ella said.

'I'll do it,' Denise said.

Ella wasn't going to argue as Denise grasped Bill's sweat-greasy face and pressed her mouth over his. She held his wrist and thought she felt a faint racing. After three breaths, his skin started to pinken and she knew that didn't happen unless the heart was still going. Good. He still had a reasonable chance.

She glanced around to find Murray looking at Weaver's desk. Denise appeared to be doing fine so she got up.

'Any note?' she asked.

'Not printed out.'

Murray nudged the mouse and the computer monitor asked for a password.

Ella looked at the staff gathered in the doorway. 'Anyone know Bill's computer password?'

They shook their heads.

'No doubt Peter will know,' she said to Murray. 'Checked the drawers?'

'Financial papers and a bottle of whisky. No cups.'

On the floor, Bill started to cough.

'Bill,' Denise shouted at his face. 'Can you hear me?'

He groaned and coughed again.

'Roll him on his side,' Ella said.

It took her and Murray plus Denise and Roger to heave him over.

'Bill!' Denise screamed in his ear.

'No need to deafen him,' Murray said.

Bill moaned. Denise burst into tears. Roger came forward and helped her up, and took her out of the room.

Ella squeezed Bill's shoulder. 'Can you hear me?'

He mumbled something.

She leaned close. 'Say that again?' *Tell me what you know.*

He mumbled again.

She glanced at Murray. 'Something about Marko.'

There was a bustle in the foyer and two paramedics and three firefighters hurried in, kits and equipment swinging from every hand.

'Excuse me,' the taller female paramedic said. 'We need to get in there.'

Ella moved reluctantly out of the way.

'What happened?' the other one said.

Ella described the situation. 'I don't know when he did it, but we weren't able to get in for maybe four minutes.' She pointed to the cut tie. 'That's what he used.'

They glanced over at it, then shone a tiny torch into his eyes and put an oxygen mask on his face.

Ella could hear Denise weeping in the foyer. She looked around for Peter but couldn't see him.

'Did anyone meet you downstairs?' she asked the paramedics.

'Some guy told us to come to the fifteenth floor.'

'He didn't come up with you?'

The paramedic shook her head. 'Are you the patient's work-mates? What's his name?'

'I'm a detective,' Ella said. 'He's a possible witness. His name's Bill.'

The paramedic called Bill's name. Ella saw his eyelids flicker. *That's right, come on back. We'll find out what you know yet.* She patted his meaty shoulder and walked out to the foyer. Murray was already there, speaking to a couple of the men. Denise sat trembling on the leather lounge near the reception desk, Roger beside her, his arm around her shoulders.

'Have you seen Peter?' Ella asked.

They shook their heads.

Denise peered past her at the paramedics. 'Is he going to be okay?'

'I think so.' Ella went behind the reception desk and pulled open the drawers. Paperclips, a stapler, sticky tape, pens and notepads. No wallet or mobile phone. 'Does anyone have Peter's number?'

People shook their heads.

Ella looked at Murray. He shrugged, clearly getting nothing useful from the pale staff.

The lift doors opened and she looked over to see a fire-fighter emerge, pushing the ambulance stretcher. No Peter.

'I'm going downstairs,' she said to Murray.

EIGHT

In the lift, Ella watched the lights flash behind the floor numbers. At ground level, she stepped out onto marble floors. The clacking of women's heels echoed in the high space, and two empty-faced men sat motionless behind the security desk. Peter was nowhere to be seen.

Ella showed her badge at the desk. 'Did you see the paramedics arrive?'

'Yep.'

'See a skinny guy meet them?'

'Yep. He had us hold the door for them.'

'Did you see where he went then?'

They shook their heads.

'He didn't hang about here, didn't go up with them?'

'No idea.'

Ella walked to the doors to the street. It was still raining. People hurried across at the lights with newspapers or briefcases over their heads, cars drove past with wipers swishing, and heavy drips fell from the joins between one building's frontage and the next. The air smelled of rain on oily asphalt and cigarette smoke. Ella looked along the footpath and saw Peter standing with his back to the wall, a cigarette in his shaking right hand, his eyes fixed anxiously on hers.

She walked over to him. 'Why didn't you come back up?'

He motioned to the ground. Four cigarette butts lay around his polished shoes. 'I don't do well with stress.' He glanced away, then back at her. 'Is he, ah . . .?'

'He's waking up,' she said. 'With a bit of luck he'll be all right.'

'Thank heavens.' Peter sucked the last out of the cigarette and dropped the stub on the ground, then twisted it flat under his toe.

'Do you know why he did it?' she asked.

'He didn't leave a note?'

'Not that we've found.'

'Huh.' He opened his cigarette packet and tapped a new one out, then held it towards her.

'No, thanks.'

He took it for himself and lit up, blowing the smoke above his head, eyes on its drift in the damp air. Ella waited and watched, her hands on her hips, passers-by brushing against her now and then, the hiss of tyres on the wet road loud behind her. Peter hemmed and hawed and scratched under his jaw with his little finger while his index and second squeezed the cigarette's barrel.

'I don't know for certain,' he said at last. 'I mean, I think he was having some kind of marital issue, so maybe it could be that.'

'But,' Ella prompted.

'But there may have been something else going on.' He scratched his jaw again, the skin turning red under his nail. He looked over her shoulder at the street and blinked, once, twice. 'I heard him arguing on the phone a few times.'

'Yesterday?' Ella said, thinking of the mysterious phone call to Marko that Roger had overheard.

Peter shook his head. 'Last Friday he got one, early afternoon I think it was. And a couple the week before.'

'Do his calls always go through you?'

'Not always. If people know his line they can call him directly. That's what this person did.'

'Which means you can't know whether it was always that person,' she said.

'No, but it was always the same pattern.' He sucked hard at the cigarette. 'I can see on my computer when he gets a call, and sometimes the number appears and sometimes it's blocked. These were always blocked. And after Bill answered, he'd buzz me and ask me to hold everything, so I knew he wasn't to be disturbed.'

'How long did he talk to this caller?'

'Five, ten minutes,' Peter said. 'Last Friday I could hear him even through the closed door. He was saying, "No, no, no!" Almost shouting it. Angry.'

The same words Roger had heard Marko saying.

'Was he saying it as if disagreeing with what the caller was saying, or trying to get somebody to stop doing something?'

'What do you mean?'

'Like if you saw somebody beating someone up and you tried to stop it, your shouts would be different than in an argument.'

He scraped his teeth over his upper lip. 'It was as if in an argument. Insistent. No. No. Angry, as if he'd had enough.'

Ella nodded. 'Did you ever listen in on the calls?'

'I would never do something like that.'

She studied him. 'You're sure?'

'Of course.' He widened his eyes, returning her stare.

'Did you ever talk about the calls with him?'

'After Friday's one I tapped on the door and asked if he needed anything. He said, "I told you I was not to be disturbed."' Peter's voice took on the large man's boom. 'I thought, fine, okay, and left him to it.'

'Then what?'

'He wandered out about half an hour later, all smiles.' Peter looked at the cigarette tip. 'I didn't bring it up.'

'And today, after we went to speak to Denise and the others?'

'He was quiet,' Peter said. 'Thoughtful. He stayed on the lounge for only a few minutes, then said he was all right and had some calls to make and I should go back to my desk. He got up without my help and really seemed fine, if a little shaken. He told me to shut the door on my way out, and I did, then at my desk I saw on the computer that he was making a call. I could see the number, it was local. I didn't think much more about it and got on with my work.'

'How long was he on the phone for?'

'I don't know,' Peter said. 'I had other screens up on the computer and didn't see when he disconnected.'

Ella estimated that she and Murray had spent fifteen to twenty minutes talking to the other staff. Weaver couldn't have hung himself too soon after he was left alone though, or he would've been dead for sure.

'We need to go up and see who he was calling,' she said.

As they reached the lifts, the doors opened and the paramedics and firefighters heaved the stretcher out. Bill Weaver's enormous belly jiggled under a white blanket while blue nylon seatbelts strained to hold him in place. Ella saw the redness on his flabby neck was turning into bruising. He looked at her and Peter from behind an oxygen mask, and tried to speak but made no sound. The paramedics pushed the stretcher across the lobby, the firefighters laden with gear falling in behind them and hiding him from view.

In the lift Ella said, 'Do you know the password to his computer?'

Peter shook his head.

★

On the fifteenth floor, Murray waited by Peter's desk. The staff had disappeared, back to their cubicles, Ella supposed, or gone out for a restorative early lunch.

Peter went behind his computer. 'The call's no longer connected.'

'Can you find the number he dialled?'

He typed something on the keyboard and frowned at the screen. 'It's something called Holder and Byron. I don't recognise the name.'

'Can you Google it?'

He typed quickly. 'It says accountants.'

'Address?'

He read out a floor and street number in Commonwealth Street, Surry Hills.

Ella scribbled it into her notebook. 'Thanks for all your help.'

Peter smiled weakly.

Murray was already walking to the lift. Ella waited until they were inside and the door had closed before she spoke.

'Bill Weaver's had "no, no" phone conversations recently too.'

Murray nodded. 'And while you were downstairs, one of the other employees – a guy named Donald Staines – told me that he'd twice seen Marko and Weaver having hushed conversations in the corridor, conversations that stopped when they saw him. I took Roger aside and asked him if he knew anything about it, and he said no.'

'Did Weaver say anything before the paramedics took him out?'

'Mumbled a bit, nothing intelligible.' Murray pushed his hands into his pockets. 'He squeezed their hands when they asked him to, and they said that showed his brain was in reasonable shape. They were going to Sydney Hospital.'

'Let's check out this Holder and Byron, and by the time we're finished there Weaver might be well enough to talk to us,' Ella said.

'I need lunch first,' Murray said. 'I'm starving.'

The rain had slowed to a drizzle. They crossed the street to a cafe and ordered sandwiches to take away. The tables were full of men and women in suits and the noise bounced off the ceiling. Ella looked out the window at the building they'd just left and thought about what might make a man try to kill himself like that. Bill Weaver knew something, and she was going to find out what.

Murray glanced at his watch. 'I'll just go outside, make a call.'

Ella grinned. 'You still haven't told me her name.'

'Whose name?' He winked and went out.

Ella checked her own phone and found a recent text from Callum asking her to call. Anticipation making her tingly, she went outside herself and took a few steps in the other direction from where Murray whispered sweet nothings into his phone.

'Hey,' she said when Callum answered.

'Thanks for calling back.' He sounded flat. 'Are you off this evening? I'm on break at seven and I need to talk to you about something.'

Horns blared on the street and she put her hand over her ear. 'Are you all right?'

'Or if you're busy we could meet tomorrow.'

A grey sludge of trepidation drowned the tingles. It didn't sound like a conversation to anticipate. If only she could count on getting overtime. But wait. 'I'm having dinner with my parents tonight. I can't really pull out now.'

'Can you drop by first? It won't take long.'

She couldn't think of another excuse. 'Okay.' Then she said, 'Want me to bring coffee from that place you like?'

'Up to you.'

Oh, this was bad. 'Are you sure you're okay?'

'I have to go.' The line went dead.

She lowered her phone. The sound of traffic on the street was loud and the passers-by walked too close. She pressed herself against the wall. It could be disputed whether she and Callum were technically even going out, but this felt like a break-up roaring straight towards her. And from the tightening screws in her chest, she knew it was the last thing she wanted.

★

Jane went out of the muster room to the ambulance, checking her phone on the way. She'd texted Laird half an hour ago, as she usually did at lunch, and he hadn't replied. *So today he's busy.*

She leaned into the ambulance and picked up the radio. 'Thirty-five's complete code twenty.'

'Thanks, Thirty-five,' Control answered. 'Head to Rozelle HQ and phone me in a couple of minutes.'

Jane looked back at Alex, who was standing in the muster room door.

He raised his eyebrows. 'Have you been naughty?'

'Not at work,' she said.

He grinned.

Her heart fluttering unreasonably in her chest, Jane waited until Alex turned into Druitt Street next to Town Hall before she dialled Control's number on her mobile.

'Trevor Gittins in HR wants to see you,' the control officer said.

'What about?'

'No idea,' he said. 'But good luck.'

She hung up and said to Alex, 'I have to see some guy called Gittins in HR. Know him?'

'Nope. What's it about?'

'It must be a complaint,' she said. 'Why else would they pull us off the road like this?'

'A complaint against you? Can't be. We've spent practically every second of every shift together for the last two months. Apart from the two weeks I was off. What did you get up to then, hmm?'

'Nothing at all.'

'Then maybe you're getting another commendation. Something to go with your bravery award.' He smiled

She looked past him at the grey sky reflected in the water of Darling Harbour. 'There was this really pissed guy we picked up at the casino, when you were off. I had to restrain him from slapping me. He could've misinterpreted. Taken offence.'

'If he was really pissed it's unlikely he'd remember anything of the night, let alone you.'

'That time frame though,' she said. 'It's enough time for the bill to arrive, and that might've provoked him. Because what else could it be?'

'Some crazy,' he said. 'Some officious nurse maybe.'

That reminded her of Trudie. 'What if it's to do with Marko Meixner? What if his wife or someone is complaining that I didn't look after him properly? What if they found something that I should've picked up, something that caused his death?' She felt uneasy, clammy. 'Maybe he had a head injury, and he had a fit on the platform and that made him fall. I knew I should've fought harder for him in Emergency.'

'It was Trudie's decision to put him in the waiting room,' Alex said. 'You didn't miss anything. I heard you in the back of the truck. You did the lot. I asked him too. He knew where he was and what was going on. You did everything you could.'

Jane frowned out the window. She felt like she had back in her early days on the job, when she'd been afraid that every patient had something extra wrong with them, something she couldn't see. For a while she'd overtreated – ECGs on fractured ankles, blood sugar tests on breathing difficulties – then slowly she'd learned to trust herself and her knowledge and particularly her experience. Over the years, she'd come to the point where every case was some combination of things she'd seen before. She'd believed Marko was either paranoid or had good reason for his fear, and whichever it was, she'd checked him fully, from head to toe, more than once. There'd been nothing to miss. She'd looked after him properly and well.

But then what was the reason for this summons?

★

The ambulance administration building at Rozelle had smelled the same since Jane had first entered it for her applicant's interview twelve years ago. The carpet had been replaced a couple of times since then, but there was still the same hint of must in the air, still the same odour of paperwork and printer ink and warm computers, of coffee and lunches and long afternoons behind desks. The corridor Jane sat in was long, and if she leaned forward from her chair she could see almost all the way to the classrooms, full of apprehensive students, at the southern end of the building. She remembered fat textbooks and exam nerves and shaky-handed fumbles in practical tests. *Don't let it be over.*

The uniformed officer working as Trevor Gittins's assistant had his leg in a cast. He sat with it stuck out sideways from the desk and resting on stacked phonebooks. He hunted and pecked on the keyboard, frowning at the monitor, and kept glancing at Jane apologetically.

'Shouldn't be much longer,' he said at least once a minute.

'Thanks,' she said in reply each time.

She took out her mobile and sent Laird a text. *Wish I was there right now.* She got up and crossed to the window. Alex was waiting in the ambulance; she could see his arm on the sill. If she couldn't be with Laird, she wanted to be there in the truck with Alex, rushing off to get vomited on by a drunk, or splattered with blood at a prang, or coughed on by an old man with tuberculosis. Anywhere other than here.

'Officer Koutoufides?'

She turned. The office door was open and a square-shouldered man of about sixty smiled at her. 'I'm Trevor Gittins. Come on in.'

Not reassured by the smile, Jane walked past him and into the office. While he was behind her she checked the screen of her mobile but Laird hadn't replied. The blank screen made her feel worse.

Gittins shut the door with a firm click. 'Have a seat.'

Jane stuffed her phone in her pocket and sat. She could feel her heart pounding in her chest. *You've done nothing wrong, so calm the hell down.*

Gittins sat behind the desk and placed his hands flat on top of a closed manila folder. His black hair was slicked down in distinct comb lines. His uniform was starched and pressed and bore the fifteen-year service medal, something that a lot of people had but few actually wore. He smelled of deodorant.

He smiled at her again. 'You look anxious.'

'I'm not,' she said. 'I just look that way. People are always telling me.'

He nodded as if he believed her. 'How's your shift been so far?'

'Good.'

'You like The Rocks?'

'Yes.'

Where was this going? The service didn't forcibly transfer people – not unless you did something *really* bad – and they didn't promote you without you applying.

'How're the nightshifts there?'

'Busy, like they are everywhere.'

She was uncomfortable under his gaze and couldn't read his face. *If he tries to touch me I'll punch his lights out.*

He smiled. 'Back when I joined it wasn't always like that. You could do your study on station, even sleep sometimes. You've been in twelve years, you would've found the same, am I right?'

'Sort of.'

'The kids that join nowadays have no idea.'

They're not the only ones.

He smiled again, then leaned a little across the desk. 'So,' he said conspiratorially.

Jane bunched her fists.

'You know why you're here, of course.'

'No.'

'Come on,' he said. 'This is us. Two foot soldiers on brief respite from the trenches. Let's just talk it all through.'

She bet he hadn't been in a trench for years. 'I don't have the slightest idea what you're referring to.'

'Look.' He tapped the service patch on his sleeve. 'I'm on your side. I know what it's like out there: maniacs in all directions, every one a hindrance rather than a help at scenes, and forget them pulling over in traffic.'

'Actually, I enjoy dealing with the public.'

'There's no TV camera here,' he said. 'No bugs in the walls. I've been in the war zone too, remember; I know what it's like. The frustrations, the upset, the anger.' He spread his hands as if in invitation. 'You can tell me. I understand.'

'I don't know what you want me to say.'

Some of the light left his eyes. 'I'm trying to help you. Giving you a chance to tell your side of the story. We can get in front of this thing.'

'Still blank,' she said. 'Are you sure you've called in the right person?'

Gittins opened the manila folder, took out a photo and slid it across the desk. 'Does that help?'

She looked at it. 'I can see it's the back corner of a car, but I don't recognise it and I don't know what it has to do with me.'

'Care to describe the damage?'

'The tail-light's broken and there's a dent in the panel next to it.' Jane pushed the photo back to Gittins, the heat starting to build in her blood. 'So what?'

He shook his head. 'You're doing yourself no favours.'

'I don't need any favours because I've done nothing wrong.'

'Is that so?' His voice had an edge now. He opened the folder again, licked the side of his thumb and flicked through a stapled collection of pages. 'This says otherwise.'

Jane put out her hand. 'May I?'

'Not yet.'

A siren wailed outside as an ambulance sped along Balmain Road.

Jane gestured to the window. 'Then can we get to the point? There are things I could be doing.'

Gittins closed the folder. 'Thursday the sixth.'

Jane said nothing.

'You remember that day?'

'Of course. It was only last week.'

'You were on a dayshift,' he said, as if she hadn't spoken. 'You were driving near St Vincent's Hospital. At three in the afternoon, at a set of traffic lights, you got out of the ambulance and abused another driver, then kicked the back of their car, causing that damage.'

'No, I didn't.'

'The complainant has witnesses. They each made statements.' Gittins waggled the folder.

'I didn't do it.' Jane leaned forward in her chair. 'I was working that day with Alex. Let me call him up here and he'll tell you the same thing. It never happened.'

'I'm sure he would.'

Jane felt the hackles rise. 'What does that mean?'

'I was working on the road when you were singing into your hairbrush at sleepovers,' he said. 'I know exactly how officers cover for each other.'

'Just because you did it doesn't mean everyone does.'

'Moderate your tone,' Gittins said.

'You moderate yours. I didn't do it, and Alex will back me up on that because it's true.'

'You're not getting off on good footing in this investigation, speaking to me in that manner and being so uncooperative.'

'There shouldn't be any investigation,' Jane said. 'How many times do I have to tell you I didn't do it?'

Gittins slapped down the folder. 'The complainant has threatened to go to the police and media on this, so I suggest you try to work with me.'

'Work with you how?'

'Admit you were in the wrong, write a statement of incident, fill out these insurance forms –'

'I will not.' Jane stood up.

'Sit down.'

'No.' There was a buzzing in her ears and her skin was hot. 'Who made this complaint?'

'Under the Service's standing orders I can't tell you that.'

'How do you know it's real?'

'Two witnesses, the photo of the damage, and I spoke to the woman myself. I believe what she says.'

'Woman,' Jane said, realisation dawning. 'She looked like me, didn't she?'

'I spoke to her on the phone.'

'Her name's Deb Bodinnar-Koutoufides, isn't it?'

'No.'

'Then that has to be one of the witnesses' names,' Jane said. 'She got one of her friends to make the complaint. It's a lie.'

'I've heard that excuse before too,' Gittins said. 'And that name is nowhere on this report.'

'So she's using a fake one,' Jane said. 'That woman hates me and will do anything to cause me trouble. She smashed windows at my house. She phones me up and abuses me.'

'And did you report that to the police?'

'No, I told my ex-husband, who's now married to her. She's behaving like this because she thinks we're seeing each other,' Jane said. 'Police can't fix that. I told him to tell her the truth about whatever it is he's been doing.'

'So you have no proof that she's done anything.'

'Feel free to come to my house and see the windows I'm having repaired.'

Gittins held out a form. 'If there's no police report, you need to start the paperwork.'

'No.' Jane took out her phone with shaking hands, saw there was still no reply from Laird, switched it to speaker and called Alex.

'Yep,' he answered.

'Can you come up?'

'On my way.'

Jane ended the call and tossed her phone on the desk in front of Gittins. 'You heard what was just said. You have my phone. I'll wait here until he arrives, then I'll step outside without speaking to him. You ask him about it and see what he says, see if he doesn't say it's a lie too.'

'If I wanted to speak to your colleague I would've called him up myself,' he said.

She glared at him. 'I'm not writing a single word until you ask him the same questions you've asked me.'

There was a tap on the door, then it opened. The desk officer stood there on his crutches. Alex stood behind him, his eyes full of questions. Words boiled up in Jane's throat but she said nothing.

'Alex Churchill to see you,' the officer said.

Gittins gestured Alex in. Jane resisted the urge to roll her eyes, the urge to shout at Gittins and tell Alex everything, and instead waited until he was inside the room before walking out with her face blank and head high.

The officer closed the door behind her and hobbled back to his chair. Jane paced the carpet before his desk, her hands opening and closing at her sides, hearing the low rumble of voices inside the office. She hated that Gittins wouldn't listen to reason, and equally hated that with her phone inside she couldn't call up Steve or the witch herself and vent her feelings.

She faced the desk. 'How do you cope, working for him?'

'I don't. I've asked to be moved.' He pushed a block of sticky notes towards her and lowered his voice. 'Write down your mobile number.'

She did so without hesitation. He peeled off the sheet and stuffed it into his shirt pocket as the voices in the office grew louder, and when the door flew open he was frowning at the keyboard again.

'Jane,' Gittins said brusquely.

Jane went in. Alex stood with his arms folded and his face like thunder.

Gittins again slid the form across the desk, this time adding a pen. 'You said you wouldn't fill it in until I listened to your partner's answers. I've listened, so now you write.'

'I just told you I was driving that day, and nothing like that happened,' Alex said. 'If you don't believe me, why won't you call Control and get them to check the case records?'

Gittins kept his eyes on Jane. 'You need to write your denial.'

'I'm not writing a thing,' Jane said. 'I'm going back to station, I'm checking the case sheets to see if we were even in the vicinity of St Vincent's that day, and I'm calling Control and asking them to fax you our truck's records.' She picked up her mobile and jammed it into her pocket. 'I suggest you read all that, talk to the supposed complainant once more, then contact me again if you still want to go ahead. But next time, I'll be asking the union to send along a solicitor.'

'This will go in your file,' Gittins said.

'And then I'll be formally requesting that it be removed.'

Jane stalked out. Alex followed. The desk officer glanced up but said nothing, Gittins's office door open behind him.

Down in the ambulance, Jane turned the aircon up high. She undid her top button and fanned her neck. 'That bastard.'

'What's his problem?' Alex said. 'Why wouldn't he listen to reason?'

'He reckons he knows we all back each other up no matter what.'

'Moron.'

Jane's mobile beeped. She didn't recognise the texter's number, but the message read *Complainant Simone Walsh* followed by a mobile number she knew only too well from the days before Deb learned how to hide it.

'It's Deb all right. The desk guy just sent me the details.' She texted back *Thanks*.

'She must know that she wouldn't get away with it,' Alex said.

'She's never been one for clear thinking.' Jane tapped her fingers on the sill. 'Can we go back via Annandale?'

Alex looked at her. 'You don't want to make this worse.'

'I've asked Steve to talk to her, but either he's not doing it or it's not working. So maybe it's time I tried.'

'She smashed your windows,' Alex said. 'And you just said yourself she's not big on the clear thinking.'

'All I want is a quiet word,' Jane said. 'How can that make things worse?'

He narrowed his eyes. 'You're kidding, right?'

'Would you please just drive?'

NINE

The offices of Holder and Byron were in a five-storey red-brick building. Ella parked down Commonwealth Street and they walked back up. The early afternoon sky was an even pale grey, and the cool air smelled clean and damp. The rain had stopped, but water dripped from the scrawny trees along the footpath and the corners of air conditioners jutting from windows. Murray strode with energy and enthusiasm, but Ella didn't even try to dodge the drips. Her ham and salad sandwich sat like a hard lump in her stomach. Worse than Callum's words in that phone conversation had been his tone. So flat. So dead. The tone of a man who's made up his mind and for whom there's no going back. It felt wrong that he might decide they shouldn't try any more. Didn't she get a say in it at all? Didn't her feelings count for anything?

She yanked open the building's front door and stomped into an empty lobby where the air was stale and smelled faintly of old cigarette smoke. The only furniture was a blue vinyl chair pushed up against the wall and piled high with a tilting stack of free local newspapers.

'Charming,' she said.

'What's with you?' Murray said.

'Nothing.'

A board by the lift listed the building's tenants without giving any indication of what they did. Holder and Byron occupied one of twelve offices all up, and one of four on the second floor. Murray pushed the lift button. Ella folded her arms and listened to the working of the machinery behind the closed metal doors, forcing Callum out of her head, trying to focus on what they might be about to learn.

The lift doors opened onto an empty hallway with thin beige carpet one shade darker than the walls. They stepped out and looked left and right. One of the glass doors to the left had a logo put together from the letters H and B, while the other was blank, the office behind it dark. The doors to the right belonged respectively to Clifford Distribution and MSL Associates.

Murray pushed open the HB door. An unoccupied desk stood near the right wall, a small silver bell and a wedge of business cards in a plastic holder on the top. Three closed doors were visible down a short corridor. The walls were empty of everything except one painted-on HB logo. The place smelled of fresh paint and felt empty. They listened to the silence for a moment, and Ella took a business card and stuffed it into her pocket, then hit the bell.

A chair creaked behind one of the closed doors, then a woman of about forty in a grey business suit looked out. 'Can I help you?'

They held up their badges. 'Detectives Shakespeare and Marconi,' Murray said. 'And you are?'

'Miriam Holder,' the woman said. 'Is there a problem?'

She came three steps closer, then stood with her feet apart and her long hands on her hips. Her fingernails were painted bright red and her eyebrows were high and taut. Her dark hair was held off her face with combs.

'Is anyone else here?' Ella asked.

'Just me,' Holder said. 'My colleagues are out.'

'How many?' Ella got out her notebook.

'Two. Juliana Scholler and Shing Wei.' She spelled the names.

'Who's Byron?'

'My ex-partner,' she said. 'He left. I bought him out and kept the name.'

'What is it that Holder and Byron do?' Murray asked.

'We're accountants.'

'Who are your clients?'

'That's confidential.' Miriam Holder smiled, but her grey eyes held no warmth.

'Who was here in the office at ten twenty this morning?' Ella said.

'We all were.'

'Did you yourself make or receive a phone call at that time?'

Her smile widened and her eyes grew colder. 'What is this about?'

'It's a simple enough question,' Murray said.

'I don't recall what time I was on the phone,' she said. 'I'm not in the habit of keeping track.'

Ella thought she heard a sound behind one of the other closed doors. 'You're sure nobody else is here?'

'Of course I'm sure.'

'Where exactly are your colleagues?'

'Out, as I said. In meetings with clients.'

Ella looked around. 'I can see why you go out to meet. You don't have the most stylish surroundings.'

Holder gave the worst pretend laugh Ella had ever heard. 'We prefer to keep our money working, not slapped onto walls or spent on comfy chairs.'

'When will your colleagues be in the office again?' Murray asked.

'Not for the rest of the day.'

'We'll come back tomorrow then.'

'I'm looking forward to it already,' Holder said.

They left the office and walked down the hall, Murray in front.

Ella said to his back, 'Did you hear that noise?'

'Which noise?'

'When I asked if there was anyone else there,' she said. 'Pay attention.'

'All right, okay. I didn't hear a thing. You think someone was there? You want to go back in?'

'No.' She pushed the lift button to go down. 'I have a plan.'

Once in the lobby, she took out her mobile and the business card and called the office number. 'Let's see who answers.'

It rang at length then voicemail picked up. *'You've reached the office of Holder and Byron. All our staff are busy at the moment. Please leave a message after the tone.'*

'Voicemail.' She hung up and jabbed the lift button. 'I bet she's busy calling someone about our visit.'

The doors opened immediately and they got back in. She felt better. There was nothing like the prospect of catching somebody out to lift your mood.

Back up on the second floor, they found the HB office door locked. The lights inside were still on, and the internal office doors were closed. Ella banged on the glass with the flat of an angry hand. 'Is she hiding or has she done a runner?'

Murray went along the corridor to the offices of Clifford Distribution and MSL Associates. 'There're fire stairs here.'

'I'll go.' Ella pushed open the heavy door and paused to listen and peer up and down the bare concrete stairwell. No sound or movement. She started down the wide flights, her heart pounding in her ears. If Holder went down here she'd done it mighty quick, which meant she had a good reason to want to avoid them.

I knew she was hiding something.

On the ground floor, she shoved open the door onto the footpath and found herself around the corner from the lobby. She let the door close and looked up and down the street, then checked around the corner too, but there was no sign of Holder.

Shit.

Back upstairs, she found Murray talking with a young woman at the front desk of MSL Associates.

'She went past a few minutes ago,' the woman was saying. 'I waved but I don't think she saw me. I thought it was odd that she went for the stairs not the lift, but then I thought maybe she wanted a little exercise.'

'And you're sure it was her,' Murray said.

The woman nodded. 'I've known her for like six months, ever since I started working here. We're sometimes in the lift together. She seems like a nice lady; we have a bit of a chat.'

'Do you know the other people who work there?' Ella asked.

'Julie something and the Chinese guy,' she said. 'She's a bit snobby. He seems okay.'

'Do you know what kind of cars any of them drive?'

'Sorry.'

'Where do you park around here?'

'On the street, if you're lucky enough to find a space,' she said. 'The building has no parking of its own. Most people get the bus anyway.'

'Including Miriam Holder?'

'I don't know, sorry.' The phone on the desk rang and the young woman put her hand on it. 'I have to get this.'

'Thanks for your help,' Murray said, and they went into the corridor. Ella heard the woman say, 'MSL Associates, can I help you?' in a high and chirpy voice before the door closed.

'No sign of Holder on the street,' she said.

Murray dug his hands into his pockets. 'Nobody in the other office saw anything.'

'Let's go and see Weaver, squeeze the situation from the other side,' Ella said. He'd better be ready: she was going to squeeze him hard.

★

Bill Weaver lay in a curtained cubicle at Sydney Hospital, red marks and bruising around his flabby neck, chunky fingers clasped over his belly, his gaze fixed on his feet under the white cotton blanket.

The nurse put the buzzer into his hand, said, 'Press it if you need me,' then pulled the curtain closed.

Ella and Murray stepped up to the side of the bed.

'How're you feeling?' Ella asked.

Weaver stared at his feet and said nothing. She wondered how long he'd wait before calling the nurse and having them kicked out.

'You're not even going to say thanks?' Murray said. 'This woman saved your life.'

A flush crept up Weaver's jowls.

'Maybe they didn't tell you,' Murray went on, 'but she reached around the door and sawed through your tie with a fruit knife.'

The flush deepened.

'Her wrist's still sore.' Murray clapped a hand on Ella's shoulder. 'She deserves a medal really, but at the very least your thanks. And an explanation.'

Ella felt embarrassed and wanted to twist out from under Murray's hand, but Weaver finally made eye contact.

'Wanted to die,' he rasped. 'Not thanking anyone.'

'Come off it,' Murray said. 'If you were serious, you'd have left the office and done it where you wouldn't be disturbed.'

Ella trod on his foot to shut him up, then leaned on the side of the bed. 'Okay, Bill. I get that you're annoyed, that you thought you'd be waking up wherever you believe you'd go, or not waking up, or whatever. The fact is, you're still here, and Marko Meixner's dead. We know that you and he were having clandestine little chats in the office hallways. What were they about?'

'I have no recollection of that.'

'What about today then? After we talked to you, you shooed Peter out of your office, called Holder and Byron in Surry Hills, then sat yourself down behind the door. We've just been to Holder and Byron, where we talked at some length to Miriam Holder. Now we're giving you a chance to tell us your version of events.'

Weaver shook his head. He fitted his thumb to the red button on the buzzer, but didn't press.

'Peter told us about your phone conversations too,' Murray said.

Weaver shrugged his meaty shoulders. 'On the phone all bloody day,' he whispered hoarsely.

'I'm talking about the phone calls that don't make you very happy. The ones made to your office from numbers that our colleagues are tracing as we speak.'

Another shrug. 'GFC. Nobody's happy.'

'Is that why you tried to kill yourself?' Ella said.

He shook his head and closed his eyes, thumb still resting on the button. 'Personal.'

Flesh bulged either side of his gold wedding band. Ella tried to picture him and the bony Miriam Holder having an affair. 'What's your wife's name?'

'Irrelevant.'

'This is a homicide investigation,' Murray said. 'Nothing's irrelevant. And in fact —'

But Weaver pressed the buzzer, and before Murray could finish his sentence the nurse bustled in. 'That's enough now. Let him rest.'

Ella looked at Weaver, but his eyes were still shut. She and Murray left the cubicle, the nurse yanking the curtain closed behind them.

They made their way through the hospital and walked outside into a cool drizzle.

'Interesting that it was the mention of his wife that made him clam up,' she said.

'One more person to look into,' Murray said.

It was ten past two. Ella figured they had time to check out Miriam Holder's home, in case she'd scuttled off there, and maybe Weaver's wife as well before they had to be back at the office for the next meeting.

'No,' Langley said, his voice crackly over Murray's speakerphone. 'Lee's hurt his knee and had to sign off, so Hossain's back here in the office. Holder and the wife can wait. I want you two to check out the parole officer before she knocks off and then see Canning.'

'Weaver's clearly lying,' Murray said.

'And he'll no doubt still be lying tomorrow,' Langley said. 'It's the probation and parole office in Chatswood for you. The officer on Canning's case is Grace Michaels.' He gave them an address on the Pacific Highway. 'You better hurry. Meeting's at five sharp.' He hung up.

Ella cranked the key hard. 'Stats, times, numbers.'

'He wants this all wrapped up today,' Murray said. 'Any money that tomorrow it'll be just you and me.'

She sighed. 'I don't bet when there're no odds.'

★

'Anywhere along here,' Jane said, and Alex pulled into the kerb.

They were in a wide and leafy street in Annandale. Shops lined the footpaths, with small offices dotted here and there among them. People walked past and glanced at the ambulance curiously. The road was still wet and the tyres of passing cars threw up a light mist that glistened on their bumpers in the weak sunlight.

Jane grasped the handle but didn't open the door. The glass front of Annandale Architects was three shops along and she stared at it, thinking. Could this make things worse?

'You really going in?' Alex said.

'Yes.'

No. I don't know.

But what else could she do? Her appeals to Steve were getting her nowhere, and perhaps this latest debacle meant the time had come for the direct approach. Some people didn't listen until you confronted them yourself, she reasoned. There was a chance this would work. And there were two other good things about it: she wouldn't still be waiting for Steve to act, and she wasn't troubling the cops. She knew how busy they were. She really didn't want to call on them until she'd tried everything herself.

'If you're not sure –' Alex began.

'I'll just go in and tell her the facts,' Jane said. 'We'll have a polite dialogue. I'll explain that she's doing the wrong thing. I'll appeal to her morals and ask her to put herself in my shoes and get her to see that she needs to stop.'

Alex looked doubtful.

'It'll be fine,' Jane said. *I hope.*

The phone calls were one thing, the glass smashing worse, but something about the complaint hinted at a whole other level of mental issues.

'You want me to come?' Alex asked.

Architects' office – shouldn't be any knives lying around. *Unless she brought one from home.* No – Deb wasn't smart enough to think Jane might confront her here.

She picked up the portable radio and opened the door. 'Back in a tick.'

She strode to the office, a nervous worm wriggling in her stomach. *Are you a man or a mouse?* She pushed the door open and stepped inside.

Deb sat bolt upright behind a wide timber desk; she looked over with a smile that froze, but only for a second. 'Good afternoon. May I help you?'

'It's time we talked,' Jane said, watching Deb's hands. Just in case.

Deb's smile didn't change. 'Did you wish to arrange a consultation with one of our architects?'

'You need to withdraw your complaint.'

'I'm sorry but I don't know what you're talking about.' Deb glanced at the computer screen. 'Did you have a particular architect in mind? Brenda Plowman has just stepped out but shouldn't be long. Jonathan Frances isn't back until tomorrow morning.'

Like that, was it? Stubborn and playing dumb.

Jane drew herself up. 'I know you put in that complaint. I know you made it up and I can prove it. You should be aware that there are serious consequences for lying like that, and if you don't withdraw it I'll do everything I can to make sure all those consequences happen. Enough with the phone calls too, and the trashing of my windows. Apart from when we talk about the kids, I don't have anything to do with Steve and I don't want to.'

Deb's eyes looked overbright. 'I suggest that you leave.'

'I'll leave when you promise to withdraw the complaint and stop harassing me.'

'Perhaps I should call the police.' Deb reached for the phone.

'Go ahead.' Jane felt more confident by the second. 'I'll report the damage you caused at my house.'

Deb's eyes took on a glint. 'You have no proof that was me.'

'Not yet maybe,' Jane said. 'But the police will talk to the neighbours, and who knows how many looked out their windows when they heard glass smashing?'

'If I get into trouble that'll affect Steve too.'

'You have to get it through your head that I don't care.' Jane stepped close to the desk. 'I left him. Can't you understand that? I. Left. Him.'

Deb's ears turned red. 'The kids then –'

'They won't care either,' Jane said. 'You either promise to withdraw the complaint, pay for my windows and leave me alone, or you call the police.'

The red spread. Deb stood up. Jane thought for half a second about taking a step back, but she was done with retreating, with trying to get along, with playing nice. Besides, the woman was behind a desk.

'Clock's ticking. What's it going to be?'

'You think you're so tough,' Deb said.

This was ridiculous. 'Time's up. Pick up the phone.'

'Marching in here in your uniform, harassing me like this.'

'I'll even dial for you.'

Jane reached across the desk for the phone, but Deb grabbed her arm. Jane tried to jerk away, but Deb's fingers dug into her wrist. Jane twisted her arm and pulled back. Deb's grip tightened.

Deb bared her teeth in a horrible imitation of a grin. 'You think you're so smart.'

The radio was in reach on Jane's belt. She could call Alex in, but how embarrassing to need backup for something like this. Deb was smaller than her too. How could she be so strong? Jane planted her feet and heaved backwards, at the same time raising her free arm to fend off any punch from Deb's other hand. But Deb locked that hand onto her wrist too, and as she was dragged forward Jane's palm smacked into Deb's chin – just as a woman opened the door and stepped into the office.

'Brenda!' Deb screeched. 'Help me!'

'Give up, Deb,' Jane said through gritted teeth.

'Come and help me!'

The woman seemed not to know what to do or say. She carried a cup of takeaway coffee, and looked around as if she needed to put it down before she could think. Jane yanked again and Deb fell onto the desk. Jane wrenched her arm free.

Deb popped up and pointed a shaking hand. 'She threatened and assaulted me.'

The woman came closer, suspicion on her face. She was short and stocky, in her early fifties.

Jane stuck out her hand. 'Brenda Plowman, is it? My name's Jane Koutoufides.' She saw recognition of the surname in the woman's eyes. 'Deb's now married to my ex, and she and I are having a couple of issues.'

'She assaulted me,' Deb said. 'You saw that. She punched

me in the face. Oh, I feel so dizzy.' She flopped to the carpet with a howl.

Now Brenda moved, hurrying around behind the desk to where Deb thrashed on the ground.

Jane sighed. The good ol' fake collapse and seizure, dependable standby of those wishing to avoid awkward conversations.

She took the radio from her hip. 'Alex, can you come in here, please? No equipment.'

He could be a witness if anything weirder happened and Brenda turned out to be under Deb's spell.

She walked behind the desk. Deb rolled and flailed on the carpet. Her skin was pink, she was having no trouble breathing, she hadn't wet herself. She was also being transparently careful not to hit her windmilling arms on the desk and chair.

Brenda glared up at her. 'Can't you do something?'

'There's nothing wrong with her,' Jane said, as the door opened and Alex walked in. She crouched beside Deb and tried to catch her flapping hands. 'Deb, it's time to stop this.'

Deb screeched again. *Trying to drown me out.* Her face was screwed up but Jane knew she was watching from slitted eyes.

'You're just embarrassing yourself. Calm down and let's talk.'

Alex came to stand near Deb's feet and she kicked at his legs.

'Enough,' Jane said, sterner. She held Deb's wrists tightly.

Deb writhed and lurched herself into a half-sitting position and tried to bite Jane's arm. Jane let go just in time and Deb's teeth scraped over the skin, leaving it wet with saliva. Jane stood up and stepped back, her heart thumping with anger.

'What are you doing?' Brenda said. 'You have to help her.'

'She doesn't need any help.' Jane took a breath to steady her voice. 'She's angry and is pretending to be sick because she doesn't want to talk to me. So we're going to walk out of here now and get back into our ambulance. We'll wait there until you come out and nod at us, which will be the signal that she's suddenly better. If this doesn't happen within a minute or so, we'll come back, and I'll call the police and have her charged with the damage she's caused to my house and with assault for biting me.'

She glanced at Deb, who still rolled back and forth on the floor but was undoubtedly listening. 'Deb, it's up to you.'

Brenda blinked and said nothing.

Jane walked to the front door, then outside, with Alex close behind her. She was steaming, but didn't speak until she got in the ambulance and slammed the door.

'That bitch.' She rubbed her arm. 'And I was being perfectly reasonable.'

Alex climbed behind the wheel. 'She got a psych problem?'

'Yeah, it's called being an attention-seeking drama queen.' Jane rubbed her arm again. There was a red band around her wrist from Deb's fingers, and a paler red mark from her teeth. 'Bitch.'

'I see what you mean about how she looks like you. Same hair, same everything. Just fifteen years younger.'

'Tells you a lot about Steve's taste, doesn't it.'

Alex chuckled, then looked out the front. 'There she is.'

Brenda had come out onto the footpath, looking a little shell-shocked. She nodded at them.

'Quicker than I expected,' Jane said. 'Can't you just picture her, pretending to wake up on the floor, saying, "Ohh, what happened? I don't remember a thing."'

Alex started the engine and pulled out. Jane looked over as they went past, meeting Brenda's perplexed gaze and seeing Deb peering out of the window behind her, then turning hurriedly away.

'Wonder if she'll put in another complaint,' Alex said.

'If she does, she'll pretty much have to admit that she gave a false name on the first one.'

Alex stopped at a red light. 'So where we going? Back to the station?'

Jane nodded, her heart harder than ever. She was going to take Deb down. 'Time to gather evidence.'

TEN

Ella turned off the Pacific Highway and parked on the side
street just past the ten-storey blue-glassed building that
housed the State Parole Authority office. She'd met a few
parole officers in her time and they'd all been like cops. You
got into these jobs to help people and because you wanted to
believe they could do right. Some officers, of course, managed
to keep that hope alive longer than others.

The sky had cleared a little and a sharp breeze shivered
the leaves in the trees along the roadside. Traffic rushed past
in a continuous stream as she and Murray walked towards the
building. A man hurried towards them from the other direction. He wore tight jeans that were faded on the thighs and
dirty sneakers with new white laces, and kept his hands stuffed
into the pockets of a thin brown jacket. He glanced up at them
then quickly back to the ground, and Ella knew he knew what
they were. He reached the door first and didn't hold it for them.

The lobby was full of the light of buzzing fluorescents.
A board on the wall listed the SPA as being on the fourth
floor. The lift button was already lit and the fire-stairs door was
slowly closing, the man nowhere to be seen.

'Doesn't want to ride with us,' Murray said. 'Fine with me.'

On the fourth floor, the lift opened onto a grey-carpeted corridor and a sign on the wall indicating that the SPA was to the right. They followed the corridor to the end, where a heavy glass door opened onto a waiting area with a reception desk. Two men and a woman sat on the brown vinyl chairs lining the waiting area, all in their early twenties. The woman had earbuds in and thumbed through tracks on an iPhone with a cracked screen. One of the men flicked through a car magazine; the other slumped with his arms folded and a beanie pulled down low on his head. Neither was the man they'd seen coming in off the street.

'Can I help you?'

The woman behind the reception desk had assessing eyes and a straight line of a mouth. Her brown hair was scraped back in a ponytail and she wore no make-up, and her black button-up shirt was baggy around her body.

Ella held up her badge and Murray said, 'We're here to see Grace Michaels.'

'Do you have an appointment?'

'No,' Ella said. 'We're from the homicide squad.'

The woman picked up the phone and pressed a couple of buttons. 'Police to see you,' she said, listened for a moment then hung up. 'She'll be out shortly. Have a seat.'

Ella and Murray stayed on their feet. Murray checked his mobile. Ella watched the waiters, all of whom she knew would be feeling her eyes on them though none of them looked up. She'd had dealings with repeat offenders, and had listened to them complain about how hard it was to get by on the outside after years in. She wouldn't like it either, she was sure. *Just another good reason not to start in the first place.*

'Officers?'

She looked around to see a thin woman of about thirty in the hall that led away from the reception area. The woman motioned for them to follow her, and they went past a couple of interview rooms then into an open-plan office area where the air conditioning was too cold and two women and two men typed or talked in low voices on the phones. The woman went towards the window. A pale-looking plant sat in a pot on the sill, casting a thin shadow onto a desk piled with papers and folders. The computer monitor showed a generic screensaver of coloured lines; a scattering of pens lay around its base, and the letters were partly worn off the keyboard. The woman sat, and Ella and Murray took the chairs beside the desk.

'I'm Grace Michaels,' she said. She wore a hint of eyeliner and lipstick, black pants and a grey shirt. Her shoulder-length hair was dark and hooked back over her ears. She wore no rings and no jewellery apart from a plain watch with a narrow black leather band.

'Detectives Shakespeare and Marconi,' Murray said. 'We're here about Paul Canning.'

Michaels nodded, her expression unchanged. 'What would you like to know?'

'He's been out how long?'

'Seven weeks.'

'How's he doing?'

'So far so good.'

'How often do you see him?' Ella asked.

'I've seen him three times so far,' Michaels said. 'The first week he was out, then three weeks after that, then yesterday.'

Yesterday. 'Did he come here?'

'The first time. The other times I went to where he lives and works.'

'What time yesterday?' Murray asked.

'Late afternoon.' She dug under the papers for a diary and flipped back a page. 'Five thirty.'

'Why so late?'

'Surprise visit,' she said. 'When they're not expecting you, you sometimes find them with people they shouldn't be with or doing things they're not meant to be doing.'

Ella could see scrawled on the diary page the address of the boatyard in Neutral Bay.'

'He's living with a woman who's taken him on as an apprentice marine mechanic.' Michaels said. 'Her name's Natasha Osborne.'

'Is that ethical?' Murray said. 'That they work and live together?'

'We have no problem with it,' Michaels said. 'Our main concern is getting them to stay away from criminal influences. We checked Osborne out completely when they said this was what they wanted to do – she's got no criminal record and has worked at this place for ten years. While I'm not sure the relationship will last, so far it seems to be working.'

'Why don't you think it'll last?' Ella said.

'These women who start up with these men while they're inside.' Michaels shrugged. 'I've seen it too often: the woman thinks she can fix him, she can be the one to save him, then one day you see her, she's got a black eye – or worse – and you wonder what it'll take before she realises who she's really living with.'

Ella nodded. She'd seen it too.

'But you haven't seen any signs of that yet?' Murray asked.

'Not yet.'

Ella rubbed goose bumps from her arms and looked up. An air-conditioning vent was right over her head. 'How did the relationship begin?'

'They were penpals first,' Michaels said. 'There are internet sites where friends of inmates put up information on their behalf. Osborne found one of these and started writing to him early last year. Later there were visits.'

'What's she like?'

'Seems smart enough.' Michaels shrugged again. 'She says she understands what he's done, and she believes everyone deserves a second chance. I told her she can call me if she has trouble. She said she wouldn't need to.'

Huh. 'What's Canning like?' Ella asked.

'Adapting fairly well, all things considered. He was locked up before the internet was widely used, before everyone had mobiles. He said it's taken him a while to adjust to the lack of bells telling him what to do every minute of the day. Some people can't adjust to that at all and need to write up their own timetable to give their day some structure, especially if they don't have a job.'

'And as a person?'

'Hardened, definitely, but he seems aware of how he has to behave to cope on the outside. He says he knows it's not about swagger and influence out here. He says he enjoys his work and wants to train up fully.'

'What were his inmate records like?' Murray said.

'He had some problems early on – many young inmates do. They get in fights, they can't stay clear of trouble. Looks like he got a handle on his temper after that, and for most of his sentence he's done all right.'

'And you said you saw him at five thirty yesterday afternoon,' Ella said. 'How long were you with him?'

'About twenty minutes,' Michaels said. 'He and Osborne were working on a motor in the workshop. I talked to them then I left.'

Ella jotted this down. Marko Meixner had gone in front of the train at ten to six, and Grace Michaels had been with Canning at the boatyard until that time. If Marko had been pushed off the platform, it wasn't Canning who did it.

'Do you have a current photo of Canning?' Murray asked.

Michaels moved the mouse and clicked to open a file. A black-and-white photo of a man's unsmiling face filled the screen. Ella studied it. Canning's hair had thinned at the front but he still combed it to the right, and while the skin under his eyes had pouched a bit he didn't appear to have put on much weight. He looked at the camera with much the same blankness of expression as in the mug shot taken on his arrest at the age of twenty.

She felt Murray's eyes on her and closed her notebook to indicate she was done. He shook Grace Michaels's hand. 'Thanks for your help.'

She nodded. 'You said you're from homicide. What did you think Canning might've done?'

'The witness who testified against him was hit by a train late yesterday afternoon,' Murray said. 'There's some confusion about whether he fell, jumped or was pushed, so we're trying to rule out possibilities.'

A sudden crash and burst of shouting cut him off. Ella's heart leapt and she jumped to her feet.

'Fucking arseholes, the lot of you!'

Michaels, Ella and Murray hurried with the other staff to the front interview room to find the man from the street screaming obscenities over an upturned table at a burly male parole officer.

The officer put his hands out in a placating gesture. 'Gary, you need to settle down.'

'Fuck you!'

'This isn't helping you,' the officer said.

'Like I fucking care?' Gary's face was bright red, his broad hands clenched, and one bright white shoelace had come undone.

Ella glanced at Murray. He was pulling up his coat sleeves.

'Sit down now or face the consequences,' the officer said.

'Fuck you! You think I'll go back inside all meek and mild? You think you can tell me to sit and I will?'

Murray pushed past Grace Michaels and Ella stepped right up beside him, the adrenaline pumping, her jaw set.

'Police,' Murray barked. 'Do as he says.'

Ella saw Gary size them up then glance back at the parole officer. 'Look,' he said in a conciliatory tone, but Ella saw his feet shift and knew he was going to try to rush them. She set her own feet a little further apart and braced herself, and felt Murray doing the same.

'Look,' Gary said again, then turned and barrelled straight at them.

His shoulder hit Ella's chest and almost knocked her over, but she was ready and grabbed his arm, twisting it behind his back. Murray kicked his legs out from beneath him and shoved him sideways and he went down in the doorway, Ella stumbling onto his back. He thrashed and swore and between them they seized his wrists and cuffed him tight. Ella saw a hand in front of her and took it as she got up. Grace Michaels turned it into a handshake. 'Thanks.'

'No worries.' The adrenaline had made her shaky but she brushed off her trousers like she felt fine. 'Glad to help.'

The male parole officer crouched beside the still-swearing Gary and talked to him in a low voice. The other officers drifted away, and Michaels motioned Ella and Murray into the hall.

'I'm sorry I couldn't be more help on Canning,' she said.

'No, you were great,' Murray said.

He was perky. The rush of put-downs always energised him. Ella, in contrast, was tired now. She checked that her notebook was still in her pocket and took a hinting step towards the front of the office. Murray glanced into the room where the officer was helping a subdued Gary to his feet.

'You can take the cuffs off now,' the officer said. 'He's fine.'

'You're sure?'

The officer nodded.

'If you say so.' Murray unlocked them and came back out with the metal jangling in his hands.

'Thanks again,' Ella said to Michaels, and they left her standing in the corridor.

★

The rain had started and stopped again by the time Ella and Murray parked by the boatyard in Neutral Bay where Paul Canning lived and worked. The place looked deserted; despite a number of boats being moored in the bay and at the dock, none appeared in use, and there were no people in sight. The low grey sky and the humidity made Ella feel flat. The water was the same colour as the sky and slid around the pylons as the wake of a passing dinghy rolled in. The air smelled of salt water, seaweed and oil.

A final few raindrops dotted the puddles as they crossed the concrete forecourt to the shed. A wide door had been pulled back and inside a radio played Lady Gaga. Ella saw the flash and spit of welding as Murray banged with the side of his fist on the wall.

A tanned and fit woman in a tight black singlet over khaki workpants came out, a spanner in her hand. 'Yes?'

Ella said, 'We're looking for Paul Canning.'

The woman turned, the long brown plait at the back of her head swinging over her shoulder as she did so, and shouted, 'Paulie!'

The welding stopped, then a man emerged from the gloom behind her. His straight brown hair had recently been trimmed and was shorter than in the photo Grace Michaels had shown them, and the pouches under his eyes were mostly gone. He was clean-shaven and tanned, and, like the woman, wore a black singlet, but with navy workshorts. They both wore black steel-capped workboots.

Canning looked them in the eye as he wiped his hands on a rag already dark with grease. 'Officers.'

'Detectives,' Murray said. 'Homicide.'

'My mistake.' Canning's voice was even. 'What can I do for you?'

Ella looked at the woman. 'Natasha Osborne, correct?'

'That's right.'

She was in her early thirties, with freckles on her cheeks and squint lines around her eyes. She looked like she was about to say more but didn't. Ella had no doubt that Canning had schooled her on how to behave, had told her how the pigs would try to rattle you but you could never let them see you cared.

'Where were you yesterday afternoon?' Murray asked.

Canning pointed his thumb over his shoulder. 'Working.'

'All afternoon?'

'Yep.'

'What time do you usually knock off?' Ella said.

'Depends on the workload,' Canning said. 'If we have a job that Nat wants to get done, if a client's on her case, then we keep going. If it's quiet, we knock off a bit earlier.'

'And yesterday?'

'We were here in the shed until six.' Canning looked at them steadily. 'But you know that already, don't you? How is Mrs Michaels?'

'What about earlier in the afternoon?' Murray said. 'Can anyone apart from Natasha vouch for you then?'

Natasha Osborne had stuck the spanner in her pocket and now folded her arms. 'I'm not enough?'

'Answer the question, please,' Murray said.

'We had no clients come in,' Canning said. 'I don't know if anyone else saw that I was here or not. I guess you'll have to trust me.'

They let that drop into the silence, then Ella said, 'How did you two meet?'

Osborne eyed her. 'We were penpals. We hit it off. Plus he was interested in my work, and I'd been thinking about taking on an apprentice for a while.' She shrugged. The straps of her black singlet were snug over her shoulders.

'What kind of cars do you drive?'

'I don't own one and I don't have a licence yet,' Canning said.

Osborne nodded across the yard. 'That's mine there. The F250 ute.'

The truck was pale blue with huge white wheels and rust bubbles along the bottom of the driver's door. A hulking piece of machinery sat in the tray.

'And you live here too?'

'Over the shop.' Canning pointed up. Ella saw rain-specked windows with white net curtains.

'When did you last have contact with Marko Meixner?' she said.

'Seventeen years, give or take,' Canning said.

'So you remember him.'

'I remember his name. I'm not going to lie and say I don't.' Canning took the dirty rag from his pocket and wiped his hands again. 'I remembered it even before the cops came a few weeks back and asked if I'd been stalking him. I'm not proud of what I did, and I can't bring the dead back to life, but I've paid my debt and now I plan to be the productive member of society I wasn't able to be before.'

'Because of the drinking and the drugs,' Murray said.

'Yes, because of the drinking and the drugs, and I don't do those any more.' Canning stuffed the rag away.

'So you didn't write any letters to Meixner while you were in jail, you didn't call him up at his home or work when you got out, you haven't been following or threatening him or planning to harm him?' Ella said.

'No,' Canning said. 'What would be the point? I'd be the prime suspect. I'd be caught and locked up again, and that's the last place I want to be. I've wasted enough of my life already. Besides, I hold no bad feelings towards the man. The whole thing is in the past and that's where it will stay.'

Ella studied him. His stance and gaze were open, his chest moving easily as he breathed, not too fast but not too con-trolled and slow either. His face was empty of tics and his hands hung apparently relaxed by his sides. Lots of prisoners got good at hiding what they really felt though – it was how you got by inside, and sometimes how you landed parole. She looked at Natasha Osborne. The woman dropped her gaze. She shifted her weight on her feet and took the spanner back out of her pocket. Ella couldn't see any bruises on her arms, but that didn't mean there were none elsewhere. 'You feeling okay? You seem on edge.'

'We've got a lot of work to do, that's all,' Osborne said. 'Clients expect their stuff fixed and we're standing here wasting time.'

Ella guessed it was more that she was uncomfortable talking to them, but there was nothing more they could do anyway. Evening was approaching, they were due back at the office, and there was nobody on the rain-soaked dock to ask about the previous evening. The cop on the original case, Paterson, hadn't called her mobile, but she hoped there might be a voice-mail on her office phone. She put her notebook away.

Murray got the signal and nodded. 'Okay, right,' he said, and walked away.

Ella took a last look at the pair, who stared back at her in silence, then followed.

★

Jane stood by the fax machine, feeding the pages in. They'd caught a case on the way back and she'd only now been able to get her proof together. Take that, she thought, and that, and that: a copy of the case sheet of the job they'd been on at the time of the alleged incident, which showed they were nowhere near St Vincent's but instead at a house in Double Bay; a summary she'd typed up of all their cases that day, showing that they only went to Vinnie's once and that was early in the afternoon, not 3 pm when she'd supposedly done the dastardly deed; and finally a statutory declaration from Alex, witnessed by the JP owner of the jewellery store across the street, stating that on every case they did that day he was the driver.

She took out her mobile. Still nothing from Laird. She typed in *Looking forward to tonight* and sent it, then checked the screen on the fax.

'All pages received,' she read out. 'Now what are you going to do, Gittins?'

'He's probably gone for the day,' Alex said.

'Then he'll have a lovely present waiting on his desk in the morning.'

Jane folded the pages and went to put them in her locker. While in the locker room, she typed a smiley face and sent that to Laird as well. It was odd that he hadn't replied at all. Even when he was flat out he'd always managed to grab five seconds to send her something. She saw in the mirror that she was frowning. *What are you, a fretting adolescent? He's just busy!*

When she came back to the muster room, Alex was staring at his mobile.

'Everything okay?' she asked.

'Mia's not answering again.'

'Ah, the teen years.'

He pressed the call button and put it to his ear. 'Every day she scares me more.'

'Wait till she can drive.'

He made a face then frowned again, and Jane heard Mia's voice as her voicemail picked up.

'It's Dad again,' Alex said, poorly controlled irritation in his tone. 'Call me back.' He put the phone in his lap and rubbed his forehead. 'Last night she started talking about her mother again. She said I should've tried harder to keep in touch, that it wasn't right that she was growing up without knowing her.'

'They're experts at making you feel guilty,' Jane said.

'And then the doubts start. Perhaps I should've tried harder. But for what? If Helen didn't want anything to do with us, why should I put in any effort to track her down?'

Jane perched on the edge of the desk. 'She was the one who left.'

'Exactly,' Alex said. 'Yet I understand what Mia means. Helen's her mum. Of course Mia wants to know her, wants to have her in her life.'

'But what more could you have done?' Jane said.

142

Alex stared out the window and didn't answer. Jane watched emotions cross his face.

'I've looked for her online now and then over the last couple of years,' he said. 'Just to see. Do you know how many Helen Churchills are out there? That's if she's even using that name still.'

'But even if you found her, even if you got them in touch with each other, what kind of mother is she going to be? Listen, Alex.' She rapped her knuckles on the desk to get him to look at her. 'Helen's an adult and she made her choices. Didn't you say she told you she didn't want that domesticated life? She couldn't be bothered to stay in touch, and never mind that you've moved a couple of times – you'd be easy enough to find. You're in the phone book, for goodness sake.'

'I wanted her to be able to call.'

'You're too soft on her,' Jane said. 'Listen. Mia will get through this stage and eventually she'll understand. She'll know what she means to you. She'll grow up and move on, and so will you.'

The job phone rang before he could reply. He grabbed it up. 'Alex Churchill, The Rocks.'

Jane watched as he scribbled down the details of a cardiac arrest in a Darlinghurst flat. She could feel her phone like a stone in her pocket; she knew it hadn't buzzed with a text but couldn't resist taking it out anyway. Five bars of service, battery close to full. Well, it was okay. Look at the time. He was probably preparing for the broadcast. There might even be a problem: someone had gone home sick and everyone was working harder to fill the gap. Or he'd left his mobile at home. No big deal.

Alex hung up the phone. 'Ready?'

Jane stood up straight and nodded.

ELEVEN

Murray looked up from his computer. 'Osborne owns that ute and nothing else, and has no record. There's no vehicle in Canning's name. Bill Weaver owns a white BMW and has no record either.'

'According to what I could find,' Ella said, turning from her own monitor, 'Weaver's worked high up in financial companies for years, and there was no mention of anything shady.' She heard Brad Langley's voice down the corridor and checked her watch. 'Shit.'

They hurried into the homicide meeting room. The lights were on, and the late afternoon beyond the windows was growing gloomier by the minute. Ella sat down next to Murray and the three other detectives, and Langley closed the door.

'Gawande, you first,' he said.

Yes, why waste time on niceties? Ella folded her arms. *It's not like we're a team or anything.* It was another thing to irk her. Paterson hadn't called. She'd ring his station again tomorrow.

John Gawande flattened his notebook on the table. 'Meixner caught a taxi from RPA to Town Hall at quarter past five. The driver, one Mohamed Shalim, said Meixner was acting strange from the beginning. First he walked past the rank a couple of times, looking in at Shalim, then when he did get in, he lay on the back seat. During the drive he kept changing the destination – first it was Centrepoint, then it was the QVB, then Hyde Park – and kept peering out the back and asking Shalim to change lanes and put his indicator on like he was going to turn. Shalim said as they were passing Town Hall, where there were hordes of people going down into the station, Meixner told him to pull over. He threw a fifty at him and jumped out and disappeared in the crowd.'

'Did Shalim think there was anyone following them?' Ella asked.

'He said the traffic was really thick and he couldn't tell,' James Kemsley said.

Gawande said, 'Then we went into Town Hall and watched more CCTV footage. We found Meixner entering the station via the stairs outside Town Hall itself at twenty to six. He looked frightened and kept checking over his shoulder, but it didn't look like he spotted the person or people he was worried about. He went into a bathroom on the concourse level and stayed there for eleven minutes, emerging very tentatively at nine minutes to six. We couldn't see anyone who had been hanging about there, but by this time the crowds were really thick. Meixner started weaving through the people, pushing and shoving a little, still looking over his shoulder.'

'It was impossible to know if he was being followed because so many people were going the same direction,' Kemsley said. 'We focused on looking for people with caps, and saw a few but none matched the man on the platform later.'

'Easy to slip one on and off,' Ella said.

'We looked for someone doing that too,' Gawande said. 'Didn't spot anyone, but not all of the station is covered by cameras, and not all the cameras are working.'

'So next thing we see is Meixner on the Bankstown line platform,' Kemsley said. 'And there's the guy with the cap, and it all unfolds: smoke, panic, push or fall.'

'Or jump,' Langley said calmly.

Ella looked at him. 'Did a witness call in to say that?'

'Not as such,' Langley said. 'There's been a number of calls but none certain one way or another, and nothing helpful about the car accident either.'

Hmph.

'Well, whatever happened, he didn't take a big leap,' Gawande said. 'We could see that much.'

'Jumps can be small.' Langley straightened his cuffs. 'As small as stepping off into space.'

Ella pressed her feet hard against the floor.

'After the incident, we couldn't spot the capped man,' Kemsley said. 'Again, the masses of people and the panic made it impossible to pick a single person out, and I'm guessing the cap was off by then.'

'So he was deliberately hiding,' Ella said.

'That's my feeling,' Gawande said.

'Let's not leap to conclusions here,' Langley said. 'Good police work involves evidence, not hunches.'

Ella bit her tongue.

'Hossain?' Langley said.

'You were right about the patrons of the Thorn and Thistle,' Aadil Hossain said. 'Nobody could remember a thing, right down to whether they'd been there yesterday afternoon or not. The staff has the same attitude. One of them recommended that George and I leave.'

'Charming,' Murray said.

'Fletcher's offsider, Daley Jones, was more talkative,' Hossain said. 'The worksite's closed because of the rain so we tracked him down at home. He said he left work yesterday at two, because his daughter was sick and his girlfriend doesn't drive so he had to take them to the doctor.'

Ella and Murray looked at each other. 'That's not what Fletcher told us,' Ella said.

Langley held up his hand. 'In a minute.'

Ella wanted to scream.

'Jones doesn't seem to like Fletcher very much,' Hossain went on. 'Says he can be a bit of a bully. Reckons if he gets offered one of the other jobs he's applied for, he'll be out of there like a shot. He's never heard him talk about Chloe or Marko Meixner, and said that he's seemed his usual self lately, not upset or angry about anything. We planned to talk to the other tradies at the worksite tomorrow, if it stops raining, and see what they say.

'George's knee started to play up then, so he had to sign off. I talked to Meixner's friends. Henry Marsden said they play tennis together most weeks, and he was concerned when Marko didn't show last night, but he knew about the pregnancy so thought maybe something was up with that. He rang Marko and left a voicemail at about eight. Never got a reply, obviously. Tim Raye and Lucas Ellison both said they hadn't heard from Marko in a week or so. Last time they spoke, he'd been talking about the baby, and wanting to buy a house and not having enough money. They assumed he was busy working extra hours to earn a bit more. None of them knew about the murder he witnessed, and none had noticed anything amiss in the last few months, the time frame in which Marko knew Canning was getting out.'

Langley nodded.

'Last thing I did this afternoon was check the toll system on the motorway between Fletcher's worksite and the city to see if his van was registered going through,' Hossain said. 'It wasn't, but he could've taken the minor roads, of course. That's it.'

'Shakespeare and Marconi?'

'Fletcher never told us that Jones left at two,' Ella said.

'He didn't tell us what time Jones left specifically, but led us to believe that they'd both been there until four,' Murray said.

Langley's eyes were flat. 'I mean, can you tell us what pro-gress you made today.'

Ella felt like steam was coming out of her ears. She seethed in silence as Murray summarised their visit to Marko's GP.

'So three suicide attempts all up,' Langley said. 'Interesting.'

'She also said he was thrilled about the baby,' Ella put in.

'Babies can add pressure,' Langley said. 'But go on.'

'Then we went to Marko's workplace,' Ella said, 'and spoke first to his boss, Bill Weaver, who then tried to kill himself when we were talking to the other staff.'

'Get out,' Hossain said.

'Hung himself with his tie on the back of his office door,' Murray said. 'Ella cut through the tie. Saved his life.'

'Nice one,' Gawande said.

Ella felt a flush creeping up her neck. 'We also met Daniel Truscott, colleague of Meixner's and owner of the car he crashed yesterday. He hadn't given Meixner permission to use it, and couldn't understand why he'd taken it as he'd never done so before.

'One interesting thing we learned is that yesterday after-noon around two or two thirty Marko was heard to get a phone call in which he sounded strange enough to catch the attention of his workmate, Roger Saito, and was heard to repeatedly say "No, no". Bill Weaver's PA said that Weaver too has had calls in which he says the same thing, the most recent last Friday.'

'Calls in which people say "no",' Langley said. 'Fascinating.'

Ella stared at her boss, impassive in his blue tie. *He hates me. He hates me and I do not care. I just want to catch who did this. And yes, maybe prove to him that Marko didn't kill himself, and that his desire to move us onto something else is completely idiotic. But mostly catch who did this.*

'Another staff member told me that he'd seen Weaver and Meixner having quiet chats in the hallway on more than one occasion,' Murray said. 'When we talked to Weaver this after-noon in hospital, he denied any memory of that.'

'And he said he tried to kill himself for personal reasons,' Ella said, trying to regain her cool. 'He got touchy when we asked about his wife though. And he made a phone call just before he hung himself, to the office of an accounting company called Holder and Byron. We spoke to one Miriam Holder there this afternoon, but she denied taking Weaver's call, then did a runner.'

'Huh,' Kemsley said.

'I know,' Ella said. 'We didn't get to visit her at home, however, but instead met Paul Canning's parole officer, Grace Michaels.'

She summarised the meeting, including details about the timing of Michaels's impromptu visit to Canning at the boatshed.

'Then we checked on Canning himself,' Murray said. 'His version of yesterday's events matched hers. He was working all afternoon, and Michaels turned up at about half past five and stayed for twenty minutes. He went on about how he'd paid his debt and was moving on. Said he held no grudge and didn't even think about Meixner.'

Langley nodded. 'The officers at Ryde told a similar story. Canning recognised Meixner's name when they spoke to him, but said he had no idea where the man lived, nor did he care. Said he's focused on work and getting his life sorted.'

'What were his alibis for the times Meixner felt he was being followed?' Ella said.

'His employer and partner, and a boatie the officers spoke to on the dock.'

Kemsley looked at Ella and Murray. 'Was he crying harassment? The ex-crims I've dealt with would be by this point.'

'He was a bit surly but polite enough,' Murray said. 'The girlfriend was surlier actually. I'm guessing he's used to being asked questions and told what to do. She's not.'

'She better get used to it quick,' Ella said. 'So we still need to talk to Weaver's wife, find and talk to Miriam Holder, trace the phone calls made to Meixner and Weaver, and check further into Fletcher and Canning. Fletcher especially, now that we know he lied in his answers.'

'Did he lie, or did you fail to ask the question?' Langley said. 'You yourself just said that he never actually stated what time Jones left.'

'Regardless, I think we should bring him in for a formal interview,' she said. 'Sooner rather than later.'

No matter what spin Langley put on it, Fletcher deserved a grilling in a small windowless room. And if she got overtime, she'd not only avoid the family dinner, she could text Callum and cancel their conversation. It might just delay the inevitable, but that was still something. But Langley shook his head.

'Tomorrow,' he said. 'Go sign off, people. Let's keep this budget in the black.'

Ella gripped the arms of her chair. 'So people can lie, and practically flee an interview, and it doesn't matter any more?'

But Langley was on his way out the door and didn't even glance around. 'Tomorrow.'

★

The unlit stairway was narrow, the carpet-covered steps creaky and sagging. Jane could hear someone panting and crying up ahead. She squinted through the gloom to an open door. She carried the Oxy-Viva and monitor, while Alex had the drug box and portable radio.

'Hello?' She didn't wait for an answer but walked straight through the door into a living room stuffed with armchairs and side tables.

'In here!'

Jane hurried into an even more cramped bedroom to find a white-haired humpbacked woman in her eighties on the floor doing CPR on a motionless man of the same age. The woman was crying as she clasped her shaky hands together over the man's bare and skinny chest, and counted aloud as she pressed down. 'One and two and –'

'Let me do that,' Alex said, kneeling beside her and doing compressions one-handed while lifting the radio. 'Thirty-five to Control. Confirm arrest, confirm backup required.'

'Copy, Thirty-five.'

The man's face was bony white, his eyes half-open in that dead stare, his lips and ears turning purple. He wore pyjama shorts and nothing else. His white hair was thin, his elbows and knees and ribs knobbly under pale skin. Alex attached the monitoring dots one-handed, switched the machine on, and ran a strip, while Jane unzipped the Oxy-Viva and pulled out the bag and mask. The woman leaned stiffly back on her knees and put her hands to her own chest, tears running down her face.

'Do you have chest pain?' Jane said, alarmed.

'It's just angina,' the woman gasped. 'Is he going to be okay?'

'How long have you had it for?'

'Since he collapsed. When I phoned you.'

Eleven minutes. 'And you did CPR anyway?'

'I wasn't going to stop just for a little pain. Please help him.'

The monitor was showing the flat line of asystole, meaning the heart muscle had stopped beating, with just the occasional intermittent blip, the agonal rhythm that signalled the last electrical activity of a dying heart. Jane and Alex exchanged a look. In this kind of situation, with a person this age who'd been collapsed for over ten minutes and had this cardiac rhythm, and who looked this . . . well, dead, the family often understood what had happened before you told them. This woman though . . . Jane couldn't shake the thought of her doing CPR for those long minutes while her own heart was cramping in her chest, and worried that to break the news to her without even trying to resuscitate him might send her into arrest too.

'Alex is going to take care of you and your chest pain while I look after your husband,' she said.

'Please don't let him die.'

The woman let Alex help her up from the floor and tottered beside him as he dragged an armchair across the living room. Jane did some quick compressions, held the bag and mask to the man's face and inflated his lungs, then did more compressions. As she worked, she saw Alex put an oxygen mask on the woman, give her an aspirin, check her blood pressure, and pop an Anginine tablet under her tongue, the two of them talking all the while. When he came back, stretching another length of oxygen tubing to connect to the bag Jane was using, she had a tourniquet in place, ready to cannulate a vein, and the intubation kit unrolled.

'Her name's Rose, his is Graham,' Alex said in a low voice as he took over the CPR. 'Married fifty-seven years. Haven't been apart since she was in hospital having their kids fifty-three years ago. They're both on blood pressure and cardiac meds, but never been admitted for either problem. He's been well lately, and collapsed suddenly without any warning. She called us, then started CPR straightaway, but she thought he might have still been breathing for a few minutes.'

It was more than likely just the final gasps for air triggered by a fading brain, Jane thought. They'd run through the protocol and see what happened. The chances that he'd live were slim in the extreme, but now they were working for Rose's sake. She would at least have the comfort of knowing that everything possible had been done.

Jane crouched over Graham's arm, palpating for a vein. Rose wept softly in the living room. For a brief second, Jane couldn't help but think of Laird, couldn't stop herself imagining growing old like this with him.

She turned Graham's arm and felt her way down to his wrist then back up to his elbow, then stripped off her gloves and tried again with her bare fingertips. His flesh was cool and soft. She found a small vein high inside his elbow, chose a twenty-gauge cannula, swabbed the site and crossed her fingers. She slid the cannula in, and after a moment saw the flash of dark purple blood in the chamber. She held the cannula in place with one hand and withdrew the plastic-sheathed stylet with the other, then went to screw the bung in but slipped, and for a second blood poured out and over her fingers. She swore under her breath, attached the bung properly, then taped it down before wiping roughly at the blood with the used swab. *No time for this now.*

'How is he?' Rose called.

'We're doing everything we can,' Alex said. 'How are you?'

'Please, just save him.'

The monitor was still showing the same flat line, with the blips getting further apart. Jane injected adrenaline through the cannula without much hope. Alex's compressions would move the drug through the bloodstream and into the heart, where it would – in a perfect world – stimulate the muscle. It'd also constrict the blood vessels in Graham's arms and legs, keeping more blood around his heart and brain where it was really needed. Survival rates of cardiac arrest outside hospital were around five per cent, and way lower at his age. In twelve years of doing the job, she could count on the fingers of one hand her saves who'd been over seventy. *Poor guy. Poor Rose.*

Alex had already started the conversation, and she knew how the rest of it would go: 'We're doing everything we can'; 'unfortunately he's not responding'; 'the damage to his heart might just be too great'. All to help prepare, to soften the blow, before you said, 'we're so sorry'. As if it could be softened.

She injected another bolus of adrenaline, followed it up with a flush of normal saline, then moved to Graham's head to intubate. She chose an eight-millimetre tube and picked up the laryngoscope, then heard Alex say softly, 'Holy shit.'

He was staring at the monitor, and stopped compressions and pressed his fingers to the soft stubbled skin of Graham's throat. He looked at Jane. 'You're not going to believe this.'

Jane reached for the other side and found a carotid pulse. Thready, but more or less regular. The monitor started to beep with each beat. She pressed harder. It was really there.

'You saved him!' Rose called. 'You did it!'

Jane glanced at Alex. He looked as stunned as she felt. She had never, ever, had someone come back so quickly after being down so long with such an awful rhythm, CPR or no CPR. She wanted to tell Rose that they had a long way to go yet, and even if his heart kept going he'd probably be severely brain damaged, but then Graham started to gasp.

'This is unbelievable,' Alex breathed.

The hair standing up on her arms, Jane dropped the tube and held the mask to Graham's face. His skin turned from white to pink and the purple congestion slowly left his ears and lips.

Rose appeared in the doorway, mask clasped to her face with shaky hands, the Oxy-Viva dragging behind her. 'Graham?'

'Please sit down, Rose,' Jane said.

She lowered herself onto the end of the bed. 'Can he hear me?'

'He's not out of the woods yet,' Jane said. 'Sometimes in cases like this, even with the good CPR that you were doing, people take a long time to wake up, and sometimes there are lasting problems.'

'But he's alive,' Rose said.

For the moment, Jane thought. But she realised his breathing was getting deeper and stronger, less gaspy, more normal. She looked down at him and was startled when he blinked. Focus came into his eyes and he looked into hers.

'Graham?' Rose said again.

He moved his hand in a decent approximation of a wave. Jane blinked back tears.

Rose fell to her knees off the bed and grasped his foot, weeping. 'I knew you wouldn't leave me.'

Graham reached up to the mask and tried to push Jane's hands away.

'Hold on,' she said. 'Take it easy. It's oxygen. Good for you.'

He lowered his hands and clasped them over his chest, looking like a man relaxing on a beach. Alex started to laugh.

Rose smiled through her tears. 'I knew that if I didn't give up he'd be all right.'

Jane tried to pull herself together. 'Graham, how are you feeling?'

He gave a thumbs-up.

'Do you know where you are?'

He folded his hands together and put them beside his head, mimicking sleep.

'Bedroom,' Alex said, his voice full of wonder.

Graham gave another thumbs-up.

'Do you know what happened?' Jane asked.

He touched his left chest over his heart then drew a line across his throat.

Alex laughed again. 'I like this guy.'

Jane heard boots in the hallway. 'Hello?' someone called.

'In here,' she said.

The crew came to the door and looked in. 'You got him back.'

'Like you wouldn't believe,' Alex said, jubilation in his voice.

Jane felt tears bubble up. She would not break down here. She had to get out.

'I have to wash this blood off my hands. Alex, can you take over here?' she managed to say, adding to Rose, 'Okay if I use your bathroom?'

She stumbled away without waiting for an answer. Through a blur of tears, she found the bathroom in a short hallway off the living room and locked herself in, her chest tight with emotion. She scrubbed at the drying smears of blood on her fingers, blinking as hard as she could. Funny how you got used to the bad stuff, the dying, the deaths, and someone coming back like this made you fall apart.

Her phone buzzed in her pocket. *Laird.* She was suddenly

craving his skin, his body, his arms around her. She looked at the message.

Sorry, Laird had written. *Shocking day, just too busy. Too exhausted for tonight too. Call you tomorrow.*

She read it again. Disappointment squeezed her heart and made her stomach sink, and she realised just how much she'd been looking forward to seeing him – and not just now, not just because of this case. She wanted to see him smile at her, she wanted to hold him, and she wanted to tell him that she loved him.

Oh God, no. Not that.

She was a grown woman. A mother of three grown children. Divorced for years, content on her own, enjoying her life, happy for a bit of fun but not interested in anything more.

So you thought.

'Dammit all to hell,' she said.

★

Ella drove angry. She didn't care what Langley said, Fletcher had lied. And Miriam Holder must have something to hide or she wouldn't have run. So why the hell weren't she and Murray on one or other of those doorsteps right now?

She wished Chloe and Audra could be present every time Langley sent detectives home, the action more or less declaring that Marko wasn't worth the cost of overtime. See how calm and composed he'd be then.

And now she had to meet Callum and listen while he told her 'it's not you, it's me' or some such thing.

She wrenched on the handbrake outside the cafe in Annandale and stormed in to pick up coffee. She wanted a plan, a list of things to say in reply, reasons why they should give it another go. But that felt ridiculous. If he didn't want to be with her, why should she continue to want to be with him? She should walk away with her head held high. But she couldn't shake the memories of the good times they'd had; the intense conversations, the connection she'd felt and was sure he felt too, the mutual understanding when it came to the pressures of their jobs. They'd clicked, there was no other way to put it. It felt like such a waste to give up on all that, to not even try to work it through.

At the hospital, she parked in the police bay. Three ambulances stood with their back doors open, the crews joking with each other while they cleaned up after their cases. She texted Callum and waited, half-hoping that he'd say he was too busy. *I'm on my way*, he replied.

Teeth gritted, she got out of the car and put the coffee on the bonnet, then straightened her back and pressed her hands against the car and looked up at the leaves moving in the wind. *Just don't let him see that it hurts.*

The doors opened and Callum stepped out. He didn't smile. She watched him cross the asphalt, heart beating in her ears, trying to read his blank expression. She lifted her chin. *I've chased killers. I've been shot. I've seen people die and I've helped bring them back to life. Whatever he says, they're only words.*

'Hi,' he said.

She handed him his coffee.

He nodded. 'Thanks.'

They leaned on the car, sipping. The paramedics clanged their stretchers and flapped clean linen and one sang along with the radio; Hall and Oates, Ella thought.

Callum faced her. 'Ella.'

Here it comes. She kept looking at the ambulances. 'Coffee's too hot.'

'I told my dad that I'm seeing you,' he said.

She turned. 'What?'

'He went very still and quiet, then he said he couldn't believe it, that I was letting him down, that you were a liar and I should stay away from you.'

She couldn't help herself. 'When did I lie?'

'He said he was confused in the interview.'

'No way,' she said. 'I remember that interview and he was not confused. He admitted everything.'

Callum put his cup on the bonnet. 'This is my father we're talking about.'

'Don't worry, I'm not likely to forget it.' She took a sip of coffee but it was bitter on her tongue. She launched the mostly full cup at a bin and missed. 'So that's why you were angry yesterday? Because of what your father said? Thanks for being honest and open with me.'

'Mum's not happy either.'

'Why the hell did you tell them?'

'It seemed important.'

'For you or for them?'

'It just was.'

'I haven't told mine.'

'Perhaps because you know that who I am doesn't matter to them,' he said.

Ella had known there would come a time when his parents would find out, and had figured it would make things awkward – awkward being an understatement – but it felt like Callum had shut down on her completely, that his parents' opinion was the most important thing of all.

'And because of that you don't want to see me any more,' she said.

'I understand why they feel that way. I knew it wouldn't be easy for them.'

'Or for you.'

He nodded and looked across at the ambulances.

She didn't know what to say. She liked him, and she felt sick that their past might loom so large over them that this was never, ever, going to work.

'The thing is,' he said, 'I don't know what I want. I sometimes wonder whether –' The pager on his belt started beeping and he looked at the screen. 'I have to go.'

'Wait.'

But he was already jogging across to the door. 'Emergency. I'll call you later if I can.'

She started after him. 'Just a second.'

But the doors closed behind him.

Ella stopped, trying to decide what to do. After a couple of months of the relationship dying off, he'd told his parents. Did that – what did that mean?

She was aware of the paramedics watching from their vehicles, of the fluttering in her chest that was either hope or fear. She could walk away, call him later. Or she could . . .

Ella went up to the doors. They slid open and she walked in. The department was lit by overbright fluorescents, and she heard a kid screeching somewhere, barked commands, someone vomiting behind a curtain. She walked down the aisle between the cubicles and found herself at the foot of an occupied bed. Callum bent over a woman's arm, tapping the skin with gloved fingers. The woman was ghostly pale and trying to push away a nurse who held a mask and bag to her face. 'You have to keep this on,' the nurse said.

Callum wiped his forehead with his wrist and looked up at the patient. 'Margie, it's okay. Just relax and breathe through the mask.' He put his hand in hers and squeezed her fingers. The woman turned her white face his way and he cupped her shoulder and smiled at her. 'Breathe and take it easy and we'll have you feeling better in no time.' He didn't look around; he had eyes only for his patient.

Ella stepped away. She liked him. A lot. And for this kind of focus as much as anything.

She headed back outside, determined that whatever happened, she wouldn't let him go without a fight.

TWELVE

Jane parked her car on the street near Laird's house at twenty
to nine. She was freshly showered, and wearing a light cardigan and a cotton dress that moved around her hips and legs
and lacy underwear when she walked. She could smell the perfume rising with the heat of her body and looked forward to
seeing his face when he opened the door. They didn't have to
do anything. They could watch TV, they could sit and have a
drink, they could just talk. He could doze with his head on her
lap. They could go to bed and fall asleep in each other's arms.
She was on nightshift tomorrow night; they could wake up
late, share breakfast, have a proper lazy morning.

The porch light was on, and she stepped up and knocked
on the door, a little breathless, weak in the elbows, a smile
spreading across her face.

The woman who opened it was ten centimetres taller than
her and whip-thin. The bulk of her blonde hair was pinned
up, the rest straggled oh-so-carelessly around her face, and she
wore a tight white velvet tracksuit zipped down just far enough
to reveal large fake cleavage. She looked at Jane with round
blue eyes. 'Yes?'

Jane couldn't think. *Lucille?* She couldn't remember enough about the photo she'd seen online. 'Is Laird here?'

'Who's asking?'

'I am.'

The woman eyed her. Jane could see now that while she was striving for early twenties, the work wasn't invisible and she was more like thirty-five. The hands would tell the true story – you could get your face lifted all the way over the top of your head, but there was nothing you could do about your hands. She shifted her glance to the woman's left hand where it rested against the open door, then saw the rock on the third finger and the wedding band beside it.

The woman held out her right hand now, and Jane saw in those hard eyes that she recognised why Jane was there. 'I'm Mrs Lucille Humphreys.'

Jane took the cold fingers automatically, managed to say, 'My mistake. Wrong address,' then turned to stumble off the porch.

'No, wait, let me fetch him.'

Lucille screeched Laird's name over her shoulder, and a moment later he looked out of the sitting room, a set of head-phones in his hands.

He gazed blank-faced at Jane. 'Yes?'

She backed away and lurched out to the street. The foot-path seemed to be tilting. She could hear Lucille's shrill voice demanding that Laird tell her her name and Laird swearing about autograph hunters.

He's not separated at all. He's still fucking married.

She staggered to her car and fumbled her keys out of her bag, then dropped them. On her knees on the asphalt, the burn of tears began and she groped between the wheels through a haze.

Once in the car, she swiped at her eyes with the back of her hand, then tore away from the kerb.

Five blocks later, she pulled over. The streetlights were smears in her eyes, and she pressed her forehead hard against the top of the wheel.

Either they were separated and he'd taken her back, or she had just been away for a while and he'd hidden every speck of evidence of her existence. Photos, her clothes, toiletries, everything. What kind of fucking bastard did that?

And what does that make me, that I couldn't see through it? That I was so taken in I'd started to fall in love?

She banged her head hard on the wheel.

When she could see again, she dug in her bag for her mobile and called her friend Tracey. She was overseas and out of contact, but Jane needed to hear her voice.

'Hey, this is Tracey. Tell me the short version and I'll call you back for the long one.'

'It's me.' Jane wiped her eyes on the sleeve of her cardigan. 'You're not going to believe what I've done. I always thought I was smart, you know? I'd never be one of those people. I wish I could talk to you. You won't get this for days but no doubt when you do I'll still need your help. Love you.'

She put the phone on the seat. She ached all over. Her mind rushed: image after image of her and Laird, the sound of his voice and his laugh, the feel of his skin against hers. The feeling she'd had this evening when walking from her car to his door; the shy and secret and now so ridiculous hope that maybe he was falling for her too, and they might have a future together, like Rose and Graham.

She jammed her hands against the horn. 'Fuck it all!'

★

Ella scraped the plates off into the bin in the corner of her parents' kitchen, then stacked them in the sink. In the dining room, her mother, Netta, tried to get a word in, but Aunt Adelina wasn't letting go of the conversation. 'So I said to the girl, don't they teach you arithmetic in school any more? And she said, "What's arithmetic?".'

Ella's father, Franco, stumped into the kitchen with the

vase of violets from the table.

'I thought they were fresh,' Ella said.

'I needed an excuse to get out.' He lifted the flowers out, tipped the clear water down the sink beside the plates, refilled the vase and thrust the flowers in again. 'God knows I love your aunty, but sometimes enough is enough.'

Adelina had come to stay while she recovered from a fall at home that had left her with a broken wrist. Ella had sat at dinner listening to her father and aunt bicker like they were children again, while her mother tried desperately to smooth things over. *No wonder she's so keen to get me here.*

'And there you were always apologising to me for not giving me siblings,' she said. 'Really, you did me a favour.'

His face softened. 'Did we?'

Ella turned to the sink and started filling it with hot water. 'Has she said when she might leave?'

'Sometimes she talks about the weekend, but doesn't say which one.' He tied up the handles of the bin liner.

'Let me do that,' she said.

'It's all right, bella. Both *my* arms work.'

She followed him outside to the wheelie bin and lifted the lid. 'Doesn't she do anything?'

'Even asked your mother to help her wash.' Franco gripped the handle, but Ella gently took it from him and started to pull the bin out to the street. He followed. 'Who needs two hands on a washer?'

She parked the bin at the kerb. Moths circled the streetlight.

Franco positioned the bin just so, then looked up. 'No stars tonight. Too much cloud. Bit more rain tomorrow – be lovely for the roses.'

Ella looked up too. The air was cool and smelled of damp grass and tree bark.

'I'm still sorry we didn't have any more after you,' Franco said. 'You were the most cute thing I'd ever seen. Dark curls, dark eyes, your little shoes.' He smiled. 'We tried, but nothing.'

Ella felt her face grow warm. 'Look, a bat.'

He didn't glance up. 'And as much as I complain about Adelina, I do love her. She's my sister.' He squeezed her arm. 'People. It's people that matter the most in life.'

She had the sudden horrible thought that he was sick again. 'Where's this coming from?'

'We worry about you sometimes. So busy with work.'

'I love my life,' she said.

'Relationships are important too,' he said. 'You know you're always welcome to bring a boyfriend to dinner. Or a girlfriend, we don't mind. Whoever you love. Either way.'

'Fine, next time I have a boyfriend I'll bring him.'

She was hot with embarrassment. All through dinner, her thoughts had strayed to Callum. She'd called him on the way here, left a message saying hi and asking him to get back to her when he could, and ever since had kept touching her phone in her pocket, hoping to feel a text arrive. Now she thought about opening up to her dad, telling him what was going on and what had happened tonight, but firstly she didn't know what to say and secondly she was frightened she might cry.

'Look, another bat.'

Franco kissed her cheek. 'I know, bats everywhere.'

★

Jane went to a drive-through bottle shop and bought a sixpack of pre-mixed rum and Coke, then sat in the car by Maroubra Beach, staring into the night darkness over the ocean and drinking. The worst thing was feeling so stupid. She took pride in being able to suss people out at work – she was always the first one to spot the faker, to recognise the crazy, to see the danger coming their way when the brawl seemed over – and here she'd acted like a twelve year old with her first crush, mooning over her memories, dreaming they'd be together forever.

She felt sick over the idiocy of her hope, and had to lower the window and lean her head on the sill. The wind tasted of the sea and blew through her hair, and she stared into it, her eyes watering, the can cold in her hands, the lace underwear making her itch, the ache in her chest raw and growing.

'Fucking bastard,' she said.

She finished the can and put it on the passenger side floor, then opened the next. Cars with thumping stereos cruised the car park but she focused on the black water. Her skin grew sticky with salt. Her ear got sore and she put her fingers between it and the sill and kept drinking. Her phone stayed silent, but she wouldn't have answered him anyway.

When she dropped the fourth empty on the floor, she started to think about going home. She felt ridiculous in the lacy underwear and wanted to strip it off and throw it away. And how come they still couldn't make these things itch-free? But she shouldn't drive. She rested her chin on her folded arms on the wheel and thought about calling a taxi, or Alex. It was only a ten-minute walk. The fresh air might do her good. She was on nightshift tomorrow, so could sleep in, then walk down and get the car late in the morning. That would be two walks in two days. Yes. Excellent idea.

She put up the windows, got out and locked the car, placed the keys carefully into her bag, then started off through the car park. The night had grown somehow darker and she kept stumbling, almost falling more than once. On the street, she focused on the power poles and walked slowly and consciously from one to the next, slapping the wood with the flat of her hand as she passed each one. 'Laird. You. Cheating. Slime.'

She stopped for a breather with her arms around a pole, and realised the pain was better. She was almost numb, in fact.

'See, I'm over you already!' she shouted. 'You bastard!'

She found her street and turned into it. It was even darker here, and so quiet. It must be later than she'd thought. She must've fallen asleep in the car. She soldiered on and reached her house at last, and rested against the fencepost for a moment. The garden and porch were pitch dark. She hadn't yet replaced the globe Deb had smashed.

'Bitch,' she said aloud.

That's what else she'd do tomorrow: call up Gittins and listen to his apology. Sleep, walk to the car, call up Gittins. It felt good to have a list. A schedule. Such a thing left a person with no time to think.

She lurched into the yard and along the path, then tripped on some kind of stick. She fell forward, her hands landing in something wet and skidding out from under her, dropping her chest down on something big. She rolled off it, sticky wetness all over her hands and neck, the air thick with a smell her alcohol-fogged brain knew well but couldn't immediately name.

What has that bitch Deb done now?

If this was a dead or injured animal, she'd kill her.

She couldn't see a thing in the darkness and reached towards the object tentatively. Her fingertips brushed what felt like skin. An arm.

'Jesus.'

The flesh was cool and firm, and the person didn't move when she squeezed. And blood, it was blood that she could smell. She felt her way cautiously, fearfully, up the slender arm and across soaked clothing to the neck. Blood everywhere, and a thready pulse.

'Jesus!'

★

Jane sat in the gutter with her dress tucked around her legs and her blood-smeared hands gripping the concrete kerb. The drying blood on her neck and chest pulled at her skin when she moved and the metallic smell rose into her face. A paramedic crew she didn't know had taken over the care of the unconscious woman, helping Jane up from the path beside her, where she'd knelt supporting her head after rolling her in the recovery position and screamed and screamed for help.

She could hear her neighbours talking in low voices behind her, one saying he'd get a towel and water and help her wash, another answering that the police were on their way and had said not to touch anything or anyone. Above her, the night sky felt endless.

A torch shone in her face then down her body. 'I'm Fran, a paramedic,' a voice said from behind the light. 'Are you hurt?'

Jane shook her head. 'I fell into the blood.'

'That's her house,' one of the neighbours volunteered. 'She's a paramedic too.'

'Really?' Fran said. 'Where do you work?'

'Rocks.'

It was too tiring to talk. She closed her eyes. She felt Fran's gloved fingers on her wrist, then the BP cuff being wrapped around her upper arm. Cars pulled up and doors slammed and people conferred in serious tones about body this and body that. The BP cuff was removed and Fran squeezed her shoulder, then someone's shoe tapped sharply against hers.

She opened her eyes and looked up.

'I'm Detective Juliet Rooney,' the woman said. She held an open notebook. 'Your name?'

'Jane Koutoufides.'

'Stand up for me, please.'

Jane tried to get up and almost lost her balance. The detective caught her arm. 'Been drinking?'

'Yep,' Jane said.

'Look at me.'

Jane blinked into her face. The street was lit by car headlights and moving torch beams. Rooney was a pale-skinned woman with cool eyes and brown hair in a smooth ponytail. Jane felt filthy standing there in front of her.

'Who is that in your garden?'

'I don't know,' Jane said. 'It was too dark to see.' *But I have a suspicion.*

'Come and look now then.' Still holding her arm, Rooney steered her past the neighbours and through her own front gate, detouring off the path and around the stick Jane had tripped on – a golf club, its head matted with blood and hair. The paramedics had the woman on their stretcher. She was collared, intubated and being bagged. The cardiac monitor beeped, IVs had been started, and a thick pad and bandage covered most of her head.

Jane stared.

'You know her,' Rooney said.

'It's Deb, my ex's wife.'

Deb's dark hair was matted with blood across her forehead and her skin was white. Dizzy, Jane took a step back.

'Why would she be here?' Rooney said.

'She thinks Steve and I are seeing each other,' Jane said, as the paramedics wheeled the stretcher away. 'She's been coming around and smashing my lights and windows. I need to sit down.'

'Did you report her?'

'I asked Steve to tell her to stop.' Jane felt the ground moving under her feet. 'It wasn't working though, because today she complained about me at work. I really need to sit down.'

Rooney led her across the lawn to the far corner of the porch. The tiles were cold through her dress. Rooney stood in front of her with her notebook. 'What was the work complaint?'

Jane described the allegation of the damage to a car and the subsequent confrontation she'd had with Deb.

'She might have bruises on her wrist. That was me, trying to restrain her.' She raised her own arm. 'She did this to me at the same time.'

Rooney looked at the fingermarks. 'What time did you finish work?'

'Six thirty.'

'Then what did you do?'

'Caught the bus home, had a shower, made myself dinner.'

'Were you here when she arrived?' Rooney asked.

'No.'

'Where were you?'

'I went out for a drive,' Jane said.

'Where?'

'Just around. Bondi way, the suburbs. I parked at the beach for a while. To look at the ocean and think.'

'About what?' Rooney said.

'Work. You know how the job can be. I had a guy under a train yesterday. I talked to some of your people then too. Detective Ellen something. Ella.'

Rooney turned the page. 'What time did you head out on this drive?'

'Around eight thirty.'

'You encounter anyone in your travels?'

'Guy at the drive-through bottle shop on Anzac Parade. I bought a sixpack of rum and Coke. He'd remember me because I was crying and he said something kind about a hard night and I told him to mind his own fucking business.'

Rooney looked at her.

'You ever think you might have PTSD?' Jane asked.

'How much did you drink?' Rooney said.

'Four cans. I don't drink much usually.' The thought of it now made her stomach spasm.

'What did you do then?'

'I left the car at the beach and walked home. It took me a while. I stumbled in here and tripped and fell on her.' She held out her hands. The dried blood was flaking off.

'What time was that?'

'Whenever the neighbours called you,' Jane said.

Rooney checked her watch and wrote something in her notebook. 'Wait here.'

Jane pulled her sticky cardigan around herself and watched Rooney talk to a blonde detective and two uniformed cops, while a crime scene officer took photos of the golf club. The lie about where she'd been hadn't been planned, but she'd realised as she spoke that she never wanted to tell anyone about Laird. She even regretted having called Tracey, but at least she could make up some story by the time Tracey got reception at Machu Picchu and called back. It wasn't like leaving Laird out of the story here made a huge difference: she *had* driven to Bondi then around the beach suburbs; she had gone to the bottle shop, then parked at the beach, then walked home. Cars had passed while she'd staggered along the road, she was almost certain, so if the police tried they could no doubt find people who'd seen her. All this checking was just the police filling in the night's blanks, putting the story together like she did in her case sheets. This happened, then that happened, and the victim was found at such and such a time by a person named X.

Rooney came back with the guy with the camera. 'Stand up,' she said to Jane. 'Hands out by your sides, palms forward.'

Jane did as she was told, shutting her eyes against the flash.

'Turn your hands over.'

More flashes.

'Stay there.'

The photographer moved in for closer shots of her hands, back and front, and of her bruised wrist.

'She bit me, too,' Jane said, pointing to her elbow. 'She tried, anyway.'

'Did you hurt yourself when you fell?' Rooney asked.

'No,' Jane said, cold now and starting to shiver.

'What about that bruise on your forehead?'

The photographer leaned in for a shot of it, then some of the blood on her neck and chest.

'Bumped it on the steering wheel when I was drinking,' Jane said.

'Uh-huh,' Rooney said.

The photographer finished and walked back to the body.

'Is that your golf club?' Rooney pointed.

Jane shook her head. 'I hate golf.'

'Know anyone who plays?'

'My ex.' Did Laird? She didn't know. 'Can I go inside now? I'd really like to shower and lie down.'

'Sorry,' Rooney said. 'I need you to come to the station for a formal interview.'

'Can't it wait until tomorrow?'

'Sorry,' Rooney said again.

Jane looked down at herself, trying to bury her feelings. *Just more box-ticking.* 'Can I at least change my clothes? Clean off this blood?' And get out of this goddamned itchy lace crap.

'Better if we go now.'

Rooney took her arm again, but this time the grip felt more like a restraint than a support.

THIRTEEN

Ella left when her mother dozed off in her armchair. Adelina had gone to bed an hour before, and Netta had visibly relaxed. The three of them had stayed in the lounge room, the TV on but none of them watching it, instead talking about holidays they'd taken when Ella was young, about pets they'd had, about weather and gardens and Sunday dinner the coming weekend.

Franco waved her off, and she settled deeper into the driver's seat as she pulled away. It was late but she didn't feel tired. There'd been no text from Callum, but she kept thinking about how he'd looked at that patient. She would talk to him tomorrow. They would sort it out and it would be good.

She stopped at a red on an empty intersection. Home was east, to the right, but she didn't feel like going there just yet. She looked in the other direction. Granville wasn't far.

The light turned green, and she sat there a moment longer, then turned left.

Half an hour later she was parked across the street and down from Simon Fletcher's ramshackle house, her car tucked between a couple of others outside the closed gate of a panelbeater's workshop. Fletcher's white van with the plastic pipes strapped to the roof was parked at the kerb in front of his house, and she could see a light behind the curtains in his front window.

Sometimes on surveillance she felt the passing of every second, but tonight she was in no hurry. She slithered down in her seat and thought about Callum. The dedication. It was what they shared. Here she was, in her car, on her own, doing what Langley should've organised. It was all about the case, about finding who killed Marko Meixner and bringing that person to justice. About doing her best to help one person, just as Callum did with a patient. Nobody could save the world, but – what was that saying? – if you've helped one person today then it's been a good day.

Fletcher's light went out. She yawned, thinking she'd give him a few minutes before starting the car and heading off, then she saw the front door open. The man himself stepped onto the verandah. He wore jeans and zipped up a dark jacket as he crossed his crappy garden to the footpath, then got behind the wheel of his van. She clutched her own wheel in excitement, and watched as he turned on his headlights and drove away down the street.

She waited until his car was almost at the corner, then started her engine and followed.

★

Alex woke fighting the sheets. He could feel the girl's dead hand in his, hear her parents' sobs in his head. Every night this happened. The psychologist said it would get better. He walked to the bathroom and rubbed his sweaty head with a towel, wondering *When? When?*

Down the dark hallway, Mia's bedroom door was open an inch. The streetlight shone through her partly open blinds. He eased into her room and stood watching her sleep. She lay curled on her left side as she usually did, her face relaxed, the quilt high around her shoulders. Every night since the crash, he'd come in here and stood like this. She never woke.

Every night that he wasn't on nightshift, that was. And on those nights, he'd asked Louise, the sleepover sitter, to come in and check on her. He'd said Mia tended to throw the quilt off and not wake up, and was prone to serious chest infections if she got cold. Louise had believed him, and told him every morning that she'd checked, that Mia'd slept fine. He knew it was irrational, but he felt it helped keep her safe.

He moved to the wall beside her desk and eased himself down onto the floor, careful of his knees that sometimes clicked. Mia breathed evenly. He lifted the back of his T-shirt to wipe the last of the sweat from the nape of his neck, and sat there watching the light lie in bands on the floor.

He'd been to more fatal crashes than he could remember. Eventually they tended to blur, for the mind's sake he guessed. This one, though . . . The dream always put him right back there, breathing the smells of oil and petrol and eucalyptus from the battered tree, seeing the twisted shell of the old car as he pulled up, getting close and finding the bodies, the young man pinned behind the wheel, head back, open eyes sightless, blood on his face from fatal head injuries caused by the caved-in roof, and in what was left of the passenger seat, crumpled against the tree, the girl. Open head wounds. Crushed chest. Dead stare. Blood all over her, and Mia's age and size. One limp white hand hung out what remained of the window. He'd called for urgent rescue though they were beyond hope, and stood holding that hand while he waited. And then her parents had arrived.

★

Jane had been inside Maroubra police station once before, when David had been caught trying to shoplift a carton of Coke at the age of fifteen. He'd been in tears, and she'd thanked the officers for giving him a fright that fortunately had stuck. The station hadn't changed much in ten years, but it felt different to be walking in covered in blood, the cops at the desk looking up at her as Rooney opened the door into the back. She could easily have been a victim, but something in their gazes made her feel like they believed she wasn't, like they recognised some action or tone of Rooney's that marked her as something else.

Unsettled, she followed Rooney through the office areas and into an interview room.

'Have a seat,' Rooney said.

Jane hesitated then sat. 'Should I be concerned about anything?'

'Like what?'

'Am I a suspect?'

Rooney's gaze was even. 'Why would you think that?'

'I would really have liked to clean myself up.'

'I can imagine,' Rooney said. 'But we won't keep you long. Sit tight and I'll be back in a minute.' She closed the door behind her with a click.

Jane sat in the chair with her hands in her lap. They hadn't said she was under arrest, and she was almost certain that meant she didn't have to stay if she didn't want to. She thought about getting up and seeing if the door was locked, seeing if she could walk out or if someone would come running and grasp her arm again. But paramedics and police worked so well together normally, it would probably look odd if she didn't want to cooperate now. Odd, as in she had something to hide. She started to pick dried blood from around her nails, then felt sick and tucked her hands under her thighs. Blood didn't usually bother her, but she didn't usually have it coating what felt like most of her skin and it didn't usually come from the comatose body of someone she knew. She hoped Deb was okay.

Minutes dragged past. She heard someone walk past the closed door, and somewhere a telephone rang five times.

She kept her hands under her thighs and tried to stay still. Her bladder was full and her nausea growing. She waited as long as she could, then got up and knocked on the door.

No answer.

She tried the knob. It was unlocked and turned smoothly in her hand. She looked up and down the corridor but there was nobody in sight.

'I need the bathroom.'

No reply.

She hadn't seen one as they'd come in from the right, so she went left. The second door she found was the female bathroom. She locked the cubicle door and sat on the loo. Now she'd get to wash her hands as well. *Thank goodness.*

The urine poured out of her like a flood. She grabbed sheets of the same government-issue paper they had at her station, stood to pull up the scratchy lace underpants, then froze at the spotting on the lining.

She hadn't had a period for four years, and now she was spotting.

She sank back onto the toilet, dismay and anxiety and fear filling her limbs with lead. She'd only spotted three times in her life, and they were called Glenn, David and Breanna.

'Jane?' Rooney said, right outside the door.

She started. 'Yes?'

'Are you okay?'

'Fine. I'm just – one minute. I'll just be another minute.'

'I'm outside in the corridor if you need me.'

'Okay,' Jane said. 'Thanks.'

She sat there trembling as the outer door closed, then looked at the spots of blood again. It might not be that, she told herself. It could be the stress of Laird, and Deb. Perhaps she had an infection. Or maybe her menopause wasn't as straightforward as she'd thought, and this was some new and exciting phase.

She tore off another wad of paper. A few more slight smears. She stared at them, then dropped the paper into the toilet, yanked up her underpants and flushed. Her dress fell around her thighs and she unlocked the cubicle door and went to the sink.

Rooney hadn't said straight out that she couldn't clean herself up, and she didn't care any more about what might look odd. She lathered her hands and washed the pink-tinged foam down the drain, then wet handfuls of paper towel and scrubbed at the blood on her neck and chest, and dress and cardigan. Her gaze drifted to her stomach where it pressed against the cotton of her dress. It bulged a little, but she was a middle-aged woman who'd had three kids.

She dumped the sodden towels in the bin and turned for more, and couldn't help glancing into the mirror as she did so. Was the bulge bigger?

No. No. It was an infection or something. It had to be.

But in the mirror, her face was pale, her eyes huge.

★

When she stepped into the corridor five minutes later, the top of her dress and cardigan were wet and stained pink but the blood was gone from her skin.

Detective Juliet Rooney pushed herself off the opposite wall. 'All right?'

'I want to go home,' Jane said.

'Beg your pardon?'

'I'm going home.' Jane stood up straight like she'd practised in the bathroom. 'I've told you everything that happened tonight, and a formal statement won't have anything new in it.'

Rooney looked at her for a long moment. 'Okay. We'll do it another time.'

'And I need a lift.'

'Sure.'

They eyed each other, then Rooney turned away. 'Come on then.'

Jane followed her through the station and outside under

the dark night sky. She felt disconnected from the world. Her fingers felt sticky, and she could still smell the blood.

As she climbed into the police car, she was horrified to catch herself putting a protective hand over her stomach.

★

The closer they got to Ryde, the harder Ella found it to sit still. And now Fletcher was turning off Lane Cove Road. He was really going there. She could hardly believe it.

She hung back as he slowed, his brakelights showing intermittently, and for the shortest second she thought he was going to drive past, but then he slowed even further and the van crept at walking pace into Amy Street.

I knew it.

She adjusted her grip on the wheel as she eased around the corner behind him. Chloe and Marko Meixner's flat was in a building about halfway down the street, but it was empty, she knew, because Chloe was still in hospital.

Fletcher crawled along the parked cars, then swung in to stop across a driveway. Ella stayed back, her heart beating in her ears, tucking her own car into a no-standing zone and hoping he hadn't noticed her. She turned off her lights and slid down in the seat, eyes on the motionless back of the van. There was a streetlight directly over it and the glow shone dully off the plastic pipes on the van's roof. Ella slowed her breathing and made herself stay calm. She could see both the driver's and passenger's doors. A breeze moved the leaves in the trees and made the light waver. The van's brakelights were still on, which meant Fletcher was sitting there with his foot on the pedal. If he got out and went up to Chloe's door, if he did something, she could go after him. If he didn't . . . well, she didn't want to show her hand.

Time inched past. Ella swore under her breath. *Get out and do something!*

But nothing happened.

Ella stared at the van's back door. What was he doing? She thought of the hang-up calls Chloe had mentioned. Maybe he was calling to see if she was home. Maybe he was thinking that if she answered, he'd hang up, then go to her door and knock. And then what?

Ella had never been gladder to know that someone was in hospital.

After a couple more minutes, the brakelights went off and the van crept out of the driveway and down the street. Ella craned to keep it in sight. She knew the streets that crossed Amy further along, knew that if Fletcher was heading back to Lane Cove Road he'd turn right at the roundabout. She twisted the wheel and started to swing out of her space, headlights still off, watching as he made the right turn.

She sped down the street, and by the time she reached Lane Cove Road was just two cars back from him at the lights. Again she stared at the back of the van, annoyed by the thought that she'd followed him here only for him to return home.

But he did still come here. That means something.

But what?

FOURTEEN

At eight the next morning, Ella stood in the autopsy suite of Glebe Morgue. Marko Meixner lay naked on the steel table, his eyes closed, his right foot placed neatly next to the stump of his lower leg, the deep lacerations and crush injuries to his chest and shoulders gaping open. She could see the red tissue and yellowish fat layers and the bright white bone of broken ribs. The blood had been cleaned off his skin and the edges of the wounds were dry, and above it all his face was unmarked and almost serene.

Ella watched the pathologist peer closely at Meixner's skin, while beside her Murray kept his eyes fixed on the ceiling. She thought again about Fletcher's suspicious behaviour the previous night: lurking outside the Meixners' building then going home. She hadn't told Murray about it. Yet.

'Now this is interesting,' the pathologist said.

Ella stepped closer. Murray glanced down then away.

'It's a recent bruise.' The pathologist pointed a gloved finger at a mark on the top of Marko's right arm.

'Are those fingermarks?' Ella said. 'As if someone grabbed him from behind?'

The pathologist nodded. 'It was a large hand using considerable force. About a week ago, I'd say. Let me keep looking and I'll see if there's more.'

Fletcher had big hands. She nudged Murray. *How about that?*

He swallowed hard and nodded without looking at either her or the body.

The pathologist examined Marko's scalp, pulled the overhead light nearer to look more closely at an area on his neck, then had his assistant help him turn Marko onto his stomach. He was stiff and his hands struck the steel table like he was making a point. Ella could see the bruise more clearly now, and stared at it, wishing for an impression of rings or some other distinctive mark.

The pathologist worked slowly down Marko's body, then stretched his back. 'There's nothing else.'

The assistant took a series of photos, including a ruler in some to indicate dimensions.

'Over we go again,' the pathologist said, and once Marko was on his back he took up a scalpel and began to cut.

Murray walked away. 'Are these his clothes?' He picked up a plastic bag of bloodstained clothing sitting on the bench.

'Yep. Mobile phone's in there too.'

Ella watched Murray pull on gloves, untie the bag, and sort gingerly through the contents. The phone he lifted out looked like an older-model iPhone. He studied the screen with a frown. 'Cracked to buggery. Won't even turn on.'

'Tech heads might be able to get something out of it.' Ella turned back to the table just as the pathologist lifted off a section of ribs to reveal blood pooled in the chest cavity underneath.

★

Afterwards, Murray sat in the car with his hands hanging between his knees. Ella started the engine, thinking of the hand-shaped bruise. The photos were in a manila folder, tucked safely down the side of her seat. She needed to tell Murray what she'd seen Fletcher do last night. She shouldn't have gone there, but he wasn't her boss. He'd be fine with it.

'It's not the death or the body that gets me so much,' Murray said. 'Or even the smell in there. Blood itself's no problem. God knows, I've waded around in the stuff. But that.' He shuddered. 'That foot sitting there. Out of place.'

Ella checked for cars and swung out. *Tell him what you did.* 'I knew a copper once who could handle the most splashy blood and guts but couldn't stand vomit.'

'Vomit doesn't bother me. Phlegm, on the other hand. Ugh.'

She glanced over at him. *Tell him.* 'What does your girlfriend do?'

He raised his eyebrows and looked out the window, and she thought he wasn't going to answer. Then he smiled. 'She works in publishing. She's an editor. The company makes educational books – school textbooks and so on.'

'Do you talk to her about this stuff?'

'Not really. She sometimes asks. I give her the clean version.'

The lights on Parramatta Road went green as Ella approached and she drove through the intersection.

'You wouldn't have that problem, I guess,' he said. 'Him being a doctor. He sees everything.'

She smiled. *Tell him!* She took a deep breath. 'Listen. I went out last night.'

He grinned at her.

'Not that kind of going out. I went to Fletcher's house. He got in his van and I followed him. He drove to Chloe's place and sat outside for five minutes then drove back home.'

The smile drifted off Murray's face. 'You can't use that.'

'I know.'

'If Langley found out, you'd be off the team faster than a . . . faster than –'

'I know,' she said again. 'But Fletcher's got pretty big hands. He'd be strong too.'

'We need to ask Chloe about the bruise when we get in.' Murray stared out the windscreen. 'It's a pity we didn't see him go there while under official surveillance.'

Ella said, 'I could call in an anonymous tip. Report a lurking van, give the numberplate.'

'Let's try pushing the point with Langley first,' he said. 'Keep the tip as backup.'

★

They reached the office ten minutes before the meeting. Murray, still pale, went to wash his face. Ella sat at her desk and picked up her phone to call Audra, but found a voicemail waiting for her.

'It's Juliet Rooney. Can you ring me back? Whatever the time.' She'd left her mobile number.

Ella called her.

'Long time no talk,' she said when Juliet answered. They'd done a course together and got along well. It was nice to hear her voice again. 'How's Randwick?'

'The beating heart of the city, as ever,' Juliet said. 'Now listen. I've got this assault and a witness dropped your name. Jane Koutoufides, paramedic. Ring a bell?'

'She's a witness in my current homicide case.' Ella summarised the situation about Meixner, the crash, the train, the old murder. 'What happened?'

'Her ex's wife was beaten unconscious with a golf club outside Jane's house last night.'

Ella struggled to process that. 'And Jane saw it? Heard it? Not — she didn't do it?'

'She found her,' Juliet said. 'She says she was out on the piss, walked home, and tripped over the woman lying in her front yard.'

'She says,' Ella said. 'You don't believe her?'

'She and the victim had been arguing, and yesterday after-noon had a fight from which they both got bruises. My question to you is: what impression did you get when you dealt with her?'

Ella thought. 'I can't see it.'

It was just an impression, they both knew that, but it was never a wasted conversation to check. It reminded Ella to call the Central Coast, see if Paterson was back on the job.

'Is she seriously a suspect?' she asked.

'We have a couple of neighbours who heard her coming down the street before she found the body and started scream-ing, and we're checking her alibi for the time before that,' Juliet said. 'But the women look almost the same, so Jane may actually have been the target.'

'Huh,' Ella said. 'Well, good luck.'

Murray arrived as Ella put down the phone. His hairline was wet and he finished wiping his hands and dropped the paper towel in the bin. 'Good luck with what?'

'Another case,' she said. Time was moving on. The meeting would start soon. 'You want to ask Chloe about the handprint bruise, or see if this Paterson guy's back from sick leave?'

He pulled his phone close. 'What's his number?'

While he dialled, Ella rang Chloe Meixner's mobile num-ber. Audra answered.

'It's Detective Marconi,' Ella said. 'How are you? How's Chloe? Are you still at the hospital?'

'She'll be discharged this morning. She's doing okay.'

'I have a question,' Ella said. 'Did Marko say anything to her about somebody grabbing him by the arm, a week or two ago?'

Audra asked the question, then Chloe came on the line. 'He didn't say anything.'

'Did you notice a bruise on him in that time?'

'No, nothing. Where was it?'

'High up on his right arm.'

'I didn't see anything, but he didn't often go around

shirtless,' she said. 'Come to think of it, he did wear a T-shirt to bed in the last week or so. Usually he wears a singlet. It's been cooler though, so I just assumed it was that. Do you think he was hiding it from me? Why wouldn't he tell me?'

'I don't know,' Ella said. 'Is everything else all right?' It seemed a ridiculous question, and when she heard Chloe start to cry she said, 'I'm sorry. I'll talk to you later.'

Audra got back on. 'Just catch whoever did it.'

Ella could hear Chloe weeping.

'I'm so sorry,' she said. 'We're doing everything we can.' *Though if we had more people, we could do more.* 'Is she okay? The baby's all right?'

'We're getting by,' Audra said. 'I better go.'

Ella hung up and looked at Murray. 'She didn't know about the bruise. She even wondered whether he was hiding it from her.' She lowered her voice. 'I should've rung in that fake tip about the van on the way here. We could've been on our way to pick him up right now.'

'We can always ring it in later. That cop's not back, by the way.'

'Have they told him we've been calling?'

'They said he's really sick.'

Sick schmick. She wanted to know what he thought, whether he felt that Canning might be capable of revenge. She knew that one murder while drunk was a lot different to following someone and pushing them under a train, and there were the intervening years to take into account too. She still wanted to ask him though.

Murray checked his watch. 'It's time.'

They went down the corridor together and took seats in the meeting room with James Kemsley and John Gawande. Langley shut the door, then introduced Annie Blackwood, forensic accountant from the Fraud Squad. She was a civilian of around forty-five, dressed in a smart magenta jacket over a black shirt and pants. She smiled at them.

'Annie will go this morning with Gawande and Kemsley to the Payton and Jones offices.' Langley smoothed his tie, today a bright sky blue. 'You boys look into tracing the phone calls made to Meixner and Weaver there, while Annie has a chat to the staff, and then we should be able to move on.'

Ella sat back in her chair and folded her arms.

'Then head out to Fletcher's worksite. Check with people other than his mate that he was indeed there until four. Talk to Fletcher himself again. See what he says when you ask him directly about what time Daley Jones left.'

That was hardly the challenge he deserved. Ella tried to speak but Langley kept going. She was definitely ringing in about the van now.

'Shakespeare and Marconi, you'll pay a visit to Bill Weaver's wife,' he said. 'A polite chat but see if you can find out what she thinks about what he did. Check in with the man himself again too. Then have another try with Miriam Holder, and her colleagues. Hopefully they'll be more forthcoming than she was.'

'They can hardly be less,' Murray said.

'Then look a bit further into Canning.'

'The post-mortem found a hand-shaped bruise on Meixner's shoulder,' she cut in. She made Murray stand up and grabbed his right shoulder from behind to demonstrate. 'It was a large hand, so most likely male. I checked with his wife, but she knew nothing about it and believed Meixner must've been hiding it from her. Fletcher has large hands. I think we should get him in for a formal interview.'

'What was the cause of death?' Langley asked.

'Blood loss from severe trauma from going under the train,' she said. 'What about Hossain? He could check out Mrs Weaver while we get Fletcher.'

'He's back on the old cases,' Langley said.

Those bloody old cases. 'But we could use him here.'

'Work fast and you might have time to do it yourself.' Langley stood up. 'Questions? Good. Back at five.'

Ella stared at his back as he walked out. Kemsley and Gawande talked to Annie Blackwood as they followed. Murray sat silently in his chair beside her.

'He won't be interested in this case until it's been unsolved for a year,' Ella said. 'What can we do? Can we go over his head?'

Murray snorted. 'You know what happens when people do that. They're back in uniform and working in some shithole, never to be seen again.'

She leaned in close. 'My tip idea looks brilliant now, doesn't it?'

★

Jane lay curled on her bed with her arms around a pillow. She'd had a three-hour doze in the spare room at the back of her house when she got home, because uniformed cops had still been doorknocking her neighbours and a news crew was filming on the street. The bastards had zoomed in on her getting dropped off by Rooney and scurrying inside, but they were all gone now. The path was wet and clean after some kind person had hosed it off, and she was back in her own bed. She wanted to sleep again, but couldn't. Her mind wouldn't shut up, bouncing between the feel of Deb's blood on her hands, past conversations with Laird, the other blood that was still coming, the pale stillness of Deb's face.

She didn't know why she felt like this. She couldn't count the wounded bodies she'd seen, touched, dealt with — hundreds probably. At least. Plenty of people that she knew too. Plenty dead as well. Some went peacefully in their beds; some traumatically, like Marko under the train. Some wanted to go, like the woman she'd saved on the roof, who went up there again later, this time at night when nobody was around, and was found twisted and cold on the ground the next morning; but most didn't, like the kids in the crash Alex went to.

How absurd that she'd got a medal for grabbing that woman while Alex got nothing except what she suspected was a case of PTSD. Just because a photographer had seen her on the roof, and Alex had been alone.

You also got Laird out of it.

And what a nightmare that'd turned out to be.

She refused to think about him any longer. She had to go get her car. Call up Gittins. But first she'd ring Steve, find out how Deb was, and then call the kids.

She'd thought that Laird might try to ring so had turned her phone off before she had her doze. He hadn't, but Steve and the kids all had, Breanna and Glenn multiple times.

Steve's phone went to voicemail. 'Just checking in,' she said. 'Hope she's doing okay. I'll try you again later.'

Breanna answered on the first ring. 'Finally! Are you all right?'

'I'm fine.' Jane covered the phone and took a deep breath. Some days she was not all right with her kids living far away. 'I had to go to the police station. They kept me for ages.'

'What happened?'

'What did Dad tell you?'

'Just that you found her unconscious outside your place, that someone had beaten her up. Who would do something like that?'

'I wish I knew.'

'Why was she even there?'

Now was not the time to go into it. 'I'm not sure about that either.'

'God, Mum, it's awful.' Breanna was crying now. 'And I'm at work, and everyone's looking at me.'

'Oh, honey.' Jane's heart ached. 'Can you go home?'

'I'll be okay in a minute.' She snuffled, then blew her nose. 'Dad was so upset. And Deb has her moments, but I guess I like her, you know? They've been married five years.'

Jane understood, though she couldn't say she had the same feelings. The events of the last few months had ruined whatever liking she'd had for Deb. But she felt for her family, and for the kids, and of course for Steve.

'I haven't talked to your dad yet,' she said. 'I got his voice-mail when I tried just now.'

'He sounded shattered,' Breanna said. 'Listen, Mum, I'm thinking about coming up. I'm going to talk to my boss and see if I can get the rest of the week off.'

'Your dad would probably appreciate that.'

'It's to see you too,' Breanna said. 'I can't imagine what it was like to find her like that, what it was –' Her voice cracked.

My soft-hearted little rabbit girl.

'I'm fine, sweetie,' Jane said, pinching her arm to keep her voice strong. 'You don't have to worry about me.'

A moment of sniffling, then Breanna said, 'I have to go. Love you.'

'Love you too.'

Jane took a moment, then tried Steve again. Voicemail. She didn't leave a message. She called both David and Glenn but got their voicemails too. They couldn't answer as easily at work as Breanna. She left messages saying she was all right, she loved them and she'd talk to them later. Then she stood at the front window and looked out. They would've taken Deb from here to Prince of Wales. She should call and find out how she was. But she couldn't take her eyes from the drying path.

Someone had come along that path last night in the dark and attacked Deb. Jane had seen beating injuries and murders before. It didn't take as much effort to cave in a skull as people might think, and Deb would have been unconscious from the first blow. Hopefully she didn't even hear them coming and had suffered not one second of fear.

But who did it? And why? And was it meant to have been her?

If I wasn't parked at the beach getting pissed, would it be my blood soaking into the grass this morning?

But she had no enemies, apart from Deb herself.

Who thought you were cheating with her husband. So what about the woman whose husband you were really cheating with?

He'd been so careful to keep any sign of Lucille out of her sight. Jane imagined he'd done the same with her; it was unlikely that Lucille had been able to find out anything to lead her here so quickly last night.

Except Laird knows where you live . . .

No. No way in the world. She knew him – okay, so it turned out she didn't know him, but she thought she knew him enough to feel certain he wasn't a killer.

If they had a prenup, and Lucille decided to leave him, he might stand to lose everything. That was motive right there.

But then he'd want to kill her, not me.

No, it'd be to stop you telling anyone what happened, idiot.

Jane grasped the window frame. None of this felt real. She didn't believe that Laird could have done it. She didn't believe anyone would want to hurt Deb, but neither could she believe that anyone would want to hurt her.

A familiar silver Lexus came slowly down the street, then pulled to the kerb outside her gate. The driver's door opened while the engine was still running, and Laird looked across the car's roof at her front door.

Jane ran down the stairs and burst outside, bolted down the path, around the wet place where Deb had lain, and onto the footpath. 'Did you do this?'

'What?' He was in a suit and tie, and wore reflective sunglasses that he didn't remove.

'A woman was attacked here last night! She looked just like me!'

'Oh, sweet pea, no, no. How could you even think that?'

He tried to touch her arm. She slapped his hand away.

'Then you're just a plain shitty arsehole, not a murdering one.'

'Come on. It's not what it looks like.'

'You told me you were separated.'

'I thought we were,' he said. 'I didn't know that she thought something else.'

'Take those ridiculous glasses off and look me in the eye when you say that.'

He removed them with obvious reluctance, glancing around as if he felt he might be recognised. 'She doesn't make me happy like you do. I swear, Jane, I've never met anyone like you.'

'Shut up,' she said. 'You weren't separated at all, were you?'

He couldn't meet her gaze. 'I wanted to tell her about you. I was trying to tell her when you knocked. We'd just sat down in the lounge room. I was about to begin.'

'That's why you were holding headphones?'

'I was psyching myself up. She's crazy. I didn't know what she'd do. That's why I had to pretend not to know you. She might've tried to hurt you.'

'Bullshit.'

'I think I'm in love with you,' he said.

Something in her heart twanged tight. 'If that was true, you would've told me upfront she was still in the picture and you wouldn't have hidden all her stuff.'

He looked about to reply when a car tore into the street. She thought for a second it would be Lucille, then recognised Steve's black Holden ute. He screeched to a stop beside Laird's car, blocking the narrow street, and leapt out with his fists clenched and his face a deep and enraged red.

Laird stepped back, looking frightened, but Steve rushed past him and came straight for Jane.

'What did you do to her?'

What the hell? 'I didn't −'

'You couldn't give me one more chance to talk to her? You had to do this?'

His breath reeked of alcohol. The hospital must've kicked him out for being drunk.

'You've hated her from the start. You happy now she's in hospital? Are you? She's unconscious, they don't know whether she'll live or die.' He shoved her into the hedge. 'You happy about that?'

'Fuck you.' She shoved him back. 'Get off me.'

He'd never hit or even pushed her before and she wasn't going to let him start now. Laird jumped in his car and accelerated backwards away from the kerb and haphazardly up the street. *Thanks a lot.*

Steve grabbed the neck of her shirt and rammed her deep into the hedge. Twigs scratched her neck and she kicked at his shin and missed.

'Bitch,' Steve hissed. He shook her, rattling her teeth.

'Get off me.' She punched his stomach. He didn't flinch. 'Get off!'

'You always were jealous.'

His eyes were crazy. She felt his hands wrap around her throat and believed suddenly that he might really try to kill her, that anyone was truly capable of anything.

She grabbed his shoulders and rammed her knee into his groin. He groaned into her face and she tore free of his grip and started to run, but at the last second he clutched the back of her shirt – not enough to hold her back, but just enough to throw her off balance so that she stumbled and fell headfirst into the gatepost and complete darkness.

FIFTEEN

Bill and Prue Weaver lived in a shining white two-storey house in a leafy street in Hunters Hill. The hedges along the front of the property were thick and sharply trimmed, and the lawn was like a bowling green, glistening from a recent and unnecessary watering. Ella and Murray followed the white paved path to the front door, where she pulled the rope attached to a heavy cast-iron bell. The air smelled of flowers and freshly turned earth.

'Money much?' Murray said.

Ella grinned, still feeling edgy from when she'd called in the anonymous tip about seeing Fletcher's van lurking in Amy Street. Because he'd never been mentioned in the news as a suspect in Meixner's death, she couldn't call the hotline, so had stood at a grimy public phone box in Meadowbank and called Ryde station instead. The constable on the desk hadn't sounded particularly interested, not even when Ella declined to give her name, but all she could do was hope that a note made it through the system attached to Fletcher's name and van, and when they were back at the office she could oh-so-casually bring his record up and say, well well, would you look at this.

There was the sound of heels on a tiled floor inside and the door was flung open. The woman who glared at them was around fifty, her ash-blonde hair loose on her shoulders, her dark denim designer jeans tight over her plump hips.

'Didn't you see the sign?' she snapped. 'No hawkers.'

Ella held up her badge. 'Mrs Prue Weaver?'

The woman's round cheeks turned brighter pink. 'Yes?'

'Detectives Marconi and Shakespeare. We'd like to speak to you about your husband, Bill.'

'I have nothing to say.' She started to close the door.

Murray put out his hand. 'It's important that we find out what's —'

'I do not like repeating myself,' Prue Weaver said. 'Kindly remove your hand.'

'We saved his life, you know,' Murray said.

She hesitated, then lifted her chin. 'Regardless. He's asked me to say nothing.'

'Why?' Ella asked.

'It's private business.' Her cheeks coloured further.

'Did he tell you what happened?' Murray said.

'Yes, he did.'

'He hung himself with his tie on the back of his office door,' Murray said, as if she hadn't answered. 'Detective Marconi here managed to get a knife through the gap and cut through the tie, then squeezed in and did CPR until paramedics arrived.'

Prue Weaver hesitated. 'Then I suppose I owe you my thanks.' She put out a plump hand.

Suppose? Ella shook it. The woman's skin was hot and damp.

'Did you know that we were there because one of your husband's employees was killed two days ago?' Murray went on. 'Marko Meixner. Did you know him?'

'I've never met the man, and I can't see how I could shed any light on anything to do with him.'

'The fact remains that his death led to our presence in the office, and our presence saved your husband's life, so a few minutes conversation is perhaps not only in order but owed, don't you think?'

Murray smiled and stepped through the doorway, Ella right behind him, Prue looking flustered in their wake.

The living room was full of oversized armchairs. A huge and gloomy painting of a bowl of fruit hung over the mantel-piece and velvet-embossed wallpaper covered every other wall. The thick carpet made the place feel padded and soundless, and the air stank of overly sweet chemicals, as if somewhere a plug-in air freshener worked overtime.

Prue stayed on her feet and didn't invite them to sit.

Murray faced her with his hands behind his back. 'You've been to the hospital to see Bill?'

'Of course.'

'Did he tell you why he tried to kill himself?'

'Suicide is no longer a legal issue, so I don't see why the police are involved.'

Ella said, 'We're concerned there may be irregularities in how Payton and Jones operate, and an attempted suicide and a death among the staff are no reassurance.'

Prue drew herself up. 'My husband would not be involved in any manner of wrongdoing.'

'He might have inadvertently become involved,' Murray said. 'We're here for his protection, if anything.'

Nice one, Ella thought.

Prue's eyes widened. 'Do you think he's in danger?'

'We just don't know,' Ella said.

'Nobody can get to him in the hospital, can they?'

'Doubtful,' Ella lied, thinking back a couple of years to the man who'd been murdered in his hospital bed right before her eyes.

'But you can understand now why we need to know what's going on,' Murray said.

Prue Weaver squeezed the mantelpiece with one ring-heavy hand and stared at the bowl of fruit as if for inspiration. 'He must never know that I told you.'

'We do our best to keep every confidence,' Ella said.

'He told me in the hospital that he's been feeling depressed and the news of the death upset him greatly,' Prue said. 'But I believe there's more reason than that. Over the last year we've been having some financial difficulties because his bonuses at work have been decreased and the value of our investment properties have dropped.'

Properties, plural, Ella thought. 'Go on.'

'Bill is a man who expects life to continually improve,' she said. 'The GFC has affected not only his clients' portfolios but our own, and Bill had to sell the properties at a loss. He said it was the best thing to do, that the forecasts weren't good and it was better to let them go now than wait and see their value fall even further.'

'These properties were where?' Murray said.

'A house in Clontarf and an apartment in Double Bay. We lost three-quarters of a million between the two, can you believe it?'

'No,' Ella said.

'The shares we own too. So much money gone.' She smoothed a finger over the gilt frame of the painting. 'It goes to show that even the most knowledgeable people aren't immune to the vagaries of the market.'

'Indeed,' Ella said.

'That kind of thing makes him feel like a failure,' Prue said. 'When I was signing the paperwork for the sales, he apologised for letting me down. I told him it didn't matter, we still have our lovely home here, we still have his salary, and one day we will come back better than ever.'

Ella nodded. Beside her, Murray coughed into his fist.

'Having said that, though, let me say this.' Prue smiled, and Ella smiled back.

For someone who wasn't going to tell them anything, she was really letting loose. *The power of the attentive ear.*

'I think things are picking up.' Prue lowered her voice, as if

Bill might somehow be able to hear. 'I stumbled across a cruise brochure in his desk drawer when I was dusting.'

Ella bet the woman had never dusted in her life. 'Is that so?'

'It's for the expensive Caribbean cruise we go on, the one he thought we couldn't afford this year. Obviously things are turning around and he's going to surprise me with it one day soon.' Her teeth shone.

'So things are looking up, but he's still depressed enough to try to kill himself?' Ella said.

'I told you,' Prue said. 'It's been a stressful year. And he was very saddened by his employee's death.'

Ella nodded, thinking that something didn't add up.

★

Bill Weaver lay in a ward bed, his huge bulk propped up on three pillows and his meaty hands clutching the raised side rails. The bruising on his throat had turned dark and Ella could hear a whistle in his throat when he breathed.

'Beautiful home you have,' she said.

He glared at them. 'You had no right to go there.'

'This is a homicide investigation,' Murray said. 'We go where we need to go. And by the way, your wife is delightful.'

'You stay away from her,' he wheezed, fumbling in the sheets for the call button while sweat burst out on his forehead.

'Prue knows about the cruise,' Murray said.

'You have no right,' Bill gasped.

'She told us a few other things too,' Ella said. 'How about you tell us your side of the story?'

A nurse hurried in and bustled them aside. She grabbed an oxygen mask from the wall and slid it over Bill's head.

'Just breathe,' she said to him. 'Nice and even.'

He flapped a hand at Ella and Murray, a clear 'go away' gesture.

'Yes, you'll have to leave,' the nurse said.

Ella said to Bill, 'Think about it, okay?' before they walked
out.

★

Jane lay dry-eyed and angry in Prince of Wales hospital's Emergency Department, her fingers going numb on the icepack she
held over her aching cheek. Her head throbbed and her neck
was sore. They'd done X-rays and now she was waiting for the
verdict. She thought briefly about asking for a pregnancy test
but couldn't stand the prospect of some cheery nurse offering
either congratulations or commiserations.

'Jane?' The curtain was inched open and Detective Juliet
Rooney looked in. 'You awake?'

Jane struggled up in the bed. The icepack fell off.

'Jesus.' Rooney peered close. 'You feeling okay?'

Jane found herself tearing up. *Stop it.* 'I'm fine, really.' She
reapplied the icepack and looked into Rooney's eyes. 'I lied last
night.'

Rooney raised a hand. 'Before you say another word, I have
to tell you that anything you say —'

'I didn't do it,' Jane said. 'I'm not confessing.'

'Even so.'

'I wasn't just driving around. I went to see my, uh, boyfriend. But his wife answered the door. That's why I was upset
and wanted to get drunk.'

Rooney sat down and opened her notebook. 'What's his
name?'

'Laird Humphreys.'

Rooney looked up. 'The newsreader?'

'Yes,' Jane said. 'And he was outside my house this morning
when Steve and I had the fight that ended in this.'

'The constables didn't mention him.'

Jane felt heat creep up her cheeks. 'He scarpered when it
kicked off.'

Rooney made a notation in her book, then looked up again. 'If we need to speak to him about last night, what will he say?'

'God knows.' Jane felt her colour deepen. 'He told his wife I was a fan or something. From what I heard before I left, I don't think she believed him.'

Another notation.

Jane shifted in the bed. She should tell Rooney her concerns. *In a minute.* 'Where's Steve?'

'At Maroubra station,' Rooney said. 'Are you going to press charges?'

'I don't know.'

'Has he ever done this sort of thing before?'

'No, God no. He can be an idiot but he's never been violent,' Jane said. 'Did you find out where he was last night?'

'The casino. For hours. Apparently he's something of a regular there.'

'Oh.' So he didn't have a girlfriend at all, he had a problem. 'How is he?'

'Apologetic, sobbing, and sobering up.'

'No charges,' Jane said.

Rooney nodded. 'Getting back to Laird Humphreys, what time did he arrive at your house this morning?'

'Around an hour ago,' she said.

'Did he come straight up and knock on the door?'

Jane shook her head. 'I was upstairs and saw him through the window. He pulled up in his car and half-got out, and was looking at the front door.'

'Or the path?' Rooney said.

'Perhaps,' Jane said, feeling the blush inch higher.

'What did he do then?'

'I ran downstairs and outside and started yelling at him,' Jane said. 'He was blustering, said it wasn't like that, he thinks he loves me.' She snorted.

'How long were you seeing him?'

'Almost four months.'

'Was he ever violent to you?'

'No,' Jane said. She looked at the foot of the bed, but could feel Rooney watching her.

'You know why I'm asking, don't you?' she said.

Jane swallowed. She felt faint. 'Yes.'

'How did he look when he saw you?'

'I don't know, I was running too fast and yelling too much.' She tried to remember. 'Stunned, maybe? Surprised?'

She knew what that suggested; knew it made him sound suspicious.

Rooney turned a page in her notebook. 'What about his wife? Do you think she knew who you were to Laird when she opened the door?'

'She knew all right. I could see it in her eyes. And she turned her hand to make sure I'd see her rings.' Jane put down the ice-pack. 'Laird said this morning that she's crazy. He claimed that he had to deny knowing me so she wouldn't try to hurt me.' She could hear Rooney's pen moving on the page. 'But how could she have found out where I lived?'

Rooney said nothing.

Jane felt herself tear up again. 'I know that Laird might not want me to tell anyone what happened. That if she divorced him he might lose a lot. Or that he could have told her my address.' She looked at Rooney. 'Do you think that's what happened?'

'I don't think anything,' Rooney said. 'It's just one of the avenues we'll look at. But you said yourself that it was dark at the front of your house, and Deb had a history of coming around and breaking things, which explains why she was there. She even brought the golf club with her – your ex identified it as one of his. And you do look very much alike.'

Jane sagged back in the bed. 'I can't believe he would.'

'People get killed for much less,' Rooney said.

It was true. Jane had seen it often herself. She tried to

picture Laird skulking in her front garden, and shook her head. The motion made her dizzy. 'I can't imagine it.'

Rooney's phone buzzed in her pocket. She checked the screen then shut her notebook with a snap. 'I have to go. I'll be in touch.'

She went out, and Jane lay back and looked at the ceiling. Her head ached. She pressed the icepack on firmly, the pain a sharp stab that she swallowed down. How could this be? She'd been so good at picking troublemakers and liars; and hiding a wife was one thing, but having a violent streak wide enough to kill a person, or let someone else do it, was a whole different issue. Sure, it wasn't necessarily true, but knowing the thought was in Rooney's head too made it impossible to dislodge from her own. And while she couldn't imagine Laird doing it, or 'helping' Lucille do it, before yesterday she couldn't have imagined him driving off while she got beaten up or being with someone else either.

★

Ella slowed the car past Miriam Holder's address near the beach in Tamarama. It was a four-storey block of flats with a daisy-filled garden along the front and a row of letterboxes all stickered *NO JUNK MAIL*. The sun shone through the windscreen and onto her hands, but her heart was warmed just as much at the thought of confronting Holder. Try to run again, she thought. Just try.

'No driveway, so no off-street parking or garage.' Murray checked the page in his notebook where he'd written down her details. 'She drives a dark blue Toyota sedan, QKM 377.'

Ella cruised along the vehicles parked by the kerb, then took them around the block, but the car wasn't there. Nor was there any rear lane or side street access. She returned to the front and pulled over.

Holder's apartment was Number 8, and there were eight buttons in the panel by the door. Ella pressed the unnamed button while Murray stepped back and peered upwards with his hand shielding his eyes.

'Top floor, probably,' he said. 'She'd have a great view.'

They waited.

Nothing.

Ella jammed her thumb against the buzzer again, annoyed but not really surprised by the lack of response. Holder was no doubt lying low. *Weasel.*

Another half-minute passed, then she pressed the rest of the buzzers, one after the other. If they couldn't speak to the woman herself, they could at least quiz the neighbours. But nobody answered in any of the units.

'How can they all be out?' Murray said. 'Where's the retired person who watches everyone and is dying to tell us what they've seen?'

'At bingo,' Ella said. 'Let's get moving to her office, see if she's there and what her colleagues have to say.'

She was annoyed not to have found Holder, but they were making great time. If they kept on like this, they'd be done before Kemsley and Gawande would be even thinking about getting out of the Payton and Jones office, and she and Murray would be able to grab Fletcher themselves. The tip on his van would hopefully be through by then, and she looked forward to making him explain himself once and for all.

When they arrived at the offices of Holder and Byron, two of the doors in the short corridor were open and Ella could hear a man talking. She rang the bell and a woman came out. She was in her early forties, tall and blonde, and dressed in a grey business suit with a white shirt.

'Ms Juliana Scholler?'

'Yes?'

Ella held up her badge. 'Detectives Marconi and Shakespeare. Is Miriam Holder here?'

'No, she's not.' Scholler had a slight accent; German, Ella thought. 'Is she all right?'

'Have you seen her today?' Murray asked.

'No, and I'm a little concerned because I tried to call her mobile a moment ago and she didn't answer.'

'Would she answer if she was in a meeting?' Ella asked.

'She had no meetings scheduled.' Scholler frowned. 'Has something happened?'

An Asian man of around thirty with trimmed black hair, black-framed glasses and a red tie came out of the back. 'Is everything okay?'

'They're detectives,' Scholler said.

The man put out his hand. 'Shing Wei, accountant. Can we help you with something?'

'We need to speak to Miriam, make sure she's okay,' Ella said. 'Do you have her mobile number?'

Scholler took a phone from her pocket, scrolled through and read out the number.

Ella jotted it in her notebook. 'And where were you both yesterday afternoon?'

'Here, until about three,' Scholler said. 'Then we both went out to meetings in clients' offices.'

'A phone call was made to this office from the office of Payton and Jones at ten twenty yesterday morning,' Murray said. 'Did either of you speak to that caller?'

'Not me,' Wei said.

'Nor me.' Scholler looked confused. 'That firm isn't one of our clients.'

'How can you be sure?' Ella said.

'They're a big money management firm with their own accountants,' Scholler said. 'We look after individuals or small businesses with just a few employees. They'd have no need for us.'

Ella said, 'How does your phone system work? If someone rings the office number, who decides who answers?'

'We each have extension numbers, so if the caller knows it and puts it in they'll come straight through,' Wei said. 'Otherwise it rings in all our offices, and the rule is that Miriam answers first, but if she's out or busy Juliana is next, then me.'

Hmm. Ella had thought it had to be a personal call from Weaver to Holder, but going by this he could've called and Holder picked up just by chance. But *why* call?

'Does the name Bill Weaver mean anything to you?' Murray asked them.

They shook their heads.

'Have you ever seen a very large man come in to see Miriam?' Ella said. 'Over six foot tall, considerably overweight, a voice to match?'

'No, sorry,' Scholler said.

Wei shook his head. 'Does he have something to do with what might've happened to her?'

'We're not sure,' Murray said.

'Has Miriam ever spoken about her friends and family?' Ella asked, thinking further afield. 'Or have you met them?'

'She's quite private,' Scholler said. 'I've never heard her talk of them, and nobody's ever come in.'

'Same here,' Wei said.

'Okay.' Murray gave them his card. 'If she turns up, or gets in touch, I'd appreciate it if you could let us know.'

'Is she in trouble?'

'Nothing like that,' Ella said with a smile. 'We just need to speak with her. Make sure she's okay, as we said, and clear up a couple of questions.'

They went out into the corridor, then into the office of MSL Associates where the same young woman was behind the desk.

'Did you find her?' she said brightly.

'Not yet.' Murray gave her his card. 'If you spot her, could you give me a call?'

The woman read it. 'Homicide, wow. Is she like a serial killer or something?'

Murray smiled. 'Thanks for your help.'

On the street, the sun shone down between the buildings

and the air was steamy. Ella checked in both directions but there was no sign of Holder. Her phone buzzed with a text.

Making cannoli. Dinner again?

We'll see, she sent back. *Lol.*

She dialled the number Juliana Scholler had given her, but it went straight to voicemail. 'Hi Miriam, call me back,' she said, and hung up.

It was highly unlikely that Holder would call if Ella identified herself, but this way her curiosity might be aroused enough to do so. Besides, if they ended up trying to track her number through mobile phone towers they needed her phone to be switched on, and every minute she spent checking voicemail would help.

'She could be at home, sick in bed,' Murray said.

'I can see on your face you don't really think that,' Ella said. 'And if she was, why not call the office and let them know? Why not answer her mobile? Why not answer the door when we buzzed?'

'Okay, okay,' he said. 'So now what?'

'Back to the car,' she said. 'I have a plan.'

SIXTEEN

Alex had been up at seven, making breakfast and lunch for the monosyllabic Mia, watching out the window as she walked down the street to the bus stop, then going back to bed in preparation for nightshift. Sleeping during the day was always a struggle, and today he couldn't stop his mind nor get comfortable enough in the bed to doze off. He shifted about unhappily, thinking about Mia. He'd known tough times would come, but he felt a kind of grief that the charming little girl who'd been so happy and so delighted with everything life had to offer now walked around like the world was ending and it was all his fault.

He was lying wide awake on his stomach with the pillow over his head when the phone rang.

'Mr Churchill, this is Helen Treasure at Randwick Girls.'

He sat up. 'Is Mia okay?'

'She's fine but in some trouble,' the woman said. 'Are you able to come down? Now?'

'I'm on my way.'

He threw on clothes and ran to the car.

At the school, he hurried down the main corridor and

found Mia slumped on a bench outside the office, her arms folded and her face closed.

'What happened?' he said. 'Are you okay?'

Tears welled in her eyes but she shook her head. 'It's nothing.'

'Sweetheart, please.' He put his arm around her shoulders and tried to pull her close. 'Talk to your old dad.'

She squirmed away.

The office door opened and a woman with a lined face and curly grey hair looked out. 'Mr Churchill, thank you for coming down. Mrs Dennison is waiting to speak to you.'

He squeezed Mia's shoulder and got up.

Dennison was the principal, and she sat behind her wide desk with her hands clasped on top. Also in the room was a young woman wearing large round glasses and pink lipstick. The air was cold and smelled of perfume and carpet cleaner.

'Mr Churchill,' Dennison said. 'This is Annabel Vesey, Mia's maths teacher. We asked you in because we're both concerned about Mia. Her marks are falling in all her classes, and now her behaviour is of concern too.'

Alex drew a steadying breath. 'What did she do?'

'She's been participating less and less in class, and this morning when I asked her a question she swore at me,' Vesey said. 'I told her to leave the room and come here to the office, and she swore again and shoved over her chair as she left.'

'That's completely out of character.' Alex could feel his hackles rise in Mia's defence. *Calm down. Be a grown-up and talk about this coolly.*

'Yes and no,' Dennison said. 'Her participation level in every class has dropped, and her science teacher has reported her for swearing also.'

'Why wasn't I told before now?'

'We did send a letter home with her a fortnight ago.'

'I never got it.' Alex grasped the arms of his chair. 'She's having some issues regarding her mother. I think she's acting out as a result.'

'We understand, Mr Churchill,' Dennison said. 'We have hundreds of girls doing the same kind of thing for the same kind of reason. But it's important that we tackle this, both at school and at home.'

'What do you need me to do?'

'Discuss all this with her, naturally,' Dennison said, 'and be clear on what behaviour is acceptable and what isn't. She needs closer supervision when it comes to homework and assignments, as very little of her work is being handed in on time. She has four assignments overdue now. Watch the time she spends on the internet too. That's becoming a problem with many students.'

Alex nodded. 'I will.' He felt a strange mix of shame and anger directed at everyone involved: himself, the two women, and Mia sitting outside in the hall. 'I will,' he said again.

'Mia is not suspended, but we will mark this down as a warning.' Dennison looked at her watch. 'The next class begins in a few minutes. I suggest you have a chat to her before you leave.'

'Thank you,' he said.

Out in the corridor, he sat down beside Mia. 'You can't swear and carry on like that no matter how bad you feel inside.'

'Who said I feel bad?'

Her eyes were dry and she kept her gaze fixed on the opposite wall, but he saw the pain and embarrassment and anger in her face. His heart hurt. *My darling girl.*

'I know you have stuff going on in your head about your mum,' he said. 'You can't behave like that though. Not to the teachers and other students, and not at home to me.'

She crossed her legs and swung her foot.

'You need to do your work too,' he said.

'I hand it in eventually,' she said. 'It's not like I'm failing.'

'No TV and no internet until you're up to date. After that you get them back, but your hours are going to be limited, and if an assignment becomes overdue you lose them again.'

'That's not fair!'

'One more word and you lose your phone as well.'

She scowled. The bell rang and students poured out of classrooms.

'Same consequence if you don't come straight home after school,' Alex said.

She grabbed her bag and stamped off down the hall.

'I'll see you this afternoon,' Alex said softly, watching her go, a girl in a uniform soon lost among a sea of them.

★

Ella made Murray drive so she could call up Langley and tell him herself.

'So as there's no sign of Miriam Holder anywhere,' she concluded, 'and we have no leads on where to check next, we're going to head out and collect Fletcher.'

'Hmm,' he said, a sound that didn't make her feel good at all. He didn't mention the tip either. 'Better to go back to her home and try again, both at her door and the neighbours.'

'But nobody was there.'

'That was then, this is now,' he said. 'Let me know how you go.' He ended the call.

She lowered the phone. 'He hung up. He said no and then he hung up.'

'Well, maybe we will get an answer at Holder's this time,' Murray said.

'That's not the point,' she said. 'There are more important things we could be doing. You know?'

Murray braked for a red and didn't say anything.

She looked at him. 'You're not going weak on me, are you?'

He didn't meet her eye.

'Murray,' she said, then her phone rang. 'Marconi.'

'Oh my God,' a woman's voice said.

'Audra?' Ella seized Murray's arm. 'Are you okay? Is it Chloe? The baby?'

'No, no.' Audra's voice was strained. 'She got a note from Marko.'

★

Jane walked out of Prince of Wales's Emergency Department and towards ICU. She switched on her phone on the way, and found voicemail messages from Glenn and David, both of which made her feel better, and four from Laird, which didn't.

'I'm so sorry to have to rush off like that –' Delete.

'Please call me back and let me know that you're okay –' Delete.

'Sweetheart –' Delete.

'If I can help in any –' Delete.

She switched it off. Her face was sore, and the bruising made it feel tight when she smiled, but those things were nothing. Deb lay in a bed in intensive care, intubated and ventilated and on IVs, and, if Steve had heard right in his intoxicated state, she might not survive.

And Laird might be to blame. And therefore so might I.

She pushed open the ICU doors. The low murmur of voices and the hiss and beep of machines filled the air. A nurse she knew looked up from the desk.

'What happened to you?' she said.

Jane flapped a hand. 'Does Deb Bodinnar-Koutoufides have visitors at the moment?'

'Only Steve.' The nurse nodded down the unit. 'Her parents and sister went for a break when we let him back in.'

'Mind if I . . .?'

'Go ahead.'

Steve sat in a chair at Deb's bedside, elbows on his knees, holding her limp fingers.

'Hi,' Jane said.

He looked around. His eyes were red. 'Hey.'

Deb's face was pale, her eyes taped lightly closed, a nasogastric tube in her nose and an ET tube tied into her mouth with white cotton tape. Bandages came low across her forehead and covered most of her head. Machines monitored her heart rate, blood pressure and oxygen saturation, while another ventilated her lungs. IV pumps and syringe drivers clicked and ticked, delivering drugs that kept her paralysed and helped control cerebral swelling. Sometimes Jane wished she didn't know so much, though being in Steve's position and not knowing anything would be terrifying.

He was looking at the bruises on her face. 'I'm sorry about that. I know you didn't do it.'

'I know you didn't mean it.' She sat in the chair on the opposite side of the bed and looked at Deb's arm where an IV was taped down, and at the red marks and slight bruising where she herself had grabbed her the day before. 'Have the police told you anything more?'

He shook his head. 'If they know something, they're keeping it quiet from me. I think they're hoping she'll wake up and be able to tell them what happened. Who it was.' His eyes kept straying back to Deb's face.

A flush heated Jane's cheeks. It was ironic, in a sick way, that Steve had accused her when she might in fact be responsible. She couldn't tell him now though. Better that he remained calm and was able to stay here in the unit with Deb. If the detectives found out that Laird or his wife had actually done it, and that therefore it was her fault, they could tell him later, and she'd deal with it then.

Steve raised Deb's hand to his cheek. 'I blame myself. I should've told her where I was going. I should've been clearer that it had nothing to do with you.'

'I was pretty clear.' Jane shifted in her chair. 'And don't forget that she chose to come around there. With a golf club.'

Steve seemed not to hear. 'I love her so much.'

That wasn't what he'd said on the phone the other day, but Jane let it slide. 'What's the latest from the doctor?'

'They're going to see about cutting back the drugs this

afternoon or tomorrow. See how she does.' He was staring at her face, tears in his eyes. 'God, I love her.'

'When she wakes up, you need to tell her the truth about what you were doing,' Jane said. 'It's better than what she was afraid of.'

'I know,' he said. 'I will.'

Jane's head and body ached. She was tired. She had a night-shift tonight, and though she could get a doctor's certificate and call in sick, she wanted to be there. She liked working with Alex and she felt like he needed her. Besides, look what happened last time she took a night off.

She went around to Steve's side and put her hands on his shoulders. 'She's tough. She'll be okay.'

He blew out a shaky breath. 'I hope so.'

★

Ella knocked on Chloe's door, heart bounding in her chest. Audra opened it and led them into the lounge, where Chloe was sitting on the sofa holding a sheet of paper inside a plastic bag.

'I made her put it in there in case of fingerprints,' Audra said.

Ella sat down. She could see Chloe had a tight grip on the page so didn't try to take it from her. Scrawled in black pen were the words, *I hoped I could escape my past, but protecting you from it is the best I can do. I love you both forever, Marko.*

'Is that his handwriting?' she asked.

'Yes,' Chloe whispered.

'And when and where did you find it?'

'It was in the letterbox this afternoon. It'd come in the post.'

'Here's the envelope.' Audra held out another plastic bag.

Murray took it. 'Envelope's from Payton and Jones, and postmarked 3 pm two days ago in the city. Chloe's name and the address are in the same handwriting as the note.'

He managed to get the envelope open inside the plastic bag and peer in.

'It's empty,' Audra said. 'I already checked.'

Ella was thinking. Marko must have written it and put it in the internal mail before he took Daniel Truscott's car. Before he took the car, but after the 'no, no' phone call, meaning he must've feared that something was going to happen.

We need those phone records, and now.

'Is there anything on the back?' Murray asked.

Chloe turned the sheet over but it was blank. A tear dripped from her cheek.

'I'll make tea.' Audra squeezed Chloe's shoulder then went into the kitchen.

'This might sound odd,' Ella said to Chloe, 'but does that sound like Marko? Would he use those words, in a sentence like that?'

'Yes. It's from him.'

Murray sat on her other side. 'And you don't know what he's talking about?'

'No.'

'Why do you think he didn't explain what he meant?' Murray asked.

Chloe looked up with a frown.

'I mean, what particular part of his past is he referring to?' Murray said. 'If he was thinking that he might not come home, why not give you more detail?'

Ella glared at him.

'To make your job easier, you mean?' Chloe said.

'No, so that you would feel bet–'

She reared up. 'You think an explanation would make me feel better? That that's all I need, then I could go on with my life?' She put her hand on her belly. 'If I have an explanation, I'll feel fine about telling our child what happened to its father?'

Audra hurried in. 'What's going on?'

'That's not what I meant at all and I'm sorry if that's how it sounded,' Murray said.

'I'm grateful he managed to send me this much,' Chloe snapped.

'I meant no offence, truly,' Murray said. 'I'm as keen to find out what happened as you are.'

'Really?' Chloe said. 'Really?'

Ella shot Murray a look then another one at the door.

'Perhaps I'll wait outside,' he said.

When he was gone, Ella said, 'I'm sorry.'

She wanted to say he was generally more sensitive than that, he didn't usually blunder around so much, but it would all sound like excuses, and no excuse made anything any better.

Chloe shook her head and wiped her eyes again.

'I'll go too,' Ella said. 'May I take that to examine for fingerprints please? The envelope too?'

'Will I get them back?'

'I promise.'

Chloe held them out, and Ella took them gently. 'Thank you.'

Downstairs, Murray was kicking the kerb by the car. The wind blew leaves up the street.

'Is she okay?' Murray said.

'No thanks to you.' She tugged at the handle. 'Unlock it, will you?'

He pressed the button and they got in.

'I just don't understand why he wouldn't explain what he meant. He wanted her to know something was wrong, he wanted to tell her he loved her and the baby, and he would've known that if something did happen there'd be a heap of questions, so why not be a bit clearer?'

'Maybe he didn't really think he wouldn't be here to explain.' She was looking at the page. 'This could apply to Canning, but not much to Fletcher. Meixner mentions his past, not hers, and he had hardly anything to do with Fletcher. So it's got to be about Canning, right? Maybe he found where Meixner worked and called him, threatened him. It could've been him that Meixner was saying "no, no" to.'

'I guess so,' Murray said. 'But Langley's going to say it's a suicide note. He'll say that escaping the past is referring to his previous attempts and psych problems.'

'So let's not tell him yet. We know that the phone call might've been part of the trigger, and Kemsley and Gawande are checking all the calls at the office now. So with that end of it covered, let's go visit Canning.'

★

Alex slept fitfully for a few hours, then woke at quarter past three. The room was stuffy and hazy in the afternoon light. He rubbed his face with his hands, then stretched and yawned so widely something popped in the side of his jaw. Mia would be home soon, and he would be showered, shaved and dressed when she arrived. They'd have another talk, and he'd supervise her homework and assignments while making dinner, then when Louise arrived at five thirty he could walk out the door knowing that all was on track.

In the shower, he washed and shaved, then turned the water as hot as he could stand it, then completely cold. He stepped out gasping, his skin tingling, certain that they'd get through this. He'd work on communication, get them both to counselling maybe – the service was always sending out brochures; he'd look into it tonight. It wouldn't be easy but they'd make it through.

He dressed in a clean uniform, then went downstairs. The clock on the microwave said it was already three forty. He put the jug on, then thought he heard a girl's voice out the front. Mia had forgotten her key again probably, and he walked through the house to let her in. The porch was empty. He went out to the street.

Two girls in private school uniforms chattered further up the footpath. He looked towards the corner where Mia walked up from the bus stop. The sun glinted off the windscreens of the parked cars and he shielded his eyes with his hand. Then around the corner appeared a figure in the Randwick uniform, a black schoolbag over one shoulder, a Slush Puppie cup in her hand, and something inside Alex loosened. As the figure drew closer, however, he saw it wasn't Mia, but an older girl who lived on the next block.

'Excuse me,' he said when she got level with him. 'Were you on the three twenty-two?'

She shot him a suspicious look. 'Yeah.'

'Do you know Mia Churchill? Was she on it too?'

'Blonde hair?'

'Brown,' Alex said.

'Don't know her, sorry.'

Alex glanced up the street. She could be at the shops, getting a Slush Puppie of her own. 'Did any other girls get off at the stop with you?'

The girl shrugged. 'Don't know.'

'Thanks,' he said as she walked on.

Down at the corner, nobody appeared. He squeezed the fencepost and stared. *So she's late. No big deal. She's angry, she's gone shopping with her friends, she's hanging out in a park, avoiding coming home. She's an angry teenage girl. That's all.*

Cars drove past and a horn blew. A breeze ruffled his hair, birds called and the sun warmed his shoulders through his uniform shirt. They were ordinary things happening in an ordinary street, but he suddenly felt that danger lurked everywhere; that he was being watched by some malevolent force that knew something had happened to Mia and was even now taking pleasure in his ignorance. He stared around, searching the parked cars for someone slumped low behind a dashboard or peering out over a back seat, for a figure on the footpath half-hidden behind a power pole, for a twitching curtain in a neighbouring house, even as he told himself not to be ridiculous.

Because ridiculous is what this behaviour is. Be sensible. Go inside and ring her.

He made himself let go of the fencepost, took one last look down the street, then stopped. Another girl in uniform turned the corner, Slush Puppie in hand. He recognised her walk.

'Hi,' he said as she got near.

Her face was guarded. 'I'm just a little bit late.'

He hated that she was so quick to be defensive. Had he caused that? When? How?

He nodded at the cup. 'What flavour did you get?'

'Blue.'

He smiled.

'I know, blue's not a flavour.' Her tone was almost hostile.

'Yes it is, and it's my favourite.'

'You hate blue.'

'Not today.' He made a grab for the cup.

'Dad.' She pulled away.

'Sharesies.'

'You are so lame.'

'You mean so cool.' He grabbed again.

A smile broke through her scowl and she ducked past him and ran into the house. He followed with a smile on his own face, thinking that from now on things would be different. He would make sure of it.

SEVENTEEN

Ella and Murray drove into the boatyard car park just as Natasha Osborne was heading out alone in the big blue ute. Ella saw the moment when she recognised them and the expression that flitted across her face. She braked hard. 'Let's follow her.'

'No, look.' Murray pointed down to the dock where a man walked with a bucket and fishing rod. 'First time we've seen someone here to talk to.'

'She made a face when she saw us.'

'You go then. Let me out.' He put his hand on the door.

Ella stopped the car and he jumped out, then she spun the wheel and headed back the way she'd come. She caught up to Osborne quickly, and saw the woman frown in the mirror. She followed her along a leafy road, through roundabouts and traffic lights, the sun shining down on them both, then the ute slowed and turned into the parking area of a small shopping centre. Osborne nosed it into a space outside an IGA supermarket and Ella pulled in next to her.

Osborne turned off the engine and got out, a green shopping bag in her hand.

Ella jumped out of her own car and followed her into the supermarket. 'How's it going?'

Osborne dropped apples into her bag, her jaw set. She wore grey shorts over black steel-capped boots, and a snug black T-shirt. She smelled vaguely of grease and oil.

'I hate grocery shopping myself.' Ella followed her past the deli. 'How's life with the ex-con?'

Lips closed, Osborne ran her tongue over her teeth. She picked up a loaf of bread.

'Men like that never change,' Ella said. 'They can promise to, they can intend to, but one day something happens and that thing inside them comes out again. That anger, that rage and fury and violence.' She saw Osborne's hand tighten on the bag. 'You know what I'm talking about, don't you?'

'You have no right to follow me,' Osborne said, her voice low and hard and angry.

'Has he hit you yet? Because he will. Probably somewhere that nobody can see. The stomach. It hurts really bad, and once you can walk upright again nobody will know.' Ella leaned close as they went into the cereal aisle. 'That's the kind of stuff he knows, and counts on.'

'This is harassment.'

'He's no good, Natasha.'

'You don't know him.'

'Neither do you.'

Osborne rounded on her beside the tinned fruit, plait swinging over her shoulder, points of colour high in her cheeks. 'What exactly do you want from me?'

She hadn't denied it.

'Tell me what he's done. I can put him away again.'

'He hasn't done anything.'

'Where is he now?' Ella asked.

'In the workshop, cleaning engine parts.'

'Where was he at five thirty in the afternoon two days ago?'

'Talking to the parole woman when she came around.'

'She look around your flat upstairs as well?'

Osborne raised her chin. 'Yes.'

'You don't like it when people go through your stuff?'

'Would you?'

Ella stared at her. 'Why don't you just tell me the truth?'

'I am,' Osborne said. 'It's not my fault that you cops don't want anyone to ever get out of prison and rebuild their life.'

'Is that what you think this is about?' Ella stepped close. 'A man is dead. His wife is pregnant. That family is what this is about.'

'Paul had nothing to do with that,' Osborne said. 'And if you had half a brain you'd be finding the real killer instead of hassling me.'

She turned and walked off. Ella went after her.

'You listen to me. One day this is all going to fall apart. You might be lucky and manage to get out in one piece, or you might be unlucky and get hurt. You could find yourself facing charges too. And when that day comes, I want you to think back to this little chat and realise that I was right all along.'

Osborne turned on her. 'And then what? I'll regret my decision for the rest of my life? I'll wish I'd never been born? You want me to go on with more clichés?'

Ella shook her head. 'Then you call me, because you want to tell me everything he did and help yourself in the process.'

She dropped her card into the green shopping bag, pushed past Osborne and through an empty checkout, then out into the sun.

Half a brain indeed.

★

Back at the boatyard, she found Murray waiting in the car park. She pulled up and he got in.

'That Natasha's hiding something.' She turned the car around. 'You should've seen her. So touchy.'

'Well, everything was calm here.' He clipped in his belt. 'The old guy with the fishing rod said he's known her for a while, says she's decent; and he's met Canning a few times and thought he was okay too. He was walking his dog here day before yesterday, in the late afternoon, and saw a woman drive up. The description he gave matches Grace Michaels. He didn't notice the plates, but I called the office and had them check the white Camry he described, and it matches hers. He didn't see Osborne and Canning, but saw Grace Michaels go into the shed and heard people talking. And he said his dog peed on the wheel of Osborne's truck, so he knew for sure that it was here too.'

'What about Canning? What'd he have to say?'

'Not much,' Murray said. 'He was cleaning some bit of machinery in a sink. He talked about the weather, said it was nice to be able to get out in it again. I asked how he was going and he said he had no complaints.'

'Don't you think that in itself is strange?' The afternoon sun was low and she flipped down her visor. 'Like Kemsley said, people like him are usually quick to start bitching when we drop in.'

Murray shrugged. 'He was busy scrubbing at this thing with a toothbrush. I kept asking questions but he didn't bite.'

They were due back for the meeting soon so she didn't have time to go back and needle Canning herself. She waited to turn onto Military Road, eyes fixed on the approaching traffic. The whole thing was disappointing. The responses from the old guy, from Canning and even from Natasha Osborne hadn't helped build her argument for the meaning of Meixner's note. This really wasn't the way she'd hoped to present it to Langley.

They got back to the office in time for Murray to make copies of Meixner's note and for Ella to hastily look up Fletcher and his van on the computer system. The information on the tip was there, and she printed it out then they hurried down the corridor.

Langley asked them to begin, and Murray summarised their visits to Prue then Bill Weaver, their unsuccessful search for Miriam Holder, and the lack of information given by her colleagues, Scholler and Wei.

While she listened, Ella watched Langley. He seemed particularly uninterested today, brushing fluff off his navy blue tie, glancing at the windows where the sun's low angle showed every smear and mark. It annoyed her.

'It does appear that Holder took the call that Bill Weaver made, but until either he decides to talk to us or she turns up, we're stymied about the relationship,' Murray said.

Ella jumped in. 'After we left there we got a call from Meixner's wife, because a note from him had arrived in the post.' She passed copies around.

Langley took one and she could see his eyes following the lines. *I hoped I could escape my past, but protecting you from it is the best I can do. I love you both forever, Marko.*

'Chloe told us it's definitely his handwriting,' she said. 'And the envelope's postmarked 3 pm on the day of his death, which means we have a timeline that looks like this. At around two that afternoon, Meixner received a phone call at the office in which he was heard to argue with the caller, saying "no, no". Sometime during the next half-hour he wrote this note and put it in the outgoing mail, then took Daniel Truscott's car keys and left without telling anyone. At three thirty-five, he crashed Truscott's car into a power pole in Wattle Street in Glebe, and told paramedics that someone was following him. As there were no signs of a head injury they felt he might have a psychiatric problem, and at RPA the triage nurse felt the same way and put him in the waiting room. At quarter past five, he got a taxi from there to Town Hall station, behaving in a paranoid manner on the way, and was seen there on CCTV, pushing through a crowd of commuters moments before he went under a train at six.'

The detectives were silent.

'We need those phone records from Payton and Jones,' Ella said to Langley. 'Is there any way we can hurry those up?'

'Telstra is glacial,' he said, still looking at the note.

You won't even tell me that you'll try?

Murray said, 'Because the note refers to events from the past, we followed up with another visit to paroled killer Paul Canning and his girlfriend slash employer, Natasha Osborne.'

Langley looked up. 'And?'

'Nothing really to report, except that we found another witness who supports Canning's alibi for the evening Meixner died,' Murray said. 'Old guy fishing on the dock.'

'Hmm,' Langley said.

'Canning complaining yet?' Kemsley asked.

'Not yet,' Murray said.

Kemsley nodded. 'I bet he's keeping it all bottled up tight. Then one day, look out – he'll explode.'

'Makes sense,' Ella said. 'The parole officer said that he'd been in trouble in prison for fighting, had anger problems, that sort of thing. She thinks now he has it under control. But if he's been planning revenge for a while, he'd want to seem like he's in control, wouldn't he?'

But Langley was waving the note gently, persistently, in the air. 'This is more likely to be a suicide note. A reference to Meixner's suicidal impulses. He's tried to fight them, but now all he can do is kill himself somewhere the wife doesn't have to be the one who either finds him or cleans up the mess. Hence the mention of protection, and hence why he first tries to crash into a pole, then takes the foolproof method at the station.'

'We don't know that for sure,' Ella said. 'His wife said he was delighted about –'

'The baby, yes, we know,' Langley said. 'Can we move on? Kemsley, Gawande, how'd you go at the office?'

'Annie Blackwood got further with Denise Pham than we'd managed,' John Gawande said, glancing at Ella as if apologising for being given the floor. 'She understood the accounting speak and gave us the summary afterwards. Basically, as in any firm dealing with large amounts of money, it is possible to hide transactions, and Bill Weaver, as the head of the office, was in prime position to be able to do so. I just got word that the warrant came through, so first thing in the morning Annie'll go back and start going through the books properly.'

'We talked again to the rest of the staff, but nobody had remembered anything new,' Kemsley said. 'Nobody had any thoughts on the "no, no" calls either. We checked on the phone records too, but they're still being processed.

'Then we went to Fletcher's worksite. The man himself was working and refused to talk to us. The foreman was initially more concerned about whether we could take details of some thefts that've been happening on the site. As with Daley Jones, he and the other contractors don't seem to like Fletcher, but none of them were certain about what time they'd last seen him that afternoon. One thought that he'd left when Jones went, which we know was around two, but he wasn't sure. Another had been at the Thorn and Thistle from around five thirty and said he didn't notice Fletcher there until about seven, but again couldn't be certain that he wasn't actually there before then.'

Ella cleared her throat. 'I have something to add about Fletcher. I happened to check his record this afternoon and found information about an anonymous tip saying his van was seen parked in Amy Street last night, in a spot not far from the Meixners' flat.'

Langley seemed to be looking at her oddly. 'Was he doing anything?'

Don't panic, he doesn't know it was you. 'Not that was reported, but I think it's a big concern. Chloe told us she's had hang-up phone calls at home before, so perhaps Fletcher was sitting there calling her. He would've got no reply because she was still in hospital then, but who knows what he might've done if she did answer?'

Langley looked unimpressed.

She forged on. 'So this means we have the big handprint on the body, the fact that Fletcher's colleagues aren't sure whether he was on-site the afternoon of the death or not, and this suspicious behaviour last night.'

Langley shot his cuff and looked at his watch. 'Tomorrow,' he said. 'We'll speak to Fletcher tomorrow, and also find Miriam Holder, review the CCTV from the train station, and chase up forensics regarding prints from the smoke bomb and so on. If the phone records are in, we'll track down the "no, no" calls. All jobs for tomorrow – back here at eight, thanks.'

This isn't right.

Ella caught Langley as he reached the door. 'What about overtime?'

'To do what? Nothing's what I would call urgent.'

'Bring in Fletcher,' she said. 'Look for Miriam Holder. Fletcher lied, Holder's avoiding us –'

'Fletcher's still working his job, so hardly likely to flee now. And I'm sure Holder will turn up.'

'But Fletcher knows we're onto him now. He might decide –'

'I very much doubt it.'

His tone was final, and he walked away. Ella folded her arms as anger sang hotly through her veins.

★

Alex finished checking the equipment in the Oxy-Viva for the start of the nightshift, and was sliding the bag back into the ambulance when the station phone rang.

'Sixteen-year-old girl on a roof with self-inflicted cuts to her arms,' the controller said, before rattling off an address in Potts Point. 'Police have been notified, but they tell me they've got nobody just now.'

'Thanks,' Alex said.

Jane peered out the back of the ambulance. She'd told him about Deb, and about Steve coming over and how she'd fallen trying to get away from him. The bruises on her cheek and forehead were dark purple in the truck's fluorescent lights.

'What we got?' she said.

'Girl on a roof with cuts to her arms.' He saw her blanch. 'I'll treat tonight.'

'I'm okay.'

'All banged up like that, you'll frighten her right over the edge.'

She closed the back door. 'But you know that I really am all right – if you need to swap or whatever.'

'I know.' He got in the passenger seat and clipped in his belt. His heart was beating high in his chest.

Jane started the engine and he told her the address. 'Want me to look it up?'

'I'm good.' She pulled out of the station and swung onto George Street heading south, then hit the lights and siren.

Evening was falling on the city and the sky between the buildings was purple and pink. Alex kept his eyes on the crowds of office workers scurrying over the road, watched the cars giving way at cross streets when Jane went through red lights, and told himself to stay calm.

The house in Potts Point was painted white with grey trim. It was three storeys high, with cast-iron balconies on the ground and first floor, then a gable with French doors and another similar but tiny balcony poking through the roof of the second floor. The doors there stood open and a woman leaned over the balcony, her hand out to a girl who sat beyond reach on the sloping roof tiles. The house's front door was red, and a man flung it open and rushed out as they pulled up.

Alex picked up the microphone. 'Thirty-five's on scene. Any word from police?'

'Not so far, but I'll call them again,' the controller replied.

'She's up there,' the man called through the ambulance's closed window. His face was white. There was blood on his shirt. Alex knew from the look in his eyes that he was the father.

He opened his door and grabbed the Viva and first-aid kit. 'What happened?'

'We found her cutting herself in the bathroom, and were

trying to stop the bleeding when she pulled away and rushed out there.' The man talked over his shoulder as he hurried back up the steps. Alex followed, Jane close behind him with the drug box and monitor. 'She won't come back in, won't even talk to us. And she's still bleeding.'

The house was lush inside. Alex got glimpses of thick carpets in neutral tones and soft furniture as they went up one flight of internal stairs then another. His thighs and lungs burned, keeping up with the dad.

'Has she ever done anything like this before?' he asked.

'She's cut herself once, about a month ago,' the father said. 'But she's never gone out there before.'

The top floor was one room under sloping ceilings with an en suite at the back. One corner was occupied by a wide desk covered with papers, textbooks and a laptop, and the pink walls were dotted with band posters. A blue school uniform lay crumpled on the floor.

Stay calm. 'Is she on medication?'

'Nothing,' the father said, as a woman came in through the French doors, tears streaming down her face.

'She won't even look at me,' she sobbed.

Alex put the Viva and kit on the floor near the doors, getting a grip on his breathing. 'What's her name?'

'Rebecca.'

He glanced at Jane, who was paler than ever, and stepped out onto the tiny balcony.

The girl sat on the tiles hugging her knees, the lower legs of her pink tracksuit pants soaked with blood. She was barefoot and her blood-streaked arms were goosepimpled below the sleeves of a thin pale blue T-shirt. Her face was pale. The air was cool and the sky darkening, lights coming on in the houses across the street, cars going along below like nothing was happening.

'Hi,' Alex said, hands sweaty.

She didn't answer. Her dark hair was pulled back in a

stumpy ponytail and he could see that her eyes were fixed on the street.

'My name's Alex. Is it okay if I call you Rebecca?'

Again she didn't answer. She was midway between the wall of the next house and the balcony, about two arm's-lengths from him. The pitch of the roof was steep, and from the gutter it was too many metres straight down onto concrete.

'Can you show me your arms, please?' he asked.

She raised one then the other, then rewrapped her legs. In the few seconds glimpse he saw enough.

'Excuse me for a second.' He turned to see Jane just inside the doors. 'She's got deep lengthwise lacerations on both arms and they're still bleeding.'

She nodded and stepped away with the portable radio. Alex could hear the mother weeping over his own thudding heart.

He faced Rebecca again. 'Thanks for showing me. I really need to put some bandages on those. Could you come over here so I can do that, please?'

She shook her head, just once, short and definitive. When she moved, he saw the shine of perspiration on her cheek. She'd lost enough blood to be in the early stages of shock, and if she continued to lose it she'd soon fall unconscious. The pitch was steep enough that once she went limp, she'd slip down and fall off.

He swallowed hard. 'Rebecca, I've been in a place like you before.'

She didn't answer.

'The pain was so bad I thought I'd be better off dead. I thought, what's the point of living when it's so hard, when every day is just more pain? I'd be better off gone, and my family and friends would be better off for not having to have me around.'

She didn't move. He saw a bead of sweat run down her neck.

'People told me that things would get better, but I thought, what would they know? How can they understand what I feel? They're just saying that.'

Behind him, Jane whispered, 'Fireys and cops are five to ten minutes away.'

They didn't have that long. He murmured over his shoulder, 'Get a rope.'

Rebecca put her forehead on her knees.

Alex gripped the railing. 'Rebecca, can you look at me, please?'

'I'm too tired.'

At least she was speaking.

'Please just turn your head so you can see me.'

She did so slowly. Her lips were blue, her eyes with dark circles, hair lank with sweat. She was shivering.

Alex felt sweat gathering on his own forehead. 'Please shuffle over here so I can bandage your arms and we can talk.'

'No.'

'Then I'll come over there.'

She shrugged.

He crouched by the first-aid kit and stuffed his pockets with pads and bandages. He could hear Jane down at the ambulance, digging the rope out of the back. She'd be back up in a minute, but when he looked back at Rebecca he realised even that was too long. Her arms were loosening around her knees, her eyes closing, one foot slipping down the tiles.

Alex climbed over the railing.

EIGHTEEN

Ella drove slowly past Miriam Holder's address in Tama-rama, looking for her blue Toyota among the cars parked on the street. The sky over the sea was a darkening shade of blue and with the window down she could hear the surf pounding the rocks around the headland and smell the salt in the evening air. People walked along the footpaths, some in suits with briefcases, some in jogging gear with impatient dogs pulling at leads. None of them paid her any attention.

Stupid Langley. She and Murray should've been in an interview room hammering Fletcher, or Canning, or at the very least both here, the two of them sharing the watching, ready to take Holder down if she appeared. Instead, Ella was here on her own, in the hope that she might see something and get to phone in another anonymous tip in the morning. Not that her call about Fletcher had got her anywhere significant, but it was better than nothing.

She cruised around the block, hands slightly sweaty on the wheel, with no success finding the Toyota, then squeezed her car into a space thirty metres from Holder's building. From there she could see Holder's windows on the top floor. She couldn't make out any movement, and there was still too much brightness in the evening to see if any lights were on, but the sky was turning deep purple beyond the unit blocks all down the street and behind her in the mirror the orange and lavender clouds were fading. It'd be dark enough soon.

She felt conspicuous as she settled into her seat, a magazine open on her lap in the hope that she looked like she was killing time while waiting for someone. She eyed the box in the plastic bag with the camping store logo that sat in the passenger footwell.

After fifteen minutes, the orange and lavender were gone and the squabbling over perches by the birds in the trees along the footpaths was dying down. Pedestrians were fewer, passing cars had their headlights on, and she could smell dinners cooking in countless kitchens. Her stomach rumbled. She stared at the windows in the top floor and thought she could see lights.

She looked around for passers-by, then reached for the box in the bag, tore off the top and lifted out the binoculars. The smell of new plastic filled the car. She reclined the seat a fraction, checked again for pedestrians, then put the binoculars to her eyes. The windows came into sharp focus even in the gloom. The curtains were open and she could see the edge of a light fitting. The globe was off, but the fitting cast a shadow on the ceiling, meaning there was definitely light coming from elsewhere in the apartment. It was steady, so it wasn't from a TV. She imagined a floor lamp or a ceiling light in another room.

She watched the light grow brighter as the outside world darkened, hoping to see movement, hoping to see Holder herself come to the window and look out at the sea.

A mosquito whined and she slapped at her neck and pressed the button to raised the windows. They'd only been open a crack, but the car quickly became too stuffy. She lowered the binoculars. There'd been no movement, but that didn't mean Holder wasn't in there. She could be hiding. And she mightn't expect the police at this time of day.

Ella opened the driver's door and got out.

The sensor light above the front door of the building clicked on as she stepped up to the panel of buttons. She pressed Number 8 and waited. After a minute of silence, she pressed it again, longer, then walked back out to near the letterboxes and looked up at the windows. No movement.

It better be the right windows.

Back at the step, she hit eight again, then seven. Then six.

'Yes?'

'New South Wales police detective,' Ella said. 'I need to get into the building. Could you open the door, please?'

'Is this some kind of joke?' the man said.

There was no security camera system. 'I'll come up and show you my badge if you like.'

A moment's pause, then the door buzzed open. Ella pushed into the small foyer, which smelled like glass cleaner, and started up the stairs. She glanced up the stairwell to see a man looking down from the third-floor landing, and she had her badge out ready when she got there.

He hardly looked at it. 'Has something happened?'

'I'm just doing a routine check as part of an investigation,' she said. 'Do you know all your neighbours?'

'Is everyone okay?'

He was around fifty, soft-shouldered as if he spent his days over a desk, wore glasses with wire frames and had a hint of whisky on his breath. From the open door behind him came the smell of lamb cutlets cooking. Her stomach complained again.

'As I said, I'm just doing some checks.' She thought she heard a noise on the next floor and looked up, but saw nobody. 'Do you know the people in Numbers 7 and 8?'

'They're both single ladies, but I don't know their names. We all nod and smile if we run into each other, but that's about all,' he said. 'One's about seventy, she lives in Number 7. The one in Number 8's younger, about forty or so.'

'When was the last time you saw either of them?'

He rubbed his chin. 'The older one I guess I saw yesterday; the younger one probably the day before. I work long hours and leave pretty early.'

'Ever hear much noise coming from up there?'

'Never,' he said. 'They're very quiet. Everyone in the building is. Very considerate.'

'And you all have to park your cars on the street?'

He shrugged. 'You get used to it.'

'Either of them get many visitors?'

'I couldn't say,' he said. 'As I said, I'm out a lot.'

'You don't hear hordes of people going up the stairs though, when you are home?'

'No.' He smiled.

Ella smiled back. 'And you don't happen to know any of their family or friends?'

'Sorry.'

'One last question,' she said. 'Did you see or hear anyone strange in the last few days? Or did anyone buzz and try to get in with no good reason?'

'No,' he said. 'You're starting to worry me a bit.'

'I'm sorry. It's nothing to feel concerned about, really. I'll just go up and see if they're in. Thanks for your help.'

She went up to the next flight, feeling his eyes on her back, then reached the top-floor landing. Unit 8 was to her right, 7 to her left. She had been looking at the correct windows. She went to 8's door and listened, but heard nothing. There was no peephole. No light shone under the door onto her shoes, but the carpet could be high enough to block it out.

She knocked.

No answer, and no sound.

She knocked again. She could feel the man downstairs still there, listening, but she got no sense that there was anyone standing behind this door, holding their breath, trying to be quiet.

She took out her mobile and scrolled through to when

she'd last called Holder's number. She pressed to call and put her head close to the door. It rang five times but she couldn't hear it in the flat. When it went to voicemail, she hung up. Okay. So maybe Holder wasn't home. If she was dead in the flat, and her phone was with her, it was on silent.

Ella sniffed near the doorframe and couldn't smell anything. Not that that meant much. In a closed apartment a body mightn't stink for a couple of days.

She crossed the landing to Number 7. This door did have a peephole, but it was dark. She rapped on the wood and again got no reply.

She headed down the stairs. The man stood in his open doorway.

'Are the ladies okay?' he asked.

'Have a good evening,' she said.

Down on the street, full night had fallen. She heard the flap and screech of bats in the trees as she walked back to her car, and got in to pick up the binoculars once more. The curtains were still open, and the same low light shone in the windows of Number 8, casting the same motionless shadow from the same light fitting. She lowered the binoculars and rubbed her face with one hand. Miriam Holder could be there, completely still and quiet, resisting the urge to look out the window and see who her caller might have been. Or she could've gone out for the night, leaving the light on for when she got back. Or she could've gone away and left the light on for security – or because she was in such a hurry that she forgot to turn it off. Or she could be dead on the floor. But whichever it was, there was nothing more Ella could do tonight.

Her mobile rang. The screen showed Callum's name. She took a deep breath. 'Hey.'

'Hi,' he said. 'I'm calling to apologise.'

She leaned on the wheel. 'I'm listening.'

'I was an idiot last night. It's all been so strange, and I thought I was dealing with it, but obviously that's not true.

So I wanted to say I'm sorry, but also ask if you'd like to come over tonight. I finish at eight. I could cook you a late dinner and apologise properly.'

'That could work,' she said.

'Is nine, nine thirty too late? And I'm in Cammeray.' He gave an address. 'That's not too far?'

It was almost seven now, and she was starving but could wait. She calculated how long it would take to drive back into the city then over the bridge and east to Cammeray, and knew she still had time for her next job. 'Sounds good.'

'Great,' he said.

'I'll see you then,' she said, and hung up with a smile and a feeling like a little butterfly stretching hopeful wings in her stomach.

★

Jane panted up to the room to find the parents alone on the balcony. She pushed between them to see Alex sliding sideways on his butt across the roof and Rebecca starting to slump down beyond him.

Oh Jesus, Alex.

Blood throbbed in the bruises on her face, but the rest of her was cold and clammy. She leaned over the railing with the rope in her hand, but didn't dare break Alex's concentration. He'd stripped his gloves off and his bare fingers gripped the edges of the tiles. She held her breath. He reached Rebecca and grabbed her by the upper arm, and she said something Jane didn't catch.

'It's okay,' Alex said to her. 'It's going to be okay.'

The compassion and anxiety in his voice brought a lump to Jane's throat. *Keep it together.* She started tying knots in the rope. One loop at this end, one loop at the other. The leaves of a nearby tree waved in her peripheral vision but she wouldn't look. Down on the street stood the ambulance, and some gawkers who'd asked her what was happening and been ignored.

The parents wept. She couldn't hear any sirens. Where were the fucking cops and fire brigade?

The rope was ready. She threw one end around herself and fed the rest of the rope through the loop so it made a slipknot around her hips, thinking briefly of the spotting that was still going on, then passed the rope between the railings and gathered it up in her hands. As long as Alex could hold onto his end, she'd hold onto hers. If it killed her.

Rebecca was weeping. Alex was trying to hold her and inch his way back across the roof at the same time. A plastic-wrapped bandage popped from his pocket and rolled down the roof, bounced over the gutter and fell. The gawkers on the street made a startled sound.

'Alex,' Jane hissed, the rope ready.

He looked over and nodded, set his feet then held out a shaking hand. Jane tossed the rope and it fell in loops across his shoulder. Rebecca moaned in his other arm. Alex grasped the rope and turned towards her, trying to tie her in, trying to tie them together or loop it around them and somehow make them safe.

Jane couldn't quite believe any of it was real. The sky was right there at eye level and making it hard to breathe. She held onto the rope as Alex struggled on the other end. There were still no sirens in earshot.

Alex slipped and slid down a couple of tiles and the mother shrieked.

Jane blinked back tears of fear and anguish and stepped out of the loop of rope. She stuffed it into the father's hands and climbed over the railing.

★

Alex could feel Rebecca start to slide out of his grasp. She was slippery with sweat and blood, and she'd passed out again so was a dead weight in his arms. He tightened his grip and pressed his boots against the tiles, but the surface was smooth and steep. The rope stretched across his chest, and he'd wrapped it around her upper arm but hadn't been able to tie it off, so if she started to fall it would simply unfurl and let her go.

Jane crouched on the tiles between him and the balcony, the rope over her back, her breathing fast and loud, sheer terror on her face. One hand gripped the mother's, the other was outstretched towards him. He was close enough to see the creases in her palm, but couldn't do anything about grasping it because it was taking everything he had to hold onto Rebecca.

'Grab me,' Jane said.

He didn't answer. He was thinking about the rope, about how to tie it off, and how to do so when he couldn't use his hands. His left was gripping the bloody waistband of her tracksuit pants and his right held her right arm across his body. He hadn't been able to get any dressings on her arms, because he couldn't hold her and bandage her at the same time, and that meant she was still bleeding. He could feel it soaking into his uniform trousers. He looked at Jane's hand, so close and yet so far.

He slipped another inch down the roof. He was icy cold with sweat and fear. Rebecca's breathing was becoming laboured.

A siren wailed in the far, far distance.

He could hear Jane saying something. Behind her, the parents sobbed.

He stared up at the early stars, barely visible in the blue and purple sky. He thought of Mia at home, texting her friends or listening to music and doodling when she should be doing her homework. He remembered the look on her face when he'd pretended to grab the Slushie, the bright feeling he'd had that things would be okay.

He slipped another inch. The gutter was just beyond his boots now. It looked flimsy. Gutters usually were, being built for rain and a few leaves, not the combined weight of a man and a girl.

I am not going to lose this one too.

Gently, gently, he lifted his left leg and hooked it around Rebecca's right. Another inch down. Jane and the parents gasped.

He planted his boots and held his breath. He adjusted his grip on her slick right arm, his fingers digging in close to her armpit, then released his hold on her waistband. The loop at the end of the rope lay somewhere between them and he felt around gingerly. He found it, grasped it, eased it out.

Another inch. His boots were almost at the gutter.

The loop was big, but the rope wasn't long enough for him to get it over his arm and up to his shoulder. He thought for a split second, then lowered his head and pushed the loop over it. The knot was good, it wouldn't slip, and as long as he hung onto Rebecca, and the rope stayed twisted around her arm as well, she wouldn't fall.

'Alex,' Jane whispered.

'Pull,' he said. 'Pull, goddammit!'

NINETEEN

Ella crept her car along the kerb until she found a gap in the trees. The moon was high and the light glinted off the ripples on the water. Security lights shone down on the concrete surrounding the boatyard. She pulled on the handbrake, turned off her headlights and engine, and lowered the windows to listen. There were bats in the trees here too, and through their squawking and her impatient stomach's growl she heard the repetitive wash and suck of water on the rocks along the shore and around the dock's pilings, the clink of wire ropes against masts as the moored boats rocked on the tide, and underneath all that, the faintest sound of music.

She raised the binoculars. In the car park, Natasha Osborne's blue Ford F250 ute looked grey. A breeze brought the smell of seaweed and salt water into the car. Ella moved the binoculars across the car park to the building, over the now-closed door to the workshop where she and Murray had spoken to Canning and Osborne, upstairs to the windows with the white net curtains. A light was on inside one room and she could see a table and chairs, and beyond it a sink and kitchen bench. Three canisters stood in a neat row beside a spice rack and an electric jug. She scanned the other windows but they were dark. She looked back to the kitchen, but could see neither Osborne nor Canning.

The breeze strengthened and she heard the music more clearly. Classical. Probably coming from a house nearby. She swept across the car park and boatyard walkways, then out to the boats. Deserted.

She put down the binoculars and yawned. Two places visited, two nil results. She hadn't expected to see much here anyway. This hour of the evening, they were probably watching TV. Or having an early night in bed.

Then a flicker of light on a boat much further out in the bay caught her eye. She lifted the binoculars again. Candles. And movement of two people in front of them. The moon slid behind a cloud then out again, and she recognised Canning and Osborne, in their dark work singlets and shorts, dancing barefoot on the deck of a large yacht. A portable CD player sat nearby. Ella could even see the green light on its top. She watched them move and sway, their arms around each other, their heads close together, the sound of violins drifting over the water.

She lowered the binoculars, feeling like she was intruding. Clouds covered the moon and turned the bay dark, making the candles stand out brighter than ever. The figures moved slowly across the light. She took one more look through the binoculars, saw Osborne lay her head on Canning's shoulder and his hand move up to stroke her hair, then she put the binoculars away.

★

Callum's apartment was in a building across the street from the Cammeray golf course. Ella parked and walked along the footpath, hearing the faint drone of cars on the Warringah Freeway, smelling the damp grass and earth from the greens, feeling the butterfly in her stomach start to flutter its wings. She'd never been here, and she studied the building with interest. She pressed the bell for Flat 3 and he answered immediately.

'Were you standing right there waiting?' she said.

'Wouldn't you like to know?' he said. 'Come on up.'

The door buzzed and she pulled it open. She went up the stairs, keeping calm and cool, and found him standing in his doorway, smiling at her. He wore jeans that sat low on his flat stomach and a snug grey T-shirt. They hugged briefly and a little awkwardly, and Ella felt the warmth of his skin and the muscles of his back under her hand.

'Come in,' he said.

The apartment had beige walls and carpet and a deep red leather lounge suite. Cream curtains hung half-drawn over sliding glass doors to a balcony. On the coffee table, a bottle of red wine and two glasses stood next to a plate of small wafer biscuits and tiny slices of cheese.

'I haven't started cooking yet,' Callum said. 'I thought a drink first might be nice.'

'Sounds good.' She sat at one end of the lounge.

Callum sat at the other and poured the wine, then gave her a glass. 'Here's to you.'

She stepped onto the limb. 'To us.' He smiled. They clinked, and Ella sipped. Her stomach rumbled and she laid her arm across it. 'How was work?' she asked.

'Busy,' he said. 'Yours?'

'Same.' She felt suddenly nervous and couldn't think what to say. She looked around at the modern art prints on the walls, the three purple tulips in an expensive-looking vase. Her stomach growled again. 'Want a hand with dinner?'

'First I owe you a proper apology,' he said. 'I should've told you sooner that I'd talked to Dad, and that was why I was angry.'

Ella nodded, both hopeful and anxious about where this was going.

'It's just that he was so furious.' He put down his glass. 'I couldn't get his expression and the way he spoke out of my head.'

Ella nodded again.

'It got me thinking about it all. Here's me with him in jail, there's you with your job and your part in the whole thing. I wondered if it's too much.'

A little breathless, she put down her own glass. 'It's a big issue to carry around.'

'It's huge,' he said. A little dent of worry appeared between his eyebrows.

He likes me, Ella thought. And I like him. 'I guess the big question is whether it's insurmountable.'

'I hope it's not.' He looked at her.

'I hope it's not too.' She smiled.

'I think if we acknowledge it, and understand it, then . . .' He trailed off.

'Me too,' she said. 'It's all about being, uh, aware.'

And right now she was so aware.

He moved forward a little, his eyes testing, measuring. She slid closer and put her hand on his cheek. His skin was hot, and when she leaned in so were his lips. His hand brushed her knee, then cupped the back of her neck. The butterfly danced.

Her mobile rang. *Shit.* She broke off and looked at the screen. She didn't recognise the mobile number.

Callum's hand slipped down to her shoulder. 'Work?'

'I don't know.' *Maybe it's Osborne, come to her senses.*

He smiled. 'I can wait, if you want to get it. Work's important.'

This relationship could be good. She held back a shiver of delight, and answered her phone. 'Marconi.'

'This is Michael Paterson,' a deep voice said. 'You've been trying to contact me?'

★

Jane straddled the balcony railing and heaved on the rope, the parents pulling alongside her. She saw the loop slip under Alex's chin and his head jerk upwards, his eyes shut tight, his teeth bared and gritted. His arms and now both legs were wrapped tightly around the sagging, unconscious Rebecca. They were unbelievably heavy and Jane's hands slipped on the rough rope.

She could see Alex's face turning dark with blood because his jugular veins were compressed, and God only knew what was happening to his carotid arteries. If they didn't get them on the balcony soon, they could both be dead. She refused to even consider whether the rope might snap. She heard Alex grunt and saw his arms tighten and pull Rebecca closer to him. She guessed he was starting to lose consciousness himself.

'Quick,' she said to the parents, though all three of them were already hauling as hard as they could. They strained and heaved and slowly dragged them up the tiles towards the balcony.

Jane leaned down but couldn't quite reach them yet. Saliva ran from the corner of Alex's mouth. His eyes were still closed and she could see his grip on Rebecca was slackening.

They pulled again on the rope and this time they came within reach. She caught hold of Rebecca's T-shirt, and then the mother was beside her on the railing, making a noise like Jane had never heard before, lifting her daughter with the strength of ten women, up and out of Alex's slackening grip and over the railing and into the house.

'Put her on her side and press against the cuts,' Jane gasped as she grabbed the collar of Alex's uniform shirt.

He was fully unconscious now, limp, his face dark, his mouth open and his tongue starting to protrude. The rope had left red marks on his throat and was tight up under his jaw. He breathed raspingly.

The father leaned over the railing beside her and seized Alex's belt, taking the weight while she loosened the rope from his neck, then she shoved one arm under Alex's and the other behind his head and inside his collar, and they dragged him onto the balcony.

When he thumped down onto the tiles, Jane could've wept with relief. Instead, she rolled him on his side, pulled off the rope, ripped open the Oxy-Viva and set up two oxygen masks. She put one on him, making sure he was breathing better and his colour was improving as she scrambled into the room where Rebecca shivered in her parents' arms on the floor. A white T-shirt and the school uniform were wrapped tightly around her forearms and all three of them were crying.

Jane slipped an oxygen mask over Rebecca's head and suddenly the room was full of uniforms – cops and fireys and paramedics – and people took over from her with Rebecca.

She found herself on her knees in front of Alex, holding his hand, brushing his sweat-soaked hair back from his forehead, and telling him as he woke up that he did it, he saved her, he saved her.

★

'Thanks for calling me back,' Ella told Paterson.

She pointed at the sliding glass doors. She didn't have anything to hide, but she couldn't focus with Callum sitting there grinning at her.

He nodded. 'I'll start dinner.'

She stepped out and slid the doors closed behind her.

'It's no problem,' Paterson was saying. 'I'm sorry I didn't get your message sooner. It's about Marko Meixner?'

'You remember him.' Ella had only given Marko's last name in her message.

'I do,' Paterson said. 'He was the taxi driver who tried to stop Paul Canning beating his supposed friend to death with a star picket. One of my first homicides. Marko laid himself over the vic's bleeding unconscious body like it was his own mother's. Got hit too. What's happening with him?'

'He's dead,' Ella said. 'Went in front of a train at Town Hall station.'

'Went? As in jumped?'

'The story's sketchy.'

'And I take it you're calling because Canning might be involved? Is he out already?'

'Seven weeks ago,' Ella said. 'Do you remember much of the case?'

'Enough that I'd be looking closely at him,' Paterson said. 'In the lead-up to the trial Marko said he was being harassed – a car was following him around when he was driving the cab, someone smashed his windows late at night, and his cat was killed. He found it drowned in a little pond in his garden. I always thought it was Canning.'

A cool breeze touched Ella's face. 'None of this is in the file.'

'That was the hard bit,' he said. 'Nobody ever saw anything. Marko didn't have a witness to the car following him, or a numberplate. Plus, Canning had alibis for every single occasion. And Marko seemed to be developing some kind of problem, anxiety or something. Schuster, who was senior to me, had an idea that it was a combination of imagination and him doing it himself, as part of his psych problem. He said it'd make us look like fools if it all went in the file.'

'He thought Marko would drown his own cat?'

'The cat was old. He said it might've been an accident.'

'Are you kidding me?'

'I wish,' Paterson said. 'Schuster was a stubborn old goat. Once he got an idea into his head that was it. I argued that we should take it seriously just in case, that Marko deserved protection because of what Canning was like as well as what he was doing for us, but Schuster just brushed it off. I wish I'd argued harder though.' He sounded pensive. 'Marko threw himself over the victim to protect him, then got up in court and identified Canning even after all that crap, and I couldn't stand up to a senior detective and make sure he was looked after. That's why I remember.'

'The situation here's a bit similar,' Ella said. 'There's some confusion over Marko's mental state for one thing, and from there the water gets muddier. But Canning himself has alibis, one in the form of his parole officer.'

'If I was you I'd check them closely,' Paterson said. 'His alibis when it came to the harassment of Marko were good, almost too good, and I remember wondering whether the people had been threatened. One was this woman I knew to say hi to, a council ranger. First she was nervy when giving her statement, and then we'd run into each other sometimes afterwards and she could never look me in the eye. I asked her once, and she got all shirty and said he got convicted so what's it matter? The others I don't remember so well, but I do know I wondered the same thing about all of them.'

'Thanks for this.'

'You're welcome,' Paterson said. 'Call me again if you need to. Good luck.'

Ella hung up and stared out across the dark golf course, at the houses on the other side. Marko had asked the police for help when he felt threatened all those years ago, but they hadn't helped him. Three weeks ago, he'd tried again and got the same result.

We let him down, and now he's dead.

She needed to solve this case. It couldn't change what had happened, but it could right the world, just a little bit.

She slid open the glass door and stepped inside. Callum stood in the kitchen, slicing mushrooms.

'You look happy,' he said.

'Just got a phone call I'd been waiting on.' She leaned against the bench. 'Found out that our suspect has threatened people in the past, and I'm thinking he might be doing it again now. I need to check him out again. Talk to his parole officer, go a bit harder on the girlfriend.'

'Parole officer?'

'He killed a guy years ago and my victim was the witness,'

Ella said. 'He got out a few weeks back and looks clean and shiny but I reckon he might've wanted revenge.'

Callum started on a capsicum. 'You don't think he's rehabilitated?'

'That's a rare event, in my experience.'

'So once a crim, always a crim.'

'Not in every single case, but in a lot of them. It's a high enough percentage to make this guy suspicious, that's for sure.'

The knife thwacked into the board. 'Why does his past record mean more than what he's doing today?'

'It's like in your job,' she said. 'Someone comes in with a history of heart attacks and the same pains, you look first at that, right?'

'They're completely different situations,' he said. 'What evidence do you have apart from what this person said on the phone?'

She paused. 'I don't see why I need to justify myself.'

'I'm not saying you do. I just think it's a broad generalisation to say that criminals never change their ways.'

'I never said that.' She stared at him. He kept chopping, his eyes on the knife.

'I'm talking about one man, not every prisoner,' she said. 'I'm not referring in the slightest to your dad.'

'Who said this is about him?'

'I'm not an idiot,' she said. 'You've never jumped to the defence of any of my suspects before.'

'We've never talked about your suspects before.'

He slapped a carrot onto the board. His cheeks were red. Ella couldn't believe they'd gone from kissing to this so quickly.

'So is this going to happen every time I do it in the future?' she said.

'You tell me.'

She took a deep breath. 'Look. Why don't we back up a bit and start the conversation again. Let me help with dinner too.'

'I'm not hungry any more.'

He dropped the knife and stalked out of the kitchen, grabbed his wine and went to the glass doors. Ella stared at his back, the blood thumping in her head. The man was full grown. He was a doctor. And here he was acting like a child having a tantrum.

Just when you think things are going well, something always happens.

She ran through her options. She could walk out now without another word. She could go over to him and squeeze his arm, try to get him to talk. She could demand he turn and face her and admit that he was touchy about his dad. Or she could simply speak to him, one adult to another.

'Callum,' she said. 'How about –'

But he opened the glass door, stepped outside and slammed it shut behind him.

She stared after him and sucked her teeth. *Like that, is it?*

She grabbed her bag off the end of the lounge and stalked out the front door, leaving it standing wide open.

★

One paramedic crew took Rebecca to St Vincent's Hospital, and another took Alex and Jane. Alex's throat and neck were sore, but as he sat for the doctor's examination he knew he was all right.

'I'm perfectly fine,' he said after the doctor had shone a light down his throat. 'Couple of Panadol and I'll be up and dancing.'

'After we do an X-ray and make sure your hyoid bone and cervical spine are okay,' the doctor said, tapping first his larynx and then the back of his neck as if Alex didn't know where those things were.

When the doctor had gone, he rolled his eyes at Jane, who sat on a plastic chair beside the bed. 'I feel like a million bucks.'

'That's great, but you scared me half to death,' she said.

He smiled at her. They'd already been down the corridor and seen Rebecca, the colour coming back in her cheeks with fluid and blood transfusions, a plastic surgeon murmuring to her parents about her arms, a counsellor sitting quietly by the bed and listening as Rebecca talked. That was the important thing, Alex had thought, watching from the doorway: she was talking.

Rebecca had looked up and seen them, and smiled, and Alex had felt like his heart was going to burst.

'A million bucks,' he said again.

TWENTY

Ella drove, snorting, back to the boatyard. Callum was being ridiculous. As if she meant that no criminal could ever be trusted again. Had she said anything, anything at all, to suggest that? She was merely stating facts. And she understood that he was sensitive about his dad, but jeez. That reaction.

She swung hard into the road down to the boatyard and had to swerve to miss a dark grey Mazda coming out. 'Idiot,' she said aloud, glancing in the rear-view as it turned out onto the road, seeing that the numberplate ended with 733. She shook her head. Morons everywhere tonight.

Natasha Osborne's pale blue truck was parked in the concrete yard. Ella pulled up beside it. The doors to the workshop shed were open again. Light shone out onto the concrete, and a light was on in the flat upstairs. Beyond the building, the bay was black with night, the boats lost in the darkness, no candles visible anywhere. A breeze ran cool fingers along her neck as she walked to the open door. 'Knock, knock.'

There was no answer.

She stepped in and let her eyes adjust. Fluorescent lights dangled on chains from the steel-beamed ceiling, and three outboard motors were clamped to the side of a long work-bench. A silent clock radio sat at the back of the bench, and tools hung neatly inside their outlines on a pegboard screwed to the wall above it, while drums of oil and grease were lined up underneath. Frames in the centre of the space held an upturned tinnie and another two outboard motors, plus a large piece of machinery that Ella guessed was an engine from inside some-thing bigger. At the back another smaller door stood open, a breeze blowing in and straight through the building.

At the far end of the shed, a flight of timber stairs led to an open door. She went up the stairs and knocked on the frame.

Inside, Canning and Natasha Osborne sat on opposite sides of a small square table covered with a yellow cloth, a bottle of red wine, two half-full glasses, and a plate of cheese and crack-ers between them. They still wore their work clothes.

'Hi,' Ella said.

Osborne chewed and stared at her, while Canning put a slice of cheese down on his plate. 'Detective.'

'Lovely place you have here,' Ella said. 'Mind if I come in?'

She stepped inside without waiting for an answer. The floor was plain boards, the kitchenette cheap white melamine with a tiny sink, the wall dividing it from the next room unpainted plasterboard with rough smears of filler over the nail holes. The breeze blew in through the open windows that faced the bay, flapping the curtains, bringing the smell of brine and seaweed. She could feel her pulse in the crooks of her arms, in the skin of her face.

'Anything in particular you're after?' Canning said. 'Maybe I can help you find it.'

'I'm just looking.'

Ella walked to the window and glanced down at the car park, then went to the open doorway into the next room. A red rug lay on the centre of the boards. A neatly made double bed with a blue quilt stood against one wall, a melamine ward-robe and chest of drawers against another, and in the corner a doorway led into a small clean bathroom. It had a combined shower/bath and the curtain was dotted with pictures of fish. The toilet lid was closed. One orange and one green toothbrush stood with a tube of toothpaste in a glass on the sink. Ella opened the wardrobe and looked at the hanging shirts and trousers, then went back out.

Osborne's cheeks were red. Canning said something to her in a low voice.

'Everything okay?' Ella said.

'You like looking through other people's stuff?' Osborne said. 'Get your jollies that way?'

Ella smiled at her. 'I wish.' She peered out the kitchen window towards the water. 'Are all those boats waiting to be worked on?'

'No,' Canning said. 'They mostly belong to people who live nearby.'

'Nice life if you can get it.' Ella looked into the sink. Another wineglass stood in the bottom. 'You just had a visitor?'

'No,' Canning said.

Ella pointed to the glass.

'That's mine from earlier,' he said.

Ella stared at him, thinking of the dark grey Mazda with the plate ending in 733. 'Really.'

'Yes,' he said. His face was empty.

Natasha Osborne picked up her glass and drank. Ella studied her, willing her to make eye contact, but she kept her gaze on the wall across the room. 'So what are you guys working on at the moment?'

'We *were* having supper,' Osborne said.

Ella saw Canning touch her foot with his under the table. 'We've been servicing outboards,' he said.

'You like the job?'

He nodded.

She glanced along the floor. 'No pets?'

'No.'

'I thought places like this usually had cats,' she said. 'You know, so much fish around. You like cats, don't you, Paul? Although I guess here, with water everywhere, there's a high risk that a cat could drown.'

He didn't blink. 'I've never been one for domesticated animals.'

Ella held his gaze. 'Some people just aren't.'

Osborne scowled. 'Do you always come into people's homes and ask such stupid questions?'

Ella smiled at her, then pushed off the bench. 'Ask Paul there what I mean. You two enjoy the rest of your evening, won't you?'

She shut the door, then walked down the stairs, back under the fluorescent lights and outside. She took a long look in the windows and tray of Osborne's truck, then turned to smile and wave at the white net curtains before she got into her car. She couldn't see them, but that didn't mean they weren't watching.

★

Alex had to wait a couple of hours for the all clear, but once that was done they went back to station, showered and changed, then spent over an hour filling out paperwork on the incident. When that was done, the supervisor told them they'd been signed off for the rest of the shift, and to go home.

Jane and Alex stood in the plant room and watched him drive out.

'Are you going?' Jane said. 'I don't want to.'

Alex looked at his watch. It was just after midnight. 'I'll wake Mia and Louise if I go home now.'

He didn't want to leave, anyway. He'd thought they would keep working, but if they weren't going to work, it would be nice to sit on station. And Jane would otherwise be going home to an empty house.

'Cup of tea?' he said.

They shut the station doors and went inside, made tea and kicked back in the recliners.

'What a day,' Jane said.

He looked at her. 'How's your face?'

'Forget about that, how's your neck? I thought I was going to kill you.'

'I never thought that,' he said. 'I thought, I'll just hang on to her and you'll pull us up. I never doubted it.'

'Well –' she began, then her voice broke, and she started to cry. She put her cup on the floor and her face in her hands and wept.

Alex squeezed her shoulder.

'I thought you were both going to die. I thought she'd lost so much blood, and I was choking you to death right there, and wouldn't be able to get you up in time. I thought –' She shook her head.

'But we didn't. You saved us both. Even with your fear of heights. You went out over that railing and you saved us.'

He knelt by her chair and put his arms around her. He felt her tears on his neck and a lump in his own throat. 'It's going to be okay.'

And it was. Not just this – everything. Saving Rebecca had fixed something that'd been broken when he couldn't save the girl in the car.

Say her name. It's not a jinx. Mia. Just like his own.

He'd done his best, but he couldn't save her. But today he'd done his best, and this time he and Jane *had* saved someone. And everything really was going to be okay.

★

He woke to the buzzing of his mobile. They were still in the recliners, Jane half-curled on her side, her hands tucked between her knees. She'd cried herself out, then they'd talked for a while, then dozed off. He could see the windows were light and realised he hadn't dreamed about the girl. He guessed it was close to seven even before he got the mobile out of his pocket and saw the time. Seven ten. Louise calling him. He sat upright.

'Louise?'

'Oh my God, Alex, I'm so sorry –'

He was on his feet, heart hammering. 'What's happened?'

'She's gone, I don't know where or when. I went to wake her up and she's gone.'

Alex turned cold.

Jane blinked up at him. 'What's the matter?'

'Was the door locked?' he said into the phone.

'Yes, it's all locked up. She must've let herself out –'

'What time did you check her?'

'Alex, I'm so sorry, I didn't. I know I tell you that I always do, but –'

'I'm on my way.' He hung up on her.

Jane was staring at him.

He said, 'Mia's gone.'

Jinx.

★

On the way into the office, Ella stopped at the cafe on the ground floor for a proper coffee. Her improved mood after needling Canning had dissipated overnight, then been killed altogether by the shouts, radios and nail guns of the builders who were back on their site next door. Callum hadn't called to apologise either. *Well, stuff him.*

Coming back out into the bright morning sunshine, she saw a car pull into the bus zone. Murray got out of the passenger door, and Ella slowed as she saw the driver's door open and a tall woman with long dark hair run around the front of the car. She laid one hand flat on Murray's tie and placed the other in the small of his back, pulling him towards her. Murray was laughing as she talked, close to his face, and they kissed.

They parted, Murray raising a hand as the woman climbed back behind the wheel and drove off.

Ella caught up with him in the foyer and they stepped into the lift together. The doors closed. He was smiling. 'Nice morning.'

Stupid love.

'That cop Paterson rang me back last night,' she said. 'Meixner was getting harassed before he testified, but Canning had alibis, all the witnesses for which Paterson reckons had been threatened.'

He faced her. 'This wasn't in the file.'

'His superior officer said it was nothing. Sounds familiar, doesn't it?' The lift doors opened and she stalked out.

'Hang on,' Murray said, following. 'What sort of harassment? How could they leave it out of the file?'

She stopped in the corridor and told him about the cat, the broken windows, the car that followed Marko, and about Paterson's colleague's response.

'You know what Langley's going to say if you tell him,' Murray said.

'What do you mean if?'

'He'll say it's more proof that it was hallucinations or whatever. Meixner thought someone was following him back then, just like he thought when he crashed Truscott's car.'

Ella shook her head and was about to speak when the lift pinged and the doors opened. A young guy holding a big flat pink cardboard box stepped out and looked both ways in the corridor, then at them. 'Uh, where would I find a Detective Marconi?'

'Right here.' Murray pointed at Ella.

The guy handed her the box, then stepped back into the lift. 'Enjoy,' he said as the doors closed.

The box was light. She could smell sugary food. She felt disbelief and annoyance in equal amounts.

'Open it,' Murray said. 'What, you think it's a bomb?'

'I don't want it whatever it is.'

'Who's it from?'

'What makes you think I know?'

'I bet I know.' He grinned. 'Open it.'

'You open it.'

He took it from her and peeled off the sticky tape that held the lid down. 'Ooh, donuts. And a note.' He handed her the sealed envelope and showed her the array of iced and sugar-dusted donuts.

She crumpled the envelope in her fist. 'Throw them out.'

'No way,' he said, and took them with him into the meeting room.

Left alone in the corridor, tense and angry, she ripped the back off the envelope and opened the card inside. The front had a picture of a red flower. Inside, in blue pen, were the words, *I'm sorry. Can we please talk? C.*

'You have got to be joking,' she said aloud, and ripped the card in half.

★

Alex stood in Mia's room, Jane silent behind him. The bed hadn't been slept in. The quilt was rumpled, as if she'd lain on it while waiting, counting down time, but she hadn't got in. That meant she'd left after she'd said good night to Louise and come upstairs. If he'd come home from work at midnight he would've checked her, and seen that she was like this, and been able to stop it all.

Louise, who'd lied about looking in on Mia each night as he'd asked, was sitting downstairs, crying. He'd told her she had to wait to talk to the police. She'd said she had her job at a childcare centre to go to, but he'd made her phone in sick.

She's gone. You thought it would all be fine. You tempted fate and thought life was good and now she's gone.

He'd thought the fear he'd felt on the roof was bad.

'Let's do this methodically,' Jane said. 'Is her schoolbag here? How about clothes? Toiletries? Does she have much money? Or a diary?'

'That won't help us find her,' he said.

'But we'll be able to tell the police how well she prepared.'

Jane went to the dresser and pulled out the top drawer, but Alex ignored her and went to the desk. Mia's desktop computer was on, and he moved the mouse to wake the screen. Homework documents, internet, email. He clicked on the email first. It asked for a password. He typed in *jdbieber1394* but was rejected. He put in her own name and birthdate in various combinations, but they were all rejected.

When Mia first got email and Facebook accounts, Alex had made it a rule that he knew her passwords, and he'd looked at both accounts a few times, but she and her friends just complained about homework and parents' rules, or raved about boys in bands and on TV. He hadn't checked for a few months, thinking he should give her some privacy; a teenaged girl didn't want her dad to know everything she thought and felt. Now, as he stared around her room, he kicked himself. He should've realised that when the posters on her bedroom wall changed, so would other things.

He took out his mobile and scrolled through until he found the name Pepper Green. It rang twice then she answered. 'Yello.' Music played in the background.

'It's Mia's dad,' he said. 'Is Mia with you? Or do you know where she is?'

'No, sorry.'

'This is very important,' he said. 'Has she been talking about running away?'

'Look, Mr Churchill —'

He thought he knew what was coming. 'I don't care about you wanting to keep her secrets, I don't care if you're worried about what she'll say to you at school. Kids die when people keep their mouths shut.'

'What I was going to say,' she said, 'is that Mia and I aren't that close any more. Like, we're still in the same group, but we don't talk much, you know? I don't know if she's got a boyfriend, or is friends with a girl from another school or what, but she's always on her phone, texting and talking to someone, and a couple of times I asked her who it was and she said it was none of my business.'

Alex's stomach dropped. 'How long has that been going on?'

'Three or four weeks.'

He thought back, but it was hard to say whether her behaviour had changed around that time. She'd been irritable and moody for months.

'And she gave you no clue?' he said. 'You never saw anything over her shoulder that gave you an idea of who it might be?'

'No,' she said. 'She was really careful.'

'Do you know her computer passwords?'

'They all used to be *rpattz86*, but I tried that a while back and they didn't work.' She sounded embarrassed. 'I know that was wrong but I was curious. And a bit hurt that she'd found another friend. I wanted to see who it was.'

'Please call me if you hear from her, or if you hear that she's been in contact with anyone else.'

'I will,' she said.

The three other girls he thought were Mia's closest friends told him similar stories, Eleni adding, 'I asked her if she had a boyfriend, and she said no and got all angry, but once I saw on her phone that she was texting "I love you".'

Alex had to breathe deep. It could be another fourteen year old, a boy too shy to hold hands even. It wasn't necessarily some older guy passing himself off as young; someone she'd met online who had designs from the start.

None of the friends had heard her talk about running away, or had seen or heard from her this morning.

He hung up. 'She's been hiding something.'

Jane looked like she didn't know what to say.

He pulled the keyboard close and started to type, but couldn't help thinking about the parents of the dead Mia, and how they'd said they didn't even know she had a boyfriend until they learned he was driving the car she'd died in.

TWENTY-ONE

Ella sat in the meeting room, arms and legs crossed, watching from narrowed eyes as Murray, Kemsley, Gawande and Hossain ate donuts. They'd offered the box to the forensic accountant, Annie Blackwood, but she'd shaken her head.

'Say thanks to your boyfriend for us,' Gawande said to Ella.

'He's not my boyfriend.'

'S'funny too,' Hossain said, 'sending a cop donuts.'

'No, it's not,' Ella said. 'It's ridiculous. It's pathetic. It's insulting, and it's an American stereotype anyway, therefore irrelevant, therefore even more ridiculous.'

Their mouths were too full for them to answer. Annie Blackwood looked down at her notes, trying to hide a smile. Ella frowned.

Langley walked in and shut the door. He didn't bother sitting down. 'Okay. Nothing new overnight from the tip lines, so here're the tasks for the day.'

'I have something new,' Ella said. 'I got a call last night from Michael Paterson, the officer on the homicide in which Meixner was a witness. He said Meixner had complained about being harassed in the lead-up to the trial. Canning had alibis, but Paterson suspected that the people who supported those alibis had been threatened.'

'Suspected?' Langley said.

She explained what Paterson had said about the council ranger. 'He said he felt the same way about the other witnesses but couldn't prove it.'

'Is any of this in the file?'

'No.'

'Why not?'

She could feel Murray looking at her. 'Because Paterson's partner thought Meixner was having some sort of breakdown and imagining it all.'

'Isn't that interesting,' Langley said. 'It's the same story all these years later.'

'I think it justifies taking a much closer look at his alibis for the time Meixner died, at least.'

'You don't trust the parole officer?'

'I'm saying it's worth looking into.'

Langley leaned forward on his hands. The end of his deep blue tie brushed the table. 'Yesterday you were obsessed with Simon Fletcher. Today you're sure it's all about Paul Canning. How about you stop trying to think and instead just follow the plan I set out?'

The other detectives were silent. Annie Blackwood stared at the floor. Ella felt herself turning bright red with humiliation and anger.

'Okay?' he said.

She could barely breathe.

He snapped his fingers. 'Okay, Detective?'

She managed to nod, the briefest nod of all time.

'Good.' He stood straight. 'Right. As I was saying, here are the tasks for today.'

★

Alex entered his username and password into the Optus homepage. Mia's phone was on his account, and when he brought up her usage page he could see that over the last month she'd repeatedly rung and texted a mobile number that he didn't recognise. He picked up his own phone with shaking hands and dialled. It rang five times then a robotic female voice kicked in: '*The person you are calling is not available. Please try again later.*'

'It's probably a boy,' Jane said, her hand resting on her stomach. 'You know what that first love is like. You want to be in touch all the time. They're probably sitting in a McDonald's somewhere, holding hands and feeling magnificent.'

Alex dialled again and heard the same message, then he hung up and called Mia's number. It went straight to voicemail, just as it had when he'd rung on the way from the station and the five times since. '*Hey, it's me. You know what to do.*'

'I love you, sweetheart, and I just want to know you're okay. Please, please, call me back.' He hung up.

'The police will be able to trace it, no worries,' Jane said. 'They can do anything these days. We'll track her down before you know it.'

Alex didn't answer. He scrolled through to another number, and called Frances and Donald. They'd been his and Helen's neighbours back before Mia was born, and quickly became her surrogate grandparents afterwards. With his own parents dead fifteen years, and Helen's busy doing missionary work in the highlands of Pakistan – or somewhere; it'd been years since he'd had any contact with them, they could be dead for all he knew – he'd been grateful for their interest and their willingness to look after Mia on the afternoons he was on dayshift.

Helen, he thought, just as Frances picked up. 'It's me,' he said. 'Is Mia there?'

'No. Is she supposed to be?'

'She's run away,' he said. 'She left sometime during the night.'

'Oh my goodness. What can we do? Have you called the police?'

'I'm waiting for them now,' he said.

'Keep in touch, won't you? Let us know how we can help,' she said.

'I will.'

He ended the call and sat for a moment with his eyes closed. He could smell Mia in the room: the honeysuckle Body Shop perfume she liked, her shampoo and hairspray, deodorant and nail polish.

'What if Helen's come back?' he said.

'After so many years of indifference?' Jane said.

He opened his eyes. 'What if she decided she wants custody but knew she'd never get it after being away so long, so persuaded Mia to run away to her?'

'But then what?' Jane said. 'She can't get her out of the country. She's got no documents so she can't enrol her in school or anything. They'd be living on the run, and surely that's not what she'd want?'

Alex scrolled through the contacts in his phone. He wasn't sure he still had the number, but there it was, towards the bottom of the list. He pressed, hoping she hadn't changed it. After three rings, he heard the voice he remembered.

'Nat,' he said. 'It's Alex.'

'Oh. Hi.'

She sounded guarded, which was understandable given the circumstances in which they'd last spoken, and the nine years that had passed since.

He said, 'I'm sorry to bother you, but I need to ask you something.'

'Um, okay. Just hang on.' She put her hand over the phone and he heard muffled voices, one of them male. *How about that.* After a moment, she came on again. 'What's up?'

'Have you heard from or seen Mia or Helen lately?'

'No,' she said. 'Why?'

He hesitated, not sure if he'd been so hopeful she'd say yes that he couldn't quite accept her answer, or if he didn't actually believe it. It seemed too fast, for one thing, and she sounded on edge. Nervous. Like she might if she was lying. 'You're sure?'

'Of course I'm sure. Why? What's happened?'

'Mia's run away.'

'Oh shit. When? How?'

He told her, then recited the mobile number Mia had been calling. 'Do you recognise that?'

'I don't, I'm afraid,' she said. 'I'm so sorry, Alex. I wish I had heard from Helen so I could help you. But she's been out of touch with me pretty much since she left you guys, and I haven't talked to Mia since the day of that birthday party.' She paused. 'I wish that wasn't true. I haven't been much of an aunt.'

There was no time to go into that now. Alex said, 'Let me know if either of them gets in touch.'

'I will,' she said. 'And Alex –' She stopped.

'What?'

'Nothing. Just . . . good luck. Keep me posted, will you? Tell me if I can help.'

'Sure.' He hung up.

'Who was that?' Jane asked.

'Helen's sister, Natasha. I thought Helen might've let her know if she was back in the country.'

'And she hasn't?'

'She said no, but she sounded strange.' He got up and crossed to the window. He felt like he was in hell. Images of kids he'd seen dead and maimed filled his head. 'Where the fuck are the police? We need that mobile number traced, we need them to find out if Helen's back in the country. What the fuck are they doing?'

'Did you check her bank account?' Jane said.

He went back to the computer, sick and tense. As he opened the ANZ website, Jane went out of the room and he heard her phoning someone called Rooney and telling him or her what had happened. He logged on, then clicked to open Mia's account page, while Jane asked Rooney if the response could be hurried up a bit.

He stared at the screen, and when she came back in he said, 'She had three hundred dollars in here, and she withdrew it all a week ago.'

Jane came around to look, then squeezed his shoulder in what he knew was meant to be reassurance.

★

Murray drove, and Ella glared out the window. Langley was unbelievable. She'd presented him with a more or less legitimate lead, and sure, she hadn't expected praise exactly, but attitude like that? Her blood boiled up all over again.

'Wakey, wakey,' Murray said, turning off the car. They were outside Miriam Holder's apartment.

She looked at the building. 'I was here last night.'

'Where?'

'Here,' she said. 'Parked here on the street, watching the flat.'

He looked as if he was about to say something disapproving, but instead said, 'See anything?'

'There was a light on inside but I didn't spot any movement. I talked to a neighbour, but he hadn't seen her either. I went to Canning's place too, but there was nothing to call in any anonymous tips over.' She turned to face him. 'There must be some way we can go over Langley's head without stuffing up our careers. Your dad could do something. Have you told him about how Langley's restricting us?'

'My dad's got no power,' he said.

'Bullcrap. It's the boys' club —'

'He doesn't. I told him already and he said there's nothing he can do.'

'So we're stuck.'

'Sorry.'

She got out and slammed her door. Her phone buzzed in her pocket. A text from Callum: *I really would like to talk.* Ridiculous that he thought he could twice behave so shittily then apologise the next day, and everything would be fine. Delete.

She stormed to the building's front door and pressed the button for Number 8, waited five seconds for the reply she didn't expect, then moved on to Number 7.

'Yes?' The woman's voice was old but bright.

'New South Wales police detectives,' Ella said. 'May we speak with you?'

'I'm on the top floor.'

The buzzer sounded and Murray pushed the door open. They climbed the stairs, going past the closed door to Number 6 where she'd spoken to the male neighbour yesterday. On the top floor landing, a woman in her early seventies, with rectangular glasses and permed and dyed black hair, waited in her doorway.

Her name was Gwen Gorrie and she'd lived there for six years. Her flat smelled of coffee and toast. The walls of her living room bore faded Elvis posters, worn Beatles' album covers, old concert tickets stapled to a ragged red ribbon that was nailed to the plasterboard, and assorted postcards featuring Graceland.

She told them that she knew all the other residents by sight and some by name. 'Some aren't too chatty, like to keep themselves to themselves.'

'How about your neighbour across the landing?'

'Miriam Holder,' Gorrie said. 'Skinny miss with a frown.'

Ella started to feel a little better. 'So you're not friends?'

'She's too curt for friendship,' Gorrie said. 'She'll paste a smile on her face and ask me to get her post if she's going away, but that's the longest conversation we ever have.'

'Are you getting her mail at the moment?' Murray asked.

Gorrie shook her head. 'Is she away? Has something happened to her?'

'When did you last see her?'

'Two days ago, in the afternoon. I was coming up the stairs with a couple of bags of groceries and I heard her come slamming into the building, then she flew up behind me and past me and into her apartment. I said hello but she didn't answer. Didn't even look around.'

'Was that uncommon?'

'The rushing was,' Gorrie said. 'The ignoring less so. She gives the impression she always has a great deal on her mind.'

'Did you see or hear her go out again later that day?' Ella said. 'Or since?'

'No, but that doesn't mean she didn't. I often have music or the TV playing fairly loudly. I wouldn't necessarily have heard her.'

'How about visitors?' Ella asked. 'Does she get many?'

Gorrie smiled. 'You mean her gentleman caller? He seems friendly. Said hello to me a couple of times. Flushed red when he did, but that could be because he's had to haul himself up all those stairs. Can't be easy when you're so big.'

Ella sat forward, hopeful. 'How big?'

Gorrie stood up and held one hand in the air, then both out to the side. 'Big. Large. Round. With a voice to match.'

Yes!

'When did you last see him?' Ella asked.

'Last week, I'd say.'

'How often was he here?'

'On and off over the last few months. Not all that often. Not regular either. Well, not that I saw anyway, but as I said, if I've got the music on I wouldn't necessarily hear.'

'What was the timing?' Ella said. 'Did he seem to be coming for meals, or to stay the night, or what?'

'The few times I saw him were different times of the day,' Gorrie said. 'There was no pattern that I noticed. The one time I saw him at both ends of the visit, he'd been there an hour, maybe two at the most.'

'How was Miriam when he spoke to you?'

'In a flap,' Gorrie said with a smile. 'Like she was embarrassed. But what do I care who she entertains?'

Ella smiled back, and got out her card. 'How would you feel about keeping the music down today?'

★

Jane made tea and toast, but Alex couldn't get any of it down. He stood at the front door until a police car pulled up, ten minutes after Jane's call. He wanted to shout at the officers but didn't.

They were calm and serious. Senior Constable Brent Mason made introductions, then listened to everything Alex and Louise said while Constable Ellis Danaher wrote it all down. Alex felt no better.

At the end, Mason nodded. 'Here's what will happen next. We'll put in a request to Immigration to find out if your ex is back in the country, and if so, what address she gave them when she entered. We'll get a trace started on this mobile number. We'll put Mia's picture into the system and alert all stations and cars. We'll let the media know too.'

'You have a recent photo?' Danaher asked.

Alex took her latest school picture from the sideboard. He was shaking, and so cold.

'Thanks,' Mason said. 'It'd be good if you can keep contact with her friends, ask them to try again to remember anything at all about who she's been in touch with, if she ever dropped a name of a new friend, anything like that.'

'I'm going to the school to ask around there,' Alex said.

Mason nodded. 'That's good. Now here's my card. My mobile number's on it. Call me anytime. I'll keep in touch and let you know the instant I hear anything.'

They stood up.

Alex said, 'That's it?'

'Once we get that information back we'll understand more about what's going on,' Mason said.

'But . . .' He didn't know what to say. He wanted so much more. But what could they do? Kick down every door in the city? Stop every vehicle? 'What about checking with the neighbours about whether they heard a vehicle last night? Finding out if a taxi picked her up? Can you hack into her email account?'

'If your babysitter heard nothing, it's unlikely a neighbour did.' Mason's voice was steady, resolute. 'And checking with taxi firms and doing computer work like that is time-consuming. I know how that sounds, but I promise you, at this point all our time needs to be spent elsewhere. We're likely to find out what we need from the first few things we'll do.'

'This is my daughter.' Alex felt Jane's hand on his arm.

'We understand,' Mason said. 'And we need to get going to find her.'

He let them go. Jane stood behind him in the doorway, and Louise sat snivelling in the kitchen. He felt lost, unanchored, bereft.

'I'll drive you to the school,' Jane said.

Louise agreed to stay at the house in case Mia came home. It was the least she could do, Alex thought, even though deep down he knew none of this was her fault.

Jane's phone beeped as they were pulling away in the car. She looked at the text and deleted it one-handed without comment. Alex pressed the heels of his hands to his temples. He felt like if he didn't get some distraction his head would explode.

'Talk to me,' he said.

'We'll find her.'

'About something else.' He rubbed his forehead hard. 'Who's Rooney?'

'The detective who's looking after Deb. So to speak.' Her phone beeped again. She deleted it again. 'I thought she might be able to give them a hurry up. I don't know if it helped.'

'Thanks for trying.'

Another text, another deletion. She was scowling.

'Everything okay?'

'You don't need to hear it.'

'I keep seeing kids' bodies in my head,' he said. 'I need to think about something else, even for a couple of minutes. Please.'

She looked in the rear-view, and adjusted her grip on the wheel, then sighed. 'Okay. You remember I told you a while back that Breanna and Alice had moved back here, that we were having dinner often, and they were always texting me?'

He nodded. His head thumped.

'They're actually still in Melbourne,' she said. 'All those calls and texts and dinners were with someone else. He asked me to keep it quiet. We'd been seeing each other for three months, and he told me he was separated, then the night before last I found out he lied.'

Alex looked at her.

'No need for pity,' she said sarcastically. 'I was an idiot.'

'I'm not pitying you,' he said. 'I'm surprised. Why did you let him persuade you that keeping it secret was a good idea?'

'I know, oldest trick in the book, right? Never eat out, never tell anyone, don't be seen in public together. But in this case it made sense for another reason. He's Laird Humphreys.'

'The guy with the ears on the news?'

'The one and only,' she said. 'I was with him the night you went to that crash, which makes me feel sick. But night before last I went to his place and his wife opened the door, then he pretended not to know me. I parked at the beach and got drunk, then stumbled home and fell over Deb. It was awful. I told that Rooney detective everything yesterday morning.' She changed her grip again. 'I think . . . I mean I don't know, but I think there's an idea that maybe Laird or his missus came around and found Deb, who happened to be there to smash more windows or whatever, and attacked her thinking it was me. Seeing as we look so alike and it was dark.'

'But they haven't been arrested?'

'Not that I've heard. Rooney didn't say anything about it before.' Her phone beeped again. 'Yesterday morning he came around and said he'd been about to break up with her, it was me he really wanted to be with. Then Steve turned up, drunk as a skunk, and started ranting at me, and Laird took off. Now he won't leave me alone. "I'm so sorry, you're the one I really love, please talk to me."' She glanced at the text and deleted it. 'Tosser.'

They reached the school. Alex motioned for her to drive through the gates. Girls in uniform walked between one building and the next, and he thought for a second that one was Mia, then she turned her head and he realised it wasn't. He wondered if the dead Mia's parents felt the same jolt and despair every day of their lives.

'We'll find her,' Jane said.

TWENTY-TWO

Ella's phone buzzed as they walked into the hospital. Callum again. *Can we talk?* Delete.

Bill Weaver closed his eyes when they entered his room. The purple bruising on his throat had yellowish edges and the skin was no longer red. Ella still heard whistling when he breathed.

'You damaged your windpipe?' she asked.

'Like you care.' He tugged the sheet up to better cover his belly.

Murray rested an elbow on the bed rail. 'Need I remind you that she saved your life?'

Weaver turned his head away.

'I thought you might've been back home by now,' Ella said.

'They won't let me out until the swelling in my neck's gone down.' His voice was scratchy and hoarse. 'They said if I lose weight that'll help. Thanks for the tip.'

'Has Miriam been in to see you?' Ella said.

He breathed for a moment, whistle in, whistle out. The buzzer hung over the rail by his hand but he didn't reach for it. 'Why would she?'

'Seems wrong if she hasn't. You two being so close, according to her neighbours.'

He shrugged, fleshy shoulders jiggling inside the white hospital gown.

'Are you worried about her?' she asked, and when he didn't answer added, 'We are, a little. We can't find her anywhere.'

'So she's gone away for a few days. People take holidays, you know.' His cheeks reddened.

Ella leaned on the rail beside Murray and touched Weaver's hand. 'Bill, look at me.'

He hesitated, and when he finally turned his head towards them his lashes were wet with tears. 'Happy now?'

'It's time to tell us everything,' Ella said.

He shook his head. 'I want you to find her first. I need to know she's okay. She hasn't called or visited, and she doesn't answer when I ring.' He gestured at the landline phone on the bedside cupboard. 'I'm worried about her. She might've done something silly, like I tried.'

Ella remembered the steely look in Holder's eyes when they'd talked to her at the office and thought that suicide would be the last thing on her mind. 'We've been to her home and office multiple times. Nobody's seen her. Where else might she be?'

'There's a boutique hotel in The Rocks,' he said. 'The Woolcott. But I've rung them and she's not there under her name, nor under the name I know she sometimes uses.'

'Which is?'

'Greta Summers.' He wiped his eyes.

'How much does Prue know?'

'Nothing.'

'How long's it been going on?'

He frowned.

'The sooner you tell us, the sooner we'll leave,' she said.

His sigh made the whistle louder. 'Six months. And I know how it looks. But this isn't some kind of low-down affair where people are just getting their rocks off. This is love.'

'So the cruise?' Murray said.

'For me and her, yes.'

'And the money from your properties?' Ella asked.

He shook his head. 'I'm not answering any more questions until you find her.'

'It's all in her name, isn't it?' Ella said. 'It wasn't the GFC at all.' *Poor Prue.*

He grasped his forearms over his stomach, the closest he could get to folding his arms. 'Find her.'

★

'I'm Alex Churchill.' Alex's voice boomed and he moved back off the microphone a little. 'My daughter Mia is in year nine.' He gestured behind him, where her picture was being projected onto a huge screen at the back of the stage. 'I need to know if any of you have seen her this morning, or if you might know where she is now. She made a new friend recently, and if any of you have any idea who that might be, I need you please to tell me.'

Below him in the hall, hundreds of girls in the familiar uniform looked back at him in silence. No hands went up.

'I really need your help. Please.'

Dennison, the principal, stepped forward to the microphone. 'If you do know something, come and see me in my office immediately following the assembly.'

'Anything at all,' Alex leaned in to add. 'Even if you're not sure whether it's relevant. Please.'

He glanced at the side of the stage. Jane stood in the wings, one hand on her hip, the other resting on her stomach. She nodded.

He looked out at the girls again. 'Please.'

Dennison said, 'Thank you, girls. Assembly is over. Go to your classes.'

It didn't seem enough. They were getting up and leaving, and nobody was even looking back. He wanted to grab the mike and shout at them, order them to speak.

Jane touched his arm. She seemed to read his thoughts. 'They're just kids.'

He had to look away from her gaze.

'If they know something, they'll come,' she said.

They were alone on the stage. Dennison was on the hall floor, walking through the students to the door. Nobody approached her. Fear tightened its grip on Alex's throat.

They waited in the office for fifteen minutes, turning down offers of tea or coffee, Alex hovering by the door, looking down the empty corridor and willing a contrite student to appear. Jane and Dennison made small talk that he couldn't focus on.

Finally, the principal looked at her watch. 'You may as well go. We'll ring you if any students come in later.'

'Can you ask the teachers to talk to them?' Alex said. 'Especially anyone who looks like they might be hiding something?'

'They already are,' she said. 'Everyone wants to find her, Mr Churchill.'

Outside, the day was bright. It felt like a travesty. He got shakily into the passenger seat of Jane's car as she climbed behind the wheel, her hand brushing over her stomach again. The bruise on her cheek was dark.

'Where to?' she said.

'Are you okay to keep on?'

'Of course. Where else would I be?'

'It's just that you look a bit pale, and you keep touching your stomach,' he said. 'Did Steve hit you during his rant?'

'No, not at all.' She started the engine, her eyes fixed on the street ahead. 'I just have anxious butterflies, I guess.'

There was something in her voice he couldn't recognise.

'Well, thank you,' he said. 'For everything.'

She reached over and squeezed his wrist.

★

The Woolcott occupied a renovated nineteenth-century sandstone building in a laneway off George Street, close to the Harbour Bridge. The front doors were dark heavy timber with long brass handles and they cut off all sound of the outside world. Leather chairs stood empty in the foyer, and two staff watched them approach from behind a long desk.

'Welcome to the Woolcott,' the younger man said. He had smooth pink cheeks and a diver's watch on his wrist.

Ella held up her badge. 'We need to speak to one of your guests.'

'What name?'

'Miriam Holder. Also try Greta Summers.'

He frowned at the computer screen and shook his head. The older man came over.

'She probably checked in two days ago, in the afternoon,' Murray said. 'She might have a car with her, a dark blue Toyota sedan, numberplate QKM 377.'

'There's nothing listed with that plate, I'm afraid.'

'She probably paid cash,' Ella said.

The men shook their heads. 'All our current guests have given us their credit card.'

'And Miriam Holder isn't the name on any of them?'

'Sorry.'

Ella put her hand on the high counter. 'What about Bill Weaver? Or William? Or even Prue Weaver?'

'Nothing even close to those,' the younger man said. 'I'm sorry.'

Shit.

'Are there any women staying here alone at all?' Murray asked.

A glance at the computer. 'All couples.'

'Any of the women in their forties?' Ella said. 'Skinny and kind of hard-looking?'

The men shook their heads. 'Nobody like that.'

Murray thanked them and they walked outside.

On the footpath, Ella said, 'You have to think that Holder would've guessed that Weaver would cave and tell us where she might be, and so she's gone to stay somewhere else.'

Murray nodded. 'So what next?'

'We have Gorrie watching the flat, and we don't know where else to look for her,' she said. 'So let's switch tracks.'

'To what?'

She didn't answer, and started for the car.

★

They stepped out of the lift in the Chatswood building that housed the State Parole Authority offices, turned right along the corridor and pushed through the heavy glass door to the waiting area. The clients' chairs were vacant and there was nobody behind the desk. Ella hit the silver bell with one finger and looked down the empty hallway to the interview rooms and desks at the back and thought about when they'd been here before, how they'd just started telling Michaels why they were checking into Canning when it had all kicked off with the parolee in the interview room. How she never really saw the look on Michaels's face when she heard what Canning might've done.

The same receptionist came out from the back and sat behind the desk, her brown hair tied back in a plait, a plain grey shirt buttoned up to her neck. She didn't smile. 'Can I help you?'

'Grace Michaels, please,' Ella said. She and Murray showed their badges.

'She's not in today.'

'Then we'll need her home address.'

'We don't give out that information.'

'It's about a homicide,' Ella said. 'We're detectives.' As if she didn't know.

'Not to anyone for any reason.' The woman's eyes were flat.

Murray smiled. 'Do you remember when we were here the other day? We got one of your clients under control?'

'Rules are rules,' the woman said.

'How long has Michaels been off work?' Ella asked.

The woman raised her eyebrows.

'That's restricted too, huh?' Ella snapped her badge holder shut. 'Thanks for your time.'

Downstairs, Ella looked at Murray. It'd be simple enough to get Michaels's home address from their own office. 'Fancy making a house call?'

⋆

Grace Michaels's house in North Ryde was on a quiet street, set back from the footpath and surrounded by trees dangling enormous strips of bark. The garage door was closed and the driveway empty. The place looked deserted, but Ella knew you always had to expect someone to be watching from a window.

She was about to get out of the car when her phone rang. She answered to hear a woman screaming. Her hair stood on end. 'Chloe?'

'Fletcher's here! He's killing Audra!'

She slammed her door and motioned for Murray to drive. 'We're on our way.'

'Help me! Oh God, please help!'

The line dropped out.

'You hear that?' she said to Murray, but he was already accelerating away from the kerb. He hit the siren and grille lights as Ella reached for the radio. They were close, only one suburb away, but there might be uniforms closer.

Murray braked hard at a red light, looked both ways, then accelerated through. 'Fucking Fletcher. We should've seen it,' he said.

'Just hurry.'

⋆

Jane held the poster against the power pole and strapped it on with clear packing tape. She turned to see Alex walk out of the bottle shop and into the bakery next door, his face tight with anxiety, a sheaf of the posters in his hands. She watched him speak to the woman behind the counter, holding out a poster and pointing out Mia's height and build and the contact information for the police and himself along the bottom. The woman nodded and took it.

Jane met him at the door. 'We should stop and eat something.'

'Oh. Yeah.' He turned back to the bakery and took his wallet from his pocket. 'What do you want?'

'I meant for your sake.'

'I can't eat.' He pulled out a ten and tried to give it to her.

'I'm not hungry,' she said.

'Sure?'

He nodded at her hand, and she realised she was touching her belly again. *For fuck's sake.*

'Let's keep going.' She looked along the street. Newsagent, chemist, travel agent, butcher. 'You do the newsagent.'

She walked into the chemist and told the sympathetic assistant about Mia.

'I saw her on the news,' he said, his eyes on the bruise on her cheek. 'Of course we'll put the poster up.'

'Thanks.' Jane glanced over her shoulder. No sign of Alex. 'I'll grab a pregnancy test too.'

'All righty,' the man said. 'Any particular brand?'

'Whichever.'

'Some have two tests in the one kit. They tend to be a little more expensive, of course, but sometimes people like to –'

'Sure, okay, whatever.'

He paused as he was putting the box into a paper bag. 'If you don't mind me saying, have you thought about getting something for that bruise? There are some amazing creams on the market now.'

'No, it's fine.' She glanced around again. 'I kind of need to get going.'

He taped down the top of the bag. 'That'll be 22.95.'

She handed over the cash and stuffed the bag into her handbag, which she then jammed under her arm. 'Thanks.'

'Good luck.'

'Huh?'

'With finding the girl,' he said.

Outside, Alex looked at her just as strangely. 'You okay?'

'This place is going to be covered in Mia's picture soon,' she said.

Her phone buzzed with a text and she lowered her head to look at the screen. Laird. *I'm so sorry, please just* . . . Delete.

She looked up. Alex had already moved on to the next pole, was lashing the tape around the poster in a frenzy. The police hadn't called. Jane hoped they were taking it seriously, not just thinking Mia would turn up of her own accord when she got hungry or tired.

★

She was collecting the next batch of posters from the photocopier when her mobile rang. It was a number she didn't recognise. 'This is Jane.'

'It's Detective Juliet Rooney. Where are you?'

'Helping Alex copy posters in Officeworks,' she said.

She watched him take another batch from the tray of the next machine and stack them on the bench. His face was white, his eyes unseeing.

'I wanted to let you know that I've talked to Laird Humphreys,' Rooney said. 'A friend arrived at his place soon after you left the other night; a friend who's a magistrate. I've interviewed him, and he says that he talked to both Laird and Lucille, then she went to bed soon after. The two men sat talking and drinking scotch until midnight.'

'Oh.'

'Laird told me to tell you he was sorry,' the detective went on. 'I asked what about, specifically, but he said, just tell her I'm sorry.'

Sorry, huh? Jane realised she was resting her hand on her stomach again. She put it on her hip instead.

'As for you, you were apparently quite the spectacle staggering home. Lots of people saw you. One of your neighbours heard you coming down the street just before she heard you scream too.'

'So you're satisfied that I didn't do it.'

'I am,' Rooney said.

'Well, thanks . . . I guess,' she said.

'How's it going there?'

'As you'd imagine.' Jane watched Alex feed the machines more money. 'I keep thinking that we should be able to do more.'

Somebody spoke in Rooney's background. 'I'm sorry, I have to go.'

'Thanks for letting me know about Laird.'

Alex lifted another batch from the tray. Jane took it from him and stacked it with the others. She guessed they had about fifteen hundred copies. 'This looks like plenty.'

'The city has four million people,' he said.

She was about to reply, then let it go. She felt useless, helpless. How many people would see the posters they'd put up? How many would actually pay attention? She'd watched an episode of Oprah once where they'd slathered a shopping centre with posters of a supposed missing boy then had the same boy wander alone from shop to shop for hours. Nobody had noticed.

Her phone buzzed. Laird. Again. *Please give me a chance to explain.*

Her thumb hovered over the delete button, then she called him.

'Thank God,' he said. 'I was really worried about you. Why didn't you answer my texts?'

The sound of his voice made her angry. 'I was busy then and I'm busy now. So if you were just checking whether I'm alive, job done.'

'Can we meet sometime?' he said. 'Start over? I miss you, and I really need to get out of this marriage. She's bad for me. Even my doctor says so.'

'I don't care about that,' she said. 'I need your help.'

'Anything at all,' he said.

TWENTY-THREE

There was already a police car and an ambulance in Amy Street when Ella and Murray pulled up. They hurried along the same path they'd walked to tell Chloe that Marko was dead. Ella could hear raised voices and saw neighbours watching from their balconies. *Let them be okay.*

An ambulance stretcher was set up near the building's front door. Audra sat on one end while a paramedic put an icepack on her wrist; Chloe wept on the other end, hands cradling her belly, while a second paramedic checked her blood pressure.

'They okay?' Ella said to the first paramedic, who nodded.

Inside the small foyer, Simon Fletcher lay on his stomach on the tiles, turning his head from side to side in an effort to see. Two constables stood beside him and a trampled bunch of flowers lay on the bottom step. Fletcher tilted his head back to look up at Ella and Murray. He wore a dark suit and tie over a white shirt, the collar of which cut into the back of his neck. He was clean-shaven, the skin of his cheeks pink as if he'd scraped too hard with a blunt razor, and a fresh bruise surrounded a graze that oozed clear liquid above his left eye.

'I didn't mean for anything to happen,' he said.

'Why'd you come here then?' Ella said.

She and Murray grasped under his arms and lifted him to his feet. 'Let's go.'

★

At the office, they put him in an interview room and closed the door. He'd been mostly quiet on the trip over, just once saying again that he didn't mean for any of it to happen, but Ella had cautioned him and he'd shut up. Now, they walked away, letting him stew a little, letting him worry.

Her phone buzzed with a message from her mother. *Dinner? Please?*

Poor Mum. *Will if I can, but probably not.*

She'd have to cope with the bickering siblings on her own.

Gawande and Kemsley came up the corridor to meet them. 'Hey, we heard you got him,' Gawande said.

'Fool was at the flat,' Murray said.

Kemsley held out some printed pages. 'Here's some ammo to help shoot him down.'

Ella and Murray leaned close to see.

'Beautiful,' Ella said, and they started to plan their approach.

★

Anticipation making her tingle, Ella closed the door and sat down opposite Fletcher. Murray uncuffed him and sat next to her.

Fletcher rubbed his wrists. 'This wasn't supposed to happen.'

'You didn't mean to go there?' Ella said. 'Or you didn't plan to end up in handcuffs?'

'I never wanted to have a fight with any lady is what I'm saying.' He put his hands on the table. The backs were scratched and the gouges were dark with dried blood. 'Is she okay?'

'Why did you go there?'

'To talk to Chloe.'

285

Murray snorted a laugh. 'You can't be serious.'

'I wanted to express my condolences, and to say that if she needs a friend I'm there for her.' Fletcher's cheeks flushed pinker.

'You're her friend,' Ella said.

'I like to think so, yes.' He smelled of deodorant over sweat and toothpaste over a dental problem. The white shirt was new, the creases from the packaging visible under the tie, and the suit was shiny on the shoulders and elbows. 'I thought about going to the funeral, then I thought that might be awkward, so I went to talk to her today instead. I took flowers. I just wanted to tell her I'm sorry.'

'Sorry because you killed him,' Murray said.

'Sorry because she's hurting,' Fletcher said. 'I didn't kill him. I was at the pub. You know that already.'

'Not so fast,' Ella said. 'We've been talking to people. You left the site early and got to the pub late. There's a gap there, between two and seven. Five hours. Long time, isn't it, Murray?'

'Long enough,' Murray said. 'Plenty long enough to get into the city, harass the man who's married to the woman you fancy, make him crash a car, push him under a train.'

'This is such bullshit,' Fletcher said. 'What am I, Superman? How'd I manage to do all that?'

'With a little help from your friends,' Murray said. 'Payback for a few favours, was it? You plumb in their hydroponic system? Let them use your place to stash guns?'

'What the hell are you talking about?'

'Wakey, wakey,' Ella said. 'Your former neighbours, the bikies. How are they doing? Tell them we said hi.'

Fletcher shook his head. 'This is ridiculous.'

'You think?' Ella took Kemsley's folded page out of her pocket and laid it, still folded, on the table.

Fletcher glanced at it then away.

'Guess what this is,' Ella said.

'Why should I? You'll tell me soon enough.'

Ella stared at him. 'I said guess.'

'Look,' Fletcher said. 'This is all wrong. I truly didn't do anything. I went there today to talk to Chloe, that's all. It's not my fault if her sister went nuts, chucked my flowers down the stairs, came at me with an umbrella. Did I hit her back? No. I don't do stuff like that. I'm a decent guy. I threw the umbrella away, and then she started hitting and scratching me. All I wanted to do was get her to calm down. Calm the both of them down. Just so I could explain myself.'

Ella unfolded the page and read out a mobile phone number. 'Recognise that?'

A flush crept up from the too-tight collar. 'That's my number.'

'And why did you use it to call Marko Meixner at his work?' Murray said.

'Okay, look. I can see how it might come across as strange, but it wasn't.' Fletcher put his hands on the table again. 'I'm going to come clean with you now, I swear. I wanted to meet the man. I know how that sounds. But I wanted to meet him and see, I don't know, who the lucky guy was. See what was so great about him.'

Ella and Murray stared at him.

'I know it sounds stupid,' Fletcher said. 'I know that.'

'So what happened?' Ella said.

'I'd heard Chloe tell someone where he worked, so I called up his office and asked to talk to him,' Fletcher said. 'I said I had some money I wanted to invest and somebody had recommended him to me, but that I couldn't meet in office hours because of work, and asked if we could meet after, like at a bar or somewhere. He asked how much money I had and I said I'd inherited a hundred grand. He said okay, we could meet. I said there's this bar just off George Street and he agreed.'

'Then what?'

'I admit I thought about trying to set him up,' Fletcher said.

'I thought about paying some girl to come onto him while he's sitting there, and getting some photos and showing Chloe, see what she thought of him then. But then I decided not to, and I went along, it was Thursday two weeks ago, and met him.'

'And?' Murray said.

'And we talked about what to do with the hundred grand. He had all these reports with graphs and shit, went on and on about shares and bonds, and I had to pretend to be interested.'

'Did he know who you were?'

'No. I said my name was Gary Smith.'

'Imaginative,' Ella said.

'He asked about what kind of returns I was hoping for, how I felt about the security of my investment, went on and on and on. And all the time I'm thinking, he has her.' He stared into space. 'He gets to go home to her.'

Ella looked at his hand on the table, the breadth of his palm. 'When did you grab him?'

He hesitated. 'I'm not proud of any of this.'

'Did we say you were?' Murray said.

Fletcher moved his shoulders in his jacket. 'He realised that I wasn't listening. He got suspicious, I guess. He said something about a waste of time and got up to walk out. I followed and grabbed him. I just wanted to tell him how lucky he was. Something like that. But he yanked his arm away and looked at me like I was a piece of shit, and I didn't manage to say anything.'

'And then what?' Ella said.

'Then nothing. He was gone. I went home. I never rang him back. Next thing you two are at my door in the middle of the night asking when did I last see Chloe and whatever.'

'That would be the night you said you'd never met or spoken to Marko.'

'So I lied,' Fletcher said. 'I guessed something had happened to him and you were looking for a reason to pull me in. I was tired and didn't feel like hanging around a cop shop for hours while you got your shit together.'

'But you're not lying now,' Murray said.

'No, I'm not, and you don't need to use that tone,' Fletcher said. 'I said I know how all this sounds.'

'It sounds like a pitiful excuse for a man trying to tell us half the truth and hoping we'll swallow the lot,' Ella said.

'It's not,' Fletcher said. 'That's all of the truth, now. That's everything I know.'

Ella smacked her hands flat on the table. 'Four months ago, you start sending Chloe Meixner flowers. Then you add anonymous notes telling her how beautiful she is, how much you fancy her. Six weeks ago, you tell her in person, at work, and that little stunt gets you sacked. Two weeks ago, you call her husband and meet him in a bar under false pretences because you want to "see what he's like". You grab him hard enough to leave a hand-shaped bruise, then you lie to us about ever having met him. And now you think we're going to believe you had nothing to do with his death because you're aware of how strange it all sounds?'

'It's the truth.'

'What about the other phone calls you made to him?' Murray said.

'I only called him once.'

Ella pulled out more pages of the office phone records. 'Here, and here, and here. You were threatening him, weren't you? People heard his end of the call, they heard him saying, "no, no".'

'That's not my number.'

'No, because by that time you'd thought about the consequences of what you were doing, you thought ahead to this time,' Ella said. 'We know what you did. We know you bought a SIM card from the 7-Eleven store in Pendle Hill, you set it up online with the fake name Chevy Johnson and the address of 171 Church Street in Parramatta, which is actually Westfield.'

Fletcher shook his head. 'It wasn't me.'

'What did you say to him?' Ella asked. 'Did you say you were going to get him?'

'I didn't say anything,' Fletcher said. 'I told you, I only rang him once.'

'What about the hang-up calls to their home? And the lurking in the garden outside their unit block?'

'That wasn't me either,' Fletcher said.

'How about when you parked outside their building, two nights ago?' she said. 'You going to claim that wasn't you either?'

He licked his lips. 'This isn't right. I'm here because Chloe was upset and I wanted to straighten everything out and have her understand that I meant no harm.'

'You're here because you were arrested for assault,' Murray said.

'I was defending myself from her sister.' Fletcher pointed at his eyebrow and his hands. 'She did that to me. Does she even have a scratch on her? No.'

'You are one big tough guy,' Murray said. 'Only *bruising* the ladies, not scratching them. Kudos, man.'

Fletcher turned red.

'What were you doing parked outside their building?' Ella said.

'I felt bad,' Fletcher said.

'Bullshit,' Ella said.

'I did. I wanted to go and see her, tell her I was sorry, but I realised how late it was and that it wasn't a good idea.'

'You went there late at night because you felt bad, but you never lurked in their garden? Is that what you're asking us to believe?'

'You can believe it or not, but it's the truth.' He sat back in his chair and glared past them at the wall. Ella and Murray stared at him for a moment, then Murray patted his pocket as if his phone had vibrated. He took it out and looked at what Ella knew was nothing.

'I'll be back in a sec,' he said, shutting the door behind him, leaving Ella and Fletcher facing each other across the table.

Fletcher glanced at her. 'So what, you're the tough one who'll kick the shit out of me now that we're alone?'

'Perhaps,' she said. 'Are you frightened?'

'As if,' he said. 'Anyway, I want a lawyer.'

'Sure. When Detective Shakespeare comes back, I'll send him to get you one. We just have to wait for him.'

She made a big show of settling in her chair. Fletcher glanced at her again, then away. He looked more anxious than ever. He touched the ball of his thumb to the lump above his eye. Ella didn't move or speak. She felt peculiarly calm. *Like before the storm.*

Fletcher couldn't settle. He shifted his chair away from the table – away from her – an inch or so. Ella watched him.

'You look like a nice lady,' he finally blurted.

Just as they'd thought. Being alone with a woman put him on edge. He couldn't stay silent. 'You think so?'

'I mean you look like you understand people. Like you get them.'

'I thought you thought I was the tough one.'

'That doesn't mean you don't see under the surface,' he said. 'I bet you sit in this little room and listen to people like me babble on every day of the week and you know just by watching and listening who did it and who didn't.'

'You're right,' she said. 'I do sit in here day after day, and I listen to dirtbags of every kind try to pull the wool, and nine out of ten come up with something way better than you just did.'

He twisted a button on his jacket. 'I didn't come up with it. It's the truth.'

'You're trying to paint yourself as a decent person who just wants to let Chloe know he's sorry for her loss, but you're right, I do see past that. I see a guy who's obsessed with a woman he can't have, so obsessed he sets up a meeting with her husband and assaults him, and then when he's dead he just can't resist visiting her.'

'Only to express my condolences. That's hardly –'

Ella leaned over the table and stared into his face, so close she could see the pores in his skin, the individual droplets of clear fluid oozing from the abrasion above his eye, the uneven alignment of his lower teeth in his open mouth. 'I see boofheads like you every day, thinking they can tell half the truth and we won't know the difference. Thinking they're smart and we're stupid. Look at you, pretending to be something you're not in your suit and tie, telling us bullshit about how much you want to help and you just want Chloe to know how sorry you are.' She widened her eyes to glare into his. 'I've met guys like you so many times before. One day you want to talk to a woman. She snubs you. Next thing you're in here charged with rape.'

'I would never . . .' His eyes filled with tears. 'I'm not like that.'

'That's what they all say.'

'No, but look.' He fumbled in his inside jacket pocket and drew out a sealed envelope. 'I wrote her a card. Look.'

Ella snatched it from his shaking hand and tore back the flap. When she opened the card, a dried pressed violet fell to the floor.

Dear Chloe, you might not believe me but I'm really sorry about your husband. I'm sorry to have given you trouble too. Love is what matters most in this world and I wish you all the best.

I won't bother you again.

Simon.

Ella flapped the card in his face. 'You're *still* making a play for her?'

'I'm not. Look, I wrote that I wouldn't bother her again.'

' "Love is what matters most in this world"?'

'I was trying to say I understood how bad she'd be feeling.' He picked up the violet. 'I couldn't get it into words any better than that. I went through seven cards to get it that good. I wanted to tell her that . . .'

'That what?'

'That I really do wish her all the best.'

'You cannot expect me to believe that.' Ella bounced the card off his chest.

He grabbed it before it fell to the floor. 'I think I love her, and I know she's not interested in me, and it hurts me that I've frightened her when I was just trying to tell her good luck, you know? I hope she's happy again one day. After I met Marko in the pub I could see he was a nice guy, and I thought, well, they're both nice, they deserve to be happy. Good for them. You know?' The tears dripped off his cheeks into his white shirt, turning it transparent. 'I know you look at me and you see this guy who digs trenches, and you think I don't care about anything, that I don't have feelings like you do, that I barge through my life without thinking about anything deeper than where's my next beer. You think you know me.' He held up the violet, then placed it on the table and dropped his hands on his knees. 'I saw today that she's pregnant. I didn't know that. I didn't want her to be upset. I wished I could make it all better.'

Ella felt like slapping him. She leaned down until their faces were almost touching. 'I don't believe a word you say.'

'It's the truth.'

'So where were you for those five hours? You weren't at the site. You weren't at the pub. You weren't at Bunnings.' She didn't know that for certain but felt sure he'd buy the bluff. 'You want me to accept that you really are a decent guy? Prove it. Tell me where you were.'

He blinked through tears, then took out his wallet, removed a white business card and slid it across the table to Ella.

'Sam's Salvage, Campbelltown,' she read.

'That's where I was for those hours. Sam's a mate of mine. We like to have a drink now and again.'

'You drank for five hours, and then you drove to the Thorn and Thistle for more?'

'I help him out in the yard too.' He looked at the table.

Clearly there was something else. 'You said you'd tell me.'

He let out a breath. 'I delivered some stuff to him.'

'What stuff?'

'From the building site. Copper wire and pipes. Stuff like that.'

'You steal things and sell them to him, is that what you're saying?'

He nodded. 'It really is the truth now. I didn't tell you before because I didn't want to get either of us in the shit.'

'You preferred us to think you killed someone?'

'I didn't think you really believed it was me,' he said. 'I thought you'd find who really did it and leave me alone. I never figured I'd end up in here.'

He looked genuinely ashamed. He looked like he was telling the truth.

'You know we'll be checking,' she said.

'I know. Just . . . tell Sam I'm sorry.'

Ella walked out and shut the door behind her. She went down the corridor and found Gawande and Kemsley with Murray, looking at his computer. They straightened. 'How'd it go?'

'He says he was flogging stuff from the building site to a mate.' She held out the card.

'The foreman complained to us that stuff had gone missing,' Kemsley said.

'Well, I wish Fletcher'd told us this way back at the beginning,' Ella said. 'Saved us a lot of time.'

Murray typed the name into a search engine. 'It's real, and the phone number matches.'

Ella felt flat and tired. She'd thought Fletcher was the one, but now found herself believing what he'd said. So who'd killed Marko? It couldn't really be suicide, could it?

'We found out something too,' Gawande said. 'Blackwood says that Bill Weaver was skimming. Looks like half a mill at least, and going up.'

Ella came back to life. 'Holy shit.'

'Maybe Meixner found out,' Murray said. 'Those secret conversations in the hallway could've been threats.'

Ella looked around. 'Where's Langley?'

'Budget meeting upstairs,' Kemsley said. 'What do you want to do?'

'Check this story out and kick Bill Weaver's butt, what else?' Ella picked up her phone.

'Yes?' Audra answered.

'It's Detective Ella Marconi. How are you?'

'All right, no thanks to that lunatic bearing flowers. Is he locked up yet?'

'He's here in our custody.'

'I mean locked up in a cell with bars and an open shared toilet and, if possible, a large gang of vicious and desperate men,' Audra said with venom.

Ella wasn't surprised at her anger. 'How's Chloe?'

'How do you think? She thought the moron was going to kill me. She was hysterical.'

'Can I speak to her?'

There was a muffled conversation, then Chloe came on the line. 'Did he do it?'

'I need to ask you something first,' Ella said. 'Fletcher claims that he met Marko in a bar on a Thursday evening two weeks ago. Did Marko mention that to you?'

'He didn't,' Chloe said. 'I remember that night. Audra and I went to the movies. He was home when I got in about nine.'

'Did he seem upset or anxious?'

'Not at all. He was watching TV. I joined him and he dozed off towards the end of the show.'

'Fletcher claims that he called Marko at the office and said he wanted to invest money but couldn't meet during business hours,' Ella said. 'They met at this bar, and he said after a while Marko realised he didn't really have any money and got up to leave. Fletcher grabbed his arm but claims nothing was said and then Marko left. We'll check all this with the bar, but if it really happened – and the bruise on Marko's arm suggests that it did – I wondered why Marko wouldn't have mentioned it to you?'

'That's probably my fault.' Chloe paused. Ella could hear she was close to tears. 'He had a drinking problem when we met.

I grew up with an alcoholic father and swore I'd never get caught in a relationship with someone like that. I fell hard for Marko, but was going to break up with him unless he stopped. And he did. But once, a couple of years ago, he went to a bar with some friends, and though he only had one beer I had such a bad reaction when I smelled it on him I guess he didn't want to tell me about it this time.'

'Did he know what Fletcher looked like?' Ella said. 'Maybe he didn't even realise it was him.'

'As far as I know, they'd never met.' Chloe blew her nose. 'So no, he probably didn't realise, if Fletcher didn't tell him. Did he?'

'It doesn't seem so.'

'And did he do it?'

'I just don't know,' Ella said. 'I'm sorry.'

Neither of them spoke for a moment, then Ella said, 'I'll keep in touch.'

'What did she say?' Murray asked when she'd hung up.

Her mobile rang before she could speak. 'Marconi.'

'Can you hear me?' a voice whispered.

Skin prickling, Ella held up her hands for the others to be quiet. 'Who is it?'

'It's Gwen Gorrie. Young Miriam's come home.'

TWENTY-FOUR

Jane stood inside Alex's open front door, watching the news crew set up in the garden. Laird must have some pull to have got these guys out to the house straightaway. Alex shifted from foot to foot on the doormat, a wad of posters in his hands. They'd already filmed him in the lounge room, holding a photo of Mia and talking about her, and now wanted some footage of him walking down the path.

'Just a few minutes more,' someone said.

Alex didn't answer. Jane could see that he was looking past the camera at the street, as if Mia might come strolling along at any moment.

'This'll get the word out,' she said to him.

He looked at her, eyes haunted. 'I keep thinking of the worst. I can't get death out of my head. Why do I do that? Why can't I believe that she's fine? It's like I'm giving up, and that means I'm letting her down.'

'You're doing neither,' she said. 'With all the stuff you've seen and done, how could you avoid thinking of those things?'

He shook his head, tears welling in his eyes. Jane hugged him.

'You getting this?' she heard one of the news crew murmur, then there was a crackle from the open doors in their van.

One man went over to listen, then came back and said something to the others. Their expressions changed.

'What is it?' Jane said.

Now Alex turned their way too.

'What is it?' Jane said again, more urgently.

'Police radio scanner,' one of them said. 'They found a girl's body.'

★

Alex could barely breathe as Jane drove down the narrow roadway into the bush in Oatley Park. News vans were already parked behind the blockade of police cars, the van behind them joining the line. Journalists waiting on one side of a stretched police tape called out questions to uniformed officers who ignored them.

He was out of the car before Jane stopped. He pushed past the journalists and under the tape and between the cars. An officer holding a clipboard saw him coming and put out her arm. 'You can't be in here.'

'I'm Alex Churchill. My daughter's missing.'

He heard Jane come up behind him. The officer took her hand off his chest.

'Wait here and I'll get someone,' she said.

Dread overwhelmed him. The trees along the road loomed. On an ordinary day, this would be a quiet and lonely place. The sun beat down on his head and his heart seemed to be missing beats. The journalists had fallen silent. He saw a group of cops look his way while the female officer spoke to them, then one came over.

'I'm Scott Chang.' He stuck out his hand. 'We don't know much right now, you understand. We know it's female and young, but that's it.'

His words seemed to come to Alex down a tunnel full of wind.

'There's no clothing and no ID . . .'

Alex couldn't see. He blinked hard but Chang was just an outline against a hazy grey background.

'. . . dental records and DNA –'

'Just let me see her.'

'I don't know if –'

'I want to see her.'

Chang looked back at the group of watching officers. 'I'll just –'

'No.' Alex shook off Jane's grip and started to walk.

He heard the whir of camera shutters, then Chang said, 'Give it a break,' and the sound stopped. The group of cops stepped aside to let him pass.

Chang touched his arm with gentle fingers. 'It's a crime scene. You need to step in certain places.'

They walked together off the roadway, then stepped up into the bush. Birds and cicadas fell silent. Alex could hear his own breath in his throat and the crackle of dead leaves underfoot. Ahead, through the trees, he saw people in white plastic suits looking at the ground.

'Step where I step, please,' Chang said.

Alex followed him in a loop around the edge of the site, then between two trees. The officers in the white suits watched wordlessly. He heard the buzz of flies and saw a young woman's naked body face down in the leaf litter, the skin purple, the long brown hair stuck to the shoulders and neck with moisture. One discoloured hand, the fingers curled loosely into the palm, was visible by her hip, which bore an irregularly shaped birthmark. There was a Tweety Bird tattoo on her right shoulder.

'Mia doesn't have a birthmark or a tattoo. And the hair's too long,' he heard himself saying. 'So are the fingernails. It's not her.' The bottom grew back on his world. 'It isn't her.'

He didn't remember following Chang back to the road, but once there Jane seized him in a hug.

'It's not her,' he said into her hair. 'She's alive.'

★

Ella pressed Gorrie's buzzer. She let them in, whispering, 'She's still here,' and they eased up the stairs.

'At least there's no fire escape this time,' Murray muttered.

Ella's heart was thudding from the harried drive over. The traffic had been its usual crazy self, making her swerve and swear in equal amounts, and Gorrie had phoned them often to whisper that Holder was still there, going into detail at one point about how she'd go out and stall her if it looked like she was leaving – 'I'll even pretend to fall and break my hip if I have to.' She'd got another text from Callum in the middle of it all too, as a bonus irritation. Now, though, as they approached Holder's closed door, Ella felt her anticipation and excitement build. *Thinks she can hide from us forever, does she?*

They took up position, Murray slightly behind and to one side of Ella. There was no sound from inside the apartment. Ella glanced back at Gorrie's door and saw the peephole was dark. The older woman would be glued to it.

She knocked on Holder's door.

No answer.

She knocked again.

Nothing.

As she turned to Murray to swear, Gorrie inched her door open and sneaked out onto the landing. She put a thin finger to her lips.

'Miriam, are you there? I'm not well, love.'

Still silence.

'I wonder if you might call the ambulance . . . ooh, dear . . .'

Gorrie let out a gasp and fell to her knees so realistically that Ella grabbed her arm. Gorrie squinted up at her in surprise, then Ella heard locks turn and Miriam Holder opened her door.

She gave a gasp of her own and was quick to slam it, but Ella was quicker, shoving her shoe in the gap. Holder let go of the door, and Ella saw a bulging black suitcase by the wall.

'Going somewhere?' she asked.

★

In the interview room at the office, Miriam Holder sat with her arms folded and her legs crossed. Her lipstick had crept into the fine lines around her mouth, worsening her scowl.

'We talked to Bill,' Ella said. 'He's quite upset.'

Holder refolded her arms. 'There's a surprise.'

'This is your chance to tell us your side of the story,' Murray said.

'I know how it works,' she said. 'I want immunity from prosecution.'

'We can't give you that,' Ella said.

'A lesser sentence then,' Holder said. 'A good behaviour bond. Not jail.'

What had they done?

'We can't make any promises,' Ella said.

'You can put it on record that I told you everything.' Holder jabbed a finger into the table. 'You can write down that I cooperated.'

'Fine,' Murray said. 'But the key word is "everything".'

'The money's in an account in the Bahamas. Here are the details.' She pulled a sheet of paper out of her handbag and slapped it down. 'Bill sold his properties and gave me the money and I put it in there. The money he skimmed from his clients is also in there, as is the money – a much lesser amount – that I took from mine.'

'And the rest,' Ella said.

'There is no rest. That's it.'

Ella leaned back in her chair. Murray crossed his legs and tweaked the crease in his trousers, then placed his hands in his lap. Neither of them spoke. The silence stretched out while Miriam Holder stared back at them.

'You can't deny that's more than he told you,' she said finally.

They didn't answer.

Holder pushed the sheet of paper towards them with one finger. 'He didn't give you that, did he? So I'm in front.'

Ella and Murray glanced at each other.

Holder made a scornful sound in the back of her throat. 'He's so weak. I knew he'd crack if anything happened. He probably told you it was all my idea, right? Don't believe a word. I went to talk to him about some investments and could see it in his eyes. We got talking, as you do, and it was him who brought up the stuff a person could do with our knowledge and access. The money you could take without anyone knowing. Put it somewhere safe, plan your way out, and boom. By the time they realise, you're long gone off the cruise ship and spending your days on your own personal beach in a place with no extradition treaty while one luscious little brown boy brings you margaritas and another rubs your toes.'

Ella felt her scalp prickle. The way Holder spoke as if it was someone else breaking the law wasn't lost on her either.

'And don't worry about the wife,' Holder said. 'She's got family money, plus she'll get that big house. Bill told me what it was like between them. They're both better off.'

'How nice of you to think of her,' Ella said.

Holder didn't blink. 'Bill planned it all. I helped carry some of it out, but he did most of it. That needs to be taken into account.'

Ella said, 'Bill was very upset that you hadn't called him.'

Holder folded her arms. 'He calls it love, I call it something else. In my version, you cut your losses and get out while you can.'

Ella stared at her. 'It really doesn't bother you that his life is wrecked, does it?'

'Mine's no bed of roses either,' Holder said. 'You think the CPA will let me stay a member with a criminal record?'

'Where does Marko Meixner fit in?' Ella said.

'What?'

'Recognise that name?'

'That's a name?' Holder said. 'Poor sod.'

'You ever met the man?'

'I have no clue who you're talking about.'

'He's one of Bill's employees.'

Holder shook her head. 'It wasn't like he took me along to work functions.'

'Did you ever go to his office?'

'He came to me. Either at the office or my place.'

'What did he say when he rang you before he hung himself?'

'A lot of gabble,' she said. 'He thought that we were going to get found out because you were there. I told him to calm down, that if you were talking about some dead guy that's all you'd be investigating.'

'The dead guy being Meixner,' Ella said.

Holder shrugged. 'Whoever. It had nothing to do with us, and that's what I kept saying to Bill. But he went on and on, like a little girl, practically in tears, certain we'd get caught and the whole plan would fall apart.'

'You did get caught,' Ella said.

'Only because he panicked.'

'So Meixner didn't know what was going on with the money?' Ella said.

'Nobody knew, and nobody would know now either, if he'd kept it together.'

'How can you be sure Meixner didn't know?' Murray asked.

'Look what Bill did when he thought he was going to be found out,' Holder snapped. 'You think he could've behaved normally if he knew one of his employees had any idea?'

Ella said, 'Did Bill tell you he was going to try to kill himself?'

'I said it was stupid. I told him to just shut up, and you lot would be gone soon enough. He went on about what would people think, he'd lose everything, Prue would get the lot, blah blah. I snapped at him. He started to cry in earnest, and I hung up.'

'And where were you going today?' Murray said.

She dug in her handbag and slapped down an Emirates ticket. 'London for starters, then who knew where.'

Sure. Ella bet Holder had researched places with no extradition treaty and had planned the next leg of her trip down to the finest detail.

'Again, you'd better be taking my cooperation into consideration,' Holder said. 'I give you all this stuff so you don't need to go looking for it yourself. How many man-hours am I saving you? You'd better be letting your boss know.'

'I'm sure he'll be delighted,' Ella said. *You'd make a fine pair.* She felt sorry for Bill Weaver, despite all his lies. 'I don't know what Bill ever saw in you.'

'A kindred spirit. Someone who loves money as much as he does. It's not my fault that somewhere along the line he started thinking he loved me too.'

'And that you loved him back,' Ella said. 'I guess a sexual relationship can sometimes make people think that way.'

'More fool them,' Holder said. 'It's a transaction like any other.'

Ella smiled. 'Actually, more fool you.'

Holder lifted her chin. Ella saw the curiosity in her eyes but knew she'd never stoop to ask.

She picked up the ticket. 'Bill told us nothing. He mentioned the Woolcott, as you'd no doubt guessed he would, but he refused to say anything more until he knew you were safe.'

There it was, crawling across her suddenly pale face: Holder's realisation that she'd dropped herself in it by assuming that he'd told them everything.

'I don't care,' she said, her mouth a tight line.

'I think you do, and deeply,' Ella said, and she and Murray walked out.

★

Bill Weaver was out of bed and dozing in a low chair. His head was back, exposing the bruising on his throat in all its colourful glory, and his chins quivered as he snored. The hospital gown barely covered his thighs and the cotton blanket draped over the top was slipping off.

Ella faked a cough and he woke with a start. 'Hello, Bill.'

'Oh. You.' He rubbed drool from his mouth.

'You look a little cold.' Murray motioned to the exposed skin.

Weaver yanked the blanket back up with a scowl.

Ella leaned against his bed. 'We found Miriam.'

His face lit up. 'She's okay? Was she at the Woolcott?'

'She's healthy all right, but she was at home, packing a suitcase.'

He frowned.

'Bit early, you're thinking?' Ella said. 'You weren't supposed to go on the cruise for a while? Sorry, but she was heading off on her own.'

'I don't believe you.'

She handed him the ticket and the bank information.

Weaver held them in his puffy hands.

Ella said, 'This is when you say "How could she do this to me?".'

'And then we answer that she's trying to get in front, to make it easier on herself,' Murray said. 'She told us about the skimming, about the plan to go on the cruise and not reboard, about the properties you sold.'

Weaver looked up at them without speaking. There was a long pause.

Ella'd thought he might've fallen apart on learning of Holder's betrayal and now felt growing unease as she tried to read his face. 'We found her, you talk. That was our deal.'

He put the ticket and bank details on the bed. 'You showed your hand a bit early though, didn't you?'

You little weasel.

'So you're just going to clam up.'

'I need to protect myself.' His eyes took on a different cast, and he looked like a hard-nosed businessman rather than a for-lorn lover. 'I need to think about my future.'

'You asked us to find her, and we found her,' Ella said. 'If she'd been trying to hang herself, I would've broken down the door and saved her, just like I did you.'

'But she wasn't,' Weaver said.

'What seems to be the problem here?'

Ella turned to see Prue Weaver in a white linen suit, Gucci handbag over her shoulder, and her arms folded over a layer of shiny dangly necklaces.

'There's no problem,' Bill Weaver said.

'That's not how it sounded.' Prue shot a look at him that could've burned a hole in a wall. 'Perhaps you could give us a minute?'

Ella and Murray walked out into the hallway. She could hear Prue's sharp voice, and caught the odd words; something about 'saved your life' and 'silly stupid man' and 'tell the truth'. Her phone buzzed. Callum: *I'm sorry.* Better, but still a delete.

'Maybe she's smarter than we gave her credit for,' Murray whispered.

Ella held up crossed fingers.

Prue Weaver came to the doorway. 'Detectives?'

They went back in.

'Bill has a question for you,' Prue Weaver said.

Weaver licked his lips. He looked somehow smaller than before. 'What did you want to know?'

Ella shot a grateful look at Prue. 'What was the topic of the conversations you had with Marko Meixner in the corridors?'

'He said he needed money, and asked for a raise. I don't have authority to give him one, and nobody higher up wanted to know about it. Then he asked if I could somehow send more work his way. But I couldn't do that either.'

'Why did he need money?' Ella asked.

'He told me his wife was expecting and asked me not to tell anyone. I wanted to help but I couldn't. And now he's dead and he'll never know his child.'

Ella ignored the crocodile tears he blinked away. 'Why didn't you tell us this when we first spoke to you?'

'All I could think about was my own skin. That you were there because you knew what I'd been doing.'

'Even when we started asking about him?' Murray said.

He nodded and wiped an eye.

The bastard was sorry for himself, not Marko. Ella glared at him. 'What about the other stuff you said about him that day? How much of that was true?'

'All of it. Marko was a fine young man. His work performance was excellent. He's going to be missed.'

But not by you, Ella thought, because you'll never work there again.

'What about the calls that you took in your office,' she asked, 'when you told Peter to leave you alone? And when he overheard you saying, "No, no!"?'

Weaver glanced at his wife and at least had the decency to blush. 'Miriam. She wanted more money. She wanted me to take increasing amounts, but I was worried about getting caught. She bullied me into most of it, you know.'

Prue said, 'Hmm.'

Exactly what I was thinking.

Ella said, 'You know that Marko got at least one similar call?'

'About stealing money?'

'No, I mean where he was saying the same thing.'

'I don't know anything about that,' Bill Weaver said.

'Would you have known if Marko was taking money?' Murray said.

'Absolutely,' he said. 'I was all over everything there. I had to be, to make sure what I was doing was hidden.'

Ella looked at Murray. This was feeling more and more like a dead-end.

'We're going to talk to you again,' she said to Bill.

'He'll be happy to help,' Prue said.

'As if I have a choice,' Bill muttered.

'I told him the choice,' Prue said to Ella. 'He could tell the truth for once in his goddamn life and I won't divorce him, or he can keep quiet and I'll take him to the cleaner's.'

The couple glared at each other. Good luck, Ella thought.

'We'll be in touch,' she said.

She and Murray walked out through the hospital.

'Now what?' Murray said.

She thumped his arm. 'Back to where we were before.'

★

Alex was outside McDonald's in Maroubra, a pile of posters tucked under his arm, wrestling with a tangle in the sticky tape, when his mobile rang. He almost dropped it in his hurry to answer. 'Yes?'

'It's Brent Mason. We've traced the mobile number Mia's been in touch with. It was bought from a service station in Mascot by someone named Shannon Pitman, who gave an address in Beaconsfield. Do you know that name or anyone in that area?'

'No.'

His hand was slippery on the phone. Jane came over with her own wad of posters and stood watching his face.

Mason said, 'There's nothing on that name in our records or in the electoral rolls, so it could be someone under eighteen. We're going there now and we'll keep you posted.'

'What's the exact address?' Alex's heart thudded in his chest, but his mind was clear and sharp as glass.

'I can't tell you that,' Mason said. 'I know what you'd do, because I'd do the same. I'll call you when we know anything. We're on our way.'

Alex hung up and told Jane what Mason had said. 'Beaconsfield's pretty small. How long would it take to find a couple of cop cars outside someone's house?'

The suburb was fifteen minutes away. Jane drove and Alex sat forward in the passenger seat, his phone in his hands, willing her to drive faster. She floored it along Anzac Parade then Gardeners Road, weaving through traffic, then swung right on the orange into O'Riordan. Alex stared down the street. No police cars in sight. Jane slowed and they looked both ways down Doody Street, then she accelerated along to Collins.

Alex looked left along it. His mouth was dry. 'Nothing.'

She turned right. Alex looked down the next street, then the next. 'There!'

Jane yanked the wheel. Two police cars were parked by the left kerb, nose to tail, two officers talking to Brent Mason in the street.

Jane pulled up and Alex leapt out. 'Where is she?'

'She's not here,' Mason said.

Alex started towards the bearded middle-aged man who stood on the doorstep of the house with a fourth officer. Mason grabbed his arm.

'No such person lives here,' he said, 'and the guy doesn't even know the name. He let us search the place. His wife and kids are inside.'

'Kids? Are they . . . Boyfriend?'

'All under five.' Mason let him go.

Alex felt faint. 'Neighbours?'

'Either elderly or young families.'

'Then why this address?' Jane said behind him. 'Where's this Shannon?'

'The whole thing was possibly made up,' Mason said. 'You can buy pre-paid SIM cards and fill in the details online, with nothing to prove you are who you say you are.'

'So there's nothing here for us at all?' Alex couldn't breathe. Spots appeared before his eyes.

'We're tracing the number through the towers, which pick up a signal when it's turned on, and we're doing the same with Mia's phone. Unfortunately, both are turned off right now, but they'll check them sometime and we'll be waiting.'

Alex felt like he was falling.

'I haven't heard back from Immigration about your ex-wife, but I'll call them again,' Mason said. 'Mia's photo's all over the web, the news sites and everywhere. Every police car on the street has it, and fireys and your lot are doing the same. One way or another, we'll track her down.'

Alex found himself walking back to the car without answering. He couldn't feel his legs, and his ears were ringing. He'd expected to find her, and instead there was nothing. Worse than nothing, because the person she'd been talking to had deliberately hidden their tracks, knowing that they'd eventually be the object of a search.

TWENTY-FIVE

Murray parked in the same place outside Grace Michaels's house. They walked up the gravel drive, their shoes crunching on fallen twigs and dead leaves swept into ridges by the recent rain, the same kind of debris spilling from the gutters on the roof. Moss coated the mortar between the white-painted bricks of the front porch and the air smelled of decaying leaf litter and damp earth. New security screens covered the windows and the door. When Ella found the handle locked, she knocked hard on the frame. Murray stood back and surveyed the street.

The door inside the screen opened. Ella could just see Michaels's shape through the thick steel wire.

'Remember us?' Ella said.

'Yes.' She made no move to open the door, and said nothing else.

'Can we talk?'

'I'm on leave,' Michaels said.

'It's very important and it won't take long.'

'I'm on leave,' she said again.

'We'd appreciate it if we could talk for a few minutes.'

'It's really not a good time. My son's sick. We were up at the hospital last night. He has asthma and he's just gone off to sleep.'

'We can talk quietly in the next room,' Ella said. 'I promise you it won't take long.'

She couldn't see Michaels's face, but after a long moment the woman unlocked the door.

'Thank you.' Ella stepped inside, past green lights flashing on a shiny new alarm keypad on the wall.

Michaels didn't answer. She relocked the screen door behind them, then closed and locked the front door. She gestured for them to go on into a living room, where a muted TV played a *Friends* rerun and a boy of around five slept curled under a blanket with his cheek on his folded hands. A framed picture of Michaels in a wedding dress, smiling beside a tall man in a suit, stood on top of the TV beside two of the boy at a younger age. A mobile phone and a cordless landline handset sat on a coffee table next to the TV remote, and a three iron golf club lay on the rug underneath.

'Practising your swing?' Ella said.

'I keep meaning to put that away.'

Michaels sat on the lounge next to the boy. She was dressed in khakis and a blue T-shirt and wore tightly laced runners on her feet. Her dark shoulder-length hair was in a ponytail. A tiny gold cross hung on a chain around her neck, and a plain gold wedding band glinted on her left hand when she stroked the sleeping boy's hip.

Murray stayed on his feet while Ella sat in an armchair.

'You're married,' Ella said.

'So?'

'You weren't wearing any jewellery when we met you at the office.'

'I keep my private life private.'

'I can understand that,' Ella said. 'What's your little boy's name?'

Michaels's eyes held hers. 'I don't mean to be rude but I'd like to get on with it.'

'Certainly,' Ella said. 'Have you seen Paul Canning lately?'

'Not since we talked about him the other day. I'm not due to see him again until next week.'

'Will that be for an arranged meeting or an unexpected drop-in?' Murray said.

'I don't know,' Michaels said. 'My diary's at work.'

'How long have you been off?'

She tucked the blanket around the boy's shoulders. 'Since he got sick. A couple of days.'

'And when do you think you'll be back?' Ella said.

'When he's better.'

'Was your husband at the hospital last night too?'

She shook her head. 'He's overseas.'

'Holiday or business?'

'In East Timor, with the army.'

'Must be tough,' Ella said.

Grace Michaels shrugged. 'It's what we know.'

Ella looked at the boy. His skin was perfect. He breathed evenly through his mouth and she could see his neat white teeth.

'He has your chin,' she said to Michaels.

Michaels raised her eyebrows. 'Is that what you came here to say?'

'What do you honestly think of Canning?' Ella asked.

'He's doing well.'

'So you think he's reformed,' Murray said.

'I do.'

Ella picked up the three iron and rolled the shaft between her palms. 'When did you get the security screens?'

'I'm not following your line of conversation.'

'I'm curious,' Ella said. 'They look new. Do you like them?'

'Do I *like* them?'

'I've seen them advertised on TV. I wondered if they're any good. Do they make you feel secure?'

'What are you trying to say, Detective?'

'Security's important when you have a family,' Ella said.

'Kids are so vulnerable. Which reminds me – when we met the other day I didn't get to finish telling you about our case, did I? The victim's name is Marko Meixner. He went under a train. He testified against Canning in the trial seventeen years ago; was key in getting him convicted, in fact. That's why we were checking Canning's alibi, which you so ably provided. Marko was a lovely guy, by all accounts. His wife's lovely too. And four months pregnant. I reckon she's concerned about security as well.'

Michaels lowered her gaze and touched her son's foot.

'I might tell her you have these screens,' Ella said. 'What's your little boy's name again?'

'Elias,' Michaels said faintly.

'Nice name,' Ella said.

'It's my father's.'

Ella nodded. 'Has Paul Canning threatened you and your family?'

'No.'

'You're sure?' Ella said.

'Of course.'

They stared at each other for a long moment.

'He's done it before.'

'He's not doing it to me.'

'We can help you,' Murray said.

'I don't need any help.' Michaels stood up. 'I think it'd be best if you left.'

Ella put down the golf club and smiled at the sleeping boy. On her way to the door, she motioned towards the new alarm keypad. 'This come with the screens in a package deal?'

Michaels unlocked the doors and held them open, her jaw tight. She kept her gaze fixed on the trees in the yard, and the second Ella and Murray were on the porch and clear, she slammed and relocked the doors.

Ella and Murray walked down the driveway.

'Are you thinking what I'm thinking?' she said.

'I believe I am.'

She stood at the car door and looked back at the house. 'Reckon she'll ever admit to it?'

'Not if he's threatened that kid.'

She checked her watch. It was time they headed back for the meeting. 'Think Langley will believe us?'

Murray just looked at her.

'I know, I know.' She got in the car. 'Let's go.'

★

Alex had gone home for half an hour, but even with Jane there the silence and emptiness was too much, so they were back out in the car, driving, looking. They'd been to two DVD rental shops, a skatepark, two McDonald's restaurants and a KFC store, various takeaway joints and the forecourts of three supermarkets where groups of teenagers sat. He'd handed out posters and asked people to call him. Either nobody had seen her, or nobody was saying.

His phone rang as Jane pulled into a Red Rooster. He recognised Brent Mason's number. 'Have you found her?'

'Not yet,' Mason said. 'And we're still trying to locate the mobiles. I heard from Immigration though. Your ex-wife, Helen, is in the country.'

'What?' Alex felt his face go slack.

'She's been back for almost a year. She's no longer living at the address that she listed on the forms when she came back in, however, and we haven't been able to trace her since then.'

Alex's head was spinning. 'What about a driver's licence? Electoral rolls? Rental agreement?'

'We've checked,' Mason said. 'We know she hasn't left, we just don't know where she is. We're thinking a press conference tomorrow and you ask her to come forward.'

'You believe she has Mia?'

'Why hide so completely unless you want to get away with something?' Mason said.

Alex thought he was going to be sick. 'I have to go.' He opened the door and put his legs out, his head hanging down.

Jane said, 'What'd he say?'

'Helen's back.'

'That's great! If Mia's with Helen, she's got to be safe.'

'But if Helen has her, she's deliberately hiding, she's deliberately doing stuff so I don't know where they are.' He was sweaty. 'Is she going to try to take her out of the country? She can't do that. She can't just come in and wreck everything like that.'

'It'll be okay,' Jane said.

'And that's if Mia really is with her,' he said. 'It could be a coincidence that she's back. She's been here for more than a year, after all, and never got in touch. It could still be some creep Mia met online. It could be anyone.' Images of the dead girl in the bush and the despair of the other Mia's parents filled his mind.

It's not a killer. Don't think like that. It's Helen.

But if that's true, how do I find her?

Nat had said she hadn't heard from Helen, but she'd sounded odd. Distinctly odd, he thought. He'd put it down to what had happened in the past, but now he picked up his phone.

'Alex,' Nat answered. 'Any news?'

'Helen's come back.'

'Really? When? Have you seen her?'

'Immigration told me.' He closed his eyes to focus on her tone, on any background noise. 'They don't know where she is though. You're sure you have no idea?'

'I really wish I did.'

There was a brief silence, then Alex said, 'I have to say I'm a little surprised at you. I thought you might've called today to see how things were going.'

'I'm sorry, I've been so busy.'

Or else she knew for sure that Mia was all right.

Alex said, 'You said earlier that you'd like to help. Can you come and put up posters?'

'I wish I could, but I've hurt my arm and I can't drive.'

Oh, really. He narrowed his eyes at Jane. 'How did you hurt it?'

'Caught it between a boat and a motor.'

'How about I pick you up?' he said. 'Drop you home after.' He felt hypersensitive to her reluctance. What was she hiding?

'I wouldn't be able to put posters up,' she said. 'My arm's really bad. How do you know if you've broken a bone?'

'Go to hospital and get an X-ray.'

Another silence, then Alex heard the male voice murmur in the background.

'I'm sorry,' Nat said, but he didn't know whether she was speaking to him or the man, and then she hung up.

He looked at Jane. 'We need to go there.'

'Where's there?'

'Boatyard near Neutral Bay.'

She nodded. 'You want to call Mason?'

'He'll tell me to stay away, that they'll check it out, and then they'll take ages to get there. Or she'll lie again and they'll leave. But I know Nat. We have this . . . past thing. I think she'll tell me the truth if I ask her face to face.'

She nodded again, then glanced at the Red Rooster store. 'Time for a bathroom stop first?'

★

Ella stared out the passenger window, trying to get it straight in her head. Ten minutes after they'd left Grace Michaels's house, she grabbed Murray's arm. 'Pull over.'

Murray braked hard and swung into a service station. 'What's −'

'Shut up for a second,' Ella said. 'It was pretty clear that Michaels is lying, right? She's got new security screens, a new alarm set-up − she's a frightened woman. That means Canning got to her, and has probably threatened her and no doubt that kid, and *that* means she's going to keep up that lie as long as she possibly can.'

'Right,' Murray said.

'So she's not going to admit it to us unless we find a way to (a) open her defences and (b) get her and her son to somewhere safe,' Ella said. 'I think if we can get her to tell us what's going on, we'll be able to crack Natasha Osborne. I reckon Osborne's either involved or she probably knows who is, because Canning couldn't do all that himself, could he? If he was following Marko, he had to have someone drive him, drop him off outside Town Hall or whatever.'

She thought of the dark grey Mazda she'd seen leaving the boatyard the night before.

Murray was nodding. 'Okay.'

'Grace Michaels would be terrified that Canning would find out she's told and then not get locked up again,' Ella said. 'We need to show her that we'll be able to get all the evidence we need to put him away for good.'

'Okay,' Murray said again.

She looked at him. 'You see where I'm going with this?'

'I think so,' he said. 'But how are you going to persuade her to talk?'

'Just get us back there.' She pulled out her phone as he drove back onto the street. When Langley answered, she laid out the case as best she could, concluding, 'I think if we can promise to keep Grace Michaels and her son safe, she'll tell us the truth.'

'You think,' Langley said. 'You don't even know for certain that she's involved.'

'Then there's no harm in making the promise,' Ella said.

'You need hard evidence –'

'And I'll get it once she knows she and her boy are safe,' Ella said.

Langley didn't answer. She crossed her fingers, and tried to stay silent, but finally couldn't resist saying, 'Nothing's lost if I'm wrong, but there's a lot to gain if I'm right.'

Murray frowned. 'Don't make it about you,' he hissed.

'And by a lot I mean the safety of a mother and child,' she added to Langley.

Another long moment of silence, then Langley said, 'Tell her we'll do what we can, contingent on her disclosing everything she knows.'

'Thanks,' Ella said. She hung up and looked at Murray. 'Can't you drive any faster?'

★

Jane sat on the toilet, her elbows on her knees and her forehead in her hands, looking at more spots of blood.

Shit.

She rifled through her bag and found a fresh pad. The pregnancy test kit was there too, silent and ominous in its paper bag. If she did it now, at least she'd know. But this was the bathroom at Red Rooster, and three teenage girls were laughing by the sinks, and Alex was walking anxious laps of the car outside, desperate to find his daughter.

She rammed the package to the bottom of her bag and zipped up both it and herself.

On the way out through the restaurant, her phone rang. Laird. She hesitated. He had helped: Mia's photo and details would be on TV soon, not just a few power poles and the internet. Practically everyone watched the evening news.

'Hi,' she answered.

'Hello,' he said. 'Has she been found yet?'

'Not yet.' She could see Alex in the car park, his head on his folded arms on the roof of the car. 'I can't really talk.'

'Once she's on our news, the other channels will pick it up,' Laird said. 'She'll be everywhere. She'll be found tomorrow if not sooner.'

'Let's hope so. I have to go.'

'You've heard something?'

'Not really.' Alex was looking her way now. 'His ex might be back, that's all. We're going to see her sister.'

'Sounds promising,' Laird said. 'Where's that?'

Alex moved to the back of the car and spread his arms in a clear *come on!* gesture.

'Some boatyard in Neutral Bay, somewhere around there.' She pushed out through the doors. 'I have to go.'

'The police know?'

'I'll talk to you later.' She hung up and hurried across the asphalt. Alex was already in the car. 'Sorry.'

He didn't look at her. 'Can we just go?'

TWENTY-SIX

The afternoon sky was turning orange when Ella knocked on Grace Michaels's door.

The parole officer opened it as she'd done earlier, keeping the screen locked. The light was on in the hall now, and Ella could see her. 'I have nothing to say.'

'We know what's going on,' Ella said.

'Nothing's going on.'

'How did he do it? Did he follow you? Did he get inside your house somehow?'

It was just a guess, but Michaels blanched.

Ella said, 'When we first spoke to him, he referred to you as Mrs Michaels. But you don't wear your wedding ring at work. You have no photos on your desk. You hide yourself well. So for him to know that, he had to have seen you somewhere else.'

Michaels's hand was white on the door. 'He might've been guessing.'

'But he wasn't, was he?' Ella said. 'We can help you. I've talked to our boss. We can take you and Elias somewhere safe until we have Canning, and we can make certain that he'll go behind bars and stay there.'

'You forget who you're talking to. I know how the justice system works.'

'Once you've told us what happened, we can get Natasha Osborne to tell what she knows too,' Ella said. 'And then we'll find the friend who helped him. We're already looking through his past associates and trying to link up a car I saw near the boatyard. Mrs Michaels, look at me. If we don't stop him now, what will happen? Is he going to feel that he can trust you forever? Will he one day decide that the risk is too great?'

Michaels was biting her lip. Tears brimmed in her eyes. Ella felt bad, but better this than she and Elias turned up dead somewhere. Natasha too.

'Don't let him get away with it,' she said.

Michaels unlocked the door. 'You'd better come in.'

In the living room, Elias was sitting up on the lounge, his gaze fixed on the TV screen where a cartoon bird danced and shrieked. Michaels motioned them past him and into the next room. They sat around a dark timber dining table.

Michaels fiddled with the cross on the chain around her neck, then looked up at them. 'I lied. Paul Canning did threaten me.' She glanced into the living room, as if checking where Elias was, then took an envelope from the top shelf of a sideboard. 'I've only handled these by the corners.'

Ella pulled a pair of gloves from her pocket and put them on before opening the envelope and taking out the four photos. Murray looked over her shoulder. The first picture showed Grace Michaels studying a packet of mince behind a supermarket trolley while Elias hung off the front. The second had them talking in a car at a red light. The third showed Elias in school uniform and climbing on play equipment with three other children. The fourth made Ella swallow. 'This is your living room.'

'Taken with a flash at night,' Michaels said. 'He was in here when we were asleep.'

Ella felt cold fingers touch her spine. 'No wonder you had to lie.'

'When did it start?' Murray said.

'The day before our first meeting,' Michaels said. 'He obviously had it all planned out. We were due to meet on a Tuesday. The pictures turned up in the letterbox on the Monday, the same day that he got out of Long Bay. I'd met with Osborne a couple of weeks before, checked out what work Canning would be doing, where he'd live and so on, and it all seemed good. She seemed all right, though a little naive about what she was getting herself into. But clearly, she or someone else followed me afterwards, back to the office, then here to home.' She shook her head. 'A parole officer based in Long Bay had been working with Canning to get him ready, and said he was doing well. He'd had some issues early on, got into fights and so on a number of times, but later made it through the violent offenders program with no trouble. None of the psychologists or anyone else he worked with had concerns, and there were no qualms whatsoever about letting him out. I'm sure he wasn't blackmailing them, because it would be almost impossible over that length of time and in that scope. I think he's one of those guys that manages to keep a lid on their rage for years, knowing that one day they'll get out and have their revenge. For them, that goal is worth any wait.'

'What happened when you met?' Ella asked.

'He came into the office on the Tuesday, all smiles, but watching me – I knew he could see I'd got the photos.'

Ella held back a shiver.

'The office was full of people, so neither of us said anything out of the ordinary,' Michaels went on. 'At the end, he said he looked forward to speaking to me again. He rang here that night and told me I had to do what he said, that the photos proved that we weren't safe anywhere, that if I loved my child at all I'd keep my mouth shut.' She was white. 'I did, but I couldn't stop thinking that I would always be a threat, like you said. I decided that I had to do what was best for now, had to protect us now, and that meant doing what he said, and when my husband got back I'd ask him to transfer interstate, and maybe then we'd be safe. I haven't told him anything because he can't get back and it would only send him crazy with worry.' Michaels looked past them to the living room where her son watched TV, her face full of fear. 'Like I feel.'

★

Langley, Kemsley and Gawande arrived soon after, and Ella and Murray met them on the verandah.

'Looks like the dark grey Mazda you saw at the boatyard belongs to the wife of one of Canning's old cellmates,' Kemsley said. 'Danny O'Hara, lives at Pendle Hill.'

'Same suburb where the SIM card was bought that made the calls to Marko's work,' Ella said. 'I bet we find that car on CCTV stopping somewhere around Town Hall station, O'Hara dropping Canning off. I bet O'Hara was the one who followed Michaels and took the photos too.'

'Good work, even though you shouldn't have been at the boatyard to see the car,' Langley said gruffly.

Ella nodded. *About time you recognised a bit of quality effort.*

Gawande had parked close to the house, and Grace Michaels walked out to the car with one arm around Elias's shoulders. He was wide-eyed and dressed in blue pyjamas and slippers and a snugly tied Star Wars dressing gown. He clutched a figurine.

'Jango Fett,' Kemsley said. 'Cool.'

Elias shot him a smile as he climbed into the back of the car. Michaels put her overnight bag in, then glanced back at Ella. 'I'm sorry,' she said.

'Don't be,' Ella said. 'And don't worry. We'll get him.'

Michaels got in and shut the door, then the car moved off down the driveway, the tyres crunching the twigs and gravel. Ella, Murray, Langley and Kemsley followed, heading for their cars on the street.

'People are meeting us at the boatyard, and water police

are on standby,' Langley said. 'He's going to feel cornered with his back to the water, and we don't want him turning Osborne into a hostage, so we're going to go in quietly and grab him before he knows a thing about it.'

Ella squeezed her hands into fists.

★

Alex walked into the workshop without knocking, Jane right on his heels.

'Nat,' he said.

She looked up from an outboard and dropped a screwdriver with a clatter to the floor. Her left wrist was heavily bandaged and she held it carefully away from her body.

'I promise you, she isn't here,' she said.

'I'm going to see for myself.'

He walked through the shed, pushed open the door to the tiny empty bathroom at the back, then headed for the stairs leading up to a closed door.

It opened when he was halfway up and a man in grey work-shorts and a black T-shirt stepped out. 'Help you?'

Alex looked up at him. 'I'm searching for my daughter.'

'Nobody up here,' the man said.

'Paulie, it's okay,' Nat said. 'He's my brother-in-law.'

'Whatever,' Paul said. 'There's nobody up there.'

Alex took a step up, but Paul took two steps down, his heavy workboots thudding on the wood, and loomed over him.

Alex glanced at Jane and Nat, who'd come over to the bottom of the stairs. Jane looked anxious, Nat outright frightened. All Alex felt was determination.

He put out his hand. 'Alex Churchill.'

Paul took it. 'Paul Canning. Now we've met, but you're still not going into my home.'

He slowly increased the pressure on Alex's hand, then bent his arm back on itself to try to force him back down a step.

Alex moved sideways instead. 'Let me go up and see, then I'll get out of your hair.'

'No.' The pressure increased more.

Alex tried not to let the pain show. 'You know that this makes you look like you have something to hide?'

'You can leave now.' He bent Alex's wrist back further. Alex had to step down.

'Is this what you did to Nat too?' he said. 'Twisted her arm until she did what you told her?'

Paul's brown eyes hardened. 'I said you can leave.'

'Let me check inside and then I will.'

A helicopter flew low overhead. Paul glanced up at the roof with a scowl.

'You can watch me while I look,' Alex said. His hand throbbed, but he would neither let go nor give in.

The helicopter came back. This time it hovered, and the downdraught rattled something that was loose in the roof.

'What the fuck?' Paul shoved Alex out of the way and went down the steps and across the concrete floor.

Alex stumbled up the steps and almost fell through the door. Inside, he saw a small sparsely furnished flat, the kitchen and living area empty of people. The bedroom, with its one double bed and small bathroom, equally so. There was no sign that Mia had ever been here.

He went back down the stairs two at a time, ready to throttle Paul for wasting his time and wanting to twist Nat's other arm until she told him where the fuck her sister was. Paul, Nat and Jane were all at the door, the women looking up at the helicopter, Paul scanning the area.

Alex grabbed Nat's arm and spun her to face him.

'Where is she?' he shouted over the noise.

Before Nat could answer, Paul shoved them back inside the shed. Jane stumbled and fell to the floor. Natasha was pushed into Alex and flinched as her arm was caught between them.

Alex put his face close to hers. 'Where?'

'I don't know! I don't know!' Natasha cradled her arm and started to cry.

Alex believed her. He needed to move on, get out of there, keep looking.

But Paul pulled the big door closed and shoved a length of rebar through the latch.

Alex grasped it to yank it out but Paul pushed him away.

'Open that door,' Alex said. 'I have to find my daughter.'

'Think I give a shit about your kid?' Paul rummaged in a bin of rags on a shelf.

Alex grabbed the rebar again. She was out there somewhere. Mason might have a lead on the phones by now. Tips might be coming in from the news broadcast. The rebar was jammed in tight and he heaved, then Paul pointed a handgun at his face.

'Back away.'

Alex could see the round black hole and Paul's finger on the trigger. 'I have to find my daughter.'

'Get the fuck away from the door.'

'Alex, you can't help her if you're dead,' Jane said behind him.

'I won't say it again.' Paul pressed the barrel to his cheek.

Alex let go of the bar and stepped back.

TWENTY-SEVEN

Bulletproof vest cinched up tight, Ella moved as part of a line across the car park, watching the workshop's open door for movement, listening for voices. She smelled the salt in the air and felt the blood pumping hard in her veins.

There were three other cars parked near Osborne's blue truck. Ella hoped no customers were about to get caught up in the situation. She was moving past the truck when the news helicopter appeared, swooping over the trees and coming low across the car park, then turning and hovering, a camera's big black lens sticking out the open door. Dust blew up in clouds and the rotor noise made the air pulsate in Ella's ears.

'What the fuck?' Langley shouted, and gestured wildly for the chopper to leave.

But it was too late. Ella saw Canning and Osborne and someone else in the workshop doorway, then saw Canning spot them and turn and slam the door shut.

She started to run, weapon held low, eyes fixed on the door, ready to duck and dodge if Canning appeared again. But the door stayed closed. She reached the corner and tucked herself around it, Murray pushing in behind her. Langley and

Kemsley took the other side of the door; Marion Pilsiger and Aadil Hossain ran to the far corner of the building.

The door was metal, and the U-shaped handle was right next to her. Langley signalled for her to test it. She grasped it carefully, heart louder than the helicopter's rotor in her ears, imagining Canning waiting inside with a weapon of his own. She tried to slide it along, then shook her head. Locked. Langley frowned.

Overhead the camera in the helicopter followed everything.

★

Jane felt Alex's rage through the tight grip of his hand. On her other side, Natasha's palm was damp with fear. Paul had shouted at them to hold hands, so he could see what they were doing, she guessed, and now he shoved them across the concrete floor to a closed door at the back of the shed. The roof rattled under the helicopter's noise, and Paul's face was wild, his eyes everywhere like he was trying to think what to do.

Natasha was weeping and trembling, her injured arm cradled against her body. Jane glanced at Alex. He glared at Paul, his face red, his jaw set.

'Where're the keys to that cruiser?' Paul barked.

'What?' Natasha said.

'The keys! The fucking keys to the fucking cabin cruiser!'

She sobbed. 'On the thing there, on the thing.'

'Fuck's sake.' Keeping the gun on them, he swept his free hand along the workbench. Tools and bits of machinery crashed to the floor.

Jane felt Alex move a little. She tightened her grip. *Don't do anything.* The cops were outside; nobody was going anywhere. It was better to stay safe as long as you could.

Paul grabbed up a set of keys and pushed past them to the back door. He listened for a moment – as if anything could be heard over the roar of the helicopter, Jane thought – then pointed the gun at them.

'Get over here,' he snapped.

★

Ella and Murray were nearing the back corner of the workshop, hoping to find another way in, when they heard Pilsiger shout, 'Police! Drop your weapon!'

Ella inched up to the corner to see Canning backing towards the dock with his arm around Natasha Osborne's neck, a handgun screwed into her temple. Walking from the other side of the shed were Pilsiger and Hossain, guns drawn. Facing Canning and walking hand in hand were the paramedics who'd taken Marko Meixner to hospital after his car crash.

'What the fuck?' Murray hissed. 'What are they doing here?'

Ella had no idea and no time to think about it.

Natasha stumbled as Canning dragged her along. Ella could see one of her wrists was bandaged. Canning had a set of keys in his hand. He was going to take a boat, and the hostages with him, she guessed. But out on the harbour, right in the middle of the entrance to the bay, waited the water police boat.

'Give it up, Canning,' she shouted over the noise of the helicopter. 'Look over your shoulder. Where you going to go?'

'Fuck you.'

'Look behind you!' she called again.

He kept moving.

They were all on the dock now: Canning and the sobbing white-faced Natasha, the two paramedics, then, five metres back, with no hope of a clear shot, Ella, Murray, Marion Pilsiger and Aadil Hossain. The helicopter hovered overhead, its blades chopping the air, the wind lashing the water and whipping the cables against the masts.

'There's nowhere to go,' Ella shouted.
But Canning kept moving.

★

Alex's mind raced. Whatever happened, he was not getting on
any boat. Mia was out there somewhere and he had to find her.
Plus he could see the water police boat bobbing on the swell and
knew Paul wouldn't be getting out of the bay, no matter what.

The noise of the helicopter was deafening. He could hardly
hear Natasha, who was almost hysterical. He felt bad for her,
but he couldn't help her directly. What he could do was get
himself and Jane out of the way of the police. And here and
now was his best chance.

Up ahead on the dock there was clear space on both sides,
gaps between moored boats. The water was grey, the surface
rumpled by the helicopter.

He squeezed Jane's hand. She squeezed back.

Keeping his eyes on Paul, he put his free hand behind his
back, fingers spread and ready to count down. Then he loosened
his grip on Jane's, and tightened it once, twice – and hoped she
understood that something was going to happen on three.

★

The grey planks of the dock clanked under Ella's feet. The
water police boat was heading towards them.

She saw the male paramedic put his hand behind his back,
fingers spread at first then folding down, one by one, little finger first.

'Get ready,' Ella murmured to Murray, as adrenaline
thumped into her blood.

As the paramedic tucked his thumb into his closed fist
he wrenched his other hand free of his partner's, gave her an
almighty shove into the water, and leapt the other way himself.

Ella now had a clear view of Canning and Natasha. She saw Canning start at the splashes, and his eyes dart between her and Murray. He was nearing the last boat, big and white with two silver motors.

'You're surrounded,' Langley bellowed on a megaphone from somewhere behind Ella. 'Water police are waiting. You will not get away.'

'Fuck you!'

Natasha Osborne flinched as he rammed the gun tighter into the side of her head.

No, fuck you, Ella thought. She was aiming straight at him now. She could see his arm and part of his chest and legs. Her breath was coming hard in her throat, her heart thundering in her chest, her hair blowing in the chopper's downdraught.

She glanced past him at the boat. The step at the back was high. He was going to have trouble getting Osborne in. She tightened her grip and narrowed her eyes.

'Give it up,' Langley shouted.

Canning reached the boat. He hesitated.

What will you do? Ella thought, her eyes fixed on his chest. Push her in first, or drag her in last?

Canning lifted his leg to climb the step. While he was off balance, Osborne kicked out against one of the motors and they both went over backwards on the planks. Ella started running, Murray pounding alongside her.

A shot rang out.

Ella expected to see a puff of blood spray and Osborne slump over motionless, but there was no blood and she was still struggling. Canning seized her neck, and as Ella and Murray reached him he raised the gun.

Ella squeezed her trigger and saw red flowers appear on his chest, flowers that spread and spread and spread.

TWENTY-EIGHT

'You don't understand,' Alex said. 'I need to go.'
The senior detective with the shaved head and blue tie stared at him. Alex stared back, soaking wet, still dripping water onto the dock. Jane sat, just as wet, on a bench nearby. The helicopter was long gone and the only sound was the slurp of water under the dock and the murmur of cops around Canning's sheet-covered body. Alex and Jane had scrambled out of the water after the shooting and attended to Canning but the blood loss was massive and the location of the bullet entry and exits meant his heart and lungs had been severely and fatally damaged. There'd been nothing they could do.

'What you need to do is sit down and wait to be interviewed,' the detective said.

'My daughter's missing and I have to find her.'

'You've reported this?'

'Brent Mason from Missing Persons knows all about it.'

'That's good,' the detective said. 'These situations are best left to us. Just as medical emergencies are best dealt with by you.'

'You're not hearing me,' Alex said. 'I'm her father and I'm leaving.'

'No, you're not.' The detective folded his arms. Alex guessed he was used to getting his way. This was not one of those times, however, and Alex stepped around him. He'd get in his car and . . . what? He wasn't sure. Nat had been his big hope. He believed her when she said she knew nothing. But he'd get in his car, find a phone and call Brent Mason, and go from there.

The detective grabbed his arm. 'I told you to sit down.'

'Let go of me.'

'This is a police investigation.'

'I'll give my statement later.' Alex tried to pull free. The cop tightened his grip. Alex bristled. 'Let me go, now, or arrest me.'

The female detective from the train hurried over. 'Alex, can I talk to you for a second?'

'I need to find my daughter.'

'Just a few minutes.'

She seemed more of an ally than the shaven-headed man. If Alex helped her now, she might help him in return. 'Fine.'

The male detective held on to Alex's arm for a few more seconds then released him.

'Over here,' the woman said, and Alex followed. She stuck out her hand. 'Ella Marconi.'

'Alex Churchill.' Her hand was warm against his cold wet skin. She was white around the eyes and seemed distracted. He said, 'Are you okay?'

'Sure.' But she couldn't hold his gaze. He saw her glance at the covered body.

'You didn't have any other choice,' he said. 'And you saved her life.'

For an instant he saw tears in her eyes, then she blinked and they were gone. 'I was just talking to Natasha. She said she's your sister-in-law?'

Alex nodded. 'That's why I came here. I thought she might know where my ex – her sister – and my daughter are. That's why I need to leave, to call Mason in Missing Persons and keep looking for her.'

'What happened in there?'

'The guy threatened us, pulled a gun, told us to walk with him out the back.' He wanted to get going. He looked at his watch but it had stopped in the water.

Ella took out her phone and dialled a number. 'Mason in Missing Persons please.' She listened, then said, 'Have him call me back straightaway, then. I'm with Alex Churchill.' She hung up. 'It'll probably be just a few minutes. After which I'll help you get out of here.'

'Deal.' Alex looked past her to where Natasha sat against the shed, her arms wrapped around her legs and her forehead on her knees. 'Is she okay?'

'She's shattered,' Ella said.

'Can I talk to her?'

'Just to say hi. Nothing about what happened.'

When he got close he heard her weeping. He'd seen her cry like that once before, on Mia's fifth birthday. When everyone else had left after the party, Alex had gone back downstairs after putting Mia to bed and found Natasha lying naked on a rug on the floor, rose petals that she must've brought with her scattered all around, candles burning everywhere. She'd reached out to him, but he'd stayed in the doorway, completely taken aback, and in that second he'd seen her face turn deep red with humiliation and shame. She'd pulled on her clothes and, sobbing, rushed past him to her car. He'd tried to call and say it was okay, there was no need to be embarrassed, and he was sorry if she'd thought he liked her that way. She never answered, or rang him back, and over the next month he'd stopped trying. He thought now that he should never have given up.

He crouched beside her and put his arm around her shoulders. 'When all this is over I'd like for you and Mia to get to know each other again.'

She looked up at him, face red and wet with tears. 'Really?'

'Of course. You're her aunt.'

'I'm sorry that I don't know where she is. I didn't even know Helen was back.'

'I know,' he said. 'We'll find her.'

'I'll help any way I can,' she said.

'For now, just take care of yourself.'

He left her sitting there and went to Ella, who was talking to Jane. 'Has he rung you back?'

'Not yet.' As she spoke, her phone rang, and Alex's heart jumped in his chest. She looked at the screen. 'Not him,' she said, stepping away to answer.

Alex sat on the bench beside Jane. She held her wet phone. 'Yours dead too?'

He nodded. When he got out of there he'd buy a new one, see if the old SIM worked. Make sure his number was available if Mia called.

Jane said, 'You know, just before that chopper arrived, Laird sent me a text asking, "Did I do good?".'

'You're kidding me.'

'He thinks we might get back together,' she said, her voice full of scorn.

Alex didn't answer. He was watching Ella on her phone. She nodded and listened and spoke, then hung up, never once looking his way.

'What a day,' Jane said. 'I always thought if I was going to stare down a barrel it'd happen at work.'

He looked at her. 'I'm sorry to get you caught up in this.'

'It wasn't like you had any idea it would happen.'

'Yeah, but you could've been shot. Killed.'

'But I wasn't.' She smiled at him. 'And smart move, going into the water like that.'

He glanced at Ella. She was on the phone again, but looking at him. A smile on her face as she hung up. He jumped up from the bench.

'They found her,' she said. 'She was with her mother, in a motel in Chatswood.'

Ella kept talking but Alex couldn't hear her properly. His ears were ringing, his vision blurry. 'She's okay?'

'She's fine. Brent's bringing her here now. Should be here any minute. After she was on the news tonight, someone rang in from the motel . . .'

Alex was walking towards the car park, his legs feeling disconnected, his heart so light.

Ella followed, still talking. '. . . heard lots of arguing previously . . . arrested and taken to Chatswood police station . . .'

He stood on the asphalt and stared at the road. He wouldn't believe it was real until he could see her, hold her.

'. . . statement from you . . .'

A police car turned into the road and came towards him. Brent Mason was behind the wheel, and smiling. A female officer sat in the back next to a smaller form. Before the car stopped, the back door flew open and Mia was out and running towards him.

He dropped to his knees and she flung herself crying into his arms. 'She wouldn't let me call you.'

'I know, sweetie, it's okay.'

She pressed her face into his neck. 'I'm sorry, I thought it'd be fun, she said it'd be an adventure, but all she did was yell at me.'

'It's okay, honey, it's all right.'

He clung tightly to her. She was really here, and he knew that everything, *everything*, was going to be fine.

'Eww, Dad, why are you all wet?'

★

Ella listened to Natasha Osborne tell the rest of her story. She'd fallen apart before, too distraught to go on. After talking with Alex, though, and hugging Mia, she'd said she wanted to talk about the rest. It had been good at the start, she said, but then she'd started to see flashes of Canning's temper, and he'd threatened her and had hit her, usually in the stomach, just as Ella had said would happen. She'd stopped then and cried some more, and Ella had the feeling there was more to it, perhaps even a rape, but didn't press her on it.

She touched her shoulder. 'What was the situation with Grace Michaels?'

'Earlier that week he said she'd be coming for a scheduled visit, but his friend needed him that day to drive up the Central Coast to where his little boy was terminally ill in hospital.' Natasha wiped her eyes. 'He said he'd told Grace and she was okay with it, her own little boy being the same age. She'd agreed to let him miss the appointment and go there even though his friend was also an ex-con and they shouldn't be together. He said we had to help Grace because she was helping him, so if anyone asked, they were all here together that afternoon.'

'Did he mention that friend's name?' Ella asked. 'Or did you ever meet him?'

'His first name's Danny and he drove this grey hatchback,' Natasha said. 'They were out for hours that afternoon, when Grace came around, and when they got back it was like they were high.'

'How was Grace while she was here?'

'Uptight and uncomfortable. I guessed that something was wrong, that he hadn't told me the truth. We didn't talk much. She hung around in the workshop looking at her watch, then left after about twenty minutes.'

Ella nodded. Her phone buzzed in her pocket but she didn't look at it. 'And your arm?'

'He got angry yesterday, over nothing, and twisted it.' She touched the bandage. 'I had to put this on myself. He said I couldn't go to hospital because people would ask questions and then he'd go back to jail. He said was that what I wanted? I wanted to say yes, but I couldn't.' She lowered her head. 'I'd wanted to help him. I thought it could be good. He seemed so nice when we were writing letters and when I visited him. And then I lied and helped him kill someone.'

'You didn't know that's what he was going to do,' Ella said. 'How about I have someone take you to hospital and get your arm looked at? Then we'll talk some more.'

She helped her stand, then they walked towards the car park. Natasha glanced once along the dock, then turned away. Ella helped her into the front seat of a uniformed officer's car, then raised a hand as they drove off.

Night was falling. An investigation team would be here soon, and there were hours of work ahead: statements, explanations, walk-throughs to demonstrate what had happened, with added pressure from the fact that it had all been filmed, and was probably online and being broadcast already. Ella was clear in her own mind about what had happened, and knew that she'd had to shoot, that she'd had no choice. Still, now that she was alone for the first time since it happened, she felt the guilt and heartache she'd been working so hard to ignore.

Canning didn't have to take hostages, she told herself, he didn't have to try to run when running was impossible. He didn't have to raise his gun like that. And Grace Michaels and her son were safe now, and that was a good thing. But she could still see the shocked look in his eyes, the spreading red on his chest. Her phone buzzed again with the text reminder. She took it out and found a message from Callum.

I've just worked out this is the second time I've done this — been an arse one day and expected you to forget it the next. I obviously have a problem, and I've made an appointment with a psychologist to deal with it. I'm sorry about behaving so badly, and about the donuts too — poor attempt at a joke there. I'm home tonight if you want to come over and slap me. I hope to see you then, though I'll understand if I don't. xox

Ella looked around. Alex Churchill and his daughter were sitting close together on a bench, heads together as they talked, Mia now and then looking like she was trying to see past him to the body. Jane Koutoufides was talking to Marion Pilsiger, making gestures like she was shoving someone, describing what'd happened in the shed Ella guessed. Langley, Kemsley and Hossain stood near Canning's body at the end of the dock. The evening was quiet except for the slap of water on the hulls of boats and the conversation of the people who were gathering behind the police tape strung across the car park. She looked at her phone.

Busy, she sent back, then sent another. *For now.*

★

Alex listened as Mia talked. Helen had found her on Facebook three months ago, and they'd been in contact regularly on their phones since. She'd apologised for being away for so long and Mia had forgiven her. It sounded like Helen had developed the idea of Mia running away over time, dropping hints about a better life, how mothers understood daughters much better than fathers, how Alex would be angry if he knew they were in touch because the break-up had been so bad, therefore Mia could never tell him.

'I felt bad about keeping it a secret, but she said you told her to leave and never come back,' Mia said.

'You don't remember, because you were only three, but one night she said she was going and she went,' he said. 'I loved her, and I wrote and begged her to come back. I would never have told her to stay away.'

'She said we could move interstate, that we'd have so much fun together,' Mia said. 'I packed my schoolbag and snuck out when Louise was asleep. She picked me up around the corner. I was so happy, and she was crying, and saying how much she loved me.'

Alex noticed she was calling Helen 'she'. Not Mum.

'It was good at first, but then I was asking where we'd go, could we get a dog when we got there, what would my new school be like, and wanted to ring my friends, and she got all

angry and shouted at me to stop asking so many questions.'
Mia wiped her eyes. 'She said couldn't I just wait and see, and
why was I always hungry, and would I just shut up and give her
some peace for a bit.'

Alex hugged her tight.

'I watched TV at first but we were in this tiny scungy motel
room and she said it was too loud,' Mia said. 'So then I got
out my phone to listen to music on my headphones but she
wouldn't let me turn it on because she said you'd send nasty
people to look for us, and I took the SIM out so that was okay
but then it went flat and the charger wasn't working and she
yelled at me when I asked if she'd buy me a new one. Then this
afternoon the police knocked on the door. She'd told me that
if anyone asked I should say my name was Airlie Green but I
wanted to come home, so when the policeman asked me I said
I'm Mia Churchill.' She pressed her head into Alex's neck. 'She
screamed and they put handcuffs on her and put her in a car.
Is she going to jail?'

'I don't know for sure,' he said.

Mia hesitated. 'Will I see her again?'

'Do you want to?'

'I don't know.'

He kissed the top of her head. He was angry with Helen,
furious, but didn't want to forbid them having contact if that
was what Mia decided she wanted. 'Let's talk about it another
day.'

She nodded against his neck. 'And Dad?'

'Yes?'

'Do you think we can get a new charger on the way home?'

TWENTY-NINE

Ella sat in the corridor outside the office, arms folded tight, legs crossed, gaze through the opposite wall. She could hear the murmur of Langley's voice and the deeper tone of the superintendent in charge of the investigation through the closed door beside her. They were going over and over what happened, just as she'd have to do when she went in. She hadn't stopped doing the same thing in her head, not even when she'd stood in Chloe Meixner's flat and told her that Canning had killed Marko – they had the detailed confession from Danny O'Hara to prove it, the man being sensible enough to do what he could to help himself – and then that Canning had himself been killed. She'd held Chloe while she sobbed – the shoulder of her shirt was still damp now – then left her in the care of Audra, hoping that the news would eventually be some small salve.

She knew word had been sent to Grace Michaels and could only imagine the relief she felt. And tomorrow she'd call Michael Paterson, although if he'd watched the late news he would've seen the footage and probably worked it out for himself. Canning had been pixelated over but the rest was clear as day, and

Ella had stood in the main office and watched over peoples' shoulders, seeing herself run up the dock then stopping to fire. At that point she'd turned and walked out of the room.

She shifted in the chair. She wanted to get out of there, but it would be hours before she was free. She wanted a hug. She wanted –

The door opened and Langley stepped out. Ella jumped to her feet.

'He's ready for you,' Langley said.

Ella nodded and went to move past but he stopped her. 'I told him I supported your actions.'

So perhaps he wasn't so bad. 'Thank you.'

'But next time, lose the stroppiness.'

'I'm sorry?'

'In the meetings and so on,' he said. 'We solve cases as a team. Stroppy individuals don't build team spirit.'

She stared at him. *He* was lecturing her on team spirit?

'It's just a friendly word of advice.' He smiled. 'Go on in. You'll do fine.'

She turned away, holding back a snort.

He thought that was stroppy? He had no idea.

★

It was close to ten when Jane let herself into her house and switched on all the lights. The place looked exactly the same, which felt strange considering everything that'd happened. She walked into the kitchen and dropped her bag and the plastic bag of her wet clothes on the table, then went to the bench and turned on the jug. Cup, coffee, sugar. Milk out of the fridge. Then scrunched-up test kit out of her bag.

Do it. Now.

Her landline rang. It was Detective Rooney.

'I heard about what happened,' she said. 'How are you?'

'Worn out,' Jane said, turning her back on the pregnancy kit.

'It was quite an evening. I'm still in the police overalls one of your colleagues lent me.'

'I have some news,' Rooney said. 'Lucille Humphreys confessed to assaulting Deb.'

'What?'

'She stayed with the magistrate and Laird for a couple of drinks, then said she had a migraine and went to bed,' Rooney said. 'She waited until they were half in the bag, then took Laird's car. His GPS records where he's been, and she worked out which was your place, drove round there, saw Deb outside in the dark and thought it was you.'

Jane had to sit down.

'She said they argued, and Deb swung at her with the golf club,' Rooney went on. 'They wrestled, then suddenly she was holding the club and Deb was motionless on the ground. She panicked and fled home. Laird and the magistrate were still drinking, and never noticed she'd been out.'

'She just walked in and told you this?' Jane said.

'I was interviewing her again today, and her conscience got the better of her. It all came spilling out. She's in the cells now, and will go before the magistrate in the morning. Not the one she's friends with, obviously.'

'How's Laird?'

'Appears quite upset,' Rooney said.

'When did you find out?'

'Mid-afternoon.'

No wonder he'd been so keen to help find Mia.

'Thanks for letting me know,' she said.

Jane hung up. She couldn't help imagining what might've happened if she'd come straight home from Laird's that night instead of parking by the ocean. Deb had brought the golf club – what had she intended to do? Lucille had brought nothing but her fury. If Jane had been home, there might've been a complicated screaming match, cops would've been called, neighbours might think she was nuts, but Deb would more than likely be fine.

She took her water-damaged mobile out of her bag, and prised out the SIM. She dug an old mobile from the junk drawer in the kitchen, inserted the SIM, and turned it on. The words 'low battery' appeared. She plugged in the charger then texted Steve. *Any news?*

He replied a moment later. *Tube's out, and she squeezed my hand when I talked to her. Good sign, right?*

Great, she sent back. *Excellent. Happy for you both.* And she was.

She picked up the kit and walked along the hall. In the bathroom, she sat on the toilet, unwrapped the stick, then held it in place beneath herself.

Three minutes, the box said. She folded four squares of toilet paper and laid them on the floor, then placed the wet stick on top. She wiped herself, zipped up the police overalls, flushed and washed and went out.

In the kitchen she made the coffee, then stood in the doorway, holding the cup but unable to drink. She tried to imagine seeing a plus sign, tried to prepare herself.

The seconds slowed. The house was silent around her. Jane stared into space, the heat of the coffee burning her hands. She thought of the tiny feet of babies, the bounding lankiness of a ten year old, the emotions stirring in an adolescent's growing heart.

She put down the cup and went into the bathroom and knelt by the stick on the floor. The sign was negative.

She took the second stick from the kit, unzipped, sat on the toilet and strained for a few more drops, then waited right there for another three minutes to see the same sign again.

She stood up. She wasn't pregnant. Her life remained her own. There'd be no new varicose veins or haemorrhoids, no sleepless nights, no cracked nipples from breastfeeding, no toddler tantrums, no first-day-of-school anxieties. No driving lessons and no groundings. No battles over clean rooms or skirt lengths. No anxious waiting up late when they first went out, no wiping tears from the first broken heart.

She placed her hand on her belly for a moment. Then she collected up the sticks and papers, dropped them in the bin and walked out.

She picked up the phone and scrolled through the contacts. 'Breanna, hi,' she said when her daughter answered. 'Were you able to get that time off? And Alice too? Because it'd be really nice to see you both.'

★

Ella lay against Callum, her hand on his chest over his still-pounding heart, his arm down her naked and perspiring back, his fingers stroking her skin.

She'd left the office after the interview and come straight here, knocking on Callum's door when the sky was turning light, and told him that she'd killed someone. He'd listened without judging, and she'd known then. Knew now.

'Question,' he said. 'Is this going to be a frequent occurrence? You coming over and jumping on me like this?'

'If I told you that it'd ruin the surprise.' She propped herself on her elbow and looked at his face in the glow of the morning sun coming through the curtains. He ran his fingers over her hip. She could feel her pulse in her throat, the blood under her skin. Her mind strayed for a moment to blood spreading like flowers but she pulled it back.

'So does this happen every time you solve a case?'

'Don't get too excited,' she said. 'You don't know our success rate.'

He tucked a strand of hair behind her ear and grinned.

Sweat had pooled in the hollow at the base of his throat. She touched it with the tip of her finger, then drew a line up through the stubble on his neck to grasp and waggle his chin. 'Life is short.'

This day, more than ever, it felt important to grab hold with both hands.